Praise for *Cemetery*

World Fantasy Award Winner
International Horror Critics Guild Award Winner
British Fantasy Award Nominee
American Horror Award Nominee

"A very fine piece of work."
—Dean Koontz

"*Cemetery Dance* is beautifully choreographed."
—Robert Bloch

"A fine home for innovative horror fiction. A home that
invites in both the talented beginner and the old pro—as long
as they bring the best of blood and shadows in their luggage."
—Joe R. Lansdale

"The best magazine in the horror field."
—*The Time Tunnel*

"Unfailingly entertaining. A great magazine."
—Joe Bob Briggs

"Hands down the best horror magazine available."
—*Mystery Scene*

THE BEST OF
CEMETERY DANCE

edited by
Richard Chizmar

VOLUME TWO

A ROC BOOK

ROC
Published by New American Library, a division of Penguin Putnam Inc., 375 Hudson Street, New York, New York 10014, U.S.A.
Penguin Books Ltd, 27 Wrights Lane, London W8 5TZ, England
Penguin Books Australia Ltd, Ringwood, Victoria, Australia
Penguin Books Canada Ltd, 10 Alcorn Avenue,
Toronto, Ontario, Canada M4V 3B2
Penguin Books (N.Z.) Ltd, 182–190 Wairau Road, Auckland 10, New Zealand
Penguin Books Ltd, Registered Offices: Harmondsworth, Middlesex, England

Published by Roc, an imprint of New American Library, a division of Penguin Putnam Inc.
Previously published as part of a hardcover edition by *Cemetery Dance*.

First Roc Printing, January 2001
10 9 8 7 6 5 4 3 2 1

 REGISTERED TRADEMARK—MARCA REGISTRADA

LIBRARY OF CONGRESS CATALOGING-IN-PUBLICATION DATA
The best of Cemetery dance / edited by Richard Chizmar.
   p. cm.
"Volume 2."
  ISBN 0-451-45813-3 (alk. paper)
  1. Horror tales, American. 2. Science fiction, American. I. Chizmar, Richard T.
II. Cemetery dance. III. Title.
PS648.H6 B45 2001
813'.087608—dc21   00-045845

Printed in the United States of America

ACKNOWLEDGMENTS

Nine years have gone into the creation of this book. It's been a long journey, and I did not make it alone. So I offer my deepest thanks to the following people who walked by my side: Kara and Max, William and Olga Chizmar, my entire family, the Wilsons, Kara's family (and thanks to Tip and Kelly, the *CD* shipping department!), Mindy Jarusek, Brian and Tracy Anderson, Steve and Dani Sines, Bill and Daniella Caughron, Bob Crawford, Jim Cavanaugh, Pondo, Roy Boy, Bob Eiring, Richard Gallagher, Tom Nugent, Ed and Carol Gorman, Marty Greenberg, Barry Hoffman, Bob Morrish, William Schafer, Tim Holt, Dave Silva, Stephen King, Shirley Sonderreger, Dean Koontz, Peter Crowther, Muffin Spielman, Adam Fusco, and each and every person who ever contributed their creative talents to *Cemetery Dance*, and – last, but certainly not least – all the good folks who supported us over the years.

This book is very special to me,
and I'd like to dedicate it to three very special people:

Mary Wilson
Nancy Chizmar
And the memory of Rita Chizmar

My sisters and my guardian angels.
Thanks for letting me be your little brother.
I love you.

For more information about Cemetery Dance:

Visit the official website: *www.cemeterydance.com*

Or write: Cemetery Dance Publications
P.O. Box 943
Abingdon, MD 21009

THE BEST OF CEMETERY DANCE

EATER

Peter Crowther

"He's a what?" Doc Bannerman slammed his locker door closed and turned to face Jimmy Mitulak.

"An eater." The word hung in the air with the dying echo of the metal door as though it were a part of the sound. "He eats his victims," Mitulak went on, hanging his black shirt on the back of his door. He shook his head and clunked his teeth together, growling.

Bannerman rolled his eyes in despair. "This fucking city, it gets to me sometimes. Gets so I think maybe I can't take any more of it."

"But still you turn in with each new shift."

"Yeah." He drew the word out lazily. "But maybe one day . . ."

"Yeah, maybe one day you'll win the lottery." Mitulak smiled. "I'll know it before you do, though, cos that'll be the day I drive down Sixth and all the lights'll be in my favor." He pulled a crumpled, brown, short-sleeved shirt from his locker and struggled into it. As Mitulak slid his holster over his head, Bannerman saw a cartoon drawing of a bowling ball with a lit fuse coming out of one of the finger-holes and the words BOWL PATROL — and, in smaller letters beneath, MITULAK emblazoned on the back.

"Nice shirt."

Mitulak turned around and squinted at him. "You serious?"

Bannerman shook his head. "No."

"My sister, Rosie. She designed it."

"I didn't know she was a designer."

Mitulak lifted his jacket of the peg and closed his locker. "She isn't," he said as he slapped Bannerman's back and made a gun sign with his hand. "Keep an eye on him, okay?"

Bannerman nodded. "I'll keep both of 'em on him."

"You'd better," Mitulak shouted over his shoulder as he opened the locker-room door. "He 'specially likes eyes."

Bannerman sneered a smile. "Who've I got?"

Mitulak was already halfway out and he didn't stop. His answer floated back through the gap between the door and the jamb, merging with the sound of footsteps already fading down the corridor to the parking lot. "Gershwin and Marty. See ya."

Bannerman changed into his shirt and pants and strapped his holster onto his belt. Then he made a last call into the bathroom and walked out into the corridor, made a right away from the back door and started up the stairs.

The holding cell where they had the beast was on the first floor, tucked against the wall in an open plan office where the uniforms could write up their collars. Just like in the movies. Above that was a flat roof, looking out onto the oily waters of the Hudson. Below, was a walk-through main desk and seven small offices. Below *that* was the locker room and the showers.

The 17th Precinct building was in a derelict area two blocks west of the Port Authority terminal and one block south of the Lincoln Tunnel. It was surrounded by warehouses filled with containers of frozen fish and electrical goods. No people. Particularly at night.

It was 3:03 am when Denny 'Doc' Bannerman signed in at the front desk and walked slowly up the corridor to the rec room.

His nickname came courtesy of a one-year spell doing medicine at N.Y.U. Medical Center. It was to there, the 18-storey Hospital building, that Denny's policeman father had taken a young punk spaced out of his head on PCP. The punk had laughed and cried, both at the same time, and, in an all-too brief second when nobody was paying him too much attention, he had pulled a two-handled telescopic wire out of his shoe, wrapped it around Jim Bannerman's neck and, with a swing of his hands, severed the big man's head and sent it scudding across the floor. Then the kid had leapt through a plate glass window, dropped two floors smashing both legs, three ribs, both collarbones and the hood of a 1983 Studdebaker before trying to scurry away across 20th Street like the stocking-clad torso in Todd Browning's *Freaks*. When the delivery van had hit the punk, witnesses said he was still laughing. Denny never went back to the hospital.

Bannerman pushed open the rec room door and cleared his throat. "Officer Bannerman reporting for duty," he said, clicking his heels to complement the officialese.

"Hey, how you doing Bannerman?" It made a change from Marty Steinwitz's usual greeting of *What's up, Doc?* which he usually supplemented with a munching chuckle a la Bugs Bunny.

"Just fine." Doc lifted the night's call-sheet from the desk. Steinwitz returned his attention to a thick slab of coagulated pizza which he lifted from a *Ssbarro* bag perched precariously in front of him, on a maze of papers and forms, alongside a polystyrene cup of milky coffee, its top edges pinched tight with teeth marks.

"What's the pizza?" Bannerman asked without turning his attention from the papers in his hand.

Steinwitz held up the steaming mess and belched. "Pancreas and large intestine."

Bannerman glanced up and grimaced. "Ho fucking ho."

Steinwitz shrugged and continued to eat, getting the mess all over the lower part of his face.

Bannerman read on. Pinned to the back of the call-sheet was the eater's record details. The guy was a bona-fide head-case. No doubt about it. The record itemized the contents of his freezer — various entrails and intestines contained in see-through bags — a wardrobe of custom-made 'clothes' and several items of undeniably avant-garde 'furniture' which included an occasional lamp fashioned out of a moldering leg stump, two torsos bound together with garden twine and used, or so it would appear, as a footstool, and three arms, suitably bent at the elbow and attached to the living room walls in a grim parody of exotic boomerangs or headless geese flying to sunnier climes.

He wanted to feel revulsion but couldn't. That was the worst part of the job right there: the way it shaved off a person's ability to shake his head at the weird and the absurd. Here, nothing was weird any more. Nothing was absurd. Things just *were*, that was all. He settled back into his chair, removed the gun from his holster for comfort and propped his feet on his desk. "There any coffee?" He opened a drawer and dropped the gun inside.

"I was just gonna make a fresh pot."

"Sure could use it."

Steinwitz nodded and bit into his pizza. "Just let me finish up my supper, and I'll get right onto it," he said through a full mouth.

Bannerman returned his attention to the call-sheet as he shook a cigarette out of a crumpled crumple-proof pack. "You seen him yet?"

"The eater?" The word came with a thick half-chewed wedge of what looked like cheese and anchovies that landed with a thud on the open file in front of him on the desk top.

Bannerman lit the cigarette and threw the burning match into a full ashtray next to his arm. "Yeah." He blew out smoke. "His name's Mellor."

"I know," Steinwitz said as he gathered the expelled food between two pudgey fingers and slid it into his mouth. Just for a second it looked to Bannerman as though it were alive, like a long, stringy worm, folded in on itself time after time and hanging with thin bubbly veils of cheese, twisting in his grip.

"What's he like?"

"What's he *like*? You mean, does he like have horns and a tail or something?"

"No, I mean what's he like? How does he talk? How—"

"Kind of deep." Steinwitz spoke in a throaty baritone, his ample chin resting on his shirt collar. "How the fuck do I know what he talks like. Go talk to him yourself, you're so interested." He lifted the glop to his mouth again and then stopped. "Hey, that's an idea. You like cooking . . . go compare some recipes." He sniggered and pulled off a piece of anchovy that looked like a wriggling worm and slurped it up into his mouth.

The call sheet said they had found the remains of 32 bodies. It had to be some kind of record. The sheet also said that some of the bodies seemed to date back a long ways but that the condition might have something to do with the lime content of the ground in which they had been buried, or something like that. Basically, not a lot could either be done or determined until they had the forensic results back. Then they might be able to pin a few names to the remains.

Bannerman shook his head and blew out smoke. "Thirty two bodies. Jesus Christ."

Steinwitz burped and wiped his mouth on the back of his hand. "*He* almost certainly wasn't one of them."

"*Who* wasn't — Oh, hey, that's funny, you know that? You ever think of going into Vaudeville?"

Steinwitz stopped eating for a second and looked straight at Bannerman. "That's what this is, isn't it?" He waved a greasy hand in a wide arc, taking in the room, the station and maybe even more beyond that. "A routine? A stand-up routine?" He seemed to produce another piece of food from the side of his mouth and started to chew again.

Bannerman shook his head and stared at Steinwitz. "I swear I don't know what's gotten into—"

"And, anyways, there's more than thirty two."

For a second, it seemed mightily oppressive in the small room. Bannerman watched Steinwitz eat his pizza. It sure had a lot of tomato on there — the stuff was all over Steinwitz's hands.

"How d'you mean, more than thirty two?"

"*Bodies*. More than thirty two *bodies*. I mean what are we talking about here?"

"I know *bodies*, okay? I mean what makes you say there are more than thirty two?"

"Because—" He paused for maximum effect. "—that's the way it is. There are more."

"Says who?"

Steinwitz smiled, his mouth a thick smear of pizza topping, and jabbed a runny finger against his chest. "Me says, that's who."

"And who are you?"

Steinwitz chewed, swallowed and stared. He smiled and said, "What about all the stuff in the freezer? Where'd that come from?"

Bannerman's shoulders relaxed. "Oh," he said, "yeah. Forgot about that."

Steinwitz wiped his mouth on a napkin and waved a finger. "Shouldn't forget about stuff like that," he said. "Gotta think about the promotions. Gotta think like Sherlock Holmes."

Bannerman threw the call sheet onto the desk. "Yeah, right. Sherlock Steinwitz."

Steinwitz laughed and stood up.

Bannerman laughed along with him, suddenly realizing that it sounded forced, unnatural.

Steinwitz said, "Coffee?"

"Yeah." Bannerman stood up and followed Steinwitz out of the room, watched him walk to the front desk. "Hey, where's Gershwin?"

Steinwitz reached across for the coffee pot and switched it on. He shrugged without turning around. "Gershwin? Oh, he went to check on the prisoner."

Bannerman shook his head. "Five'll get you ten he's on the goddam telephone again. Who's he call at this time of night, anyway?"

"Beats me."

"I'll go and get him down here."

"'Kay."

"You got the phones geared to come in down here?"

"The phones are fine."

Bannerman turned and walked along the corridor, away from the front desk. He pushed open the swing doors and started up the stairs. A half a minute later he walked into the squad room and paused, looking around the main office.

The desks were strewn with piles of papers, cardboard cups partly filled with cold coffee and greaseproof paper packages of unfinished deli feasts. He figured that the Marie Celeste probably looked a lot like this. Round-backed chairs sat at angles to desks, a television set picture glowed in the corner — Lee Marvin smashing a new car into thick concrete pillars, each impact making no sound at all — while a radio across the office advertised second-hand cars at knockdown prices. Bannerman smiled at the timing and looked across at the far wall. At the cage. It was empty.

He stepped into the squad room — suddenly wishing he hadn't removed his gun — and walked slowly between the desks, keeping his eyes wide. Then he saw the figure, lying on the bunk at the back of the cage, wrapped in a thick blanket, his face turned to the wall. He hated the relief he felt. He just hadn't been able to see Mellor because of the surrounding desks. That was all. What the hell was wrong with him?

"Hey, Gershwin? You on the goddam telephone again?"

There was no answer.

What seemed somehow even worse was the fact that Mellor hadn't moved.

Bannerman turned his full attention to the figure and called again, louder. "Gershwin?"

Still nothing.

He walked over to the cage and stared at the prisoner. *Was* he moving? Could he see the faint traces of the man's back rising and falling? Maybe he was in a deep sleep. After all, it must have been one hell of a day.

On the radio, a woman with a come-to-bed voice started talking about McCain's pizzas like they were sex aids.

Pizzas. *Ssbarro* closed at midnight. And yet the pizza that Marty had been eating had looked hot, or warm at least. He remembered seeing it steaming. Bannerman frowned. The microwave. That was how he had done it. The frown disappeared. What was *wrong* with him?

He turned off the radio and the television set and lifted a plastic mug from a nearby desk, rattling it across the bars of the cage, like he had seen Jimmy Cagney do a thousand times. "Hey, Mellor — you want anything?"

"How about a plate of liver 'n' eyeball risotto?" said a voice behind him.

Bannerman spun around to see Marty Steinwitz holding out a steaming mug of coffee.

"I brought it up to you in case you'd gotten involved with the prisoner. Here."

Bannerman took the coffee and nodded thanks. He took a sip. It tasted good and strong, though there was a faint metallic undertaste.

Steinwitz sat down heavily and rested his feet against an open desk-drawer. "That good?" he asked.

"Mm, hits the spot."

"New blend," Steinwitz said. "Chicory and soya."

"Ah." Bannerman nodded, feeling inexplicably easier.

"You seen Gershwin?"

Bannerman shook his head.

Steinwitz made a clicking noise with his mouth and then thrust a finger between his teeth and his cheek. "Maybe he's out in the storeroom," he said around the finger.

"Yeah." Bannerman took another sip of coffee, swallowed and noticed a piece of grit on his lip. He picked it off and studied it, then threw it into a nearby basket. "Guy's out like a light," he said looking across at Mellor. The figure had not moved during their entire conversation, he was sure of it.

"You ever wonder what makes them do it?"

"Kill people?"

Steinwitz nodded and clasped his hands on his stomach. "And eat them. That's the thing. Eating *people*."

Bannerman shrugged. "Maybe he gets a charge."

"A charge?"

"Yeah, you know — a thrill, kind of. Some kind of sexual turn-on." Bannerman drained the coffee and put the mug on the desk. "I can't figure it."

Steinwitz sighed and moved his hands behind his head, cradling it. "You ever wonder what it tasted like? Human meat?"

"Same as any other meat, I guess." Bannerman walked across to the cage and held onto the bars, rattling them, making sure they were securely locked.

"I think it's power."

"Huh?"

"The reason he does it. Maybe it gives him some kind of power, an edge. Maybe—" He stopped talking and turned his head sharply.

Bannerman followed the other man's gaze and looked at the door. "What? What is it?"

Steinwitz sat up on his chair. "Thought I heard something."

"Like what?"

"Dunno. Wait here a minute." Steinwitz stood up and walked across the room. When he reached the door, he opened it slowly and looked out. He turned back, shrugged, and mouthed *Wait*. Then he stepped out and closed the door behind him.

Bannerman waited.

Suddenly, the precinct house seemed impossibly big and him inside it impossibly small. Impossibly small and *very* vulnerable. He waited a little longer and then shouted, "Everything okay?" but there was no answer. What had Steinwitz heard? Bannerman wished his partner had at least given him some idea before he had just gone off like that. It wasn't like him. It wasn't like him at all. Damn me for leaving the fucking gun downstairs, he thought.

He strained to listen. He strained so hard he imagined he could hear the clock near the front desk ticking. But that was two sets of doors, a flight of stairs and two corridors away. Maybe it was his watch. Bannerman lifted his arm and looked at the watch-face. It was a little before four am. He lifted it all the way to his ear and listened for a gentle ticking. There was no sound.

He turned around to the cage and watched Mellor's body for signs of movement. Had he moved? Had Mellor turned around and watched him while he had been watching the door? He didn't like to think that.

He didn't like to think of Mellor quietly turning around, quietly standing up and oh-so-quietly shuffling across the cage towards his back. His unprotected, unsuspecting back. Sure there were bars between the two of them but were bars enough? Maybe the prisoner could have reached through those bars and grabbed him . . . maybe he could have ripped his— He shook his head and scattered the black thoughts away like crumbs from the table. "Hey, Mellor!" He banged on the bars again. "Hey, sleeping beauty . . . rise and shine. Come on!"

The body just lay there, didn't move a muscle.

He was dead. That was it. The guy had up and died on them. Here they were, jumping at the slightest sound, and all because of some guy lying dead in the cage, stiffening up right now, probably. Maybe he should check on him.

Bannerman looked around for the keys and saw them hanging from the hook on the wall beneath a large, hand-drawn sign that said POKEY in big letters. He walked across and lifted the keys, feeling something slide in his stomach as he held their coolness in his hand. He jingled them and watched for some sign from Mellor. Nothing. He walked back to the bars and rattled the keys across them. Nothing.

He shuffled through the keys until he hit on the right one and then inserted it into the lock, started to turn it slowly.

"Hey, I ain't sure you wanna be doing that, man," said Gershwin from the door. "I ain't sure you wanna be doing that *a-tall*." He slammed the door behind him and strolled across the squad room. Bannerman watched him, suddenly aware of the dumb look he must have on his face.

"Where you been? Didn't you hear me calling you?"

Gershwin frowned, raised his shoulders and splayed out his hands. "Hey, I'd heard you, man, I'd've answered. What's up?"

Bannerman pulled the key from the lock and checked the cage-door again. Just to be safe. "I'll tell you what's up," he said. "Marty heard something downstairs and—"

"Wasn't anything."

"Wasn't—"

"I just saw Marty, downstairs. He said to tell you it wasn't anything."

"What *was* it?"

Gershwin answered with a shrug. "He didn't say. The wind? Who knows, man? Nothing."

"Where is he now?"

"Downstairs. He's still downstairs."

"What's he doing?"

"He didn't say."

Bannerman rubbed his face with his hands. "God, I don't know . . . This whole thing is spooking me."

Gershwin sat down at the desk that Steinwitz had been sitting at and pulled open the desk drawer, propped his feet on it. Just like Steinwitz. He clasped his hands behind his head and smiled. "What whole thing is that, man?"

Bannerman watched him for several seconds and then smiled.

"What's funny?"

Bannerman laughed.

Gershwin's face broke into a wide smile. "What is it, man?"

"It's you . . . you guys . . ." Bannerman shook his head.

Gershwin joined in the nervous laughter, only his contribution didn't seem to sound quite so nervous. "*What*?"

Bannerman felt the smile slip from his face and, as it slipped, he watched the smile on Gershwin's face slip, too. Yeah, *what*? he thought. What the hell was so funny? "Nothing," he said. "Forget it." He turned to the cage and felt Gershwin's eyes watching him. He rattled the bars, though he knew there would be no response. Then he looked across at the squad room door.

"You want another coffee?" Gershwin said.

It was like somebody had encased Bannerman's back in ice. He wanted to ask how Gershwin had known he had already had a coffee; he wanted to ask why Gershwin sat right down at the same desk as Steinwitz; how he'd known which drawer to pull out; how he'd propped his feet up in just the same way as Steinwitz; how he'd clasped his hands behind his head, just like Steinwitz again. But then he didn't want to ask those things. There was a large part of his head that said, *No, let's not play their game; let's not show them we're falling for it.* And there was a small part of his head, a tiny, darkened part, where the sun never shone and where things — even the most ridiculous things — were simply accepted . . . where questions were never asked. That part said, *Don't let him know you know.*

Know what? said the big, rational part.

Just don't let him know, came the answer.

Bannerman heard Gershwin stand up from his chair. "I said, you want another—"

"No!" Bannerman turned around quickly and, just for a second, the other man seemed to falter. "No," Bannerman said, calmer now. "Thanks."

"Is anything . . . wrong?"

Bannerman winced inwardly at the suspicion in the question. It oozed suspicion. He'd blown it. He glanced back at the door, irrationally considering his chances of making it. Then he looked back and started to laugh. At first, it was forced but then it just seemed to flow naturally. The ease with which it flowed amazed him. Hysteria, he guessed. He laughed so loud and so hard that it hurt. He leaned back against a desk and folded his arms across his stomach. "Is *anything* wrong! Hell, is anything *right's* more the question," he said between laughs that came dangerously close to out-and-out sobs. "We're holed up here," he said, "the three of us, with some whacko who eats people for a hobby—" He pointed to the body in the cage (*Who is it*? that dark part of his head wondered) "—and the dude up and dies on us while he's in custody." He took a deep breath. "Now, how's that gonna look in the morning? Huh?"

Gershwin watched him, his head tilted slightly to one side.

"I'll tell you how it's gonna look," Bannerman said, standing up and walking towards the other man, hoping he wouldn't be able to hear his heart thudding, "it's going to look . . . *bad*." He laid emphasis on the last word like it was cement.

Gershwin continued to watch.

Bannerman turned around and started towards the door, mentally counting the steps, mentally humming, mentally praying, mentally waiting.

"Where are you going?"

"To tell Steinwitz we have a problem," he said without stopping. "A fucking big problem." He pulled open the door, holding his neck so tight that the muscles would ache for days. If he was lucky. He walked along the corridor to the stairs, forcing himself not to run, forcing himself not to turn around.

The door clicked shut behind him. There was no other sound. Walking down the stairs, he muttered to himself. He wasn't sure what he was muttering but he made sure the word 'problem' cropped up in it several times, and the phrase 'up and died on us', too. He imagined that

Gershwin was right behind him, could almost sense his breath on his exposed neck . . . breath from his open mouth . . . his *wide* open mouth.

He walked along the downstairs corridor as loudly as he could. Bannerman, man with a mission, man without fear. Yeah! "Hey, Marty?" he yelled. "Marty, we got a problem. It's a fucking big problem, mi amigo." He kept walking. Through the downstairs doors. Towards the main desk. Still walking. "Marty," he yelled again, "you listening to me? You hear we got a problem?"

There was no answer. Of course.

The precinct house doors loomed ahead of him.

He kept on walking.

"Yeah, the problem we got is—" He reached the doors, reached out . . . "It's big, Marty. It's—" His hand touched the handle, grasped it firmly, and turned.

The doors were locked.

"It's one big fucking problem," he said in a soft voice that somehow seemed very alone.

Bannerman looked down at the lock and saw there were no keys. He hadn't expected any.

He turned around, half-expecting Gershwin to be standing watching him, a knife and fork in his hands, chanting *Chow time!* over and over. The place was empty.

He started to walk back the way he had come, mentally cursing the security of the station: barred windows, steel doors . . . you name it. "Hey, Marty? You gone back upstairs?" he shouted. Then, his voice lower, "What the fuck is the lieutenant gonna say when we hand over a dead body, for crissakes?"

Halfway along the corridor he turned into the side office he and Steinwitz — or whoever Steinwitz was *now* — were in earlier. He was still muttering when he picked up the receiver. Still muttering when he jabbed the numbers. But he stopped muttering

—the phones are fine—

when he heard the silence from the earpiece. He had always thought that statements like *The silence was deafening* were ridiculous. But here it was, real, honest-to-God deafening silence. That explained what had been bothering him earlier: no incoming calls. No complaints about domestic fights; no robberies; no shootings or knifings. *Just . . . eatings*, the dark part of his head observed.

He replaced the receiver as gently as he could and leaned on the desk-top with both hands. Then he saw the file on the desk, the file that Marty had been looking at while he ate his pizza. There were stains all over it. He leaned over and read upside down: HOBBIES — Music, golf and cooking

That was

—hey, that's an idea. You like cooking . . . go compare some recipes—

his own personal file. Steinwitz had been reading his own personal fucking file! Bannerman reached out to pick up the file and throw it across the office but managed to stop himself. Instead, he pulled open the drawer of the desk he was sitting at. His gun wasn't there. He checked to make sure it hadn't slid to the back, but the drawer was completely empty.

He straightened up and considered his position. It didn't take long. Locked doors, barred windows, dead telephones, no gun all the other firearms were locked up in a metal cabinet that only the lieutenant had a key for.

Steinwitz was walking along the corridor when Bannerman stepped out of the office. "What you—" Steinwitz started in Gershwin's Brooklyn drawl; then he cleared his throat and said, "What're you doing down here?" The replacement nasal tone was Marty Steinwitz's.

"Looking for *you*," Bannerman said, all but placing his left hand on his hip and wiggling his right index finger like a fourth-grade schoolteacher. He hoped Steinwitz's dialect-slip hadn't been intentional — which would mean Steinwitz wanted him to comment on it — and he hoped that, if it were unintentional, Steinwitz wouldn't think he had noticed it.

"Problem?"

Problem? Bannerman wanted to ask where Steinwitz had been, wanted to rub his nose in it. But

—don't let him know you know—

he didn't dare.

He forced himself to walk up to Steinwitz, stand right in front of him, like he was going past, then he stopped. "I was looking for you."

Steinwitz glanced at the office Bannerman had just left and returned his attention to his face. "I was taking a dump."

Bannerman nodded. "Thank you for sharing that with me. Was it a good one?"

Steinwitz pulled a face and rubbed his stomach. "Think I might've eaten something disagreed with me." (Was that the hint of a smile tugging at the edges of his mouth?) "What's up?"

Bannerman slumped back against the wall and thrust his hands — his increasingly sweaty and shaky hands — deep into his trouser pockets. "Oh, nothing much. Nothing except we've got a dead prisoner in the cage."

Steinwitz narrowed his eyes and watched him. "Dead?"

He's playing for time, Bannerman thought. He's weighing up what kind of a threat I am to him. He's wondering if he should stop the game right now. Does he know I know the phones are dead? Does he know I've tried the doors? Does he know I've seen that he was reading my personal file? Does he know I've been looking for my gun? He looked deep into Steinwitz's eyes, searching for a sign, a sign that he was wrong, that he was being stupid and everything was A-okay. But though the eyes were Marty's eyes — a conviction that came to him not without an element of surprise; after all, why would he study another man's eyes, even over the many years he had known him? — but then again they weren't. They were the right color, sure, but they were darker and without depth. Fish eyes, lacking in . . . soul. He nodded. *He knows*, said the voice in his head. "Yeah, dead. Why don't you go see?"

Steinwitz watched him, shuffled from one foot to the other.

"Gershwin's up there," Bannerman added.

Steinwitz smiled. "Better take a look then, I guess."

"Why don't you do that." He stood up from the wall and started back to the main desk.

"You not coming up?"

Bannerman replied without turning around. "Yeah. First I'm gonna brew up some fresh coffee. Looks like it's going to be a quiet night."

"That's the way I like it," Steinwitz said softly behind him.

Bannerman nodded slowly as he walked towards the coffee maker and, just for a second, he felt like giving up. He felt like turning around and telling Steinwitz, *Okay, you win. But kill me first. okay?* But he didn't think that whatever it was that occupied his friend's body now would observe such a display of generosity. Such *weakness*. He kept walking and felt a wave of relief when he heard the door at the end of the corridor behind him swing closed.

As he reached the desk he turned to look behind him. Steinwitz had gone. He leaned against the counter containing the coffee maker, coffee and various mugs, and forced himself to think. What now? He looked up at the front doors, checking for signs of a key hanging somewhere next to them. Nothing. He looked across at the barred windows and, though he couldn't see them, thought about all the empty warehouses in the streets beyond. No life anywhere.

He had to get out.

Suddenly, he jolted upright. Downstairs! He could get out from the basement. What had taken him so long? He switched on the hot water and then walked calmly but quickly across to the stairs to the basement. Checking the corridor to the stairs leading up to the squad room, he placed his hand on the door leading to the basement, grimacing as he expected it to be locked.

The handle turned.

The door came open.

Another quick check to see that the corridor was clear and he slid inside and started down the stairs.

As he traveled down the air got fresher, cooler. He ran, now, taking steps two and three at a time. When he reached the bottom he stopped and looked back up the staircase. Saw the spare key hanging beside the door. Bannerman bit into his bottom lip as he considered running back up the stairs to lock the door. Would he get halfway up and the door suddenly open, though? *Chow time!* He decided against it and turned to the corridor leading past the changing rooms to the back door. Halfway along he stopped and listened for sounds of footsteps coming down the stairs, accompanied by Bernard Herrman's shrieking violins. But all was quiet.

He reached the back door, took the handle in his hand, turned the dead-lock and pulled. It opened.

"Where the hell *you* going?" Jimmy Mitulak said.

Bannerman stopped dead and stared.

"What the hell's the *matter* with you?" Mitulak said.

"What are *you* doing here? You should be home."

Mitulak frowned. "I forgot something. What are you, my mother?"

"What did you forget?" Bannerman said backing down the corridor.

"My bowling shoes. We got a match tomorrow — *today* now. Look, what the hell's the matter?"

"You could've picked them up in the morning."

"Doc, what *is* this? I gotta be in Buffalo by— Hey, since when do I gotta tell you everythin—"

Bannerman grabbed hold of Mitulak's jacket and pulled it open. "You still got your gun on."

"Yeah, I still got my gun on. Come on, now, what's—"

"Get inside."

Mitulak stepped warily into the corridor, still frowning. "Let me see it." Mitulak frowned some more. "The gun, let me see your fucking gun." Mitulak smiled and started to shake his head. "Jimmy, I'm not playing around here. Let me see the gun." Mitulak flipped the harness catch and removed the gun, held it out to Bannerman. "I hope I'm not going to regret this." Bannerman took it gingerly, checked the cartridge. It was full. He secured the cartridge and handed it back to Mitulak with a visible sigh of relief.

"You wanna tell me what's going on?"

"He's out."

"Who's out?"

"The eater, Mellor. He's loose in the station."

"What?!"

Bannerman nodded. "But . . . it gets worse."

"How worse?"

"He's disguised."

"How can he be disguised? There's only you and—"

"He's disguised as Marty."

"Marty?"

"And Gershwin."

Mitulak started to laugh. "Hey, I don't know what you're smoking, Doc, but how about passing it around."

"Listen to me, goddam it!"

Mitulak's smile faded.

"He's taken their appearance. I know, I know," he said as Mitulak looked at him like he was going mad. "It sounds crazy, but he has."

"How?"

"How the fuck do I know how. Maybe he's a fucking Ymir or a face-hugger . . . maybe he can assume the identity of whoever he eats . . . you know? Like the Indians? They ate the hearts of their enemies because they thought it gave them their enemies' strength. Maybe this guy gets the full thing . . . hair, face, looks . . . everything."

"He's *eaten* Gershwin and Marty?"

Bannerman shrugged. "Maybe. All I know is that they're never together."

"Never together?"

"Never together in the room at the same time. And when Gershwin came into the squad room he sat down in the same chair as Marty . . . propped his feet on the desk just the same way as he had been doing a few minutes earlier. And . . . yeah, and Mellor's dead. In the cell. He doesn't move or speak or anything."

"You just said that Mellor was loose."

"Jesus Christ! He *is* loose. But he's left his body in the cell, curled up so it's facing the wall."

"You sure it's him? In the cell?"

"Sure as I can be without going in there and checking him out."

"You haven't checked the body?"

"Hey, I've seen *Silence of the Lambs*, okay? I wasn't going to go in there and have him wearing my head like a Halloween mask."

Mitulak thought for a moment. "But, if Mellor's out and about, what's the problem with going in the cell?"

Bannerman was breathing heavily, almost panting.

"Well?"

"I wasn't sure then. I'm sure now. Okay? I didn't want to go into the cell when I thought that, maybe, Mellor was playing possum. But then all these other things happened-"

"Like Gershwin and Marty sharing a chair?"

"Yes! It sounds crazy . . . I *know* it sounds crazy, okay? But my gun."

"Your gun?"

"It disappeared. And Marty was reading my personal file . . . and the phones are dead . . . and the front doors are locked . . . Look, we have to do something, Jimmy."

Mitulak made noises with his mouth as he considered. Bannerman shook his head and ran both hands through his hair, turning around and walking to and fro in the corridor.

"Okay."

"You believe me?"

"Let's say I believe *you* believe, and leave it at that for now. Maybe it's worth checking it out."

Bannerman suddenly felt as though all of his problems were over. Then, just as he felt like hugging Jimmy Mitulak, he remembered that they still had to confront Steinwitz. Or Gershwin. Could he move both of them at the same time, this eater? He didn't think so. It would be one or the other.

"So what do we do?" said Mitulak, interrupting Bannerman's thoughts.

Bannerman glanced longingly at the back door and then turned to face him. "We go up."

Mitulak nodded. "Right." He slipped off the safety catch on his gun and hefted it slowly in his hand, like he was weighing it. "Right," he said again. "You lead the way."

Bannerman turned around and walked back along the corridor to the stairs.

Taking the stairs slowly, stopping after every couple of risers to listen for any sound of movement, took time. In fact, it took too much time. Halfway up, Bannerman started to wonder what Steinwitz was doing up there. Had he discovered that he Bannerman — wasn't there? If so, where did he think he'd gone? Surely by now he would have checked all the possible hiding places — there weren't many, for crissakes — and would probably have concluded that he was downstairs. If so, then why hadn't the eater come down after him?

He stopped and listened: all quiet. He pressed on.

Maybe Steinwitz had suddenly remembered the downstairs door, and had gone out from upstairs and snuck around the back of the parking lot to wait for him outside. Shit! Maybe the eater had tried the door and discovered it was open . . . then sneaked in, sneaked along the downstairs corridor, taken a look around the corner of the staircase, real quiet, and seen Mitulak and him creeping up the stairs.

Bannerman stopped again and turned his head slowly. There was only Mitulak behind him. The rest of the staircase was empty. He shook his head and carried on. Two steps further and he was at the top, his hand on the door handle.

"Hey . . ."

Mitulak's sharp whisper near-on made Bannerman jump out of his skin. He held onto the handle tightly and hissed, "What?"

"You want maybe I should go first?"

"Why?"

"Because I got a gun. If this guy is round the corner when you open the door — and if he knows you're onto him — he's gonna start shooting as soon as we show ourselves."

It made sense. "That makes sense," Bannerman whispered, and he changed places with Mitulak, staring intently at the door handle while neither of them was holding it.

When they were in place, Mitulak gently turned the handle and pushed. The door crept open silently.

"See anything?" Bannerman whispered.

"Nothing." Mitulak pushed the door a little wider and stepped onto the top step, folding his body into the door, his gun flat against the handle.

"Anything now?"

"Just wait, for—" He stopped.

Bannerman drew in his breath. "What? What is it?"

Mitulak jammed his head between the door and the jamb and tried to look up the corridor to the right.

"What is it?" Bannerman asked again.

"It's Marty."

"Jesus Cri— Where? Where is he? Can he see you?"

Mitulak pushed the door wider and looked around it to the left. Then he stepped back and turned to Bannerman.

"Now I believe you."

"Huh?"

"It's Marty. He's dead."

"Dead?"

Mitulak nodded. "Far as I can make out."

"Where is he?"

"Lying on the floor right in front of us."

"Any sign of Gershwin?"

Mitulak shook his head. "God. Marty. Dead." The three words came out slow and punctuated into tiny sentences, each with a poetic, grim resonance.

"What do we do now?"

"We go out. What else can we do?"

Bannerman grunted. There was nothing else.

"Ready?" said Mitulak.

"Ready."

"Right!" He pushed open the door and ran, crouched over, to the main desk on the left.

Bannerman stepped up onto the top step and looked around the door-edge. Marty stared up at him. He was naked, lying facedown on the floor about fifteen feet from the door, his head tilted to one side like he was watching the basement door. His legs were splayed out behind him, his arms stretched in front of him. One half of his face had gone, exposing teeth and gums and part of his cheek bone. His left arm ended just above the wrist in a fray of skin and cartilage. There was no blood.

Bannerman closed his eyes and blinked away the tears, then opened them again. The horror was still there. He pushed open the door and stepped out into the corridor without thinking.

"Hey," Mitulak whispered loudly. "What the hell you doing?"

Bannerman didn't answer. He walked across to Marty Steinwitz's body and looked down at it. There was a folded piece of paper lying on his back. He bent down.

"What is it?" Mitulak whispered.

Bannerman read the words on the note, four lines, carefully typed on one of the machines up in the squad room:

game over
you have gun now
now weer even
lets finnish it

He waved the sheet to Mitulak. "Come read it yourself. He knows you're here."

Mitulak stood up from behind the desk, warily watching for any signs of movement from anywhere. "Huh? How's he know I'm here?"

"He knows I've got a gun." Bannerman shrugged. "How the hell do I know how he knows anything?"

Mitulak reached him and took the note. He read.

Bannerman turned Steinwitz's body over and jumped back. "Jesus H. Christ!"

Mitulak looked up from the note and then down at the body. The whole of Steinwitz's chest had been ripped open, pieces of snapped bone jutting out.

Bannerman said, "He's eaten his heart."

Mitulak said nothing.

"Let's go. He's waiting for us."

Bannerman led the way along the corridor to the doors.

They pushed open the doors together and looked up the staircase. Gershwin was hanging from one of the lights. He, too, was naked, his chest similarly destroyed and both legs gone from the knees. As they got closer, they saw that his eyes were missing. A note taped across his stomach read:

**getting warmer
the end is neye**

Neither of them said anything.

At the top of the stairs, his heart pounding fit to burst out of his own chest, Bannerman turned the handle on the door.

"Wait . . ."

Bannerman turned.

"Let me go first. I'll go left, over towards the cage, you go right." Bannerman nodded.

"Right!" said Mitulak.

Bannerman threw open the door and both men fell into the room, crashing in two directions behind the desks nearest the door. The hail of bullets Bannerman had expected didn't come.

Bannerman lifted his head above the desk and looked around. He couldn't see anything.

Mitulak did the same.

"Hey . . ." Mitulak said.

"What?"

"I thought you said the guy was dead in the cage."

Shit, Bannerman thought . He knew what was coming next but he had to respond. "He was."

"He ain't now, man," said Mitulak. "Cage is empty."

Bannerman stood up slowly, staring around the squad room. "He's gone back to his own—" He stopped. Over by the far wall, Mellor was sitting against a radiator. He still had the blanket wrapped around him, like an Eskimo or an Indian Chief. Pulled down over his head was a large, brown evidence bag, one side of which was blown apart and stained a red so dark it looked almost black. The wall behind the bag looked like somebody had thrown a pizza at it.

"What is it?" Mitulak said.

"Just wait where you are," Bannerman said. "And cover me." He moved to the side and walked slowly around the desk. As he moved, more of the body came into view. Mellor was holding a gun in one hand. In the other hand was another note. He looked around at Mitulak. Mitulak frowned and mouthed *What*? Bannerman shook his head. *Cover me*, he mouthed. Mitulak nodded and waved the gun.

Bannerman edged his way along the side wall, keeping Mellor in sight all the way. At last he had reached a point where there were no more desks to provide cover. But he had watched the body very carefully and there was no sign of any movement. Either the guy *was* dead or he could hold his breath a very long time.

He crouched down onto all-fours and crept the final few feet towards the body. When he reached it, he leaned over and took hold of the barrel of the gun and gently pulled.

"You okay?" Mitulak whispered.

The gun came away, and Mellor's fingers plopped against his stomach.

"Yeah, I'm okay," Bannerman said. He put the gun in his pocket and reached for the note. Behind him, he heard Mitulak moving between the desks.

Bannerman unfolded the note, a roster sheet, and looked at the other side. It was blank.

"You still okay?"

Bannerman nodded, frowning. "He left a note."

"What's it say?"

"It doesn't. It's blank." He turned it over. It was this week's roster. He looked at the grid and the penciled names in the boxes. One of them was ringed, the one for tomorrow — *today*, now. The box was for 10 am; the name in the box was J. Mitulak.

Bannerman looked at the evidence bag, reached up and lifted it off. The eater had left just enough of the face for Bannerman to recognize who it was, even without the eyes. "Jimmy . . ." he whispered, sadly. Behind him, he heard desks moving as though something large was making its way across the floor.

He saw it all, now, in his mind's eye.

He reached into his pocket and lifted out the gun.

Then he discovered that the cartridge was missing.

"Let's eat," said a voice behind him. It didn't sound like any accent or dialect he had ever heard before.

TYRANNOSAURUS

Norman Partridge

She sat in the back of the police car. The deputy sat up front, his face too white in the harsh glow of fire engine headlights. Her ex-husband's car stood in stark silhouette between the two county vehicles. With its trunk sprung open, the scorched Honda reminded her of a dinosaur skull.

Jaws open wide, ready to snap.

Tyrannosaurus, the killer dinosaur. That was the one it resembled.

"Can't we do this in the house?" she asked. "It was self-defense. You have to believe that. If I hadn't ended it tonight, he would have come back again."

"We have to get your story, Mrs. Rose."

"I changed my name after the divorce. It's Janet Perkins."

"Okay, Ms. Perkins."

"Can't we do this inside? I want to see my son."

"It won't take long. Really. Just a few questions. And it has to be done."

"Okay . . . Okay. Let's get it over with."

"The man in the Honda is your ex-husband?"

"Right. I told your boss that the bastard would come after us. Parole. What a stupid idea. After what he did to Sean in that motel room, and the threats he made—"

"Sean? That's your boy's name?"

She nodded. "And I hate to admit it, but Jack Rose was Sean's father."

"You say that Rose made threats—"

"Not recently. A tabloid reporter got under his skin before the trial. Jack exploded—just verbally, but an explosion nevertheless. He wised up after that, especially when he went in front of the parole board. But how they could look at the pictures of Sean in the burn ward and let Jack out of jail, especially when he'd made those threats . . . It just doesn't make sense."

"Yeah. I remember the story. I followed it in the papers. How brave your boy was, undergoing all those skin graft operations. I want to tell you, that's real bravery."

"Thanks. He's a tough kid."

The deputy nodded. "Why don't you take me through what happened tonight, step by step, and then we'll see where we go from there."

She looked through the window. A light mounted on the fire engine scanned the gravel driveway. The tire still lay to one side of the charred Honda, half hidden by the tall weeds that bordered the driveway. The jack lay next to it. So did the empty gas can. Firemen scurried around, their faces masked against thick black smoke.

"I'm glad the windows are up," she said. "The smell must be—"

"Let's talk about tonight."

"Okay." She took a deep breath. "I finished work at seven. I'm a bartender at the Iron Horse, and the boss takes over for the night shift."

"That's a long commute. Why don't you live in town?"

"Part of the plan. First I changed my name, then I went rural. I figured it would be tougher for Jack to find us out here in the boonies. Besides, I like it here. We've got a few neighbors, and they watch out for us."

"But what about Sean? Didn't you worry about leaving him alone?"

"Sean's independent. I'm not raising him to hide like a bug under a rock. He doesn't want to live that way and neither do I, though sometimes I get so scared that I want to start running again." She sighed. "I just can't give in to that fear, though. It's hard enough on Sean—getting around in a wheelchair, looking the way he does—without me trying to mother-hen him."

"Yeah. I see what you mean."

"Anyway, it was almost dark by the time I got home. I saw Jack from the road. I blocked the driveway with my truck. Then I got my

.38 out of the glove box and headed after him. I've got a permit for the gun."

"Where was he?"

"Let's see—I heard the Honda's trunk slam as I got out of the truck . . . Yeah. Jack was behind the Honda. He'd parked it on the far side of the barn so Sean couldn't see him from the house. I guess he'd just finished changing the tire, because I saw the flat lying in the weeds near the driveway. The jack was there, too. There was a gas can in between, with the lid still on it. It was just dumb luck. If Jack hadn't had the flat, he would have torched the house with Sean in it and been out of here before I showed up."

"Did Jack see you coming?"

"Yes, but I shot him before he could do anything. In the shoulder." She smiled. "I'm a good shot."

"Just wounded him?"

"Right. He got in the car and started the engine. That's when I shot the front tires. I hope I got the one he'd changed." She sighed. "Then I walked up to him, keeping the gun aimed at his head the whole time."

"How did he react?"

"He laughed. Called me Sigourney Weaver. Said that I might as well go call the cops. Then he started making promises again."

"More threats?"

She nodded. "He said that he'd be back, that they probably wouldn't even lock him up this time because he hadn't done anything but violate the restraining order. Then he got back to the old stuff. How he'd burn down the house some night while we were asleep. Look, I just couldn't take it anymore."

"That's when you shot him the second time?"

"Right. I'd rather not say where."

"We don't have to go into that right now."

"Good. Anyhow, I turned away, and when I saw that gas can lying there I really lost it. I grabbed it. Jack saw me coming and tried to get out of the car, but I shot through the door. Hit him again. I don't know where, but it hurt him bad, because he started to cough up blood." She shrugged. "That's when I heard the sirens—I guess someone reported the gunshots—but they didn't stop me. I opened the can and poured gas all over him. He just sat there, grinning that crazy grin of his. Look, I don't have to describe the rest of it, do I?"

"No." The deputy stared at the Honda.

She looked at it, too, but saw only tyrannosaurus jaws. "It was self-defense. He really would have come back."

The deputy nodded.

"Can we go inside now?"

"In a minute," the deputy said.

Outside, the night was alive with the sound of machinery. She watched as a fireman opened the dinosaur's brainpan with some kind of gas-powered saw. Her ex-husband was inside, burnt and shriveled. A man took photos of the corpse, then of the gas can and the tire. A van drifted by, long and white, silent and slow.

"Your ex-husband lied to you," the deputy said. "About not doing anything tonight, I mean."

She swallowed, her throat suddenly dry.

The deputy sighed. "The other time, the first time, Rose took Sean somewhere before he hurt him. A motel, you said. Right?"

She didn't answer.

"Those Japanese cars have awfully small trunks. The tire you saw—it wasn't flat. And the jack and the gas can—Rose wasn't using them. He had to get everything out of the trunk. He had to make room . . . for the wheelchair . . . for . . ."

The deputy's voice cracked.

Sean's mother started to cry.

"Near as we can tell, Sean was gagged. He couldn't cry out." The deputy couldn't look at her. "Rose lied to you, Ms. Perkins. Remember that. You couldn't have known."

Long and white, silent and slow, the coroner's van rolled past the police car.

But the monster's skull remained.

VACATION

Matthew Costello

Jack went out to check the car—yet again. He tried to believe that he was overly preoccupied with the dangers, that he was letting himself get way too jittery.

He shut the door behind him, the back door to their house. He shut it tight and then looked at it.

I don't want anyone coming out while I'm looking around. No, he thought, I don't need them nervous . . . Christie, and the kids. For months, he had balked at the idea, the very *concept* of taking a vacation. Under the circumstances, it was crazy.

But Christie came to him. She put her arms around him, pulled him close, and said:

"Jack—do you know how long it's been . . . how long it's been since we've gone *anywhere*? They say it's safe, that the area is secure. It's a safe family place. The kids haven't seen a lake, any water to swim in . . . for so long."

Jack nodded. He didn't tell her many of the stories from work. There was no point in telling Christie just how badly things seemed to be going. The city was gone. Completely gone . . . New York—the Big Apple—was history. There was no question about it.

Oh, there were some spots, some key sectors that were under control. All of lower Manhattan was fine, supplied by ships on a daily basis, girded by a ring of soldiers and artillery.

And there was a broad strip running up the West Side, nearly to the George Washington Bridge. That was okay. There were still restaurants there, still places where you could go out to eat.

Instead of being eaten.

But the rest of the city was controlled by the others, the Can Heads. They were there and they were spreading . . .

Jack's own sector ran from North Yonkers, just up to the suburbs of Westchester. Westchester itself was a maze of twelve-foot mesh fences and checkpoints. The Can Heads were being contained, that was the official line. In fact, the President announced that in each of the big cities the Can Heads were confined. Yes, and soon they'd be rounded up and placed in camps. Any aggressive action by them would be put down by violent means.

Contained . . . rounded-up . . .

No fucking way.

The real orders were simple. Kill them. In fact, if you even suspected someone of being one of them, you were to blow their fucking head off. And like sharks, they'd waste some time feeding on their own. Food is fucking food. And Jack knew that—despite orders quite to the contrary—he and the other cops were taking the dead bodies and poisoning them . . . leaving them for the others.

Anything, Jack thought, anything to cut down their numbers.

Anything to reduce the sick feeling that there were more of them than us. More of them—and growing, all the fucking time, more and more of them.

Jack turned away from the back door. No one was coming.

He looked at his car. It had been an ordinary station wagon. But then Jack had fitted it with all the necessary items. There was metal shielding to protect the tires from a sniper. The windshield and side windows were all reinforced safety glass, strong enough to stop a bullet. The underbody was protected by a steel shell.

And Jack had helped himself to a nice array of weapons and ammunition from the station, all now secreted below the spare tire, a small armory.

He crouched down. He checked his last modification to the car, the one that made his mouth go dry and cottony. He felt the wires running from the gas tank, to the front, and up—into the dashboard. He fingered the plastic strip covering the wires, holding them flush to the underside of the car.

There was no way it wouldn't work—
If he ever needed it.
No way . . .
Jack heard the back door open. He quickly got up and he heard Simon bickering with his sister, fighting over who got to ride in the back seat, the one that faced to the rear. They both hated it but Jack didn't want them sitting together, squabbling all the way Upstate . . .
The luggage sat on the roof rack. Jack stood up . . . straightened his pants.
It was time to leave on their vacation.

◆   ◆

"I've packed some sandwiches, and juice—"
Christie was sitting beside him. She patted his arm, and Jack smiled, looking out the windshield. It was a beautiful day, with a bright sun sitting in a deep blue sky. It looked like there'd be cool mornings and evenings, while the days would get just hot enough . . .
"What kind of sandwiches?" Simon bellowed from the back of the wagon.
Jack could guess this.
"Peanut butter and—"
"Oh, yuck—I'm sick of peanut butter. God, I hate—"
Jack looked up to the rearview mirror, to the back of Simon's head. "Simon—ease up, will you? It's just for the trip up. We'll have some good meals at the camp."
"I doubt that—" Simon muttered.
Jack chewed at his lip.
Laurie, his little girl, was playing with her doll's hair, grabbing a great hunk of hair and pulling it through a tiny hair band. She didn't get involved in the discussion.
Of course, Jack thought, Laurie has always lived this way, she was *used* to the way food was these days. Real meat was a rarity, a special item. Mostly there was beans and pasta, and even peanut butter was getting expensive.
The Great Drought killed the farm belt. Not just wounded it, there wasn't just a bad harvest. It killed it dead. Year after year of drought transformed the nation's bread basket, turning it dry, letting the prehistoric desert in the west slither east, claiming the farmland.

Things were bad here. But in California—a confidential police report said—things were way beyond bad. The whole state might be gone. The first state to be controlled by the Can Heads . . .

Not much news got out of California these days.

"Relax," Christie said. And she gave his thigh a squeeze. Jack looked over. She was wearing a pretty summer dress, great red flowers, with bare arms. Her legs were already tanned from hours spent in the garden in their backyard, coaxing tomatoes and raspberries out of the rocky soil.

He smiled. "Okay," he said. "I just got to turn the switch. Turn the switch, and start the vacation. Try to have some fun."

Every few blocks, leading to the highway, he saw a sector patrolman. It was reassuring, but it was also disturbing. It said that even here, even two dozen miles from New York, from the big city, there was danger.

Even here . . .

There was a certain route that had to be followed to the highway. Most of the entrance and exit ramps had been sealed. Now there were only a few ways on and off the Thomas E. Dewey Thruway. You could only enter—or exit—with a pass. And the Emergency Highway Police, a new division of the State Police, would shoot to kill.

"You have the papers?" he said.

Christie popped open the glove compartment.

"All set."

Jack slowed. There was a car in front of him. The highway itself, its six lanes visible just ahead, was deserted.

Not much traffic these days.

Jack inched forward. He looked at the highway. On either side there was a tall mesh fence, topped with spirals of barbed wire. How much fucking protection in that? Jack thought. What the hell good could that do?

Someone could just as easily lob something at us, some explosive, something to stop the car and—

Jack looked down, at the dash, at the switch just near the steering column.

"Jack—they've moved up. Go on . . . the booth is empty."

He nodded, and eased the station wagon up to the booth. There was no toll. All the considerable fees—from entry point to exit point and back again—had been paid weeks ago.

The guard, an automatic rifle slung over his shoulder, stepped down to the window.

"Hi, folks. How are you doing today?"

Making small talk. It was a technique. Sometimes they could look normal, almost act normal. But if you talked to them for any length of time, if you chatted to a Can Head, you'd *know*.

Shit, you could sense it—or maybe even smell it on them, on their clothes, on their breath. You'd maybe see a red dollop marking their shirt, the sign of Cain. And still smiling, you'd try to back away, lowering your gun, hoping you could blow the fucker away before he—

"Going on a vacation, eh?"

"Yes," Christie said, smiling, "our first with the kids. We're going to the Paterville Family Camp."

The guard nodded, looking at Jack. "Yes, I hear it's nice up there."

Jack had trouble engaging in the chit-chat, the little routine the highway cop had.

"Have there been any reports?" Jack said, "any trouble, on the way up?"

The guard laughed, as if it was a silly question.

"No. Nothing for weeks. Been real quiet. I think we've got them on the run. And you've got a good steel mesh fence there. I wouldn't worry."

The guard scanned the back of the wagon, checking out the children.

"You have a nice vacation," the guard said, backing away.

He went back to his booth and opened up the gate. It took forever for the whirring engine to sluggishly get the gate up. Then Jack pulled away, onto the highway.

He drove for miles, silent now, glad that Christie let him be quiet. And the only company on the road was a few lonely-looking cars, then a truck, a giant dairy truck.

Couldn't have milk in it, Jack thought. No way there was milk in that truck.

Christie turned on the radio, but the stations were already mostly static, and the warming sound of voices and old music—the only kind available these days—vanished.

✦   ✦

Laurie had fallen asleep, and Simon had crawled forward, searching for more chips and juice. He groaned when Christie told him that he was out of luck.

"But I'm hungry," he said.

He was always hungry. No matter how much they stuffed into him, there didn't ever seem to be enough to stop him from whining about more food.

"That's all we had," Jack said. "And besides—we're almost there, Simon, now just sit quietly."

Jack looked left. He thought he saw something, by the side of the highway. And he did, a curled shaving of black, a tire. A retread that exploded, probably stranding a car. He passed more of the tire, another black chunk, just to the side of the road. Just a failed retread, he thought. That was all. Or maybe it was something else. Maybe someone had their tires shot out from under them. That would be nice—lose your tires, and then rumble to a jangly stop, pulling off the deserted highway.

Maybe it happened at night.

And then you'd have to wait, in the dark—wait to see what climbed over the fence, or cut through it. You'd lock yourself in the car, of course. You'd do that. But that wouldn't help, that would only make it worse. You'd have to watch them, prying you out, like opening a can.

Once, on his patrol, Jack found a car like that. There was nothing left inside, it had been picked clean, no seats, no bones, nothing. Like a metal clam scraped clean by a giant set of teeth. There was just the red spatters—on the ceiling, on the floor, on the broken glass.

Dried spatters where it hadn't been licked clean . . .

Now—he looked at the fence, gleaming, silvery and secure.

Christie touched his arm.

"It's the next exit, Jack. It's just ahead."

He looked at her, and she smiled at him.

"We're almost there . . ."

Moving onto the country roads, they left the security of the highway, with its twelve-foot-high fence, its curled barbed wire.

Jack felt exposed.

"Lock the doors," he said.

Christie pushed down her button, then she reached behind and pushed down Laurie's button.

"Simon, lock your door."

His son shook his head and pushed down the button.

The blue sky was now dotted with big, grayish clouds that drifted across the sky, blotting out the sun. Jack felt chilled sitting in the car.

We're up in the mountains, he thought. Gets cold up here. I wish there was more sunlight.

They passed a house, a small wooden house all burned out. Ugly black beams jutted into the air to support a roof no longer there. He wondered what had caused the fire, and what had happened to the people inside. Then an old gas station flew by, two ancient pumps sitting outside. There seemed to be a general store inside the station, signs advertising Bud Light, Marlboro . . .

Jimmy Dean's Pork Sausage.

"How far to Paterville?" he said to Christie.

He didn't do a very good job of keeping the edge out of his voice.

"Just a few more miles," she said. "You turn off just ahead, onto Old Sanfellow's Road. Then the camp is just up a hill. There's a map . . . see."

Jack nodded. Good. We're close. The camp touted its security. Its 24-hour security force. Its electronic surveillance and electrified fence.

Maybe when I'm in there, when my family is behind all that security, maybe then I'll be able to relax, Jack thought.

But he doubted it.

"Good to see you folks." The fat man looked up to the sky. "It *was* a beautiful day." The man smiled. "Some nasty clouds kinda snuck in." He clapped his hands together. "No matter, let's get you to your cabin and start your vacation."

Jack watched the man lower a hand to Laurie's head and rustle her hair. "How's that sound?"

Laurie smiled.

The man, Camp Director Ed Lowe, is doing his best to put us at ease, Jack knew. Must get a lot of paranoid people coming here. He's trying his best to radiate as much warmth as possible.

They walked to the cabin, past the dining hall and a large room that
Lowe pointed out was the family rec room.

"We got ping-pong, pool, even some video games," he said.

He came close to Jack. "You seem a bit jittery, friend. Any trouble
on the way up here?"

Jack shook his head. "No." He forced himself to smile. "Nothing
at all. It's just—"

Jack looked around at the camp, at the people he could see down
at the lake . . . kids jumping into the now-gray water from a diving
platform. Little toddlers dashing around on the thin strip of beach,
happily falling down onto the sand. It looked wonderful.

He took a breath. And he said:

"I'm a cop . . . I'm in charge of one of the sectors. Right on the city
border."

Lowe made a big "O" with his mouth. "Oh—I see. I guess you've
seen a lot, Jack. Some real bad stuff." Lowe clapped a hand around
Jack's shoulder. "I hope that we can help you forget that stuff here."
Then, tighter, pulling Jack real close. "I hope that you and your family
have a real good time here."

The cabins, a line of small brown cabins that stretched from the
beach, around the curve of the lake, into the woods, were just ahead.

Jack looked behind him, and he saw his kids, open-mouthed,
grinning, eager to get in the water, to have fun, to play.

And Jack took a breath.

✦   ✦

"Knock-knock?"

Jack looked up from his suitcase. A man and a woman stood at the
screen door to their cabin. Laurie and Simon had already torn off to the
beach while he and Christie unpacked.

"Hi, folks," the man said. "I hope we're not interrupting but me,
and Sharon, we saw that you just arrived. We're—" the man looked to
his left—"right next door, and we thought we'd welcome you."

Christie touched Jack's arm, squeezed it. He looked at her. Her
smile said, *relax.* Stop being a cop. Invite the nice people in.

Jack went over to the screen door and opened it.

"Hi," he said. "We're still getting settled here."

The man looked at the room, taking in the open luggage, the beds filled with clothes.

"Oh, don't want to disturb you. Just being friendly."

Christie came forward, her hand extended. "Oh, no—thank you. That's very nice." She saw so few people these days . . .

She introduced herself and Jack.

"We're the Blairs," the man said. "Tom and Sharon . . . Our two kids are probably down at the lake already. You're going to like it here. It's safe . . . and it's fun."

Tom Blair grabbed his wife's hand and squeezed it tight. "We're having a real nice time here. You folks are going to *love* it."

People being friendly . . . it was hard for Jack to accept the concept. There wasn't any room for friendliness in this world. Not anymore.

"How long have you been here?"

Tom Blair said, "Three days. And we're signed up for two more. Gonna hate to leave."

His wife spoke, quietly, a woman with a whispery voice, as if she could be scared of the world. "Maybe you'd like to have dinner with our family. Everyone sits at these big tables."

"Very homey," Tom said.

Christie nodded. "Sure. We'd love to."

Tom Blair winked. "See you then."

The dining room was filled with noisy kids and babies crying and the clatter of cheap silverware clanging against plates.

Laurie and Simon had had a great time swimming. Laurie only wading to the edge of the lake, while Simon swam to the float and dove off.

Now, though, they were complaining about the food. There was a lot of it, but it was a pasty bean mixture. A gloopy dish that had Simon rolling his eyes and pushing his plate away.

"*This* is good food?" he said.

"Simon . . . " Jack said.

"Yeah," Tom Blair said. "The cuisine's not quite up to what the brochure said. But it's filling—and there's plenty of it."

"Oh, goody," Simon said, and the Blair kids, two boys, ten and nine, both laughed.

"There's a lot of people here," Jack said. "They must do some business . . ."

"Yes," Blair said. "But you know there's one thing that confuses me. Last night, I—"

But Ed Lowe was at a podium in the front of the room and his amplified voice suddenly filled the hall.

"Good evening, Paterville families! And let's welcome the newcomers!"

On cue, the hall resounded with a hundred voices booming, "Welcome newcomers!"

"Now listen up, families. I just got the updated weather forecast for tomorrow," Lowe said. "And it's going to be *beautiful*. And for tonight, we're having a sing-along by the big fireplace, and there will be games for the kids in the rec room."

Jack looked around as Lowe spoke. He saw so many families, so many kids. After years of leaving his house and stopping Can Heads—killing them—this all looked so peaceful, so safe.

Then—he thought:

Why don't I feel safe?

Tom Blair stood up.

"Maybe we'll see you at the sing-along?"

Jack nodded.

"Yeah," he said. "Maybe you will . . ."

"You're not sleeping," Christie said.

They had made love. First, they'd read books, waiting for the kids to fall asleep. And then Christie had shut her light off, and then his light, before she slid under the covers, working on him, making him hard.

While he listened.

There were noises outside.

He heard noises outside.

He thought that he heard gunshots, the sound of gates opening or shutting, or someone yelling—

No. It's just the sound of the woods, the lake. A screeching, the wind rustling leaves.

The sounds faded—and he had moaned.

"You're not sleeping," Christie said. He looked to her and her eyes glistened wetly in the blackness, catching the light.

"I—I can't sleep," he said.

It wasn't the first time he had trouble sleeping. Not by a longshot. And it was getting to be a problem . . .

She nodded. "Are you worried? I mean, how safe do you want us to be?"

"No. Everything looks fine here. Couldn't be better. Still—there's something that bothers me."

She made a small laugh. "Well, when you figure it out, be sure and tell me. But now I'm going to sleep. I want to enjoy the sun and the water tomorrow."

She turned away.

The room was cold. In minutes, he heard her rhythmic breathing, a reminder that he couldn't sleep, that sleep would only come when he was too tired to think anymore, to wonder . . .

What's bothering me?

◆　◆

He was in bed, rubbing his eyes. The door to the cabin was open. It was morning . . . that fast. Morning.

Christie stood there, cute and sexy in a great two-piece bathing suit. Jack wondered: When was the last time I saw her in a bathing suit?

He leaned up on one elbow.

"I'm taking the kids down to the beach." She peered over her sunglasses. "See you there, sleepy head?"

"Yeah, what time—?" He turned left. It was after nine. "I'll see you there."

The screen door slammed shut.

Jack sat up in bed. And then he remembered. He remembered his night, all the thoughts he'd had, until he finally came to one thing he could hold onto. The one thing that really bothered him . . .

The people, all those families in the dining hall.

Some of them—a lot of them—acted as if they'd been here a long time, as if this wasn't a vacation place, some new place to visit. They acted—what?

As if this was their home.

Maybe it was just a strange feeling. Maybe it was just his cop paranoia, seeing strangeness, sickness everywhere.

He got up, pulling on his jeans and a T-shirt. He went to the screen door. He heard kids playing by the beach.

Then he looked left, to the cabin where the Blairs were staying.

It's a crazy idea, he thought. Crazy—but it wouldn't hurt. It wouldn't hurt to ask Tom Blair if he had the same feeling.

I could laugh about it, Jack thought. You get crazy ideas when you're a cop. Pretty damn funny . . .

He walked down the wooden steps to the ground and hurried over to the Blair's cabin. He walked up the wooden steps and knocked on the door . . . and it swung open, ajar, creaking . . .

A woman was inside, but it wasn't Blair's wife.

"Oh, I was looking for the family staying here."

The woman looked up at him. She was putting clean sheets on the bed. She had a cart with towels, small wrapped packets of soap. Jack looked at her face, her eyes.

She looked as if she had been caught doing something.

The woman shook her head.

Then she smiled, quickly. She put a smile on her face.

"Oh, they left. They left the Camp. They had to leave."

The words came fast. Too fast.

I know when people are lying. I *know* that. Always have.

Jack was about to say something, about how the Blairs were staying a few more days, and she must have made a mistake. But he looked around the room. The cabin was empty. No luggage. Swept clean. They were gone.

Jack's throat felt tight. He nodded. "Oh—okay," he said. He turned back to the door.

He felt the woman watching him while he opened the screen door, then let it slam shut behind him. There was no morning sun outside, no nice day, like Ed Lowe predicted. Instead, it was cloudy, cool.

Jack thought of his family, down by the water, swimming with the other families . . .

He put on shoes and grabbed his wallet, his car keys . . .

Because that's all we need, he thought. That's all we need.

If it isn't too late. Oh, Christ, if it isn't—

✦   ✦

He reached the beach. He saw Simon diving, clumsily, without any grace. Boy doesn't get any practice, he thought. Not enough fucking practice 'cause there's not too many safe places to swim, not too many pools you'd send your kids to—

He felt a hand on his back.

"You have a good night's sleep, Jack?"

Jack turned around and saw Ed Lowe, standing there.

He nodded. "Fine. It was . . . very comfortable."

Lowe smiled. "The mountain air. Makes you sleep like a baby."

Lowe came closer. The wind changed. The Director nodded towards Jack's family. "They're having a good time. You did the right thing coming here."

Jack smiled back. He knows, he thought. He knows I saw the empty cabin, and that I asked questions, and now—now—

"We have a nice place here," Lowe said. "A real nice place for families."

And Jack looked at Lowe's eyes, at the runny egg whites lined with red, then down to the coils of fat around the man's neck. His big, strong-looking hands, with pudgy fingers.

Jack licked his lips. He doesn't look—

"Maybe this is *your* kind of place?" Lowe said, moving even closer, the wind carrying his smell to Jack's nostrils.

No. You don't get that fat on beans, on soy paste, on—

The smell. Jack knew what it was. He got it a lot, on the streets. It was the smell of meat, the tangy scent of blood. Lowe's lips were red, a Santa Claus red, rosy cheeks and beet red lips.

Jack watched Lowe run his tongue across his teeth, searching, scouring.

There was something there, something stringy, dangling from a tooth.

Jack couldn't breathe. The smell, the voices squealing by the water. He felt his car keys pressing into his thigh.

"Well—if you'll excuse me. I've got to—"

Jack walked past Lowe, forcing himself to breathe regularly. It's okay, he told himself. Lowe doesn't know anything. Jack walked over to Christie, sitting in a chair low to the sand.

"Get Laurie," he whispered to her.

Christie turned around. "What? Jack, what do you—"

He put a hand on her shoulder and squeezed tightly. "Please. Don't raise your voice. Please, be—"

He turned around, expecting to see Lowe there, watching, spying on him. *I'm not crazy, am I?*

Then back to Christie. "Get Laurie and walk to the car. I'll call Simon and follow you . . ."

"Whatever for? What are you—"

He pinched her shoulder, enough to cause some pain, enough to let her know that she should just fucking *do* it.

When Jack stood up, he saw people watching him, looking.

Welcome newcomers . . .

He moved to the edge of the lake just as Simon surfaced.

"Simon! Come here."

For a moment it looked as if the boy wouldn't come, that he'd make Jack shout to him while everyone watched. But then Simon kicked back and swam to him.

Jack waited, while the cool breeze off the lake played with his hair, while—all of a sudden—it got quiet on the beach.

"What's up, Dad?"

Jack leaned down close to Simon. He whispered.

"Simon. Don't respond to what I say. Don't do anything. If you understand, just nod a bit."

"Yeah, but—"

Jack shook his head. "Quiet! Don't say a word. Just—when I start off the beach, you follow me. Do you understand?"

Simon nodded.

There was no sound on the beach now, and Jack's whisper felt thunderous.

"Just follow me back to the car, as fast as you can. Don't look back, don't do anything . . ."

The boy was shivering. He wasn't stupid, and Jack's tone had cut through his annoyance and confusion.

"Now, good . . . ready . . ."

Jack stood up straight, turned, and walked off the beach, moving fast, not running, but walking with big strides while Simon, barefooted, trotted to keep up.

✦   ✦

He was afraid that when he got to the car, Christie and Laurie wouldn't be there, or maybe—God—their car wouldn't be there.

There were only a few cars there.

That was it. All along, and I didn't understand that, he thought. All those people, and only a few cars.

Welcome newcomers . . .

But Christie was there. And Laurie was sitting in the back. The locks were down. But when Christie saw him she leaned across and opened the driver and then the passenger door.

Jack picked up his pace. He dug out his car keys.

"Ow!" Simon said. He must have stepped on a stone, Jack thought, but he didn't stop.

He popped open the back door, and then his door.

"Get in," he said.

They slammed their doors together. Jack stuck the key in the ignition and turned it, fearing that it wouldn't turn over, that the car's insides had been trashed.

That's what I'd do, Jack thought. Rip the guts rights out.

But the car turned over. He pushed down the lock on his door, and Simon copied him. Jack looked back to the lake, to the trail leading to the beach, but he didn't see anybody following.

He pulled away.

And Christie—took a breath—and said: "Now can you tell me what this is about?"

Jack looked back at Laurie. He tried to protect her, to keep the badness away. But Christie needed to know.

"They're here," he said. "God—in this camp."

Christie laughed. "You've lost it. Now I know it. Why on earth do you—"

He looked at her as he pulled onto the gravel road leading to the gate out.

I'll ram right through that fucking gate if I have to, he thought.

"The Blairs. They were staying for two more days, and now they're gone."

"Their plans probably changed, Jack. Why do you—"

"The chamber maid cleaning their room—she was hiding something. I can tell, Christie. I know when people lie. It's my job."

"Mommy," Laurie said. "Daddy's scaring me. Tell him to stop—"

"Then this Ed Lowe guy tracked me down. As if he had heard that I found out something, that I *suspected*. Fat Ed Lowe . . . How the hell do you think he got so fat? And—God—I smelled it. On his breath. I tell you, I smelled it. And his teeth. They weren't clean, they were still filled with stringy bits of—"

The gate was ahead, just around the curve, past a tall stand of pines.

"Dad—hey, Dad, there's somebody—" Simon leaned forward, pointing at the road.

The road . . . filled with people.

They were carrying things. Sticks, bats, and—catching the dull gray morning light—silvery things. Ed Lowe was in the front, and there were children there, too.

He thought of what Lowe said.

A good place for families.

As if he was saying: You could live here too. We could *use* someone like you.

Jack had guns, but there were too many of them . . .

"Hold on," he said, and he floored the car.

Which was exactly what they wanted him to do. They had prepared for him.

They parted, exposing the gravel road, and the giant tree trunk spread across it. The car rammed into it and then stopped dead.

There was a popping noise, the sound of the tires being hacked.

Primitive. Prehistoric. The way you'd bring down a mastodon.

Laurie was crying, bleating, "Daddy, Daddy . . ."

Simon, sweet boy, good boy, whispered to him, so calm. "Should I get the guns, Dad?"

Simon had found them. Simon had been worried, too. He knew his Dad had brought guns . . .

Christie grabbed his leg. "Oh, God, Jack. Oh, no—"

Last year, when the food ran out, when the meat stopped, something had happened. People changed. There was no explanation for the sudden outbreak of packs, a cult of cannibalism. There were just a few small groups—Can Heads, the newspapers called them. Except one scientist said yes, this was probably the way the dinosaurs vanished.

Feeding on each other . . .

As if some switch had been thrown, some end-of-the-world switch. After all the suffering, the homeless people, the poverty, the hunger. Some final switch was thrown. And this was the way it would end.

They were smashing at the car's windows.

The safety glass didn't shatter, but a web-like mesh of cracks appeared. Eventually it would give out.

They surrounded the car. Jack saw the other families, their mouths open, wet lips, teeth exposed. They were angry. This probably wasn't how they liked to do it. This was probably too undignified.

Christie was crying.

"Jack, please. Our babies . . ."

The back window gave out, and now he heard the voices, the snarling of the Can Heads, this new species, human cannibals ready to feed on their prey.

Jack turned and looked at his wife.

Then back to Laurie. She had her hands over her ears, and she was crying, hopelessly trying to drown out the screams, the horrible sounds.

He heard them on the roof. Crawling on the roof. It was a feeding frenzy. Jack had imagined what it would be like—to be caught by them—and now it was happening.

We fell in the trap . . . he thought.

He looked at Christie. Her eyes begged for him to do something.

I will . . .

"I love you," he said.

The window by Simon caved in. The boy yelped, and screamed, "Dad!"

There was no more time.

Jack fingered the switch by the steering column.

For a moment he thought: What if it doesn't work? Oh, God, what if somehow it doesn't work?

He threw the switch.

The battery fired a spark into the over-sized gas tank.

There was the tiniest second of hesitation—and then the explosion ripped from behind him, with searing heat, burning, painful—the screams of his family mixing with the roar.

Merciful . . .

Ending everything in one blessed, white-hot flash of pain.

And then the screaming, the crying, the smashing, all vanished. . .

And the gravel road was quiet.

A TASTE OF BLOOD AND ALTARS

Poppy Z. Brite

In the spring, families in the suburbs of New Orleans – Metarie, Jefferson, Lafayette – hang wreaths on their front doors. Gay straw wreaths of gold and purple and green, wreaths with bells and froths of ribbons trailing down, blowing, tangling in the warm wind. The children have king cake parties. Each slice of cake is iced with a different sweet, sticky topping – candied cherries and colored sugar are favorites – and the child who finds a pink plastic baby in his slice will enjoy a year of good luck. The baby represents the infant Christ, and children seldom choke on it. Jesus loves little children.

The adults buy spangled cat's-eye masks for masquerades, and other women's husbands pull other men's wives to them under cover of Spanish moss and anonymity, hot silk and desperate searching tongues and the wet ground and the ghostly white scent of magnolias opening in the night, and the colored paper lanterns on the veranda in the distance.

In the French Quarter the liquor flows like milk. Strings of bright cheap beads hang from wrought-iron balconies and adorn sweaty necks. After parades the beads lie scattered in the streets, the royalty of gutter trash, gaudy among the cigarette butts and cans and plastic Hurricane glasses. The sky is purple; the flare of a match behind a cupped hand is gold; the liquor is green, bright green, made from a thousand herbs, made from altars. Those who know enough to drink chartreuse at Mardi Gras are lucky, because the distilled essence of the town burns in their bellies. Chartreuse glows in the dark, and if you drink enough of it, your eyes will turn bright green.

Christian's bar was way down Rue de Chartres, away from the middle of the Quarter, toward Canal Street. It was only nine-thirty. No one ever came in until ten, not even on Mardi Gras nights. No one except the girl in the black silk dress, the thin little girl with the short, soft dark hair that fell in a curtain across her eyes. Christian always wanted to brush it away from her face, to feel it trickle through his fingers like rain.

Tonight, as usual, she slipped in at nine-thirty and looked around for the friends who were never there. The wind blew the French Quarter in behind her, the night air rippling warm down Chartres Street as it slipped away toward the river, smelling of spice and fried oysters and whiskey and the dust of ancient bones stolen and violated. When the girl saw Christian standing alone behind the bar, narrow, white, and immaculate with his black hair glittering on his shoulders, she came and hopped onto a bar stool – she had to boost herself – and said, as she did most nights, "Can I have a screwdriver?"

"Just how old are you, love?" Christian asked, as he did most nights.

"Twenty." She was lying by at least four years, but her voice was so soft that he had to listen with his whole cupped ear to hear it, and her arms on the bar were thin and downed with fine blond hairs; the big smudges of dark makeup like bruises around her eyes, the ratty bangs, and the little sandalled feet with their toenails painted orange only made her more childlike. He mixed the drink weak and put two cherries in it. She fished the cherries out with her fingers and ate them one by one, sucking them like candy, before she started sipping her drink.

Christian knew the girl came to his bar because the drinks were cheap and he would serve them to her with no annoying questions about ID or why a pretty girl wanted to drink alone. She always turned with a start every time the street door opened, and her hand would fly to her throat. "Who are you waiting for?" Christian asked her the first time she came in.

"The vampires," she told him.

She was always alone, even on the last night of Mardi Gras. The black silk dress left her throat and arms bare. Before, she had smoked Marlboro Lights. Christian told her that only virgins were known to smoke those, and she blushed and came in the next night with a pack of Camels. She said her name was Jessy, and Christian only smiled at her joke about the vampires; he didn't know how much she knew. But she had pretty ways and a sweet shy smile, and she was a tiny brightness in every ashen empty night.

He certainly wasn't going to bite her.

The vampires got into town sometime before midnight. They parked their black van in an illegal space, then got hold of a bottle of chartreuse and reeled down Bourbon Street swigging it by turns, their arms around one another's shoulders, their hair in one another's faces. All three had outlined their features in dark blots of makeup, and the larger two had teased their hair into great tangled clumps. Their pockets were stuffed with candy they ate noisily, washing it down with sweet green mouthfuls of chartreuse. Their names were Molochai, Twig, and Zillah, and they wished they had fangs but had to make so with teeth they filed sharp, and they could walk in sunlight as their great-grandfathers could not. But they preferred to do their roaming at night, and as they roamed unsteadily down Bourbon Street, they raised their voices in song. Molochai peeled the wrapper off a HoHo, crammed as much of it into his mouth as he could, and kept singing, spraying Twig with crumbs of chocolate.

"Give me some," Twig demanded. Molochai scooped some of the HoHo out of his mouth and offered it to Twig. Twig laughed helplessly, clamped his lips shut and shook his head, finally relented and licked the creamy brown paste off Molochai's fingers.

"Vile dogs," said Zillah. Zillah was the most beautiful of the three, with a smooth, symmetrical, androgynous face, with brilliant eyes as green as the last drop of chartreuse in the bottle. Only Zillah's hands gave away his gender; they were large and strong and heavily veined beneath the thin white skin. He wore his nails long and pointed, and he wore his caramel-colored hair tied back with a purple silk scarf. Wisps of the ponytail had escaped, framing the stunning face, the achingly green eyes. Zillah stood a head and a half shorter than Molochai and Twig, but his ice-cold poise and the way his larger companions flanked him told onlookers that Zillah was the absolute leader here.

Molochai and Twig's features were like two sketches of the same face done by different artists, one using sharp straight angles, the other working in curves and circles. Molochai was baby-faced, with large round eyes and a wide wet mouth he liked to smear with orange lipstick. Twig's face was angular and clever; his eyes tracked every movement. But the two were of the same size and shape, and more often than not they walked, or staggered, in step with each other.

They grinned and bared their teeth at a tall boy in full Nazi uniform who had veered directly into their path. From a distance Molochai and Twig's filed teeth were unremarkable except for the film of chocolate that webbed them, but some small bloodlust in their eyes made the boy turn away, looking for trouble somewhere else, somewhere that vampires would not trouble themselves to go.

They made their way through the gaudy throngs to the sidewalk, steadying themselves against posters that screamed MEN WILL TURN INTO WOMEN BEFORE YOUR EYES!!!, pictures of blondes with tired breasts and five-o'clock shadows. They stumbled past racks of postcards, racks of T-shirts, bars that opened onto the sidewalk and served drinks to passerbys. Overhead, fireworks blossomed and turned the sky purple with their smoke, and the air was thick with smoke and liquor-breath and river-mist. Molochai let his head fall back on Twig's shoulder and looked up at the sky, and the fireworks dazzled his eyes.

They left the sleazy lights of Bourbon Street behind, swayed left onto dark Conti and right onto Chartres. Soon enough they found a tiny bar with stained-glass windows and a friendly light inside. The sign above the door said CHRISTIAN'S. The vampires staggered in.

They were the only customers except for a silent little girl sitting at the bar, so they commandeered a table and slammed down another bottle of chartreuse, talking loudly to each other, then looking at Christian and laughing, shrugging. His forehead *was* very high and pale, and his nails were as long and pointed as Zillah's. "Maybe —" said Molochai, and Twig said, "Ask him." They both looked at Zillah for approval. Zillah glanced over at Christian and raised a languid eyebrow, then lifted one shoulder in a tiny shrug.

No one paid any attention to the girl at the bar, although she stared at them ceaselessly, her eyes bright, her lips moist and slightly parted.

When Christian brought them their tab, Molochai dug deep in his pocket and produced a coin. He did not put the coin in Christian's hand, but held it up to the light so that Christian might look well at it. It was a silver doubloon, of the same shape and size as those thrown from Mardi Gras parade floats along with the treasure trove of other trinkets – the beads, the bright toys, the sweet sugar candy. But this doubloon was heavier and far, far older than those. Christian could not make out the year; the silver was scarred, tarnished, smudged with Molochai's sticky fingerprints. But the picture was still clear: the head of a beautiful man with enormous sensuous lips. Lips that would be as red as blood were they not carved in cold, heavy silver. Lips pricked by long, sharp fangs. Below the man's face, in ornate letters, the word *BACCHUS* curved.

"How – how do you come?" Christian stammered.

Molochai smiled his chocolatey smile. "In peace," he said. He looked at Zillah, who nodded. Molochai did not take his eyes from Zillah's as he picked up the empty green-and-gold chartreuse bottle, broke it against the edge of the table, and drew a razor-edge of glass across the soft skin of his right wrist. A shallow crimson gash opened there, nearly obscene in its brightness. Molochai, still smiling, offered his wrist to Christian. Christian pressed his lips to the gash, closed his eyes, and sucked like a baby, tasting the Garden of Eden in the drops of chartreuse that mingled with Molochai's blood.

Twig watched for a few moments, his eyes dark, his face lost, almost bewildered. Then he picked up Molochai's left arm and bit at the skin of the wrist until the blood flowed there too.

Jessy watched with eyes wide and disbelieving. She saw her dignified friend Christian's mouth smeared with blood, trembling with passion. She saw Twig's teeth at Molochai's wrist, saw the flesh part and the blood flow into Twig's mouth. Most of all she saw the lovely impassive face of Zillah looking on, his brilliant eyes like green jewels set in moonstone. And her stomach clenched, and her mouth watered, and a secret message traveled from the softest fold between her legs to the deepest whorl of her brain – *the vampires! The VAMPIRES!*

Jessy stood up very quietly, and then the bloodlust she had wanted so badly was upon her. She leapt, tore Molochai's arm away from Twig, and tried to fasten her lips to the gash. But Molochai turned furiously on her and batted her away, hard across the face, and she felt the pain in her lip before she tasted the blood there, her own dull blood in her mouth. Molochai and Twig and even kind Christian stood staring at her, bloodied and wild-eyed, like dogs startled at a kill, like interrupted lovers.

But as she backed away from them, a pair of warm arms went around her from behind and a pair of large strong hands caressed her through the silk dress, and a voice whispered, "His blood is sticky-sweet anyway, my dear – I can give you something nicer."

She never knew Zillah's name, or how she ended up with him on a blanket in the back room of Christian's bar. She only knew that her blood was smeared across his face, that his fingers and his tongue explored her body more thoroughly than any had before, that once she thought he was inside her and she was inside him at once, that his sperm smelled like altars, and that his hair drifted across her eyes as she went to sleep.

It was one of the rare nights that Molochai, Twig, and Zillah spent apart. Zillah slept on the blanket with Jessy, hidden between cases of whisky, cupping her breasts in his hands. Molochai slept in Christian's room above the bar with Christian and Twig cuddled close to him, their mouths still working sleepily at his wrists.

Below, far away on Bourbon Street, the mounted police rode their high-stepping steeds through the crowd, chanting, "Leave the street. Mardi Gras is officially over. Leave the street. Mardi Gras is officially over," each one ready with a sap for a drunken skull. And the sun came up on the Wednesday morning trash in the gutters, the butts and the cans and the gaudy, forgotten beads, and the vampires slept with their lovers, for they preferred to do their roaming at night.

Molochai, Twig, and Zillah left town the next evening after the sun went down, so they never knew that Jessy was pregnant. None of them had seen a child of their race being born, but they all knew that their mothers had died in childbirth. They would not have stayed around.

Jessy disappeared for nearly a month. When she came back to Christian's bar, it was to stay for good. Christian gave her the richest food he could afford and let her wash glasses when she insisted on earning her keep. Sometimes, remembering Molochai's blood smeared around Christian's mouth, remembering Zillah's fragrant sperm inside her, Jessy crept into bed with Christian and sat on top of him until he could make love to her. He would not bite her, and for that she beat at his face with her fists until he slapped her and told her to stop. Then she moved quietly over him. He watched her grow gravid through the sweltering oily summer months, lazily shaping her tight distended belly and her swollen breasts with his hands.

When her time came, Christian poured whiskey down her throat like water. It wasn't enough. Jessy screamed until she could scream no more, and her eyes showed only the whites with their silvery rims, and great gouts of blood poured from her. When the baby slipped out of Jessy, its head turned and its eyes met Christian's: confused, intelligent, innocent. A shred of deep pink tissue was caught in the tiny mouth, softening between the working gums.

Christian separated the baby from Jessy, wrapped it in a blanket, and held it up to the window. If its first sight was of the French Quarter, it would know its way around those streets forever – should it ever need such knowledge. Then he knelt between Jessy's limp legs and looked at the poor torn passage that had given him so many nights of idle pleasure. Ruined now, bloody.

So much blood to go to waste.

Christian licked his lips, licked them again.

Christian's bar was closed for ten nights. Christian's car, a silver Bel Air that had served him well for years, headed north. He drove up any road that looked anonymous, along any highway he knew he would not remember.

Little Nothing was a lovely baby, a sugar-candy confection of a baby with enormous dark blue eyes and a mass of golden-brown hair. Someone would love him. Someone human, away from the South, away from the hot night air and the legends. Nothing might escape the hunger for blood, might be happy, might be whole.

Toward dawn, in a Maryland suburb full of fine graceful houses, dark grassy lawns, long sleek cars in sweeping driveways, a tall thin figure draped in heavy black clothes stooped, set a bundle down on a doorstep, and went slowly away without looking back. Christian was remembering the last night of Mardi Gras, and the taste of blood and altars was in his mouth.

The baby Nothing opened his eyes and saw darkness, soft and velvety, pricked with sparkling white light. His mouth drew down; his eyebrows came together in a frown. He was hungry. He could not see the basket that cradled him, could not read the note in spidery handwriting pinned to his blanket: *His name is Nothing. Care for him and he will bring you luck.* He lay in the basket snug as a king cake baby, pink and tiny as the infant Christ in plastic, and he knew only that he wanted light and warmth and food, as a baby will. And he opened his mouth wide and showed his soft pink gums and yelled. He yelled long and loud until the door opened and warm hands took him in.

MR. GOD

Thomas Tessier

Rex nearly threw up when he finally saw the damn things. He thought about changing his mind—but the upside was too good to pass on. Joey brought in a cardboard banana carton, set it down on the kitchen table and removed the lid. They were in a plastic bag packed with ice and sawdust: a dozen monkey heads. There was a lot of blood, still wet, and stringy bits of mangled flesh that trailed away from the coarse black hair.

"A dozen?" Rex asked.

"Yeah, a baker's dozen," Joey replied with a brief laugh.

"How much did he settle for?"

"Three hundred."

"You're sure they're not rotten?"

"He did it while I waited."

"Okay. Good." Then, "What kind are they?"

"He didn't say."

"Probably doesn't matter."

"Nah. Monkeys are monkeys."

Rex went to the refrigerator and took out a pitcher of high-protein milkshake that he had prepared earlier. Then he removed one of the monkey heads from the bag. It was damp, and the short hair had a stiff, wiry feel. He put it down on the butcher board and stared at it for a few seconds.

"You sure?" Joey asked.

"Sure I'm sure."

"Okay."

Joey turned away to get a beer from the fridge. Rex picked up the hammer and tapped the monkey head a couple of times to get an idea of how hard it was. Then he gave it a firm blow, and the skull cracked audibly.

"Perfect," Rex said.

"You got a nice touch, boss."

Rex gently pried the pieces of bone apart. He used a fork to separate the layers of brain tissue that looked like grey mud with a blush on it.

"Did he tell you what the hyper-whaddaya . . . "

"Hypothalamus," Joey supplied.

"Right."

"He told me it looks kinda like a pea, only a little fatter. And lumpy. It's lumpy."

"Yeah, here it is."

"At the bottom of the brain?" Joey asked, still reluctant to look directly at what Rex was doing.

"Yeah, sort of."

"That's it."

"Small, but packed with goodies." The only way to do it was quickly, so Rex put the fork in his mouth and then pulled it out. The gland sat on his tongue, cool and slimy. Rex became aware of an unpleasant odor rising through his nasal passages from within. He took a large gulp of milkshake, and then swallowed.

"No problem," Rex said, reaching into the plastic bag. "One down, twelve to go."

The trouble is, Rex thought as he drove down the Hutchinson River Parkway, I take so much goddamn stuff that it's impossible to tell what helps and what doesn't. D-ball, Anadrol, Hexalone, Bolasterone, Dehydralone, Triacana, Human Growth Hormone . . . not to forget the monkey glands (but only that once). And something *was* working, because Rex was finally beginning to put on that crucial extra muscle that would lift him to the highest level.

Rex had been to all the main events but one. The regionals, Mr. America, Mr. Galaxy, the Night of Champions, Mr. Universe, but always as a spectator, never a participant. He was so well-built and handsome that he had acquired a minor cult following as the next can't-miss star on the bodybuilding scene. People told Rex that he was crazy not to start entering the major events, but he had his own schedule.

He had never been to Mr. God, the most prestigious event in the world. He had stayed away on purpose. He wanted to be sure he was absolutely ready. Rex intended to make his debut at the next Mr. God—and to win it. That would be an amazing coup—his first major event, his first first, and the best event there is. All of the other prizes would inevitably fall to him after that. Had anybody ever launched a new reign in such a dramatic fashion? Never. It would be one for the record books.

He took a familiar exit and drove into the Bronx. As usual, Dr. Jack's office was empty. The receptionist, Carmella, smiled warmly as she always did. She was reading a magazine, trying to stay awake until the phone rang or something happened. Carmella wanted Rex, but he didn't want her. Too skinny, small tits. And Rex had a serious problem.

"Hello, Rex," Dr. Jack said without rising. He sat behind a battered wooden desk that was cluttered with pill bottles, sample drugs and stacks of trade literature. "Looking good."

"Yeah, but I'm not feeling good."

"What's the problem?"

"My nuts are disappearing."

"Oh," Dr. Jack said with little concern.

"They used to be as big as peaches, Doc, but now they look like a couple of peanuts. You want to see?"

"No, I'll take your word for it," Dr. Jack said with a calm smile. "It's a common side effect."

"And I don't have any sex desire left," Rex continued. "Not any, none, zero. No boners, nothing."

"Right."

"Well, can you do something for me?"

"It'll come back, and your testicles will regain their size, when you stop taking all the steroids."

Rex shook his head. "No can do, Doc."

"I didn't think so." Dr. Jack shifted in his chair. "Well, I can give you some Halotestin. That should boost your sex drive a little. Maybe some Clomid too. Women use it to increase their fertility, but in men it has the effect of increasing the body's testosterone output. I've found that the two work well together. They'll get the old carnal juices flowing again."

"Great," Rex said.

"But you'll have to keep on taking them, as long as you're still on the other stuff. Otherwise, it soon wears off."

"What doesn't?" Rex asked with a bitter laugh. "I have to keep on taking *everything*. By the way, I need some more Hex and Bola. You know, I can feel that stuff working the minute I take them. It's like an electric charge in my muscles."

"Be careful with that shit. It's toxic."

"It's the only way," Rex said.

"Do you know Louie Ginacora?"

"Louie Gee? Sure," Rex replied. "Met him once or twice, at events in Manhattan. Why?"

"He died Saturday night."

"You're kidding. What the hell happened?"

"He just won Mr. Northwest States, and they had to carry him off the stage—once the curtain came down, of course. And less than an hour later he was dead. Dehydration."

"Diuretics," Rex said.

"You got it. He had a temp of a hundred and ten. He cooked himself to death."

Rex shrugged. "Diuretics are for piss artists."

Dr. Jack smiled obligingly. It was an old gym joke. "What are you aiming for, Rex?"

"You wouldn't believe me if I told you."

"Come on."

"Twenty-inch arms and calves, thirty-inch thighs, sixty-inch chest. Perfect symmetry."

"Jesus."

"Yeah." Rex smiled. "Mr. God."

"Connie?"

"Yes. Rex, is that you?"

"Yeah. Is your husband home?"

"Of course not, he's at the office."

"I'll be right over."

"It's been more than a month since I heard from you," Connie said in mild protest. "Rex? Rex?"

He got to Greenwich in less than fifteen minutes, and pulled into the secluded driveway that led to Connie's house. She tried to look both annoyed and uninterested.

"I was sick," he said by way of explanation.

"You still could have called."

"I think I did, once."

She had just closed the front door. They were in an elegant foyer. Rex grabbed her, lifting her white tennis skirt. She had a suitably discreet air of lingering sweat.

"Rex, not here. At least let's—"

"This can't wait, babe."

"Oh my God, it's like a crowbar. You poor man." She moved quickly, undoing his pants. "Here, lie down and let me take care of you. Were you thinking of me all the way over here?"

"I sure am."

✦   ✦

"You know, you taste different."

"Do tell," Rex said lazily.

"No, really. I mean it."

"I'm on a better diet now."

"You know something else?"

"What?"

"You're ready again."

Rex lifted his head and looked down across his belly. "I'll be damned. Doc was right."

"What was it—five minutes ago?" Connie said in amazement. "If that. Wow, I'm flattered. And this time I'm going to enjoy it, oh so slowly."

She removed her panties, licked her fingers and rubbed them between her legs—did that a couple of times until she was good and moist. Then she squatted over him and gently lowered herself until she could steer him inside.

"God, you're even bigger and harder than the last time."

"Yeah," Rex murmured happily. A few moments later she came to a sudden stop, and he opened his eyes. "What's the matter?"

"Rex, you're bleeding. From the nose."

He wiped his hand across his face and saw a bright red smear of blood. Then he could feel it trickling over his lips.

"I get nosebleeds," he said. "It's no big deal."

"Do you want me to get an ice-pack or—"

"It can wait." He held his head in a position so that the blood continued to drop into his mouth. There had to be protein in human blood, and Rex hated to lose any. But sometimes he just had to let it go: "Don't stop," he gasped.

"Okay," Connie said gratefully. "Ooooh-kaaay-baaaby!"

"Seven sets today," Rex said proudly as he dug into the huge platter of spaghetti and meatballs. "Seven sets and eight meals. Whaddaya think of that?"

"Don't overdo that weightlifting," Joey said.

"Yeah, I know. Man, I love your mother's sauce."

"One more month. Don't peak too soon."

"I know, I know." Rex gulped down a mouthful of shake. "Oh man, you know how many times I got laid today? Ten."

"Fuckin' hell."

"Too much," Rex said. "It doesn't take long, but it takes a little organizing, you know? I can't afford the time, but now I just see a woman and boing, I'm ready."

"Poor bastard."

Rex laughed. "That shit Dr. Jack gave me sure does the job, but I think I'll ease it down a notch. I don't even have to give it a thought, no fantasies, nothing like that. Just, boing, bang, and on to the next one."

"I kinda like the fantasy part," Joey admitted.

"Yeah? Like what?"

"It's always the same. I'm in the confessional at St. Joe's and Patty Fitzsimmons is sitting on my bone. She's wearing that plaid skirt and knee socks. Her white blouse is off, and—"

"Hey, come on, I gotta finish this meal."

"Sorry. That reminds me. I got a call from Dickie-boy this afternoon. Can you do Sunday?"

"You bet," Rex said quickly. "I was thinking about him. My cash is getting low, so this is perfect."

Dickie-boy was one of several contacts Joey had made in the New York gay world when Rex decided to work fulltime on his body. Rex did parties. Like an exotic dancer at a bachelor stag. Sort of an I-am-Adonis-and-you-may-worship-my-body act. The gay boys were wealthy, and paid very well. It was a job, nothing more—virtually his only regular source of income. Rex didn't have to touch them and there was no real sex, but he did let them stroke and caress him, and when the payoff was rich enough he'd let them suck or jack him off. Encores were extra.

"Great," Rex said, pushing the empty platter away.

"Anything else?" Joey asked.

"No, call it a night. See you tomorrow?"

"Yeah, I'll be here about five. Okay?"

Joey was a great help, a devoted friend. He had a day job, delivering parts for an auto supply company in Queens, and he put in countless hours a month helping Rex with any odd errand that needed doing. They'd been friends since grade school. Rex meant to see that Joey got a hefty share of the riches that would soon come flooding in after Mr. God.

"Five's fine," Rex said. "I'll be here."

"I'll just take care of these dishes."

"Thanks, Joey."

Rex stood up and took a step away from the table. He felt a wave of sudden dizziness surge through his head. Sweat seemed to erupt on his face. He grabbed at the back of the chair to steady himself, but knocked it over.

"Jesus, boss." Joey caught Rex as he started to tilt, and managed to get him to the sofa. "Lie down here, boss. You got a helluva nosebleed, it's really pumping out."

Rex tried to move, but couldn't. He was aware of something cold and wet being pressed against his face. He was swallowing a lot of liquid, reflexive gulps. It was hard to breathe. Then he lost track of everything.

✦   ✦

"What the hell is this?" A roar.

"Pardon?"

"Is this list accurate?" the ER intern demanded.

"What list?" Rex asked in a subdued tone.

"The nurse asked you what medicines you're taking, and you rattled off—*this*?" He waved a sheet of paper angrily.

"Yes, sir."

"All these steroids and androgens? Clomid, for God's sake? Halotestin?"

"I might've forgot one or two."

The intern gaped at him, then sought refuge in the piece of paper again. "I don't even know what some of this shit is. What the hell is Parabolin?"

Rex smiled weakly. "Para, yeah. You take a sip of that and your lips feel like sparklers for a couple of hours. You feel it in your muscles like you're wired to an outlet."

"Oh, really? Well, let me tell you something, Hercules, and you listen good. The next time you start spouting blood, you can save us all a lot of time and trouble by driving straight around to the back of the hospital. That's where the morgue is."

Rex didn't get a chance to formulate a reply. The outraged young intern stomped out of the cubicle and disappeared. Touchy son of a bitch, Rex thought. That's what honesty gets you.

✦   ✦

"You're all alone, Doc?" Rex said as he hobbled through the doorway into Dr. Jack's private office.

"Hello, Rex. Carmella's at the post office. Come in, come in. You're looking a bit delicate."

"I am." Rex eased himself into a chair.

"What's the problem?" Dr. Jack asked in a tone of voice that made it clear he knew perfectly well what the problem was. "Did the Halotestin and Clomid help?"

"Oh, Jeez, yeah. That stuff works great," Rex said. "I've been hopping around three counties like a rabbit on fire."

"Ah, good." Dr. Jack smiled.

"But I've been having these damn nosebleeds, and every one of them is a little worse than the last time."

"Right."

"One minute I'm fine, then suddenly blood's flying right out of my face. I mean, I'm really hosing the stuff, Doc."

"You have to cut back," Dr. Jack said. "That's the only way you'll get the nosebleeds to stop."

"Any one thing in particular?" Rex asked hopefully.

"The whole menu, I should think. How can anybody know what this or that drug is doing to you, when you take so many, and in such reckless combinations?"

"Two and a half weeks, Doc," Rex said pleadingly. "Two and a half weeks to Mr. God."

"You'll probably be fine till then, but as soon as it's over you have to give your body a rest."

"Sure, sure," Rex agreed with obvious relief. He tapped his chest. "Fifty-nine and a quarter, Doc."

"Very good. You aren't experiencing any other problems?"

"Just a little dizziness—that comes with the nosebleeds. And I woke up in the middle of the night a couple of times in the last week, with these shooting pains in my sides. Like real bad cramps, you know? I figure that's just from the way I eat—I'm putting away eight meals a day, plus snacks."

"Stand up, Rex, and lift your shirt." Dr. Jack came around the desk and examined Rex's abdomen, gently palpating and probing the flesh. Then he pressed one spot, and Rex sank to his knees with a gasp of pain. "Mm-hmmn."

"Jeez, Doc," Rex muttered. "What'd you do?"

"That where you've been feeling the—cramps?"

"Yeah, in and around there."

"Sit down." Dr. Jack returned behind the desk and took his own seat again. "You've probably got some cysts growing in your liver. It's a common occurence among people who take steroids on a regular basis."

"Cysts? Is that bad?"

"They'll stop growing if you stop—"

"And if I don't?" Rex cut in.

"They'll keep growing, destroying your liver, and eventually they'll explode and kill you."

"Can you operate?" Rex hated the thought of a scar on his body. "Can you just, like, cut 'em out?"

Dr. Jack laughed. "No. But you can relax for now, because they've probably just started. You'd be in a lot more pain all the time if they were advanced. And as for your liver, a person can get by all right as long as there's about twenty percent of it still functioning."

"Oh, good. I can taper off later."

"Sure," Dr. Jack said agreeably.

"Doc, I need something to juice me up for the extra sets of exercises I have to do. I get tired and lazy, and I can't afford that now, when I'm less than three weeks from Mr. God."

Dr. Jack nodded. "I can give you some Ritalin. Just don't take too much of it or you'll find yourself ripping doors off of their hinges."

"Gotcha."

Rex closed the door behind him as he stepped back into the reception room. Carmella had returned from the post office. She was standing by her desk with her skirt up in her hands, so that the electric fan cooled her legs and crotch. She glanced back at Rex, then turned and dropped her skirt—but not before he could get a look at her thighs. Not as thin as he had thought. Nicely curved, in fact.

"Hi, Rex."

"Hi."

"This heat's something, isn't it?"

"Yeah."

"I keep asking him to get an air-conditioner for this room, and he keeps saying that he will, but he never does."

She sat back against the edge of the desk, legs apart. She held the front of her blouse and fluttered it back and forth in a fanning motion. He could see the curve of a breast.

"Rex, you're going to be Mr. God. I know it."

"Thanks."

Rex shuffled toward the door, but hesitated when he came to Carmella. He was hunched over slightly, moving awkwardly.

"Are you all right?" she asked with concern.

"Oh yeah, it's just a little . . . embarrassing."

"What?" A hand on his arm.

"You're so pretty today, and . . . " He glanced down.

"Rex . . . " She saw the enormous bulge in his pants. "Come in here with me." She steered him into the adjacent supply room and locked the door. She smiled. "Show me your chest?" Rex pulled his

T-shirt over his head. Carmella's eyes widened, and she ran her hand adoringly over the layered muscles. "Fabulous. And can I see your legs?" Rex kicked his shoes off and carefully tugged his slacks and underpants down, stepping out of them. He struck his best pose, proudly rippling his muscles in a dazzling cascade of sweat-slicked flesh. Like everyone who saw him naked, she was awed not just by his body, but also by its complete lack of hair. Hair belonged on the head, nowhere else. He turned and presented his backside to her, continuing to flex in sequence. She went down, taking his lower body in her arms, stroking him, kissing him, pressing her face to his skin everywhere.

He stood there, and let her.

It's always like this, he thought dreamily. They want to be all over you, they'd be in your skin if they could. To touch you and touch you and never stop touching—it was like adoration, a surrender to worship. Because you are more physical, more real, more alive—and more than merely human, a higher form. No, not a god—but godlike, a nearly perfect incarnation. This is what they wanted to touch, to feel, to hold to themselves, to take in their bodies and mouths—gay boys and ordinary women alike—a touch of the glorious, the purely physical. Everything that they have lost and will never find again.

✦   ✦

"How can I go onstage like this?"

"No problem," Joey said comfortingly. "You're going to have to smile, right? So your mouth is open. If you have to swallow, do it as part of another movement, so it doesn't look like you're gulping."

"Yeah, but what if I start dripping?"

"Suck it down, boss. Suck it down."

Rex was lying on the table. Joey used tweezers to withdraw a wad of bloody cotton. He dropped it in a plastic bowl and went for the next one. It was a workable idea, the only one Dr. Jack had been able to suggest.

Joey had bought a white cotton men's shirt, and washed it in warm water with no soap or detergent. Then he cut it into thin strips a few inches long, rolled them up while they were still damp, and chilled them in the refrigerator for a couple of hours. When they were ready, cold but not yet stiff, he used a Japanese chopstick to gently push them up Rex's nostrils, packing them in tightly. Twice a day, and it worked.

"But what if some of it oozes through and drips down my face and chest?" Rex persisted anxiously.

"Well, then you'd better do a quick twirl and wipe it off," Joey suggested with a laugh. "Don't worry, I'll put a fresh load in ten minutes before you go on. You'll be fine."

"I'll be fine," Rex echoed lamely. "Where's Carmella?"

"Making coffee, and a shake for you."

"I need her."

"Coming up." Joey packed in the last wad of cotton.

Like Joey, Carmella was devoted to Rex. She'd given up her job with Dr. Jack to be with Rex all the time. He needed her six to ten times a day, and it was much more convenient this way. It meant that Connie, and several other women in the area, no longer heard from Rex. But that was their hard luck.

Joey disappeared. Carmella appeared. It took less than two minutes, and Rex felt mildly relaxed.

"You know, your cum is kind of green now."

"Yeah, sure."

"No, really. It's greener than it was."

"It's just the light."

"I don't think so . . . It tastes different, too."

✦   ✦

"You sure?" Joey asked.

"Last round," Rex said, smiling. "Twenty-four hours. This shit'll be kicking in real good by then."

"You're sure."

"Sure I'm sure."

"Okay."

Rex took the first of a long line of pills, popped it in his mouth and washed it down with spring water. Alongside the pills were several plastic thimbles containing various liquids. He was not taking a chance. It was all there, everything except monkey brains. He had to laugh. He had done a few silly things on the way. Like monkey brains. Or trying to inject Beladron straight into his thyroid. The things you do, the money you pay. But all of that was behind him now. Next stage, Mr. God.

The official measurements were taken. Rex was dizzy, and could hardly stand or see. Black spots detonated silently across his vision, whether his eyes were open or shut. It took all his concentration to stay on his feet. It seemed as if he had to force himself to breathe. But he was aware of the oohs, and then the loud cheers and cries of approval. He hit every one of his targets. "You did it, boss," Joey shouted enthusiastically as he helped Rex stagger off the stage.

Perfect symmetry.

Rex was lying on a table in the dressing room. His head was buried in ice packs, only his mouth open to the air. The hideous nosebleeds and headaches were driving him crazy. Joey had just packed his nose with cold cotton, and stepped out of the room to let Carmella finish the prep. Rex tried to relax, concentrating on the exquisite movements of Carmella's hands as she jerked him off. He came quickly, but then Rex felt too sleepy, too subdued, and he was afraid that would come across onstage. He sat up and looked around anxiously.

"I want Ritalin, Para and Prima."

Carmella rooted through the tote bag and came up with them. She never questioned him, like Joey did, and he appreciated that. He popped the Ritalin, then sipped the Para and Prima. His mouth flared as if it were on fire, his lips jangled with electricity. Carmella finished taping his genitals. She slipped his shorts on and tugged them in place.

A knock on the door: "Five minutes."

"Come on," Rex muttered, waiting for the Ritalin to kick in. "Come on, damnit."

Another knock. Rex stood up. The muscles in his arms and legs were sizzling, and his chest was stitched with pinpricks of fiery light. In the tunnel, he stopped and flexed once, and his body felt like a symphony. Rex smiled and tottered on. He was aware of Joey nearby, a hand on his arm, and Carmella, a hand on his back. The silk robe fluttered in the air as he moved, like a thousand kisses on his body. Ahead—the noise, the light. He felt as light as air.

The crowd was primed, ready for a new star, and some of them gasped loudly in awe when Rex made his entrance. Women shrieked with pleasure, men roared their approval. It went on and on, and Rex realized dimly that they didn't want to stop. They were on their feet, trying to show that as far as they were concerned the winner was onstage now. Mr. God. Rex had never heard of such a fantastic reception by an audience at any event, ever.

He flexed once, just a quick flash, silencing the hall in an instant. He felt like a conductor. A long breathless pause. He began to flex in sequence, but something went wrong immediately. His skin turned into a suit of crimson beads as blood welled up in every pore. Lightning branched through his brain, showers of pain washing over him. He flexed automatically, and the blood sprayed from his body—and it was replaced at once by more. If they see this, Rex thought absurdly, I'll lose. He launched into the full sequence, but in his nervousness he rushed it, and his movements were forced, jerky. Blood continued to fly out of him, the pain was overwhelming, but he held his place. A moment later two security men wearing medical masks approached cautiously, but the Ritalin was surging through him now and Rex easily flung them into the crowd—which was screaming with horror and delight.

He tried to stick to his program, but blood in his eyes made it difficult to keep his balance. He changed position, and his feet now felt incredibly spongy. Something wrong, he repeated to himself, his mind a fog.

His body heaved once, then several more times, his diaphragm rocketing breath up into his head—and Rex felt the cotton wads shoot out of his nose in quick order. He caught a blurry glimpse of one of them as it unraveled slightly in the air. Blood washed freely down his face and chest now.

He could still hear, and the happy roar of the audience was gratifying. He had seen it in their faces—they loved him. He remembered that.

His flesh appeared to dissolve or melt from within, and Rex slowly sank to the floor. Bones gently pushed through his skin, which was turning into something soft and butter-like. Rex oozed out of himself, muscles still flexing automatically—but in a gradually diminishing pattern as they liquified.

Eventually, all that was left of Rex was a collapsed heap of bones in a large pool of radiant protoplasm—in which isolated ripples and flickers could still be seen an hour later.

DRIVE-IN DATE

Joe R. Lansdale

The Play Version

CHARACTERS: Merle and Dave and a Woman's Right Leg, complete with Belled Ankle Bracelet

PLACE: A Drive-in Theater somewhere in Texas

TIME: Now

SCENE ONE

Lights go up on two men in the front seat of a car. A rear view mirror hangs down and from it dangles a little, stuffed, silver armadillo. Our duo is dressed in Western clothes, have on cowboy hats. They're in their forties, average-looking. Dave is on the driver's side. Merle on the passenger's. There's a speaker in the driver's window and a wire goes from the speaker to a metal pole beside the car. On the seat between them are two tubs of popcorn, couple boxes of chocolate almonds, and two tall wax paper cups of coke. It's night, of course, but it's fairly bright because the movie hasn't started yet and the lot lights are on.

DAVE: I like to be close so it all looks bigger than life. You don't
          mind, do you?

MERLE: (PAUSE) You ask me that every time. You don't never
          ask me that when we're driving in, you ask when we're
          parked.

DAVE: Don't like it, we can move.

MERLE: (SLIGHTLY EXASPERATED) I like it. I'm just saying,
          you don't really care if I like it. You just ask. When you
          ask me what I like, you could mean it.

DAVE: You're a testy motherfucker tonight. I thought coming to
          see a monster picture would cheer you up.

MERLE: You're the one likes 'em, and that's why you come. It
          wasn't for me, so don't talk like it was. I don't believe in
          monsters, so I can't enjoy what I'm seeing. I like some-
          thing that's real. Cop movie. Things like that.

DAVE: I tell you, Merle, there's just no satisfying you, man.
          You'll feel better when they cut the lights and the movie
          starts. We can get our date then.

MERLE: I don't know that makes me feel better.

DAVE: You done quit liking pussy?

MERLE: Watch your mouth. I didn't say that. You know I like
          pussy. I like pussy fine.

DAVE: Whoa. Aren't we fussy? Way you talk, you're trying to
          convince me. Maybe it's buttholes you like.

MERLE: Goddammit, don't start on the buttholes.

          (DAVE LAUGHS, PLUCKS A PACK OF CIGARETTES
          FROM HIS POCKET, SHAKES ONE OUT AND LIPS IT.)

DAVE: I know you did that one ole gal in the butt that night.
          (REACHES UP, TAPS THE REARVIEW MIRROR.)
          I seen you in the mirror here.

MERLE: You didn't see nothing.

DAVE: (GRINNING AROUND HIS CIGARETTE) I seen
          you get in her butthole. I seen that much.

MERLE: What the hell you doing watching? It ain't good
          enough for you by yourself, so you got to watch
          someone else get theirs?

          (DAVE SNICKERS, POPS HIS LIGHTER, AND
          FIRES UP HIS SMOKE.)

DAVE: (SMIRKY) I don't mind watching.

MERLE: Yeah, well, I bet you don't. You're like one of those
           fucking perverts.

          (DAVE ISN'T BOTHERED BY THIS AT ALL. IN
          FACT, HE'S BECOME A BIT DISTRACTED.
          THE LOT LIGHTS GO OUT. A SILVERISH
          GLOW FILLS THE CAR, FLICKERS OVER OUR
          PAIR. TINNY MUSIC FROM THE SPEAKER.
          A VOICE: "HOWDY PARTNERS, TRUCK ON
          DOWN TO THE SNACKBAR . . . . ")

DAVE: (CUTTING THE SOUND OFF THE SPEAKER)
          Heard all that shit I want . . . I'll turn it up when the
          movie starts. Won't be long now. (SLAPS AT HIS
          NECK.) Goddamn skeeters. Man, that cocksucker was
          big enough to straddle a turkey flat-footed.

MERLE: Maybe we could just forget it tonight.

DAVE: Listen, you don't like this first feature, the other'n's
           some kind of mystery. It might be like a cop show.

MERLE: I don't mean the movies.

DAVE: (SLIGHT CONCERN) You saying you ain't up to the girl?

MERLE: I'm saying I'm in a funny mood.

    (DAVE THUMPS HIS CIGARETTE OUT THE WINDOW.)

DAVE: (TRULY CONCERNED) Merle, this is kind of a touchy subject, but we're friends, so I'm gonna ask it. You been having trouble getting a bone to keep?

MERLE: (ALMOST ANGRY) What!

DAVE: It happens. I had it happen to me. (HOLDS UP A FINGER) Once.

MERLE: I'm not having trouble with my dick, okay?

DAVE: You are, it's no disgrace. It'll happen to a man from time to time.

MERLE: (ANGRY) My tool is all right. It works. No problem. It's just a mood or something. Feel like I'm going through one of them mid-life crisis or some kind of thing.

DAVE: (REASSURING) Mood hell. Let me tell you, when she's stretched out on that back seat, you'll be all right, crisis or no crisis. What you need, Merle, is to lighten up. Lay a little pipe. You don't ever lighten up. Don't we deserve some fun after working like niggers all day?

MERLE: You got to use that nigger stuff? It makes you sound ignorant . . . . Will, he's colored and I like him. A man like that don't deserve to be called nigger.

DAVE: He's all right at the plant, but you go by his house and ask for a loan.

MERLE: I don't want to borrow nothing from him. I'm just saying
          people ought to get their due, no matter what color they
          are. Nigger is an ugly word.

DAVE: Hell, you like niggers so much, next date we set up, we'll
          make it a nigger. Shit, I'd fuck a nigger. All pink on the
          inside, ain't it?

MERLE: You're a bigot is what you are.

DAVE: That means I don't want to buddy up with no coons, then
          you're right . . . . But let's drop the niggers. We ain't
          never gonna see eye to eye on that one . . . . Thing is,
          Merle, you do have to learn to lighten up. You don't
          you'll die. That's what's wrong with you. You're tense.
          Listen here: I got an uncle, and he couldn't never lighten
          up. Gave him a spastic colon, all that tension. He swelled
          up until he couldn't wear his pants. Sumbitch had to get
          some of them stretch pants, one of them running suits, just
          so he could have on clothes. He eventually got so bad they
          had to go in and operate. You can bet he wishes now he
          didn't do all that worrying. He didn't get a better life on
          account of that worrying. He didn't get a better life on
          account of that worry, now did he? Still lives over in that
          little shit-hole apartment where he's been living, on
          account of he got so sick from worry he couldn't work.
          They're about to throw him out of there, and him a grown
          man and sixty years old. Lost his job, his wife, and now
          he's doing little odd shit here and there to make ends meet.
          Going down to catch the day truck with the winos and the
          niggers — pardon me — the Afro-Americans . . . . Before
          he got to worry over nothing, he had him some serious
          savings and was about ready to put some money down on a
          couple of acres and a good double wide, one of them finer
          mobile homes.

MERLE: Shit. I was planning on buying me a double-wide, that'd
          make me worry. Them old trailers ain't worth a shit.
          Comes a tornado, or just a good wind, and you can find

those fuckers at the bottom of the Gulf of Mexico next to the regular trailers. Tornado will take a double-wide easy as any of the others.

DAVE: You go from one thing to another. I know what a tornado can do. It can take a house too. Your house. I'm not talking about mobile homes here, Merle. I'm talking about living. It's a thing you better amend to. You're goddamn forty years old. Your life's half over . . . . I know that's cold to say, but there you have it. It's out of my mouth. I'm forty this next birthday, so I'm not just putting the doom on you. It's a thing a man's got to face. Before I die, I'd like to think I did something with my life. Hear what I'm saying, Merle?

MERLE: Hard not to, being in the same car with you.

DAVE: (CONCILIATORY TONE) Hey, I'm getting kind of horny thinking about her. You see the legs on that bitch?

MERLE: Course I seen 'em . . . . You don't know from legs. A woman's got legs is all you care, and you might not care about that. Couple of stumps would be all the same to you.

DAVE: No, I don't care for any stumps. Got to be feet on one end, pussy on the other. That's legs enough. But this one, she's got some good ones. Hell, you're bound to've noticed how good they were.

MERLE: I noticed. You saying I'm queer or something? I noticed. I noticed she's got an ankle bracelet on the right leg and she wears about a size ten shoe. Biggest goddamn feet I've ever seen on a woman. I never did care for a woman with big feet. You got a good looking woman all over and you get down to them feet and they look like something goes on either side of a sea plane . . . . Well, it ruins things.

DAVE: She ain't ruined. Way she looks, big feet or not, she ain't ruined. Besides, you don't fuck the feet . . . . Well, maybe *you* do. Right after the butthole.

MERLE: You gonna push one time too much, Dave. One time too much.

DAVE: (GRINNING) Come on, I'm jacking with you. Take it easy. Look here, you haul your ashes first. That'll take some edge off.

MERLE: (SLOW TO ANSWER, BUT THE IDEA IS BEGINNING TO APPEAL TO HIM.) Well . . .

DAVE: (MAGNANIMOUS) Naw, go one. It's dark enough. Nobody can see.

MERLE: All right . . . But, one thing . . .

DAVE: What?

MERLE: Don't do me no more butthole talk, okay? One friend to another, no more.

DAVE: Bothers you that bad, okay. Deal.

(MERLE TURNS AND LEANS OVER THE BACK-SEAT AND SNATCHES UP A BLANKET AND PULLS IT INTO THE FRONT SEAT. DAVE IS LOOKING INTO THE BACKSEAT, GRINNING. MERLE CLIMBS INTO THE BACKSEAT. HE'S ON HIS KNEES. HIS HANDS ARE OUT OF SIGHT, BUT IT'S OBVIOUS HE'S STRUGGLING SLIGHTLY. AFTER A MOMENT, HE COMES UP WITH A WOMAN'S SHORT DRESS AND TOSSES IT INTO THE FRONT SEAT. THIS IS FOLLOWED BY BIKINI PANTIES.)

(DAVE PICKS UP THE PANTIES, PUTS THEM OVER HIS NOSE, SNIFFS, DRAPES THEM ON THE GEAR SHIFT.)

(MERLE LIFTS A WOMAN'S LIMP, CHALKWHITE
LEG INTO VIEW AND HOOKS THE ANKLE ON
THE SEAT. AROUND THE ANKLE IS A LITTLE
BRACELET WITH TWO MINIATURE GOLD BELLS.
THEY TINKLE SLIGHTLY AS THE FOOT FALLS
INTO PLACE.)

MERLE: Look at that foot. Foot like that ought to have a paper bag
          over it.

DAVE: Like I said, it ain't the feet I fuck.

          (MERLE UNFASTENS HIS BELT AND PANTS,
          STARTS TUGGING THEM DOWN. HE LOWERS
          HIMSELF INTO POSITION —)

MERLE: (OUT OF SIGHT) She's already starting to stink.

DAVE: (LOOKING BACK INTO THE BACKSEAT) You can't
          get pleased, can you? She ain't stinking. She ain't been
          dead long enough to stink, and you know it. Quit being so
          goddamn contrary.

          (DAVE SHAKES HIS HEAD, LIGHTS UP A
          CIGARETTE AND BLOWS SMOKE OUT THE
          WINDOW. HE ROAMS AN EYE TO THE REARVIEW
          MIRROR, REACHES UP CASUALLY AND ADJUSTS
          IT. HE GRINS, PUFFS AT HIS CIGARETTE.)

MERLE: (STILL OUT OF SIGHT) And don't be looking back here
          at me neither!

          (DAVE'S GRIN DEPARTS. HE SWITCHES UP THE
          SPEAKER. THE MOVIE IS STARTING. WE HEAR
          EERIE HORROR MOVIE MUSIC. HE TURNS HIS
          ATTENTION FORWARD TO WATCH THE "SCREEN."
          HE CASUALLY PLACES HIS CIGARETTE BETWEEN
          THE DEAD WOMAN'S TOES. HE REACHES OVER
          AND TAKES A BUCKET OF POPCORN AND PUTS IT

IN HIS LAP AND STARTS TO DIG IN.)

(CAR SHAKES. THE WOMAN'S FOOT VIBRATES
ON THE BACK OF THE SEAT.)

(AS THE LIGHTS FADE, WE CAN HEAR THE
LITTLE GOLDEN BELLS ON HER ANKLE
BRACELET STARTING TO RING. AND IN THE
DARKNESS THEY RING, AND RING . . . AND
GRADUALLY FADE AWAY.)

SCENE TWO

(MERLE IS BACK IN THE FRONT SEAT. DAVE IS
STILL BEHIND THE STEERING WHEEL. THE
WOMAN'S FOOT REMAINS VISIBLE. THE TOES
HAVE THREE CIGARETTE BUTTS BETWEEN THEM
AND THEY ARE BLACKENED FROM HAVING BEEN
BURNED. IF THIS IS VISIBLE TO ONLY A SMALL
PORTION OF THE AUDIENCE, GOOD ENOUGH. WE
CAN HEAR SCREAMING AND THE GROWL OF A
MONSTER FROM THE SPEAKER. MERLE'S BELT
IS UNFASTENED AND HE REACHES TO FASTEN IT.
HE LOOKS SULLEN.)

DAVE: How was it?

MERLE: It was pussy . . . . Hey, turn that shit off.

DAVE: What you want me to do, read lips?

MERLE: Bad enough I got to watch this shit without hearing all that
         noise with it . . . . Hell, you're gonna take a turn anyway.
         What do you care what you miss?

DAVE: (HE TURNS THE SPEAKER TO SILENCE) Yeah, well,
         all right. But this ain't half bad. You don't get too good a

look at the monster though . . . . That all the pussy you gonna get?

MERLE: Maybe some later.

DAVE: Feeling any better?

MERLE: Some. I think maybe we had a hole cut in the backseat back there, it'd be good as I just got.

DAVE: Bullshit. You're just down, man . . . . Want a cigarette? You like a cigarette after sex, don't you?

MERLE: All right.

         (DAVE GIVES MERLE A COFFIN NAIL, LIGHTS IT WITH A LIGHTER. MERLE SUCKS SMOKE IN DEEPLY.)

DAVE: Better?

MERLE: Yeah, I guess.

DAVE: Good. I'm gonna take a turn now.

         (DAVE CLIMBS OVER THE SEAT.)

MERLE: (STARING AT THE SCREEN AS IF INFINITELY BORED. SPEAKS WITHOUT LOOKING AT DAVE.) Got to be more to life than this.

DAVE: (ON HIS KNEES IN THE BACKSEAT, UNFASTENING HIS PANTS) I been telling you, this is life, and you better start enjoying. Get you some orientation before it's too late and it's all over but the dirt in the face . . . . (HE MAKES A SLIGHT ADJUSTMENT IN THE POSITION OF THE WOMAN'S FOOT.) Talk to me later. Right now this is what I want out of life. Little later, I might want something else.

(DAVE LOWERS HIMSELF INTO THE BACKSEAT. BEAT. THE FOOT BEGINS TO SHAKE, THE BELL STARTS TO RING. GRUNTING SOUNDS FROM DAVE.)

MERLE: (LOOKS AT THE VIBRATING FOOT, LOCKS HIS GAZE ON IT. AN UNPLEASANT EXPRESSION CROSSES HIS FACE.) Bet that damn foot's more a size eleven than a ten. Bitch probably bought shoes at the ski shop.

DAVE: Hey. I'm doing some business here. Do you mind?

(DAVE LOWERS HIMSELF OUT OF SIGHT. THE FOOT STARTS TO MOVE AGAIN. CAR ROCKS. THE BELLS RING. LIGHTS FADE, AND IN THE DARKNESS WE HEAR —)

DAVE: Give it to me, baby. (LOUDER) Give it to me! (LOUDER YET. VERY EXCITED. ALMOST BREATHLESS.) Am I your Prince, baby? Am I your goddamn King? Take that anaconda, bitch. Take it!

MERLE: For heaven's sake!

SCENE THREE

(DAVE CLIMBS INTO THE FRONT SEAT, GETS POSITIONED.)

DAVE: (SMILING; SATISFIED) Good piece. (HE USES HIS FINGER TO THUMP THE BELLS ON THE WOMAN'S ANKLE BRACELET.) Damn good piece.

MERLE: You act like she had something to do with it.

DAVE: Her pussy, ain't it?

MERLE: We're doing all the work. Like I said, we could cut a hole
           in the seat back there and get it that good.

DAVE: That ain't true. It ain't the hole does it, and it damn sure
           ain't the personality, it's how they look. That flesh under
           you. Young. Firm. Try coming in an ugly or fat woman
           and you'll see what I mean. You'll have some troubles.
           Or maybe you won't.

MERLE: (DEFENSIVE) I don't like 'em old or fat.

DAVE: Yeah, well, I don't see the live ones like either one of us
           all that much. The old ones or the fat ones. Face it, we've
           got no way with live women. And I don't like the courting.
           I like to know I see one I like, I can have her if I can catch her.

MERLE: I was thinking we ought to take them alive.

DAVE: (LIGHTING A CIGARETTE) We been over this. We take
           one alive, she might scream or get away. We could get
           caught easy enough.

MERLE: We could kill her when we're finished. Way we're doing,
           we could buy one of those blow up dolls, put it in the glove
           box and bring it to the drive-in.

DAVE: I've never cottoned to something like that. Even jacking
           off bothers me. A man ought to have a woman.

MERLE: A dead woman?

DAVE: Best kind. She's quiet. You haven't got to put up with
           clothes and makeup jabber, keeping up with the Jones'
           jabber, getting that promotion jabber. She's not gonna tell
           you "no" in the middle of the night. Ain't gonna complain
           about how you put it to her. One stroke's as good as the
           next to a dead bitch.

MERLE: I kind of like hearing 'em grunt, though. I like being kissed.

DAVE: Rape some girl, think she'll want to kiss you?

MERLE: I can make her.

DAVE: Dead's better. You don't have to worry yourself about how happy she is. You don't pay for nothing. You got a live woman, one you're married to even, you're still paying for pussy. If you don't pay in money, you'll pay in pain. They'll smile and coo for a time, but stay out late with the boys, have a little financial stress, they all revert to just what mama was. A bitch. She drove daddy into an early grave, way she nagged, and the old sow lived to be ninety. No wonder women live longer than men. They worry men to death . . . . Hell, that was his wife put it on him. Wanting this and wanting that. When he got sick, had that operation and had to dip into his savings, she was out of there. They'd been married thirty years, but things got tough, you could see what those thirty years meant. He didn't even come out of that deal with a place to put his dick at night.

MERLE: All women ain't that way.

DAVE: Yeah they are. They can't help it. I'm not blaming them, it's in them, like germs. In time, they all turn out just the same.

MERLE: I'm talking about raping them, though, not marrying them. Getting kissed.

DAVE: You're with the kissing again. You been reading *Cosmo* or something? What's this kiss stuff? You get hungry, you eat. You get thirsty, you drink. You get tired, you sleep. You get horny, you kill and fuck. You use them like a product, Merle, then when you get through with the product, you throw out the package. Get a new one when you need it. This way you always got the young ones, the tan ones, no matter how old or fat or ugly you get. You don't have to see a pretty woman get old, see that tan turn her face to leather. You can keep the world bright and fresh all the time. You listen to me, Merle. It's the best way.

MERLE: Guess I'm just looking for a little romance. I had me a
            taste of it, you know. It was all right. She could really
            kiss.

DAVE: Yeah, it was all right for a while, then she ran off with
            some fella, and I bet some other swinging dick's come
            along since then and she's run off with him, and she'll
            keep running off until she's too old and ugly to hook some
            man other than the one she's got last, and she'll worry that
            poor sonofabitch to death.

            (DAVE LOOKS AT MERLE, SEES HIS COMMENTS
            ARE PAINFUL TO HIS FRIEND.)

DAVE: (SWEETLY) Don't think I don't understand what you're
             saying. Thing I like about you, Merle, is you aren't like
            those guys down at the plant, come in, do your job, go
            home, watch a little TV, fall asleep in the chair dreaming
            about some magazine model cause the old lady won't give
            out, or you don't want to think about her giving out on
            account of the way she's got ugly. Thing is, Merle, you
            know you're dissatisfied. That's the first step to knowing
            there's more to life than the old grind. I appreciate that in
            you. It's a kind of sensitivity some men don't like to face.
            Think it makes them weak. It's a strength, is what it is,
            Merle. Something I wish I had more of.

MERLE: (TOUCHED) That's damn nice of you to say, Dave.

DAVE: It's true. Anybody knows you, knows you feel things
            deeply. And I don't want you to think I don't appreciate
            romance, but you get our age, you got to look at things a
            little straighter. I can't see any romance with an old woman
            anyway, and a young one, she ain't gonna have me . . . .
            unless it's the way we're doing it now.

MERLE: (CONSIDERING) Yeah . . . I guess you're right.

DAVE: (THROWS A NOD AT THE BACK SEAT) Hey, she
            wasn't really so bad, was she? I picked all right, didn't I?

MERLE: (TRYING TO BE PLEASANT) 'Cept for them slats she
            has, she was fine.

DAVE: Good enough. (NOW HIS VOICE GOES FLAT.) Well,
            let's take the bitch to the dump site and throw her out . . . .
            Time they find her, the worms will have had some pussy too.

MERLE: You're a good friend, Dave. I ain't much to talking
            sentiment, but I want you to know that . . . The talk and
            all, it done me good. Really.

DAVE: (SMILING) Hey, it's all right. Been seeing this coming
            in you for a time, since the girl before last . . . . You're all
            right now, though. Right?

MERLE: Well, I'm better.

DAVE: That's how you start.

MERLE: But I got to admit, I still miss being kissed.

DAVE: (LAUGHING) You and the kiss. You're some piece of
            work, buddy . . . . I got your kiss. Kiss my ass.

MERLE: (GRINNING) Way I feel, your ass could kiss back, I just
            might.

DAVE: (LAUGH) I bet you would. Tell you what. Let's let this
            movie go to hell, dump the bitch, go on over to the house
            and watch a little *Dirty Harry*. I got it on tape.

MERLE: Deal.

            (MERLE REACHES OVER AND SLAPS THE
            WOMAN'S FOOT OFF THE BACK OF THE SEAT.
            SHORT FURY OF BELLS. A THUD. DAVE REACHES

TO START THE ENGINE AND THE LIGHTS GO OUT
AND WE HEAR THE MOTOR IN THE DARKNESS,
ALMOST GROWLING LIKE AN ANIMAL, MOVING
AWAY IN THE DISTANCE, AND THEN THERE IS
SILENCE AND —)

CURTAIN

DESERT PICKUP

Richard Laymon

"All right!" He felt lucky about this one. Walking backward along the roadside, he stared at the oncoming car and offered his thumb. Sunlight glared on the windshield. Only at the last moment did he manage to get a look at the driver. A woman. That was that. So much for feeling lucky.

When he saw the brake lights flash on, he figured the woman was slowing down to be safe. When he saw the car stop, he figured this would be the "big tease." He was used to it. The car stops, you run to it, then off it shoots, throwing dust in your face. He wouldn't fall for it this time. He'd walk casually toward the car.

When he saw the backup lights go on, he couldn't believe his luck.

The car rolled backward to him. The woman inside leaned across the front seat and opened the door.

"Can I give you a ride?"

"Sure can." He jumped in and threw his seabag onto the rear seat. When he closed the door, cold air struck him. It seemed to freeze the sweat on his T-shirt. It felt fine. "I'm mighty glad to see you," he said. "You're a real lifesaver."

"How on earth did you get way out here?" she asked, starting again up the road.

"You wouldn't believe it."

"Go ahead and try me."

He enjoyed her cheerfulness and felt guilty about the slight nervous tremor he heard in her voice. "Well, this fella gives me a lift. Just this

side of Blythe. And he's driving along through this . . . this desert . . .
when suddenly he stops and tells me to get out and take a look at one of
the tires. I get out—and off he goes! Tosses my seabag out a ways up
the road. Don't know why a fella wants to do something like that. You
understand what I mean?"

"I certainly do. These days you don't know who to trust."

"If that ain't the truth."

He looked at her. She wore boots and jeans and a faded blue shirt,
but she had class. It was written all over her. The way she talked, the
way her skin was tanned just so, the way she wore her hair. Even her
figure showed class. Nothing overdone.

"What I don't get," he went on, "is why the fella picked me up in
the first place."

"He might have been lonely."

"Then why'd he dump me?"

"Maybe he decided not to trust you. Or maybe he just wanted to
be alone again."

"Any way you slice it, it was a rotten thing to do. You understand
what I mean?"

"I think so. Where are you headed?"

"Tucson."

"Fine. I'm going in that direction."

"How come you're not on the main highway? What are you doing
out here?"

"Well . . . " She laughed nervously. "What I'm intending to do is
not . . . well, not exactly legal."

"Yeah?"

"I'm going to steal cacti."

"What!" He laughed. "Wow! You mean you're out to lift some
cactuses?"

"That's what I mean."

"Well, I sure do hope you don't get caught!"

The woman forced a smile. "There is a fine."

"Gol-ly."

"A sizable fine."

"Well, I'd be glad to give you a hand."

"I've only got one shovel."

"Yeah. I saw it when I stowed my bag. I was wondering what you
had a shovel for." He looked at her, laughing, and felt good that this

woman with all her class was going to steal a few plants from the desert. "I've seen a lot of things, you understand. But never a cactus-napper." He laughed at his joke.

She didn't. "You've seen one now," she said.

They remained silent for a while. The young man thought about this classy woman driving down a lonely road in the desert just to swipe cactus, and every now and then he chuckled about it. He wondered why anybody would want such a thing in the first place. Why take the desert home with you? He wanted nothing more than to get away from this desolate place, and for the life of him he couldn't understand a person wanting to take part of it home. He concluded that the woman must be crazy.

"Would you care for some lunch?" the crazy woman asked. She still sounded nervous.

"Sure, I guess so."

"There should be a paper bag on the floor behind you. It has a couple of sandwiches in it, and some beer. Do you like beer?"

"Are you kidding?" He reached over the back of the seat and picked up the bag. The sandwiches smelled good. "Why don't you pull off the road up there?" he suggested. "We can go over by those rocks and have a picnic."

"That sounds like a fine idea." She stopped on a wide shoulder.

"Better take us a bit farther back. We don't wanta park this close to the road. Not if you want me to help you heist some cactus when we get done with lunch."

She glanced at him uneasily, then smiled. "Okay, fine. We'll do just that."

The car bumped forward, weaving around large balls of cactus, crashing through undergrowth. It finally stopped behind a cluster of rocks.

"Do you think they can still see us from the road?" the woman asked. Her voice was shaking.

"I don't think so."

When they opened the doors, heat blasted in on them. They got out, the young man carrying the bag of sandwiches and beer.

He sat down on a large rock. The woman sat beside him.

"I hope you like the sandwiches. They're corned beef with Swiss cheese."

"Sounds good." He handed one of them to her and opened the beer. The cans were only cool, but he decided that cool beer was better than no beer at all. As he picked at the cellophane covering his sandwich, he asked, "Where's your husband?"

"What do you mean?"

He smiled. It had really put her on the spot. "Well, I just happened to see that you aren't wearing a ring, you understand what I mean?"

She looked down at the band of paler skin on her third finger. "We're separated."

"Oh? How come?"

"I found out that he'd been cheating on me."

"On you? No kidding! He must have been crazy."

"Not crazy. He just enjoyed hurting people. But I'll tell you something. Cheating on me was the worst mistake he ever made."

They ate in silence for a while, the young man occasionally shaking his head with disbelief. Finally, his head stopped shaking. He decided that maybe he'd cheat too on a grown woman who gets her kicks stealing cactus. Good looks aren't everything. Who wants to live with a crazy woman? He drank off his beer. The last of it was warm and made him shiver.

He went to the car and took the shovel from the floor in back. "You want to come along? Pick out the ones you want and I'll dig them up for you."

He watched her wad up the cellophane and stuff it, along with the empty beer cans, into the paper bag. She put the bag in the car, smiling at him and saying, "Every litter bit hurts." They left the car behind. They walked side by side, the woman glancing about, sometimes crouching to inspect a likely cactus.

"You must think I'm rather strange," she confided, "picking up a hitchhiker like I did. I hope you don't think . . . well, it was criminal of that man to leave you out in the middle of nowhere. But I'm glad I picked you up. For some reason, I feel I can talk to you."

"That's nice. I like to listen. What about this one?" he asked, pointing at a huge prickly cactus.

"Too big. What I want is something smaller."

"This one ought to fit in the trunk."

"I'd rather have a few smaller ones," she insisted. "Besides, there's a kind in the Saguaro National Monument that I want to get. It'll probably be pretty big. I want to save the trunk for that one."

"Anything you say."

They walked farther. Soon, the car was out of sight. The sun felt like a hot, heavy hand pressing down on the young man's head and back.

"How about this one?" he asked, pointing. "It's pretty little."

"Yes. This one is just about perfect."

The woman knelt beside it. Her shirt was dark blue against her perspiring back, and a slight breeze rustled her hair.

This will be a good way to remember her, the young man thought as he crashed the shovel down on her head.

He buried her beside the cactus.

As he drove down the road, he thought about her. She had been a nice woman with obvious class. Crazy, but nice. Her husband must've been a nut to cheat on a good-looking woman like her, unless of course it was because of her craziness.

He thought it nice that she had told him so much about herself. It felt good to be trusted with secrets.

He wondered how far she would have driven him. Not far enough. It was much better having the car to himself. That way he didn't have to worry. And the $36 he found in her purse was a welcome bonus. He'd been afraid, for a moment, that he might find nothing but credit cards. All around, she had been a good find. He felt very lucky.

At least until the car began to move sluggishly. He pulled off the road and got out. "Oh, no," he muttered, seeing the flat rear tire. He leaned back against the side of the car and groaned. The sun beat on his face. He closed his eyes and shook his head, disgusted by the situation and thinking how awful it would be, working on the tire for fifteen minutes under that hot sun.

Then he heard, in the distance, the faint sound of a motor. Opening his eyes, he squinted down the road. A car was approaching. For a moment, he considered thumbing a ride. But that, he decided, would be stupid now that he had a car of his own. He closed his eyes again to wait for the car to pass.

But it didn't pass. It stopped.

He opened his eyes and gasped.

"Afternoon," the stranger called out.

"Howdy, Officer," he said, his heart thudding.

"You got a spare?"

"I think so."

"What do you mean, you think so? You either have a spare or you don't."

"What I meant was, I'm not sure if it's any good. It's been a while since I've had any use for it, you understand?"

"Of course I understand. Guess I'll stick around till we find out. This is rough country. A person can die out here. If the spare's no good, I'll radio for a tow."

"Okay, thanks." He opened the door and took the keys from the ignition.

Everything's okay, he told himself. No reason in the world for this cop to suspect anything.

"Did you go off the road back a ways?"

"No, why?" Even as he asked, he fumbled the keys. They fell to the ground. The other man picked them up.

"Flats around here, they're usually caused by cactus spines. They're murder."

He followed the officer to the rear of the car.

The octagonal key didn't fit the trunk.

"Don't know why those dopes in Detroit don't just make one key that'll fit the doors and the trunk both."

"I don't know," the young man said, matching the other's tone of disgust and feeling even more confident.

The round key fit. The trunk popped open.

The officer threw a tarp onto the ground and then leveled his pistol at the young man, who was staring at the body of a middle-aged man who obviously had class.

FYODOR'S LAW

William F. Nolan

They were at nearly every street corner in Greater Los Angeles, standing or sitting cross-legged in their ragged, dirt-stiffened clothing, their faces stubble-bearded, eyes slack and defeated, clutching crude, hand-lettered cardboard signs:

HOMELESS!
HUNGRY!
WILL WORK FOR FOOD
PLEASE HELP???
GOD BLESS YOU!!!

Today he would help one of them as he had helped many others. He took no credit for this; it was simply his way, his personal contribution. He felt a real sense of pity for them. Society's outcasts. The dispossessed. The lost ones.

Dostoyevsky's children.

The one he selected was standing on the south corner at Topanga Canyon and Ventura, in front of a hardware store. He was very tall, well over six feet, and of indeterminate age. Under his ragged hat and twist of beard he could be thirty, or forty, or even fifty. They all had old faces; they'd lived too long on the dark side, seen too much, experienced too many horrors. The pain of existence etched their skin.

He pulled the long blue Cadillac to a whispered stop at the curb and ran down the passenger window, beckoning to the tall man. "Over here," he called, waving. The sun flashed rainbow colors from the diamond ring on his left hand.

The ragged figure approached the car.

"Get in . . . I have work for you." The driver's name was Conover—James Edward Stanton Conover—and he lived alone in a hillside home on the other side of the Santa Monica Mountains in Bel Air. He was wealthy by inheritance, had no need for work, and although he considered himself a professional artist, had never attempted to sell any of his creations. Every other year he traded in his Cadillac for the latest model. He always drove Cadillacs; his family had never driven anything else. His great-grandfather, in fact, had owned the first Cadillac in Los Angeles.

"You gonna help me, huh, mister?" The bearded man was leaning down to peer inside the car at James Conover.

"Right, I'll help you." Conover opened the passenger door. "Please, get in. We'll drive to my place. I have some work for you."

"I can fix anything," declared the tall man, tossing his hat and grimed knapsack into the seat behind him. "Do your plumbing. Repair your roof. Tile your patio. Weed your garden. Paint or plaster. You name her, mister, and I can do her."

Conover smiled at the man as he put the blue Cadillac into drive, rejoining the eastbound traffic stream along Ventura Boulevard. "You're a regular Jack of all trades," he said.

"That's my name," said the ragged man. "Jack. Jack Wilbur."

"How did you acquire all these remarkable skills, Mr. Wilbur?"

"From my Pap," replied Jack Wilbur. "We come here from Tennessee, me an' my Pap, after Ma took sick an' died. My brother an' little sis, they stayed on in Willicut, but we come out here to the Coast, the two of us." He stared at Conover. "Ever hear of Willicut?"

"Can't say that I have."

"It's fifty miles north of Chattanooga. Little bitty runt of a town, but full of good folks. My brother, he owns a feed store back in Willicut. That's how come he stayed there."

"Where's your father now?"

"Pap's in jail," said Jack Wilbur. "He done a violent act, an' they arrested him."

"What kind of violent act?"

"Well, ole Pap, he drinks some. We was in this pool hall in North Hollywood, an' Pap was takin' on whiskey. He gets mean when he drinks, an' pretty soon he's into a bustup with a trucker over one of the pool hall ladies. Killed him, Pap did. Just smashed his head right in."

"And you witnessed this?"

"Sure as hell did. But I couldn't stop what Pap done. All happened too fast. One minute the pair of 'em are yellin' over this blondie, an' the next ole Pap is layin' this pool stick alongside the fella's head. Split it open like you do a cantaloupe. It was a sight, I'll tellya. Blondie was screamin' like she was havin' a fit an' the police come an' hauled Pap off and now he's in jail."

"How did you end up on the street? It would seem that a man with your variegated skills could support himself."

"Well, I sure tried. But unless you work for some company it's tough findin' jobs that pay much. Since I lack me any kinda formal schoolin', no company will take me on. Believe me, mister, I'm no bum by nature. No siree, not Jack Wilbur. Back in Willicut I worked regular from when I was just a nipper, an' I had respect. Nobody called Jack Wilbur a bum in Willicut."

"After your father's incarceration, why didn't you return home—to be with your brother and sister?"

"Naw!" The bearded man shook his head. "I can't go back now. For one thing, I gotta earn enough money to show all them locals I amounted to somethin' worthwhile out here in California. Our family's always had a lotta pride, an' I can't go low-tailin' home like some kinda whipped hound. It's bad enough, what happened to Pap."

"I understand," nodded Conover. "I really do."

They were on the freeway, taking the connector to the southbound 405, headed for Bel Air. The sleek blue car purred along at sixty, smooth and steady.

"Real nice machine you got here," said Jack Wilbur. "I plan to buy me one a'these soon as I get back on my feet so to speak."

"You seem confident that it will happen."

"Betcha. Man like me, with all my talents, I'm fair bound to come out a winner. Just a matter of time. An' I'm only thirty, so I got me some time."

"I take it you've never been married."

"Nope—but I come real close once. There was this sweet little thing over to Haines—that's near Willicut—an' she just about roped me for sure, but I slipped away clean. Lucky I got shut of her when I did. Hell's bells, marriage should be for when you're ready to settle down and raise a flock a'kids." He chuckled. "Me, I'm a natural born ramblin' man. Been through sixteen states. That's another reason I don't want to go back to Willicut. It's what's on the other side of the hill that always takes my fancy."

"I admire your spirit," said Conover.

"What kinda work you got for me?"

"I live on a steep hillside," said Conover. "Lots of thick, fast-growing brush and trees up there. Dangerous in the fire season. I need this brush cut back from the house."

"I can do that easy," said the bearded man. He hesitated. "But I got no cuttin' tools. You got those?"

Conover nodded. "Everything you'll need is in the garage. Don't worry."

Jack Wilbur grinned. "Hell's bells, mister, that's one thing I never do—is worry. With me, things always have a way of workin' out fine."

And Conover repeated: "I admire your spirit."

James Conover's angular, flat-roofed, two-story house, at the top of Bel Air road, hovered at the edge of a heavily-brushed canyon like some huge stone-and-glass animal. Below the overhanging cast-steel deck the ground fell away in a steep drop that made Jack Wilbur dizzy.

"Geez!" he muttered, peering down. "Aren't you scared?"

"Of what?" asked Conover, standing beside him on the deck.

"Of this whole shebang ending up at the bottom of the canyon! I mean, a big quake could be murder."

"This structure is supported by steel construction beams sunk deep into granite, considerably below the surface soil. There's no need to fear earthquakes, let me assure you."

"Well, I'd say you got some guts, livin' in a place like this. Fine for an eagle maybe, or a buzzard."

Conover smiled thinly. "I happen to appreciate the view. On a clear day you can see forever."

Wilbur shrugged; it was apparent he didn't recognize the reference. "'Bout time for me to get crackin' on that job you mentioned."

"No rush," said Conover. "I spend a lot of hours alone up here and I could use some company. How about a drink before beginning your labors?"

Wilbur looked uncertain. "Pretty early in the day for booze," said the tall man. "I usually don't start till the sun's down."

"Then make an exception," urged Conover. "I have some excellent imported brandy. Aged to perfection." He saw Jack frown. "You do drink brandy?"

Again, Wilbur shrugged, uncertain. "Hard whiskey's more my style."

"All right, then, I have some Black Irish that should be suitable." He moved to the tinted glass door leading into the den and slid it back. "Please . . . " He waved Wilbur inside.

The den was richly paneled in carved oak with a fully stocked bar at the far end. Conover nodded toward a leather-topped stool as he moved behind the bar to fix their drinks.

Jack Wilbur scowled at his image in the bar mirror, rubbing a slow hand along his bearded chin. "Boy, I look kinda ragged. Need me a trim."

"Here you go, Jack," said Conover, placing a glass of Black Irish whiskey in front of Wilbur. He walked around the bar with his own drink, moving to a deep red-leather couch. "Let's make ourselves comfortable."

They settled into the couch and Conover, after a sip of whiskey, asked Wilbur if he had ever met any professional artists.

"You mean guys that do pictures?"

"In general, yes."

"Well, I never met none personal. Artists don't show up much in Willicut, I guess. Pap told me once that when he was in Chicago, he shook hands with the comics guy who did Dick Tracy."

Conover smiled. "If you'll wait here," he said, "I have something to show you."

He walked out of the den and returned with a thick scrapbook handsomely bound in levant morocco. He placed the book, unopened, on the coffee table in front of Jack Wilbur. Then he resumed his seat on the couch, taking another sip of Black Irish.

"What's in there?" asked Wilbur. "Pictures of your family?"

"Not exactly," Conover replied. "But they are photos. Of my art."

"So you're an artist, huh?"

"Correct." Conover smiled. "But not in any conventional sense of the term."

"What does that mean?"

"It means I'm not a painter or a sketch artist. I do montages."

Wilbur looked confused. "Mon what? I never heard of 'em."

"A montage is made up of various separate components. The artist uses these components to achieve a particular design. Actual three-dimensional objects are often utilized in the overall work."

"You're way over my head," said Jack Wilbur.

"You'll understand exactly what I'm referring to when I show you the photos."

"Well, I'm not much for art an' that's a fact. Never been in no museum." He hesitated. "Do these . . . mantoges of yours . . . do they hang in museums?"

"No, I destroy the originals after I photograph them," said Conover. "They exist only in this book."

"Well, I admit you got me curious. Let's have a look at 'em."

"In due course," Conover told him. "First, I must explain certain things."

"What things?" asked Jack Wilbur, taking a solid belt of whiskey.

"Let me begin by outlining a unique personal philosophy." He leaned forward, eyes bright, excited. "Have you ever heard of Dostoyevsky?"

"Nope. He an artist, too?"

"Indeed, yes—and a very great one—but his art was that of the printed word. Fyodor Mikhailovich Dostoyevsky. Eighteen twenty one to eighteen eighty one. Critics have called him Russia's greatest novelist."

"Russian, huh?" Wilbur shook his head. "No wonder I never heard of the guy. Hell, the only book writer I know about is Ernie Hemingway an' I never actual read anything of his—but how I know about him is because of his boozing. He sure loved to get smashed, ole Ernie did."

"True enough. Many great writers have fallen prey to the evils of alcohol."

Jack held up his whiskey glass, now three-quarters empty. "If this stuff is evil, then I guess I'm one bad dude." Grinning, he took another swallow.

"Of course, a multitude of critics have attempted to define the essence of Dostoyevsky's work, but the most perceptive analysis comes from a gentleman whose name I fail to recall at the moment. His words, however, are very clear in my memory: 'The extremes of man's nature, his spiritual duality, the conflict between conventional morals and the overwhelming urge to move beyond such constrictions, forms the core of all of Dostoyevsky's major novels.' Beautifully put, I'd say."

"This kinda talk is given' me a headache," declared Jack Wilbur.

Conover smiled. "Bear with me, Jack. There's a point here that applies directly to both of us—but I have to reach it in my own way. Will you indulge me?"

"Go ahead," said Wilbur.

"Dostoyevsky's greatest work, in my opinion, is the novel he published in eighteen sixty-six, Crime and Punishment."

"The title sounds okay," admitted Wilbur. "You do a crime, you get punished for it—like my Pap."

"The novel's lead character," continued Conover, "is an embittered scholar named Raskolnikov. He murders two women, one of them for money. At least that's what he thinks is his motive. However, money is not Raskolnikov's true reason for the crime. In fact, he hides the stolen loot and never profits from it."

"That's crazy," declared Jack Wilbur. "If he went to all the trouble of knockin' off some dame for her dough, then why didn't he spend it? Sounds like the guy was a real dummy."

"On the contrary, he was a brilliant man," said Conover. "His violent action perfectly reflected the author's personal philosophy. It was through Raskolnikov that Dostoyevsky developed what I choose to call 'Fyodor's Law.' You know, when the novel appeared, it was considered quite controversial. It shocked many people."

"How come?"

"Dostoyevsky boldly declared that truly extraordinary people are not bound by conventional moral standards. He wrote of a higher 'law of nature' unknown to the untutored mass of humanity. This law permits the extraordinary individual to commit violent acts, including murder, in order to advance beyond, to transcend ordinary boundaries."

"That's a hell of a thing to put in people's heads."

"Allow me to quote directly from memory," Conover continued, ignoring Wilbur's negative comment. "Raskolnikov speaks of a 'right to crime,' and adds: 'If such a one is forced, for the sake of his idea, to wade through blood, he can find within his conscience, a sanction for wading through blood.' The author, of course, was not advocating such extreme behavior for everyone—only for the truly extraordinary individual."

"Horseshit," muttered Jack Wilbur.

Undeterred, Conover went on: "If the individual is clever enough, his actions will never be discovered by the law. For one thing, a dead body is the primary proof of murder. But what if the body simply vanishes?" He spread his hands. "No corpse, no provable crime."

"Bodies don't vanish."

"Ah, but they can," argued Conover. "All one need do is saw the corpse into small parts and then burn each part to a fine grey ash. Quite simple, actually."

Jack Wilbur stared intently at him. "This is pretty heavy stuff," he said slowly.

"It's time to open my scrapbook," said Conover. He flipped back the heavy cover to reveal, within the book's pages, a variety of color photos—of human body parts arranged on brightly painted boards in bizarre designs.

"My art," Conover declared proudly. "Unfortunately, for obvious reasons, I am unable to preserve the originals. Sadly, I am forced to burn each montage after I have completed it. But at least I have this book of photographs. Arms, legs, hands, ears, noses . . . they all comprise my basic artistic materials."

"Christ!" breathed Jack Wilbur, staring at one of the photos. "That's a guy's dick!"

"Yes," nodded Conover. "I am sometimes able to utilize genitalia to splendid effect. But every body part is potentially usable." He pointed to another photo. "Here we have a loop of bowel tract, actually part of the small intestine, surrounding a freshly-severed heart. Quite original, don't you think?"

Jack Wilbur stood up, backing away from his host. "What I think, mister, is that you're one sick son of a bitch!"

"Sit down, Jack," said Conover sharply. "I laced that drink of yours with a potent pharmaceutical drug that will render you totally helpless within a very short period."

"I don't believe it," said Wilbur.

"Trust me. I'm quite adept at this by now. Very soon your lungs will begin to tighten. With every breath they will expand less, restricting the oxygen available to you. Then black spots will appear before your eyes as you gasp for air. You'll fall to the floor and lie there for a minute or two, conscious but unable to move. And then your heart will stop and it will all be over."

"You plan to cut me up in pieces an' use me for one of your damn pictures?"

"Precisely," nodded Conover. "I'm actually doing you a service—helping you to make something special out of your otherwise miserable life. You shall serve the cause of true artistic expression. A noble end to your mundane existence."

"How can you just go around killing people?" gasped Jack Wilbur. His skin was red and flushed with heat.

"After the first time it becomes quite easy. One's first murder is always somewhat disturbing. Now all I feel is a sense of exhilaration." He checked his wristwatch. "Time's up, Jack. The poison kicks in very suddenly. No use your attempting to fight it. Just let . . . " He stood up eyes wide. "Just . . . let it . . . . "

James Conover staggered, clutching at his throat. He choked, gasping for breath. Then he fell to his knees, toppling sideways to the polished peg floor of the den. Lying on his back, he stared sightlessly at the ceiling, conscious but totally paralyzed.

"Well, Mr. Conover," said Jack Wilbur as he removed the fallen man's wallet and slipped the diamond ring from the middle finger of his left hand, "your back was to me when you put that stuff in my glass, but I could see what you was doing in the mirror. When you went to fetch your book of sicko pictures I switched glasses. Guess the joke's on you, huh?"

There was no physical response from Conover, but Jack caught a faint flicker of shocked understanding in the dying man's eyes. Then they began glazing over. Conover had, at best, another few seconds of life.

Jack Wilbur bent over him, leaning close, smiling. "Fuck you, Mr. Conover," he said softly.

He removed the man's car keys and gold wristwatch, walked out to the shiny blue Cadillac, and motored away down the hill, whistling.

The sun was very bright and the Los Angeles air was smogless and sweet.

Jack Wilbur felt "truly extraordinary."

FIVE TO GET READY, TWO TO GO

Hugh B. Cave

The whole country knew Leonard Wurner was responsible for the verdict. The shrewdest defense attorney money could hire, he probably could have persuaded a jury to declare Caiaphas innocent of blame in the Crucifixion of Christ, had there been a similarly flawed system of justice in those days.

And the father of Chris Kimball, one of the four young men in the car that night, had been wealthy enough to hire Wurner to defend all four of them.

So in the end all four had been acquitted except for a probationary light sentence for having drunkenly disturbed the peace. And Henry Christian Seaton's beloved great granddaughter, only six years old, was fated to use a wheelchair for the rest of her life.

Eighty-two years old and rapidly failing in health at this time, Henry sat in his retirement-home apartment and pondered the matter, growing more and more angry by the hour. And at last, after weighing all the pros and cons, he arrived at a decision.

It would be quite unconscionable, Henry told himself, for him to face his Creator without having first done what he could to right such a heinous wrong. He must act while there was still time.

It was 8:30 of a Tuesday morning, after an almost sleepless night, when Henry reached this decision. Leaving his bed, he shunned the casual clothing he would normally have worn down to breakfast in the home dining room and, after a shower and shave, got dressed to go out. He had not been leaving the home too often of late, but still had his car in the parking lot and a license to drive it.

As he passed through the dining room where other residents of the home were breaking their fast, many of them glanced at him in curiosity. A crony of his, Jeff Thorpe, said with a frown, "You going somewhere, Henry?"

"Just shopping," Henry replied.

Getting into his car, he backed it out of its slot by using the rear-view mirror—he was too stiff these days to turn his head that far around—and very carefully drove the mile and four tenths to the center of the city. There he left the car in a parking garage while completing his tour on foot. The items he required were not sold in supermarkets. They were so hard to find that noon overtook him before he was finished, and he had to pause for lunch.

He happened to be near the downtown branch of the university at that time, and there were students in the restaurant. While he sat there over his cream of broccoli soup, some at a nearby table kept glancing in his direction and putting their heads together. Finally one of them, a handsome youth well over six feet tall, stood up and walked over to him.

"Sir . . . aren't you Professor Seaton, who used to teach physics at the U?"

"Yes, I am."

"Sir, it's an honor to meet you." Impulsively the youth thrust out his hand. "I've just been reading a book on your exploits as a demolition expert. When you were a Navy Frogman in the big war, I mean. Wow! What a story!"

"Thank you." Henry shook the youth's hand and watched him return to his companions. Why, he wondered, did some young men turn out like that and others like the four he was concerned with? Perhaps he should have specialized in psychology instead of physics.

It was nearly four when Henry finished his shopping. Returning to his apartment, he worked on his project until supper time. Then, after dining with Jeff Thorpe and another of his cronies, he worked on it again until, just after midnight, he was finally satisfied with it.

The following morning he again arose early, again skipped breakfast, and drove out to his place on the lake.

Watson Lake was nine miles out in the country and about two miles long. His son and grandson, with their families, occasionally used the cabin there in summer, but he himself had not visited it since selling his city residence and moving into the retirement home. He was surprised to find a number of new and expensive houses at its more open southern end. The more swampy narrow end where he had built his cabin many years before was unchanged, however. Apparently people today valued a view more than the privacy he and his beloved Emma had sought.

At the cabin itself, which he had assembled weekends with the help of admiring students, he discovered a window broken and signs of intrusion. The culprits, he guessed, had probably been youths of the kind who had crippled his little great granddaughter while she innocently rode her tricycle on the sidewalk in front of her home.

He thought about that while collecting the empty beer cans and fast food containers scattered about the place and carrying them outside in trash bags. Then he transferred five straight-backed chairs from other rooms to the cabin's living room and arranged them in a semicircle facing the living room's lone table, which was of local pine, rectangular in shape, and had a lamp on it. The lamp still functioned, he discovered to his satisfaction. Even after moving to the nursing home, he had faithfully continued to pay the electric bill here so that his children and grandchildren might use the place when so inclined.

These chores finished, he nailed a sheet of plywood over the broken window on the inside, and made sure that all other windows and both outside doors were locked. Then, after a final walkabout to assure himself that the cabin was indeed ready, he departed. He had not brought with him the items purchased in the city the day before. Leaving those here unguarded could be unwise. He would bring them when he came again. Returning to the city, he arrived at the home in time for supper again but somewhat weak from hunger because this time he had eaten no lunch.

"Where in the world have you been, Henry?" he was asked by eighty-six-year-old Mildred Stockton, one of the two women at his four-place table. "We've hardly seen you these past two days."

"Well . . . I went out to my old cabin at Watson Lake."

"But how nice! And was it full of memories?" They all had memories, Henry had discovered. Memories sustained them, along with visits from loved ones. And he was no different. At least once a month he was renewed in spirit by visits from his loved ones. Most uplifting had been the visits from his six-year-old great granddaughter who with her gossamer golden hair and sky-blue eyes reminded him so much of Emma. But who now, he reminded himself bitterly, would never again be able to run across a room and climb onto his lap.

"What did you do out at your cabin?" asked his crony and longtime chess opponent, Jeff Thorpe, who was seated across from him. "Must have been something pretty special, to keep you out there so long."

"Oh, I just puttered around a bit."

"Remembering," said Mrs. Stockton with a knowing smile.

"Well, yes. That too."

They dropped the subject.

Henry ate his supper, then went up to his apartment, sat for an hour or so in silence thinking about what he had done and what he planned to do, and finally went to bed.

The following day—day three—he drove to the city again and after leaving his car in a parking lot, walked several blocks to a six-story building on Front Street. There he took an elevator up to the fifth floor, walked along a hall to a door marked N. J. PELTON, PRIVATE INVESTIGATOR, and opened it.

A dark-haired man wearing metal-rimmed eyeglasses looked up at him from behind a desk, took in a breath, and shot erect with a hand outthrust. "Prof Seaton!" said Nick Pelton through a grin of delight. "Well, hel-lo! What is this?"

The shaking of hands took an unusually long time. Then Henry accepted an invitation to "Sit, sit!" and leaned toward his former student. "Nick," he said, "I need a job done."

"My kind of job?" said Nick Pelton, obviously puzzled.

"Your kind of job. At least, I'm sure you'll know someone who can do it." Henry reached into his jacket pocket and brought forth a small plastic container that had once held prescription medication. Opening it, he let a small, black object of metal and plastic fall into his cupped other hand and extended that hand across the desk. "You know what this is, I'm sure."

Nick Pelton took the object from Henry's hand and examined it. "A bug?"

"An electronic listening device, yes. I want it planted in the office of a prominent attorney, Nick. Cost is no object."

"But—"

"Not by you personally, of course. I'm sure you don't accept such assignments. But in your line of work you must be acquainted with people who do." In his eagerness, Henry leaned so far forward he had to clutch the edge of the desk to steady himself. "All I'm asking, mind you, is that you find someone who can let himself into this lawyer's office and place this where the man will think it's been there awhile, eavesdropping on his conversations. It doesn't actually have to work."

With his elbows on the desk and his square chin resting on upthrust knuckles, Nick Pelton thought about it. "Who's the lawyer?" he asked at last. "The guy who got those punks off after they ran down your little girl?"

Henry nodded.

"And you want him to think you've been privy to what went on in his office while he was defending them. That it?"

"Something like that, Nick."

Nick Pelton lifted his gaze to Henry's face and was silent a moment. "All right, Prof," he said at last. "I think I know a man who can do the job. How much time do we have?"

"Well, I won't set a time limit. But the sooner the better." Because, Henry thought, I may not be around a whole lot longer, if those last tests at the hospital were worth the small fortune they cost me.

"I'll get right on it and call you," Nick Pelton promised.

"Thank you, Nick." Rising, Henry had to clutch the arms of his chair to maintain his balance.

"You feeling all right, Prof?" the private eye asked with a frown of concern.

"Just a little tired. I've been more active than usual these last few days."

"Better be careful." Rising, Nick came around the desk, put a hand on Henry's arm, and walked him to the door. Opening the door for him, he shifted the hand to Henry's shoulder. "Yeah, Prof, be careful," he said again. "A whole bunch of us wouldn't want anything bad to happen to you."

Henry drove home with a smile on his lips that belied the increasing weariness in the rest of his body. But when a young tailgating driver impatiently blew a horn at him for not going fast enough, then shouted an obscenity while zooming past, he thought of the four young men who had crippled his little great granddaughter, and his smile became something else.

Eight days later, at two in the afternoon, Private Investigator Nick Pelton phoned Henry at the home. "It's done, Prof," said Nick.

Henry had nearly stopped hoping. Now he took in a breath that all but caused his lungs to explode. "You mean it? You've succeeded?"

"You want to hear how we did it?"

"I certainly do!"

"Well, this fellow I hired—never mind his name; that's between him and me—he phoned your Leonard Wurner for an appointment to discuss a cooked-up problem. It's gonna cost you something for that, and he had to wait a whole week to get the appointment—which is why I've been so long coming back to you. But the rest was easy. He just sat there, and when the guy had to answer a phone call, our boy sneaked a hand out and stuck the bug under the edge of the desk."

"Where under the edge of the desk?" Henry asked breathlessly.

"Huh?"

"Where, precisely? I need to know so I—"

"Oh. Under the right-hand corner, he said."

"The right-hand corner from where he was sitting?"

"Yeah, sure."

"Bless you, Nick." Henry was so elated he could scarcely speak above a whisper. "Send me a bill and I'll get a check off to you by return mail. And Nick—"

"Yeah, Prof?"

"Whoever he is, thank him for me. He'll never know—neither of you will ever know—how much this means to an old man on his last big assignment."

"Prof, I'm just glad I could help out," Nick said. "Like I told you, there's a whole lot of us will never forget all you did for us in college."

Henry hung up and glanced at his watch. It was now ten minutes past two. He consulted a bit of paper on his telephone table for a number he had long ago looked up and written down. He dialed that number.

"I should like to speak to Mr. Wurner, please," he told the woman who responded. "It is a matter of great importance."

She asked his name.

Henry had long since selected a name. "My name is Jason Carver. Mr. Wurner does not know me."

She told him Mr. Wurner was not in.

"When do you expect him back?"

"Not again today," she said.

A patient man now that he knew the first step in his plan had been completed, Henry did not make another call until eight o'clock that evening. Then, after looking up the attorney's home number, he dialed that. Again a woman's voice answered.

"This is Jason Carver," Henry said, trying hard to sound uncompromising. "Let me speak to Mr. Wurner."

"Jason who?"

"Carver."

He heard the woman call "Leonard!" and presently the voice of Leonard Wurner boomed in his ear. It was familiar enough. All through the trial of the four young men who had crippled his beloved great granddaughter, Henry had occupied a courtroom seat and blazed with inner fury at the sound of that particular voice. Now he responded to it by saying with deliberate slowness, "Mr. Wurner, I am calling about your recent defense of Bernard Tolbert, Wayne Rowan, Chris Kimball, and Ervin Wicks."

There ensued a long silence, after which Attorney Wurner said in a guarded voice, "Who are you?"

"One who has studied that case very carefully, Mr. Wurner. One who is convinced that you induced those four young men to lie about their being drunk that night."

Again a silence. "You've been reading too many supermarket tabloids," Wurner growled.

"No, Mr. Wurner, I haven't. I have been listening to several taped conversations you had with those four young men in your office."

This time the silence seemed endless, and there was a definite change in Wurner's tone when he finally interrupted it. "You've been listening to—what?"

"Tapes, Mr. Wurner, of your talks with those four clients of yours. All of your talks with them, because the device was planted in your office the day after you were hired to defend them. With your reputation for obstructing the course of justice, I was all but certain you would persuade those four unrepentant young men to perjure themselves. If you doubt what I am saying, Mr. Wurner, look under the right-hand front corner of your desk when you go to your office tomorrow morning."

Another silence ensued. This time Henry was the one who terminated it. "Do that, Mr. Wurner," he said. "Because I shall call you again at your office at precisely ten o'clock tomorrow morning, and unless you are prepared to discuss this, I shall at once deliver the tapes in question to Judge Blakiston." And Henry hung up.

After such a conversation sleep was impossible, of course. He went to bed and lay there hour after hour, thinking about what he had done. Over and over he asked himself if he could have made some small mistake that would give Attorney Wurner a way out. What his punishment might be if Wurner were able to turn on him, Henry did not even consider. He was old and ill. But the plan itself must not fail, or he would die a crushed and defeated man.

He dozed off, finally, a little after three a.m. and awoke just after nine. After a light breakfast of orange juice and toast in the dining room, he returned to his apartment to make his ten o'clock phone call exactly on time.

Leonard Wurner answered the call on the first ring, as though he had been sitting with a hand hovering over the phone, waiting in a cold sweat for it to come alive.

"What do you want from me?" he demanded hoarsely.

"That is something for us to decide upon in conference," replied Henry. "Do you know Lake Watson?"

"Of course."

"The road that goes around it, called Watson Lake Road?"

"Yes, yes, I've been out there any number of times! What—"

"There is an old cabin out there," said Henry. "Number one-four-one Watson Lake Road. White—or it was once—with a gray trim and a red brick chimney. I have arranged for the temporary use of it and will be there waiting for you at three o'clock tomorrow afternoon."

"Why tomorrow, damn it? Why not this afternoon, so we can get this idiocy over with? I have other things to do, for God's sake!"

"The most important thing you have to do, Mr. Wurner, is to contact those four young men you defended. Because you are to bring them with you."

"What? How do you expect—"

"Or there will be no discussion," Henry finished firmly. "Three o'clock tomorrow, and there must be five of you, without fail. And don't even think about trying to take the tapes from me by force, Mr. Wurner. Copies are already in the possession of friends who will promptly deliver them to the proper authorities if anything happens to me."

Henry hung up. For a few minutes he simply sat there gazing at the phone, reviewing in his mind what had been said. All was in order, he decided. But, of course, he would not wait until tomorrow afternoon to drive out to the cabin. Wurner just might decide to go out there ahead of time and attempt to set up some sort of trap.

Bone-weary at this point, Henry locked his apartment door behind him and trudged down the stairs. Curious glances from some of his fellow residents followed him as he plodded past without turning his head. Jeff Thorpe glanced up from a game of chess and paused in the act of moving a pawn. "Henry, you going out again?"

Henry could not walk past an old friend without stopping. "Well, yes, Jeff," he said. "I'm afraid I have to."

Scowling, Thorpe shook his head. "You look awful tired, Henry. Whatever you're up to, you really should slow down and rest."

"I know I should, Jeff. But I can't rest until I'm finished." Henry's smile was forced. "Go on with your game. I'll play the winner tomorrow."

He trudged on, with both players staring after him. "Now I wonder where in the world he's off to at five past eleven in the morning, so close to lunch time," said Jeff Thorpe. "Something's driving that man, Al. No doubt about it."

They watched Henry go out the door, then shrugged and resumed their game. In the parking lot, Henry got into his car and began the nine-mile drive out to his cabin at the lake.

Leonard Wurner arrived at the cabin at five minutes to three the following afternoon in a car befitting his reputation as one of the country's most expensive attorneys. With him were the four young men he had defended in court. Leading a silent parade to the front door, Wurner knocked.

"Come in," responded the voice of Henry Seaton. "It's not locked."

Wurner turned the knob and saw the speaker seated behind a rectangular pine table at the far end of a thirty-foot-long living room, with five empty straight-backed chairs facing him in a semicircle. "Come in, all of you," Henry repeated, beckoning. "Sit, please."

In his dark-green jacket and yellow sport shirt, with dark, deep circles under his bulging eyes, the lawyer somewhat resembled a large frog as he went to the center chair and lowered himself onto it. The four youths who went to the other chairs were four of a kind—seventeen to nineteen years old, casually but expensively dressed, with a collective sneer in the slouchy way they accepted Henry's invitation.

On the table was a tape recorder. Beside it lay a shiny black box the size of a pack of cigarettes, with a single red button in its center. Next to that was a similar but longer box with five green buttons in a row. Henry reached out and turned on the tape recorder, then let his hand hover over the box with the single red button.

"Very well," he said. "We seem to be ready. Shall we proceed?"

No one answered him. The Frog, lips tight and bulging eyes unblinking, simply stared. The four young men grinned at one another and made little snickering sounds behind tightened lips as though struggling not to laugh.

"Good," said Henry. "First, then, let me tell you why you are here. My name is not Jason Carver. It is Henry Christian Seaton, and I am the great grandfather of the little girl you four young men struck with your car and crippled for life. Before my retirement I was a professor of physics at the university. Before that, in World War Two, I was a demolition expert in the navy. And this red button"—he carefully lifted the smaller black box from the table and held it up so they could see it better—"will blow this cabin sky high if I touch it. Or if one of you should attempt to rush me or shoot me or whatever, and I dropped the box or fell with it. So be very careful to make no sudden moves, or all of us—all of us, I repeat—will die."

The four youths stopped snickering. Leonard Wurner's eyes became even more prominent, resembling small doorknobs.

"Now, Mr. Wurner, let me tell you what I know from having recorded your conversations with these four young men. First, though they may have had a beer or two, they were definitely not drunk that Saturday. They were simply irresponsible, uncaring, half-wild youths driving wildly around the city in search of excitement. Therefore your defense—that they had been drinking heavily all morning and taking turns at the wheel, and simply did not remember who was driving when the car climbed the curb and struck the child—your anticipated clever defense was a damned lie and all of you know it. Do I hear any arguments?"

Henry's gaze traveled across all five faces, lingering for a few seconds on each.

No one answered.

"Very well," he went on. "So now, before the second hand on this watch of mine has ticked off one minute, you will tell me who was driving the car that day or I press this button." With his right hand holding the black box a few inches above the table, he raised his left to bring the watch on that wrist to the same level and began to count the passing seconds. "Five . . . ten . . . fifteen . . ."

"Wait!" cried Leonard Wurner in a voice that resembled a frog's croak. "This is idiotic! Even if we tell you who was driving, you can't reopen the case!"

Henry stopped counting . "Really? Why can't I?"

"If you knew anything about the law . . ." Wurner stopped to wipe sweat from his forehead. "And you can't use what's on that tape you recorded, either. Evidence obtained that way is worthless. No court in the land will allow it."

It was Henry's turn to be silent. Lowering his watch hand but not the black box, he stared back at the attorney in a way that apparently gave the latter added courage.

"Put the damned box down, Seaton," Wurner advised through slack lips, with something like a grunt of relief. "You don't have a legal leg to stand on here, even if we tell you who was driving."

Still Henry only stared.

"You know something?" the attorney continued, now with a smile of derision twisting his face. "You went at this all wrong, Seaton. All wrong, yes. Now if I'd been in your shoes, with your abilities, and wanted to know which of these kids was driving the car that day, let me tell you how I'd have gone about it." The voice had shed its rough edge of fear and was now the persuasive boom Henry had listened to day after day during the trial. Though still seated on his straight-backed chair, the great Leonard Wurner spoke as though striding back and forth before a jury. "With your know-how, old man, I wouldn't have rigged that device up to blow this whole stupid cabin sky high. No! I would have turned each of these chairs into a death chair, with a high-voltage electric charge of some limited but deadly explosive hidden under the seat of each. And having determined which of these kids was the driver of the car by his reaction to the situation—an easy decision for one who can read faces—if, of course, you are able to do that—I—well I—" Actually daring to smile now, Wurner let a shrug finish what he probably thought of as a closing courtroom summation.

"Oh, but I do have that ability," Henry said quietly.

"What?"

"I do. *That* young man is the one who ran down my little girl and crippled her." Henry pointed to the seated youth at the right end of the semicircle: Chris Kimball, whose father had put up the money for the defense.

The indicated youth, his long dark hair in a ponytail, folded his arms on his chest and threw his head back and laughed, but the laugh had a quaver of fear in it and his clenched hands suddenly began to shake. The others, including their attorney, looked at him in stunned silence.

"And, Mr. Wurner, I actually set this meeting up in the way you've suggested," Henry added.

"You . . . w-w-hat?" Wurner stammered.

"Like this." Reaching out, Henry grasped the larger black box with the five green buttons on it and slid it toward him across the table top. Looking straight at the young man who had driven the car, he put his forefinger on the number five button and pressed.

Parts of the chair on which Chris Kimball sat suddenly gave off sparks and began to glow. Kimball's mouth flew open in a silent scream. His body shook convulsively. His hands flapped like the wings of a wounded gull struggling vainly to take flight.

The other three young men leaped to their feet and raced for the door, causing the old cabin floor to shake as if in the grip of an earth tremor. Leonard Wurner simply sat where he was in a state of shock.

"Don't move, Mr. Wurner," Henry said, as the sound of car doors slamming filtered into the cabin from outside, followed by a screeching of tires on gravel as the machine took off. Henry's forefinger now hovered over the middle green button.

Wurner stopped looking at the dead youth and turned his bulging eyes toward Henry, but was still too shocked to speak.

"Are you surprised?" Henry said mildly. "You shouldn't be, you know. Our entire justice system needs a sort of electric shock treatment. One day, perhaps, this country will have sense enough to do away with people like you. Perhaps with all courtroom lawyers. In my opinion, a panel of, say, five impartial judges ought to ask the questions; then there would be no 'my-lawyer-outsmarted-your-lawyer' verdicts and the word 'justice' might mean something again. In any case, utterly unscrupulous attorneys such as you, Mr. Wurner, should never be allowed in a courtroom. Don't you agree?"

Attorney Wurner's mouth quivered, but nothing resembling speech emerged from it.

"Now," Henry said, "the time has come for me to leave, and I think it only fair for you to come with me." Pushing aside the box with the five green buttons, he reached for the smaller one.

Too late, Attorney Leonard Wurner realized what was about to happen. With a cry of "No, No!" he leaped to his feet and staggered off balance toward the door. But before he could reach it, Henry's finger pressed the button that was red.

The ensuing thunderclap sent the cabin roof hurtling skyward and blew its walls apart. Wurner was aware of that. He was also aware that something terrible had happened to some part of him below his waist. At that point he lost consciousness.

When he came to, he sensed that he was on a stretcher in some kind of ambulance, with attendants hovering over him. And, again, that something was terribly wrong with his legs. He then passed out a second time.

When next that brilliant legal mind was able to function, it told him he was in a hospital bed, and it was correct. There he was to stay for weeks, and when able to leave the bed at last, he still had to remain in the hospital while learning how people with useless legs—people like the beloved great granddaughter of Professor Henry Christian Seaton—managed to get around in wheelchairs. But something more than Leonard Wurner's legs had been destroyed in the explosion. His booming voice, once so admired for its well-known power to influence the thinking of juries, had been reduced to a struggling whisper.

In that small, feeble voice, which would certainly never again sway a jury, he nevertheless insisted that he knew what had happened at the cabin and who had caused it to happen. And the three young men who had been lucky enough to escape were adamant in declaring him correct in his identification of the person responsible.

Professor Henry Seaton, they confirmed, had been the man seated there at the cabin table.

A columnist on one of the city newspapers contradicted them. "If Professor Seaton was there at the cabin," he wrote, "how do Attorney Wurner and the other three explain what happened the day before when, apparently on his way out to the cabin, Seaton stopped at Kelley's Roadside Cafe? Amos Kelley says Seaton came into the cafe and asked for coffee, saying he felt very tired. With Kelley and two customers at the counter watching him, Seaton carried the coffee to a booth. Half an hour later, suspecting something wrong, Kelley went to the booth to investigate and found him asleep, and was unable to wake him. A call to the hospital brought an ambulance, and it was determined that Professor Seaton had died there in the cafe of a heart attack.

"How, then, could the professor have been at his cabin a day later, doing what Leonard Wurner and those three young men say he did? To this reporter it sounds about as reasonable as some of Attorney Wurner's well-known outrageous claims in court."

At the retirement home, Jeff Thorpe finished reading those words aloud to another of Henry's friends. "Al," he said, frowning, "do you remember how Henry answered me when you and I were playing chess and he came by?"

The other shrugged. "You know me and my memory."

"When I told him he looked tired and ought to stop and rest? You don't remember? Well, he said—and I recall his exact words—he said, 'I just can't rest until I'm finished.' That's it. That's what he said. 'I just can't rest until I'm finished.' Think about it, Al. Just think about it."

SECRETS

Melanie Tem

When Christy didn't answer to her knock, as she'd known she would not, Grace felt justified in pushing open the door. The music struck her in the face, but she held her ground.

Still half-expecting the door to be locked and barricaded, although that wasn't possible now, she was a little taken aback to find herself actually on the threshold. At first she just stood there and said, "Christina! Answer me!" again. Despite all the times she'd been forced to come in here, it remained a private and alien place.

But she had to go in, for her daughter's sake and her own, and certainly Christy wasn't going to stop her now. Sometimes a mother had to do unpleasant or dangerous things, even things that were morally wrong, in order to save her child. Grace had already had plenty of experience with that sort of maternal obligation, and would soon have more. Her throat tightened at the thought. When you loved someone, when you were responsible for them, you couldn't allow them to keep secrets from you.

"Oh, leave her alone, Gracie," Vic used to tell her. "You can't get inside her head no matter what you do." Grace was terrified that that might be true.

"You read my diary!" She heard Christy's voice in the music, although Christy couldn't possibly be speaking to her now. "You listen in on my phone conversations!" She hadn't denied it; she had done all those things, and she would do more.

Music, the diabolical and incomprehensible music that Christy wouldn't turn off day or night, was obscuring any other sounds from the room, if there were any. Sometimes it seemed to be blurring Grace's vision, too, and the feel of things; it left a foul taste in her mouth.

The tape now had been one of Christy's favorites. The name of the group was Devil's Handmaiden. Grace had made it a point to memorize their blasphemous names and learn how to recognize one from another. She knew individual performers, too — the girls with layered faces, the boys with secret pasts. They were none of them what they seemed to be, of course, or what they wanted their audiences to think they were.

Grace could have sung along:

> Bring him to me
> Suck him to me
> Semen, blood, and flame
> Make him hold me
> Make him come, and
> Tell his other name.

"Chris-*ty*!" Grace called again, although she knew it was pointless. "Turn that thing down!"

She could have sung along, but she didn't. The lyrics were tempting, the tune catchy, the beat hypnotic, but by now she recognized the work of the Devil when she heard it.

And anyway, the words on the surface weren't the true message of the song. The true message was always hidden, cleverly subliminal. Only people who knew the codes and were willing to take the risk could face the Enemy head-on. Grace was more than willing.

"Christy, I'm talking to you!"

Grace took a deep breath and stepped into her daughter's room. Old smoke — from incense, cigarettes, marijuana — made her cough and almost instantly gave her a ringing headache. The floor was littered with piles of clothes, tape cases, straws, long thick pins like hatpins, wads of paper. From the bookcase that hid Christy's bed from the door glowed layers of graffiti, lipstick over spray paint over grape juice, messages and designs so obscured by each other that meanings had multiplied beyond Grace's comprehension. The heavy crooked curtains dimmed the morning sunlight. Grace resisted the familiar urge to fling open the curtains and window, knowing from long and bitter experience that the evil secrets in this room would not be aired out so easily.

The music soared from its continuous tape. It was one of Satan's many voices, intended to keep her from understanding her child. It said things to her that made her sick, things that most other people couldn't or wouldn't hear. Sometimes Satan sang in Vic's voice, or Christy's, or her own.

Frightened, Grace allowed herself to retreat. What she had to do this morning wouldn't be easy, even though she knew it was the right thing to do, her duty to her daughter. She needed more time to prepare, to gather her strength and courage.

She backed up and closed Christy's door. The music muted a little but was still louder than any other sound, including her own heartbeat and her own thoughts. Holding her breath, she pressed her ear against the door as she had so many times before, and now couldn't stop herself from swaying with the rhythm and lip-synching the brisk words:

> *Born to play*
> *Died to say*
> *Come again another day.*

Knowledge of what lay beyond the door, beyond the bookcase partition in her daughter's room, forced itself into Grace's consciousness before she could stop it, and she gasped and pressed her palms against the door frame for support. The music didn't stop.

"It's just music," Vic had tried to tell her twenty years ago. Or, "It's a *positive* thing. It's about love and peace." She'd smoked a lot of dope, taken a few acid and mescaline trips, and even so she hadn't realized until much later — until she had a daughter who listened to a different generation of music, and whose body and mind and soul Grace as her mother was responsible for — who Jude and Alice were.

The tape ended. Before it looped over the other side, Grace hurried into the kitchen, humming under her breath.

She switched on the radio over the counter. It was always tuned to one of the numerous oldies stations, and she came in on the middle of "Knights in White Satin." Singing loudly, half-dancing from the counter to the sink, she finished up the breakfast dishes. There weren't many. It had been a long time since she and Christy had eaten a meal together — a long time, for that matter, since Christy had come out of her room.

The pictures of Vic and Christy on the side of the refrigerator caught her attention. Hands in the dishwasher, she stared at them one by one.

From down the hall in Christy's room and from the radio inches from her face, music poured its dark secrets; she could very nearly decipher them now just by listening in a certain way.

There were dozens of pictures:

Christy as a baby, here laughing and there crying at something forever out of camera range. Vic asleep; Grace had crawled across the bed and held the camera as close as she'd dared, hoping to capture some dream image or thought wave through his eyelids, but the flash had awakened him and he'd pushed her roughly away.

A young, bearded, pony-tailed Vic, with slightly glazed eyes and earphones on his head. Grace remembered how she, with youthful naiveté, had pressed her ear against the outside of the earphones while he was wearing them, hoping to hear what he heard. Like nearly everything else in those days, it had turned into a kind of foreplay, and she never had been able to detect anything but a subaudible vibration.

Christy's high school graduation picture, posed and smoothed, her very expression looking air-brushed. Christy and Vic caught in an eternally private conversation on the front porch swing; she'd snapped the picture from the other side of the living room window, and they never did tell her what they'd been talking about.

Grace dried the last saucer and put it away. She thought she heard movement in the back of the cupboard or in the wall behind it, and when she stood on tiptoe to run her fingers back there she seemed to feel an irregularity in the surfaces that hadn't been there yesterday when she'd done her every-other-day cleaning of cupboards and drawers. Even the house she lived in had secrets from her.

The music on the radio had ended and a man was reading the news. The voice had a thick, choked vibrato, as though he had something caught in his throat, some story he was keeping to himself. Grace had known for a long time that news had hidden messages, that certain words and phrases stood for other things they didn't say. But she didn't have time now to try decoding it.

She turned off the radio, leaving herself alone with the muffled music from Christy's tape. Taking a deep breath, she reached for the butcher block knife holder, a wedding present from her sister. Over the years it had proved to be true that the knives never needed sharpening; even so, she worried now that none of them would really be sharp enough.

Hefting a long thin paring knife, her hand brushed against something and sent it rattling into the sink. Vic's bones and teeth, half a dozen small chunks she'd saved from his ashes. Because they'd come from actually *inside* him, she felt close to him when she held them in her palm or touched her tongue to them. One by one she picked them out of the drain and put them back into their clear plastic bottle on the windowsill, where light could shine through. Her hands were trembling from this reminder of the secrets Vic must have taken with him to the grave.

He'd had plenty of secrets. One time, for instance, he'd gone out and bought himself six new white shirts, identical to each other and to the ones already in his closet; Grace hadn't known about it until days later, when she'd happened to find the tags and straight pins in the trash. Sometimes when she got back from an errand the TV would be warm, and when she confronted him about it he'd say, "Oh, some dumb show. What's wrong with that?" Often — at dinner, in bed, at a school function for Christy — she'd know from the look on his face that he was thinking about something else; "a penny for your thoughts," she'd say, trying to keep it light, or, directly, "What are you thinking about, Vic?" Always, he'd frown and say, "Nothing."

But even after having lived with that for eighteen years, Grace had been shocked and vindicated to discover after his death his greatest and longest-running secret, of which she had had no inkling. On her dresser — beside the jewelry box with the false bottom that he'd given her for their seventh anniversary, among the dozens of plastic sandwich bags that held nail clippings and curls of his hair and scraps of discarded clothing — was a shoebox full of his love letters to and from women whose names she'd never heard, whose existence she'd never guessed.

That was never going to happen to her again. She was not going to be ambushed. Christy had been slipping away from her for years, and now had taken the final, irremediable step. Time was running out, and she was going to find out now, once and for all, what was inside her daughter's head.

But she was not quite ready. Her heart was pounding in her ears and her hands weren't steady enough. There was one more step to take in preparation. She slipped the knife into her apron pocket and went into the living room.

The room was certainly more comfortable than it used to be. Vic would hardly recognize it. Christy wouldn't be coming in here at all anymore.

Grace veered away from that thought and anxiously surveyed the room for things she'd missed. She'd boxed up for Goodwill any books she hadn't personally read from cover to cover, including two full sets of encyclopedias; until the truck had come to pick them up, she'd still been uneasy with all those secret words in her house. She'd taken down any photographs that had her in them; staring back at the versions of herself that the camera had caught, she never could reconstruct what had been going through her mind at the time. She'd had the fireplace opened that had been hidden in the wall, not so she could use it but so that things couldn't hide in there; even so, last winter a bird had gotten trapped in the chimney and, once the fluttering and frantic chirping had stopped, Grace had kept imagining the feathers and tiny hollow bones.

Feeling reasonably safe, she crossed to the stereo, knelt, pulled *The Magical Mystery Tour* from the record rack, slipped it out of its rainbow cover with the 24-page picture book that never had seemed to her to have much to do with the songs. Her hands were trembling so that she had trouble finding the spindle. She'd had the turntable and LPs since college, high school, junior high. Christy, when Christy was still speaking to her, used to make elaborate fun of such old-fashioned stuff; although she'd admitted to liking some of the 50s and 60s music on the radio, she'd no more have watched a black-and-white movie.

Thinking about that time not so long ago, when she had known a little of what her daughter was thinking, brought tears to Grace's eyes. For most of her life, Christy had been easy to read and had welcomed the attention.

"You seem worried," Grace would offer, and that was all it would take for the child to crawl into her lap and tell her all about the dead bird on the sidewalk or the playground bully.

"Are you nervous about the test tomorrow?"

"I'll bet you're excited about the new kittens."

"It makes you mad when we won't let you do something, doesn't it?"

During those years Grace had felt terribly close to her daughter. It had been almost as though Christy had never left her body or her mind.

Then, around junior high, things had changed. Vic had died by then, taking some secrets with him and leaving others behind for her to find, and Grace was on her own, scrambling to understand the hunted look that would come over Christy's face whenever she'd say something supportive or attentive like, "You're not really upset about homework. I know what this is all about. This is about boys."

"I have no private life! You know everything about me!"

"I was your age once. I remember—"

"You can read my mind! Stay out of my mind!"

Then came the silences and the absences, the cryptic messages for Christy on the answering machine from people who didn't identify themselves, the coded notes deliberately left out for Grace to puzzle over. Then came the drugs, which hopelessly muddled everything. And now Christy was dead, but that was still a secret.

Grace turned the stereo on, wincing at the labored noises it made, and lowered the needle onto the first track of Side 1. The record was scratchy and dusty, but it took only a few bars— ". . . coming to take you away" —before she was hugging herself and dancing around the room, which, for all her exorcisms, was filling up with secrets again.

She danced and sang along with "Fool on the Hill" and "Flying," "Blue Jay Way" and "Your Mother Should Know," remembering most of the words. But when she heard the first few jaunty-melancholy notes of "I Am a Walrus," spreading abruptly into a stirring dissonance, she stopped still and listened.

"I am he as you are he as you are me as we are all together."

That used to make perfect, luminous sense, and anyone who didn't get it had been hopelessly straight. She remembered the high of believing that — through music, through love — people could actually come to understand each other. She remembered dancing in an intimate crowd to just this music, grooving and making love to this music in flickering multicolored darkness with lovers whose names and histories and even whose secrets didn't matter because the music said the truth.

Now it said nothing. Grace listened intently all the way through the song, and it was sheer nonsense. "Koo-koo-ka-choo." She remembered when she'd thought she could decipher the bits of conversation at the end, important messages about life and love and the future of the world. Now it was garble.

The true messages in the Beatles' music had always been hidden, waiting for those who knew and cared enough to tease them out. In the 60s, she'd dismissed that notion as establishment paranoia or acid-induced delusions of grandeur, but as her head had cleared in the

ensuing twenty years she'd realized that it was true. After all, she had
heard for herself any number of times the secret of "The White Album"
— which, of course, had turned out to be a lie.

When she knelt again in front of the stereo, the knife in her pocket
thumped awkwardly against her thigh, but for now she ignored it. She
moved the needle back to the beginning of the last track and then
quickly, before those first notes sounded, began rotating the record
backwards.

At first she heard only unintelligible rasps and screeches and, afraid
that just since yesterday she'd somehow lost the ability to hear the secret
message, she fought down panic. To give herself stamina, she thought
of Christy dead in her bed of a drug overdose, accident or suicide. She
kept spinning the record faster and faster until the muscles of her upper
arm were shaking from the strain and she had to support her right elbow
with her left hand.

Finally she heard the words that had been imbedded in this song
for her to discover at this time and place in her life. "Peel away," it said.
"Peel away." She knew it was the voice of God.

Grace listened to the song backwards. Once was all she needed.
Then, very carefully, she set the needle back on its armature and turned
the stereo off. In the sudden silence, the music from Christy's room
came to her like the wail of a mad infant, demanding something of her
that she could not comprehend, nattering secrets to itself in an alien
tongue.

Grace moved rapidly now, purposefully. This time she didn't
bother with the charade of knocking on her daughters door, and she
hardly hesitated at the threshold. The smoke made her cough. Her head
ached. The music numbed her ears, tongue, fingertips. She pushed her
way through the debris on the floor and around the bookcase. When she
saw Christy's body on the bed, she cried out wordlessly and fell to her
knees, reminding herself again and again what the Beatles had instructed
her to do.

Christy's body was cold and rubbery. Things seemed to be seeping
out of it; her soul, maybe, or body fluids. Christy still had secrets inside
her head and heart. Grace didn't know where to start.

Devil's Handmaiden was chanting joyously when Grace took a
deep breath and inserted the point of the paring knife into Christy's
temple. There wasn't much blood. She made a long slit and then, as

the music spoke secrets to her, she peeled a thick strip of flesh away and rose to peer inside her daughter's head.

WITH THE WOUND STILL WET

Wayne Allen Sallee

In this city, you get used to the word *unseasonable*. It's always one or the other, too cold or too warm for the norm. On Tuesday, 16 January 1990, it was 53 degrees at ten in the morning, and by that time, I had already heard the "U" word on a half-dozen weather reports over the radio. With the temperature, balmy for Chicago, being what it was, fog had fallen over the streets like a coffin lid. The rain would come soon enough.

When Louden called me just before noon, I had already turned on the kitchen lights. Clay Louden was a staff reporter for the *Northside Herald,* and he had tossed the idea of doing a story on me to the city room a few weeks back. He got the go-ahead, and had called to say that the fog outside would make for some great photo shots to accompany the piece. Graceland Cemetery was just across the elevated tracks from my apartment on Belle Plaine.

The horror of the day would come later, with the rain. But, there in the fog that was thick as a brain fugue, the two of us had some serious thoughts on death while we wandered past the rows of tombstones. The subject matter was right there in front of us, but Clay was first to make mention of the gravesites. Many housed the remains of Chicago's last century of movers and shakers, and we both scanned inscriptions to find a stone with CASSDAY or NESS, hoping to find a "prop" for me to stand against.

Clay noticed how so many of the interred had been dead more than seventy years, and that many of the stones had most likely gone unvisited in years, all the family members dead or incapacitated by now. It has always been my belief that more gravesites are recognized by complete strangers than by family members, over the course of years. Who hasn't looked at other stones when paying respect to their own dead? Who hasn't touched another concrete cross in hopes of leaving behind some of their own private griefs? The dead don't care.

We shot through a roll of b & w, with a couple of wide-angle shots near the Gorshin Needle for effect and it certainly was eerie enough. The trees with their bare branches were like minimalist sketches, the ground itself stretching back into a thin-lipped bloodless grin. When we left the cemetery, the dew on the grass had soaked my jeans past the ankles.

Driving down Petit Boulevard, Clay mentioned that he would pop for a hot chocolate at the White Castle on Belmont, and ask me a few questions over the sliders, instead of doing a phone interview later.

The interview wasn't going to happen that easily though, because as we turned onto Broadway, we found ourselves at the scene of an accident. Though it hadn't begun raining yet, the streets were slick, and you could see the skid marks where the Ford Econoline van had smashed into the rear of a Liquid Carbonics truck.

The fire engines and ambulance could be heard in the distance, from opposite directions. Clay looked at me and reached for his camera case in the back seat, telling me to flip the visor down over the passenger seat. Pinned to it was a green and white PRESS card, identifying Clay as working for Virlik Publications, the State of Illinois emblem affixed to the lower right corner.

"It's my job," Clay said to me, almost apologetically. We parked in the lot of a Dunkin' Donuts. I followed him to the twisted mess.

My job, too, I thought. With my horror writings, there are all kinds of ways to get away with being ghoulish. As I'm writing this, I don't know if the guy Clay photographed will live. His head completely shattered the windshield. Black hairs were stuck to webbed glass by streaks of blood.

I looked down to his ruined face, the left side sliced away as cleanly as in any passage I could ever hope to write. I was transfixed in wondering how it was his eye did not fall free of its socket.

Louden snapped an additional role of film, it took so long to cut the guy out of his seat. He knew the men from the Wellington Street firehouse, so they let him click away from all angles, as long as their work wasn't impeded. I helped a bit by taking down names and descriptions. This, to justify my standing there close enough to see the steam coming away from the blood in the guy's chest, instead of back with the other gaping monsters in the lot across Broadway.

The rain started coming down as we trotted back to the car. I wasn't beyond shivering as we drove on to White Castle.

"Sometimes you get lucky," Clay said, grinning at me.

"Right place at the right time." Hey, it sells papers. No one bought the *Herald* for its articles on neighborhood bake sales and church bingo extravaganzas. Those "news" items were simply a bonus to the carnage.

We were even more soaked by the time we crossed the lot into the restaurant. Clay sprung for the hot chocolate and we ended up making a pass on the sliders when we saw what the grill looked like. The styrofoam cups still read HAPPY HOLIDAYS.

"How's this look to you so far?" Clay let me read as he went back to the counter for a plastic stirrer. I read the opening line to his article from the tiny note pad he carried: *Hunched over the journal on the elevated trains or buses like a pained cadaver, he grips his pen like a lunatic playing she-loves-me-she-loves-me-not with the limbs of a dead rodent . . .*

"I like it," I said. And I did. An unusual beginning for an article in the *Herald,* but it rang true. Every time I write a story, I tear out another piece of my heart.

We were sitting near the front windows; in the distance, because the fog had let up when the rain came, we could both see the flashing cherries of the fire engines, still at the scene even after the body was removed.

Clay took down all the basics for the article — they were doing the article because I was a neighborhood resident for a quarter-century — and then asked me, apologizing for it ahead of time, where I came up with my story ideas.

I told him that much of what I write is based on fact, that if a certain thing occurs to me at just the right time, well, the subject matter, or possibly the emotion it creates in me, is enough to get me going. In many cases, I told him, I write something to answer a question in my mind. Louden grinned again, his teeth big and white against his full, black beard.

It was funny—I didn't mention it aloud — but, there we were, talking about terror and sitting across the aisle was a young woman with three children, playing with french fries. Straight out of a television commercial.

Clay was still conscious of it, though. Agreeing with what I said about subject matter in my stories, he said how a lot of the photos he took stayed with him. He was still thinking about the crash.

We tied things up quick, Clay wanting to get back to the darkroom with his rolls of film — I couldn't help but think of how one roll was staged, the other mercilessly not — and I had to get back to a story I was working on about my days doing PR work for an Elvis impersonator, "Only The Dead Know Graceland."

As we walked back to Louden's Sentra, I saw the woman and her children following close behind. Clay was just starting the defogger and wipers when a van pulled into the lot. A flash of lightning illuminated a sky as dark as night now. I thought of lungs filled with cancer, just to avoid a bad feeling. Somehow I knew what was going down. Maybe Clay did, too, though I never asked him. He had gotten it all down in the paper for the 18 January edition. The neighbor knowing where to find the wife of the maimed man, how she took the kids out for burgers every Tuesday after Morgan the Private Pre-School had let out its classes. How the neighbor had been one of the gapers back at the scene, not knowing at first who the victim was because he was driving a different company van that day, and then how she learned that it was her friend's husband after one of the firemen mentioned his name to the responding beat cop.

Louden didn't care that the downpour was soaking his camera. We both had our jobs to do. The lightning flashed again and the rain battered my face. The wind came in from the lake and already the simple act of opening my mouth to breathe made it feel like my face was rictusing.

There was a low rumble of thunder, but the next flash came from Clay Louden's Konica. When I shut my eyes, the image remained. The horrified woman, her mouth sliced open by scream, her children staring up at her . . .

As clean and neat as any passage I could ever hope to write in my career.

PLAINCLOTHES

Steve Rasnic Tem

I wore the uniform eight years, and although I didn't really want anyone to take too much notice of the fact, I enjoyed wearing it. It made me feel a part of something, I suppose, and it also provided me with ready-made definition. When they saw the uniform, people knew how to relate to me, and I knew how to relate to them. That's no small advantage in a world that has become unnecessarily complicated.

Once I put the uniform on it was as if I had assumed the mantle of authority, donned the mask of the super-hero. I was still a vulnerable human being, certainly; I had no unusual powers or perceptions. But the uniform set me apart from the rest of the city just the same. It gave me a certain responsibility, a mission.

So although detective was what I had wanted since the beginning, losing the uniform dampened my enthusiasm for my new job somewhat. Wearing the suit suddenly brought me dangerously close to everyone else in the world. My resemblance to the man selling insurance, the commercial ad model, and the lay minister made me profoundly uncomfortable. When I first made detective I had a partner who wore loud suits. Barker had been reminiscent of a car salesman short on his quota. You could actually see the civilians backing away when Barker approached them with his blunt instrument questions.

Barker had never learned any better, and eventually died in one of his tacky suits, when he walked in on a warehouse burglary.

I was lucky enough to find a uniform within the suit, an attitude that could be pulled on with the pale blue shirt and gray slacks. People treated me with some deference, because they could tell that I had a mission.

But when I finally went all the way, when I went into plainclothes, I didn't look as if I had a mission because missions are not part of normal people's lives. I did have a *job*, of course, but in this sense I was really no more than a serviceman, a handyman, an odd-job man. My task was to blend in, to fade, to maintain a steady level of minor accomplishment. After a time, I began to forget why I was filling out the reports the department required. All my assignments began to blur together.

Once again the captain had extended my assignment: at least another six weeks of walking the four miles of Park Square. I'd been at it almost a year already; other officers in my division were beginning to talk. Had I fouled up again? I had a good arrest record — when I was a plainclothes the citizens acted normally around me, unselfconscious about theft, muggings, and rape. All I had to do was pull out a gun, show my badge, and the arrest was made. Perhaps I was eccentric — certainly *now* I would be called eccentric — but at the time there were several in the department as eccentric as I (although since I've left the force I've heard rumors of a purge of those individuals). But was I being singled out? I wondered sometimes if the captain had any idea what I was doing, or what was meant to be accomplished. But then again normal people seldom know what is meant to be accomplished by their actions — they just go through the motions.

Or maybe my continuing reassignment to Park Square was instead a vote of confidence in my abilities. I had become so familiar with the Square, and the bums and the homeless and the helpless who lived there, and with the shadowed places where they did what they felt they had to do.

Of course, I should have been a lot more careful. I had never had the right people skills, the ability to make people like me and listen to me. Everything had grown so complicated. I could never tell what people wanted from me anymore. Maybe that had been the jogger's problem as well. Maybe that was what kept the jogger running around the Square every night, always in danger of being mugged or raped, but never stopping. The captain kept ordering me to get her out of there, that it was too damn dangerous, but I had to catch her first and I never could. None of us could.

But I suppose I had no real reason to complain. I already suspected that patrolling Park Square was the only job I could do anymore. I had the routine down pat. I wondered if the jogger had any other options, any other places she could run.

Still I periodically attempted to see the captain, to talk to him about why he continued to assign me to the same monotonous task, but they wouldn't let me past the front desk. They said he was busy. They said he was home in bed. Sometimes they said they had no idea where the captain might be — they said they hadn't seen him in days. Sometimes I wondered if the captain would have seen me if I had still been in uniform. Out of the uniform I more than lacked authority; at times I felt like the worst kind of anarchist. But I was in no position to force the issue with the captain — I could not afford to lose my job. I had grown far too dependent of it. But still, I craved explanation.

My objection to this assignment was largely a matter of principle. For I liked patrolling the Square. The captain had ways of impressing his own sense of morality and dedication on his men, and I'm sure that in part I was just accepting his authority. But I liked patrolling there. I wanted to take on every criminal there, as my personal responsibility.

Majorie used to call that "avoidance."

"You spend all your time out on the beat so you don't have to talk to me! So I won't know you don't even have any small talk left!" Sometimes when she talked like that her lips would pull back, showing her teeth.

"It's my job. When we were first married you thought that was important."

"That's because I thought it was a job. Now I know it's some kind of obsession with you. Any time things get a little rough around here, we have a fight, you put on that ratty-looking coat of yours and head down to the Square. You've spent half our marriage in the Square!"

I just sat there, feeling a great deal, but frozen, not knowing what it was I was feeling, but still intending to keep a tight lid on myself. I couldn't let go. I didn't even comprehend most of our arguments anymore.

"You're afraid of me. I can't stay with a man who's afraid of me!"

Was it true? I knew I was scared to dance with her. And I had to keep the lights out when we made love. I was too self-conscious even to hold her hand in public. "I can't help it," I managed to say. "All the men in my family . . . my father . . . well, we're all like that."

She looked disgusted. "Quit the job."

"I can't"

"Quit the job or quit me. You can't have us both. You don't have any friends; you want to lose me, too?"

"It's my responsibility. My personal responsibility."

That was as strong as I could get with her. So she'd left. Women had always terrified me, and I'd envied them. They seemed to say what they pleased. They could cry when they wanted to.

Park Square is bounded by Tremont and Mayer Avenues, Eighth and Tenth Streets. Ninth Street ends in an untended morass on each side of the old park. There are small leaks in the sewer systems at each end of the park, left unrepaired for many years, and the resulting rich loam is choked with low-hanging chestnut and walnut trees, wrapped in a spiny tangle of briars, weeds, and vines. On hot nights in the late fall a stroller is assaulted by the odor of an exotic blend of rotting walnuts and chestnuts, and the faint aroma of sewage. It resembles nothing I can remember, and has a disturbing way of remaining with you long after you've gone home, making you wonder if it's something you have smelled before, but the memory since suppressed. You become convinced that you have visited the park in your dreams.

The police didn't venture into the heart of the old park anymore. The captain had made that decision several years before when he took over the job. He said he would take full responsibility for that decision, but none of the expected flak materialized. None of the other city departments — Parks and Recreation, Sanitation, the Mayor's office — would have anything to do with the park either, so they had no cause to complain. The expected public outcry never materialized; people seemed to be all too ready to let that part of the city go. At one time someone had proposed bulldozing the whole mess. I don't know whatever happened to him, or to his plan. There was a new park, with a lake, on the north end of the city — "new," even though it had been built some ten years ago — and everyone went there.

Sometimes you could hear loud, discordant noises in the park, or see a fleeting silhouette, and as usual there were rumors that some people had actually moved in there, living off the land, the animals, and each other. But I'd never seen any proof. No one I knew had ever been in there. All the park lights had been destroyed a long time ago, and the power cut off to the posts, and to the ancient sprinkler system. The lighting on the bordering streets had never been the best; it's of an old series, tied piecemeal into the new system. Some of the lamps burn brown; some street corners lie in complete darkness.

I'd walked these bordering streets for a very long time — the same amount of time it took to destroy my marriage — every weeknight, and some weekends during the summer when apparently the captain felt the streets were the worst, although I'd personally never heard him say that. As far as I was concerned it wasn't a matter of better or worse. Park Square was always the same: a bad place to be.

And quite familiar to me by then; despite the ugliness, it has become strangely home, like a small town within the city limits.

My back-up team that week was Jones and Reynolds. I didn't know exactly what it was they had done to deserve this, although I had heard Reynolds had been pretty rough his last few cases, and that Jones had a bad reputation from his days with the vice squad. Most nights I didn't have backup, but assaults were up a hundred percent in the surrounding neighborhoods, and apparently the captain thought there might be a Park Square connection.

Jones and Reynolds obviously hadn't yet become acclimated to this part of town. Jones was short and blond, looking sunburnt even in winter. He looked like a little boy sitting in his daddy's car. Reynolds was dark and quiet, with a pervading nervousness making him look a lot thinner, a lot frailer than he actually was. I'd never seen anyone else on Park Square who looked remotely nervous, even the obvious crazies. Jones and Reynolds didn't look like cops out on the street, but they did stick out. They didn't belong. Most of the time I'd make them stay in the car, parked at Tremont and Tenth in one of the better lit parts of the neighborhood. They couldn't see me most of the evening, but I could check on them once every hour or so.

The streets are never crowded around the park; you're liable to run into no more than two dozen people over the entire four square miles in any one night. But those two dozen made you nervous enough; some nights they felt like a crowd. Sometimes I even got a twinge of claustrophobia out on the street.

On that night after I left Jones and Reynolds in the car I started out Tenth Street at a leisurely pace. I usually walked on the side of the street away from the park, beside the old rows of storefronts. Occasionally I'd stop and look into the dusty display windows, or turn into a doorway and peer through the glass with my hands cupped binocular-fashion around my eyes. Other nights I wouldn't stop at all, but would stuff my fists into my black coat pockets, wrap my collar around my neck, and stride with an air of purpose tinged with furtiveness up the street, never looking directly into anyone's face, although occasionally turning around after they'd left me to catch a glimpse of the retreating form. The ones who stared into every window and the ones who trudged around eyes-to-the-sidewalk: these were two of the three classes of night strollers here. The third class was the stalkers: eccentric, anomalous, and ultimately surpassing imitation.

The first walker I encountered that night was a man in his mid-fifties. Gray hair, heavily lined skin, penny-colored eyes. His nose was running; I was hearing sniffles louder than I thought was possible. I noted that the man seemed to be wearing a tuxedo beneath his shabby gray tweed coat, then I promptly forgot all about him.

Occasionally, I would do more than pretend while looking into the shop windows, and actually made a concerted effort at cataloguing their contents. Most were empty; all I could see were curtains of dust and cobwebs, broken furniture shrouded in a lacy film. But occasionally there would be a store open at least part of the week — say Monday, Wednesdays, and Fridays, or Thursdays only, nine until twelve, but more often Hours by Appointment Only.

I could remember one store from that evening, a dealership in human prosthetics, open one to five on Tuesdays, I stopped at first because I saw an arm in the window, thinking perhaps someone had stuffed a body in there as a kind of macabre joke. But it turned out to be a rather realistic prosthetic arm attached to a paler mannequin. I supposed this was purposeful, to emphasize the naturalness of the limb by contrasting it to the mannequin's artificiality.

Scattered around the mannequin were hearing aids in their boxes, a display case full of artificial eyes, hands, fingers, feet, and toes, breast replacements for post-mastectomies, ears, noses, and a model for an artificial larynx. A rather ghoulish assortment, I thought, and with all the dust and the dirty window, it was difficult at first to tell them from the real things. The fact that there seemed to have been no attempt at an aesthetic placement of the items made me think of some slaughterhouses I'd seen.

A woman in a sweat suit passed me at a fast trot. "Miss! Miss!" I didn't even try to catch her. I'd tried before and there was just no contest – she was like a gazelle. It was hard to believe she'd be in any danger from a few drunk and malnourished derelicts.

The increase in assaults in surrounding neighborhoods had been attributed — by the press — to a number of individuals: the most recent being "The Beast," said to run about hunched over, snarling, and possessed of a foul odor. The name brought to mind other, similar characters discussed, and named, by the press over the last several years: The Strangler, The Slasher, The Bruiser, The Mangler. Like a team of wrestlers. They'd supposedly plagued this part of the city for years. But after a few weeks of publicity the career of each individual always faded into obscurity, until the next character was singled out and anointed, and stories of the earlier criminals were recalled for comparison's sake.

I'd always had my doubts, as had others in the department. With the heavy increase in street people over the last ten years conflicts were bound to emerge. Some of these citizens see scruffy individuals looking for a handout and they imagine that rape and murder is imminent. And the press feeds the hysteria.

Women in the surrounding subdivisions, encouraged by their husbands or boyfriends, or on their own, were taking self-defense courses and buying door alarms, mace, and whistles. A city likes to protect its women. Patronizing, but true.

The Beast dressed in army fatigues and old tennis shoes, and, despite the snarlings he made, supposedly never had much of any expression on his face. Apparently he just walked out of the bushes, grabbed somebody, slobbered on them and shook them up a little, stole something if they had it, then shambled back into the bushes and trees.

So far there was nothing that really tied The Beast to Park Square, but people said the captain had his suspicions, even though he never let me in on any of them. No doubt it was the rumors of homeless people living deep inside the Park. Not that he was really convinced The Beast was truly dangerous — I don't think any of us thought that. But we needed to catch him anyway, and the Park seemed a good bet.

In any case, Park Square was my beat, my duty. And if The Beast came out of there he was my duty as well. I needed to track him down, expunge him from the park. I needed to do it by myself. I suppose I imagined that somehow getting rid of people like The Beast would make Park Square a nicer place, that the snarled vegetation and the smell would clear up eventually, and that the park would once again be the

pleasant place it must have been in the beginning, the pastoral retreat it
was meant to be.

I quickened my pace after I left the prosthesis store, crossing the
next side street, and leading towards the intersection of Mayer and
Tenth.

*What's holding you there? You care more about that damn Park
than you care about me!*

A large dark form ambled out of the alley ahead of me, making me
gasp involuntarily. I wondered if he had heard me; it wasn't a good idea
to let anyone in this neighborhood know you were scared. It draws some
types like a bad smell. As he came closer I recognized him: a large,
crudely featured man who took a walk around the park once a week,
although the specific night of his walks varied. I had thought several
times about warning him of the dangers, but figured his looks alone
would scare off any average mugger.

I stopped right in front of him. He looked up slowly, his small eyes
beginning their careful examination of me. When his eyes reached my
face he blinked several times. Before I could say anything he had started
across the street to the opposite sidewalk at a stumbling trot. He veered
once into the shadows bordering the park. I heard an inarticulate cry,
then I saw him running as fast as he could carry his bulk into the dimly-lit
corner beyond. He passed through the spot of light there, then continued
on into the dark block following.

I shouldn't have stopped him in the first place. He could have
blown my cover. No one greets anyone in Park Square.

As I rounded the corner of Mayer and Tenth I squinted into the
dark, rain-shiny corridor of Mayer Avenue. At this point I had to cross
the street and walk on the Park side, as the sidewalk had been torn up
several years ago, barriers erected, but no repair work had ever been
completed. This was the worst part of the patrol; I often found myself
walking at a faster clip than I should have, but since almost no one ever
traveled this section anyway, I suppose it didn't make much difference.

I found myself hunching my shoulders involuntarily as I walked,
stooping over. It was an old habit; I'd done it as a teenager every time
I was embarrassed, or afraid. It had always made my father angry. He
always said a real man kept his posture.

The branches and scrub etched a sharp silhouette against the sky,
with but an occasional whiff of cloud behind, or more frequently a strand

of fog in front, to break the image. There was a slight breeze in the street, but the park vegetation remained perfectly still.

The jogger passed me again, pumping her legs aggressively, violently. I couldn't tell if her expression was angry or determined. I found I needed to ignore her, but could not. I could feel my back tightening up, anticipating her return, her feet pounding up behind me.

You're afraid of me! How can I live with a man who's afraid of me?

I heard a whispering, stopped and looked around, then saw that it had begun to sprinkle rain. I pulled the collar of my coat up, holding one hand against my throat. I wanted to protect my neck, my jaw for some inexplicable reason.

It was an old Navy peacoat, form-fitting, but the shoulders were a bit too large; they stuck out as if padded. I'd seen several men in the square wear similar coats. That kind of coat made the shoulders seem a bit more aggressive — manly, I guess you would say.

Many of the streetlights were out on Mayer's east end. It made the park look even darker, blacker, like a sore on the city. I was suddenly convinced that originally there must have been buildings where the park was now. A whole community perhaps. Then one day the growth started, maybe in someone's damp basement, or from some microscopic spore under an old refrigerator. It expanded, assimilated stones, bricks, parts of buildings, then buildings themselves. Finally it swallowed everything. The only thing the city officials could think to do was put a fence around it and call it a park.

I thought about Jones and Reynolds, wondering if they were still back there, or if they had bugged out on me as soon as I was out of sight. I didn't trust them. I didn't trust the captain. I didn't trust anyone. You just can't count on people; you have to be careful.

You don't have any friends; you want to lose me, too?

Turning onto Eighth I passed several men: looked like a priest under one coat, then a man I thought was naked under his, then a man with a black bag — a doctor? — all looking straight ahead, their faces pale and drawn. What brought them out here every night?

Then a woman in a nurse's uniform. A man all bandaged up. A postman still in uniform, a bag of letters over his shoulder. What was *he* doing out tonight? I should have stopped wondering by this time; I saw this sort of thing all the time. But it still unsettled me.

There were so many shadowy figures, forms that could have been men *or* women. It was hard to distinguish them in the dark.

All strolling casually, walking the Square. All silent, steady, eyes straight ahead or down at their feet.

A large station wagon was parked at the curb. A man, a woman, and a small child were inside. It had stalled; he was trying to start it. They were really out of place in this neighborhood. I went up to the driver's window to offer my help.

The man took one look at me, frantically played with the ignition, pumping the gas pedal, and then suddenly roared off in a cloud of acrid smoke.

It made me angry. I'd just wanted to help. Things had gotten far too complicated for people just to simply trust anymore.

Then she was there again, jogging, the woman in the sweat suit, short-cropped hair, strained looking face, and sunglasses, sunglasses in this light. But as she passed me I realized she was running full-out, probably as fast as she could manage. I started to follow, picking up speed, soon discovering I had to use all I had.

"Hey, wait!" I cried. She glanced back once, her mouth opening, but no sound coming out. I thought maybe she was frightened of me. "I just want to help!" She kept running.

I ran as fast as I could, alternating yellow, brown, gray, black flashing past me, making me dizzy. How could she run so fast?

We passed by the row of storefronts. We passed the lost mailman. I turned my head. We passed by the car with Jones and Reynolds. Reynolds lay across the hood, bleeding from his ears. Jones' face had been pushed through the windshield.

The jogger turned her head around and snarled at me.

Shambling down the sidewalk, away from the car that held the two bodies of my backups, was a hunched-over figure. Army fatigues. Tennis shoes.

The woman was still running. I stopped, pulled out a pistol, and yelled for The Beast to halt. He picked up speed, turned once and threw a rock in my direction. I fired a warning shot. He crossed the street toward the park.

The jogger intercepted him halfway across the street. The Beast turned and stared at her. I was busy taking aim.

But then she started unzipping her sweat suit, then, *my god*, she pulled it off. The Beast stood frozen.

Suddenly a knife was glinting in his hand, looking more like silvery smoke than steel. I squeezed off a shot.

And he kept coming at her.

I shouted and ran toward the two. I needn't have bothered. She pulled out her own knife, also strangely smoke-like, and slashed him into bloody threads. She was a lot quicker than he.

When I reached her side I was speechless, just looking down at this man and what she had done to him. For the first time I noted how much he resembled me: the broad shoulders, the largeness of him, the face gone wild and crude.

She turned, her eyes still wide, forearms held stiffly raised to shoulder height. And first slashed into my coat sleeves, cutting out the shoulder seams neat as surgery. Strangely, all I could think about was how she had ruined my suit, and how my suit had become my uniform.

Then she slashed into my shirt sleeve, my arm, then across my chest. It was all too quick; at first I felt very little pain. I was confused, disoriented; I turned back to the man's body, then stumbled back to face her, then turned again. I found I couldn't protect myself.

Then I thought it must be because I looked so much like him, like one of the enemy, just like an ordinary citizen, and in her excitement she had mistaken me for one of them. She'd attacked me because of my appearance alone. My broad face. My largeness.

"Not me . . . not *me!*"

But then I saw her angry face: angry, savage. She just didn't understand. She didn't hear. And her face, too, was a face vaguely like my own. I felt like a child again, trapped in a hall of mirrors.

So now you might say that I've gone as far as I can go in plainclothes. I'm a shadow inside shadows, just like everybody else. I live with her now, the jogger, deep inside the park. I don't pretend it's a real relationship, but obviously I'm not yet ready for one of those. Just ask my ex-wife. This one — at least she knows what to do for my wounds. And she keeps me in line. I keep one eye open at night.

I still hear rumors that the captain is going to do something about cleaning up Park Square. I've heard I've been reported dead. It may be true. I haven't left the park for months. And I believe the park is growing, tendrils and roots breaking up the asphalt, overhanging branches pushing into the empty store windows, the streets filling up with people who don't understand what's going on anymore, and don't know where else to go.

THE PATTERN

Bill Pronzini

At 11:23 P.M. on Saturday, the twenty-sixth of April, a small man wearing rimless glasses and a dark gray business suit walked into the detective squad room in San Francisco's Hall of Justice and confessed to the murders of three Bay Area housewives whose bodies had been found that afternoon and evening.

Inspector Glenn Rauxton, who first spoke to the small man, thought he might be a crank. Every major homicide in any large city draws its share of oddballs and mental cases, individuals who confess to crimes in order to attain public recognition in otherwise unsubstantial lives or because of some secret desire for punishment; or for any number of reasons that can be found in the casebooks of police psychiatrists. But it wasn't up to Rauxton to make a decision either way. He left the small man in the company of his partner, Dan Tobias and went in to talk to his immediate superior, Lieutenant Jack Sheffield.

"We've got a guy outside who says he's the killer of those three women today, Jack," Rauxton said. "Maybe a crank, maybe not."

Sheffield turned away from the portable typewriter at the side of his desk; he had been making out a report for the chief's office. "He came in his own volition?"

Rauxton nodded. "Not three minutes ago."

"What's his name?"

"He says it's Andrew Franzen."

"And his story?"

"So far, just that he killed them," Rauxton said. "I didn't press him. He seems pretty calm about the whole thing."

"Well, run his name through the weirdo file and then put him in one of the interrogation cubicles," Sheffield said. "I'll look through the reports again before we question him."

"You want me to get a stenographer?"

"It would probably be a good idea."

"Right," Rauxton said, and went out.

Sheffield rubbed his face wearily. He was a learn, sinewy man in his late forties, with thick graying hair and a falconic nose. He had dark-brown eyes that had seen most everything there was to see and had been appalled by a good deal of it; they were tired, sad eyes. He wore a plain blue suit, and his shirt was open at the throat. The tie he had worn to work when his tour started at 4:00 P.M., which had been given to him by his wife and consisted of interlocking, psychedelic-colored concentric circles, was out of sight in the bottom drawer of his desk.

He picked up the folder with the preliminary information on the three slayings and opened it. Most of it was sketchy telephone communications from the involved police forces in the Bay Area, a precursory report from the local lab, a copy of the police Telex that he had sent out state wide as a matter of course following the discovery of the first body, and that had later alerted the other authorities in whose areas the two subsequent corpses had been found. There was also an Inspector's Report on the first and only death in San Francisco, filled out and signed by Rauxton. The last piece of information had come in less than a half-hour earlier, and he knew the facts of the case by memory; but Sheffield was a meticulous cop and he liked to have all the details fixed in his mind.

The first body was of a woman named Janet Flanders, who had been discovered by a neighbor at 4:15 that afternoon in her small duplex on 39th Avenue, near Golden Gate Park. She had been killed by several blows about the head with an as yet unidentified blunt instrument.

There were no witnesses, or apparent clues, in any of the killings. They would have, on the surface, appeared to be unrelated if it had not been for the facts that each of the three women had died on the same day, and in the same manner. But there were other cohesive factors as well — factors that, taken in conjunction with the surface similarities, undeniably linked the murders.

Item: Each of the three women had been orphaned non-natives of California, having come to the San Francisco Bay Area from different parts of the Midwest within the past six years.

Item: Each of them had been married to traveling salesmen who were home only short periods each month, and who were all — according to the information garnered by investigating officers from neighbors and friends — currently somewhere on the road.

Patterns, Sheffield thought as he studied the folder's contents. Most cases had one, and this case was no exception. All you had to do was fit the scattered pieces of its particular pattern together, and you would have your answer. Yet the pieces here did not seem to join logically, unless you concluded that the killer of the women was a psychopath who murdered blonde, thirtyish, orphaned wives of traveling salesmen for some perverted reason of his own.

That was the way the news media would see it, Sheffield knew, because that kind of slant always sold copies, and attracted viewers and listeners. They would try to make the case into another Zodiac thing. The radio newscast he had heard at the cafeteria across Bryant Street, when he had gone out for supper around nine, had presaged the discovery of still more bodies of Bay Area housewives and had advised all women whose husbands were away to remain behind locked doors. The announcer had repeatedly referred to the deaths as "the bludgeon slayings."

Sheffield had kept a strictly open mind. It was, for all practical purposes, his case — the first body had been found in San Francisco, during his tour, and that gave him jurisdiction in handling the investigation. The cops in the two other involved cities would be in constant touch with him, as they already had been. He would have been foolish to have made any premature speculations not based solely on fact, and Sheffield was anything but foolish. Anyway, psychopath or not, the case still promised a hell of a lot of not very pleasant work.

Now, however, there was Andrew Franzen.

Crank? Or multiple murderer? Was this going to be one of those blessed events — a simple case? Or was Franzen only the beginning of a long series of very large headaches?

Well, Sheffield thought, *we'll find out soon enough.* He closed the folder and got to his feet and crossed to the door of his office.

In the squad room, Rauxton was just finishing a computer check. He came over to Sheffield and said, "Nothing on Franzen in the weirdo file, Jack."

Sheffield inclined his head and looked off toward the row of glass-walled interrogation cubicles at the rear of the squad room. In the second one, he could see Dan Tobias propped on a corner of the bare metal desk inside; the man who had confessed, Andrew Franzen, was sitting with his back to the squad room, stiffly erect in his chair. Also waiting inside, stoically seated in the near corner, was one of the police stenographers.

Sheffield said, "Okay, Glenn, let's hear what he has to say."

He and Rauxton went over to the interrogation cubicle and stepped inside. Tobias stood, shook his head almost imperceptibly to let Sheffield and Rauxton know that Franzen hadn't said anything to him. Tobias was tall and muscular, with a slow smile and big hands and — like Rauxton — a strong dedication to the life's work he had chosen.

He moved to the right corner of the metal desk, and Rauxton to the left corner, assuming set position like football halfbacks running a bread-and-butter play. Sheffield, the quarterback, walked behind the desk, cocked one hip against the edge and learned forward slightly, so that he was looking down at the small man sitting with his hands flat on his thighs.

Franzen had a round, inoffensive pink face with tiny-shelled ears and a Cupid's-bow mouth. His hair was brown and wavy, immaculately cut and shaped, and it saved him from being non-descript; it gave him a certain boyish character even though Sheffield placed his age at around forty. His eyes were brown and liquid, like those of a spaniel, behind his rimless glasses.

Sheffield got a ball-point pen out of his coat pocket and tapped it lightly against his front teeth; he liked to have something in his hands when he was conducting an interrogation. He broke the silence, finally, by saying, "My name is Sheffield. I'm the lieutenant in charge here. Now before you say anything, it's my duty to advise you of your rights."

He did so, quickly and tersely, concluding with, "You understand all of your rights as I've outlined them, Mr. Franzen?"

The small man sighed softly and nodded.

"Are you willing then, to answer questions without the presence of counsel?"

"Yes. Yes."

Sheffield continued to tap the ball-point pen against his front teeth. "All right," he said at length, "Let's have your full name."

"Andrew Leonard Franzen."

"Where do you live?"

"Here in San Francisco."

"At what address?"

"Nine-oh-six Greenwich."

"Is that a private residence?"

"No, it's an apartment building."

"Are you employed?"

"Yes."

"Where?"

"I'm an independent consultant."

"What sort of consultant?"

"I design languages between computers."

Rauxton said, "You want to explain that?"

"It's very simple, really," Franzen said tonelessly. "If two business firms have different types of computers, and would like to set up a communication between them so that the information stored in the memory banks of each computer can be utilized by the other, they call me. I design the linking electronic connections between the two computers, so that each can understand the other; in effect, so that they can converse."

"That sounds like a very specialized job," Sheffield said.

"Yes."

"What kind of salary do you make?"

"Around eighty thousand a year."

Two thin, horizontal lines appeared in Sheffield's forehead. Franzen had the kind of vocation that bespoke of intelligence and upper-class respectability: why would a man like that want to confess to the brutal murders of three simple-living housewives? Or an even more puzzling question: If his confession was genuine, what was his reason for the killings?

Sheffield said, "Why did you come here tonight, Mr. Franzen?"

"To confess." Franzen looked at Rauxton. "I told this man that when I walked in here a few minutes ago."

"To confess what?"

"The murders."

"What murders, specifically?"

Franzen sighed. "The three women in the Bay Area today."

"Just the three?"

"Yes."

"No others whose bodies maybe have not been discovered as yet?"

"No, no."

"Suppose you tell me why you decided to turn yourself in?"

"Why? Because I'm guilty. Because I killed them."

"And that's the only reason?"

Franzen was silent for a moment. Then, slowly, he said, "No, I suppose not. I went walking in Aquatic Park when I came back to San Francisco this afternoon, just walking and thinking. The more I thought, the more I knew that it was hopeless. It was only a matter of time before you found out I was the one, a matter of a day or two. I guess I could have run, but I wouldn't know how to begin to do that. I've always done things on impulse, things I would never do if I stopped to think about. That's how I killed them, on some insane impulse; if I had thought about it I never would have done it. It was so useless . . ."

Sheffield exchanged glances with the two inspectors. Then he said, "You want to tell us how you did it, Mr. Franzen?"

"What?"

"How did you kill them?" Sheffield asked. "What kind of weapon did you use?"

"A meat tenderizing mallet. One of those big wooden things with serrated ends that women keep in the kitchen to tenderize a piece of steak."

It was silent in the cubicle now. Sheffield looked at Rauxton, and then at Tobias; they were all thinking the same thing: the police had released no details to the news media as to the kind of weapon involved in the slayings, other than the general information that it was a blunt instrument. But the initial lab report on the first victim — and the preliminary observations on the other two — stated the wounds of each had been made by a roughly square-shaped instrument, which had sharp "teeth" capable of making a series of deep indentations as it bit into the flesh. A mallet such as Franzen had just described fitted those characteristics exactly.

Sheffield asked, "What did you do with the mallet, Mr. Franzen?"

"I threw it away."

Where?"

"In Saulalito, into some bushes along the road."

"Do you remember the location?"

"I think so."

"Was Elaine Dunhill the last woman you killed?"

"Yes."

"What room did you kill her in?"

"The bedroom."

"Where in the bedroom?"

"Beside her vanity."

"Who was your first victim?" Rauxton asked.

"Janet Flanders."

"You killed her in the bathroom, is that right?"

"No, no, in the kitchen . . ."

"What was she wearing?"

"A flowered housecoat."

"Why did you strip her body?"

"I didn't. Why would I —"

"Mrs. Gordon was the middle victim, right?" Tobias asked.

"Yes."

"Where did you kill *her*?"

"The kitchen."

"She was sewing, wasn't she?"

"No, she was canning," Franzen said. "She was canning plum preserves. She had mason jars and boxes of plums and three big pressure cookers all over the table and stove . . ."

There was wetness in Franzen's eyes now. He stopped talking and took his rimless glasses off and wiped at the tears with the back of his left hand. He seemed to be swaying slightly on the chair.

Sheffield, watching him, felt a curious mixture of relief and sadness. The relief was due to the fact that there was no doubt in his mind — nor in the minds of Rauxton and Tobias; he could read their eyes — that Andrew Franzen was the slayer of the three women. They had thrown detail and "trip-up" questions at him, one right after another, and he had all the right answers; he knew particulars that had also not been given to the news media; that no crank could possibly have known, that only the murderer could have been aware of. The case had turned out to be one of the simplest ones after all, and it was all but wrapped up now; there would be no more "bludgeon slayings," no public hue and cry, no attacks on police inefficiency in the press, no pressure from the commissioners or the mayor. The sadness was the result of twenty-six years of police work, of living with death and crime every day, of looking at a man who seemed to be the essence of normalcy and yet who was a cold-blooded multiple murderer. *Why?* Sheffield thought. That was the big question. *Why did he do it?*

He said, "You want to tell us the reason, Mr. Franzen? Why you killed them?"

The small man moistened his lips. "I was very happy, you see. My life had some meaning, some challenge. I was fulfilled — but they were going to destroy everything." He stared at his hands. "One of them had found out the truth — I don't know how — and tracked down the other two. I had come to Janet this morning, and she told me that they were going to expose me, and I just lost my head and picked up the mallet and killed her. Then I went to the others and killed them. I couldn't stop myself; it was as if I were moving in a nightmare."

"What are you trying to say?" Sheffield asked softly. "What was your relationship with those three women?"

The tears in Andrew Franzen's eyes shone like tiny diamonds in the light from the overhead flourescents.

"They were my wives," he said.

SEESAW

David L. Duggins

"Gimmie a push!"

Again. And again. All afternoon. Ted cursed. He supposed there were worse fates than having to spend an entire Sunday afternoon baby-sitting your five-year-old sister. But he couldn't think of any. He gave Cybil another push as she swung back toward him.

They were the only two people in the park. Ted heard the high, whiny hum in his ears that meant there wasn't enough noise. He wished for a loaded-up Walkman.

"Higher!" Cybil shrieked.

"Can't push you higher," Ted said flatly. "Mom would kill me."

"No fun then," Cybil whined. "Let me off!" Want to go on the merry-go-round."

Ted grabbed the chains and slowly walked forward, stopping the swing. Cybil was halfway to the metal platform by the time Ted had brushed the dust from his hands.

"Come on, come on!" she shouted.

"Come on, come on," Ted said in a tired voice. He looked up through the quiet air into the bright gold eye of the summer sun. An autumn-chill wind suddenly shot through the playground. He shivered as he gave the merry-go-round a spin.

School again tomorrow, Ted mourned. And this is how I spend my last weekend of summer vacation.

"Off, off!" Cybil suddenly shouted. "Gonna get sick."

Ted brought the carousel to an abrupt halt, seriously concerned for a moment. His sister had gone very pale. "You okay?"

She nodded, thumb in mouth. "Uh-huh," she said.

"Not going to throw up?"

Cybil shook her head. "Seesaw!" she screamed suddenly, jumping into the air. "Wanna go up and down on the seesaw!"

"Okay, gotcha," Ted said, grabbing her hand. This was humiliating. If the guys should walk by, see him bobbing up and down on one end of a big board with his little sister on the other end, he would be the belly-laugh of the school.

He tipped one end of the board to the ground, allowed Cybil to climb on. She looked very small on the wide seat, like a much older girl on horseback.

"Up and down and up and down!" she cried.

Ted reluctantly moved to the other side of the board, plopped his butt down. The wood was hard, unyielding . . . but somehow welcoming.

His legs were straight. He bent them, then straightened quickly, and the board didn't just pivot upward; it sailed up into the clear blue, into the moveless golden orb of bright summer. It delivered him up into the fire and the light. For a moment, he was blinded.

"Whee!" Ted heard Cybil yell happily, far away. He blinked. His end of the board floated like a feather to the ground, the descent dozens, hundreds of feet. He heard Cybil's faint squeal of delight as she rose up into the expanse of crystal sky . . . and then her cries of delight faded to silence as she ascended beyond the range of his hearing.

Ted fought to keep his feet on the ground, stop the motion of the board. He'd almost gotten sick himself; he still felt dizzy. He closed his eyes, felt his toes lift away. He pushed his weight down heavily on the board, felt it return to a stable, horizontal position. Cybil's wails of disappointment grew steadily louder.

Ted opened his eyes.

The playground was filled with children — swaying pendulums on swingsets, scampering simians on the monkeybars, spinners on the merry-go-round, missles on the slide, running, skipping, jumping.

Then Ted saw the man. He knew even before the man stood, before he began to walk toward the monkey bars, before he reached beneath his long overcoat, that there was something wrong with him. His eyes were cavernous, glowing like witchfire-filled knotholes in a willow tree.

His face was pale and neutral, but those eyes held a twinkle of devil-clown mirth.

Where did all these people come from? Ted wanted to ask.

By the time the question was fully formed, the man had already drawn the sawed-off shotgun from under his coat, pushed the barrel into the blonde curl-flow of a little girl climbing the slide-ladder, and pulled the trigger. The headless body flopped from its perch, spuming dust, spitting blood.

In the time it took Ted to gain full comprehension of what was happening, the man blew another little girl off the top of the monkey bars, reloaded, and cut a running boy in half, firing both barrels.

The rest of the children were scattering now. The man sought them out in all their many hiding places. The gun boomed throaty metal thunder again. And again. The smell of gunpowder became cloying. Ted coughed, gagged. White smoke obscured his vision.

He whirled. The man was gone. The playground was a slaughterhouse.

The bodies became translucent, then transparent, then faded entirely. The bloodstains sank into the earth, dissolving into swirling dust, whipped into oddly familiar shapes by the icy wind.

"Why did you stop?" Cybil whined. "It's no fun when you stop in the middle."

She stood, sat down hard on the wooden seat.

And the seesaw went up. Ted screamed. He felt hi_ _ soaring, up into the cold, cyclic eye, the uncaring cyclops star_ _ _e of blue, a gaze that knew all times as one. He stare_ grassless plain of the playground and saw a wi_ whirling toward him.

Toward his sister.

A glint of polished metal shone through on itself.

He wanted to tell Cybil that he knew what wo_ came down again, and before. But she wouldn't unde_ _ad not seen. And she did not see now, as the dust cloud solidi_ _nned, loaded fresh shells into the shotgun and moved around to her s_de of the seesaw.

Ted reached the apex, hung timeless for a heartbeat. *It's safe up here. I could stay here forever and no darkness would touch me . . .*

Ted began his second descent.

The cold sun was muted by a thin skim of cloud.

Cybil's cries of delight rang in the afternoon air, mingling with the building chorus of dozens, hundreds of screams.

Ted and Cybil intersected at an invisible point in space. He heard himself shout a warning, expecting to see the man behind her, ready to use the shotgun, claim her before she could rise beyond the darkness, the foul influence.

The man was not behind her. Cybil's bright smile remained undiluted. Ted shot a glance around the playground, saw no one.

Then he heard the double hammerclick from directly behind him. Cybil's smile suddenly reversed itself, drew down, flaired outward. Her cry became a piercing wail.

Ted rose up, sat down hard, as Cybil had done.

She'll be up there, safe up there with the ancient sun . . .

Cybil's chest exploded.

Her ruined body jerked backward. The momentum sent Ted up again. His hands were like claws rising up into the sanctuary of that globe of light, trying to take hold.

The light was far, far away. The darkness below beckoned.

The seesaw fell again.

Ted felt two hot, gritty circles of pressure against the back of his neck.

He heard a hot, hissing chuckle.

His feet touched ground.

TRIAL BY FIRE

Barry Hoffman

Word swept through town like a raging inferno. Stores closed; the diner emptied; patrons poured out of the pool hall and Cavanaugh's Bar.

"They've caught the fucker," said one.

"They're bringing him in now," echoed another.

"Praise the Lord," a third whispered, a nine week long nightmare apparently at an end.

They waited in fevered anticipation and a hush fell as Sheriff Everett Manders surveyed the crowd with some trepidation before he unveiled the suspect who held their rapt attention. An emotionally charged, volatile group of friends and neighbors, he thought, that could easily turn into a lynch mob. He wasn't looking forward to this confrontation. Sighing, he opened the back door and helped the handcuffed 23-year-old Lonnie Burkett out of the car.

"I knew it," bellowed Cecil Holloway, when he saw the youth. "Had to be him. He and his ain't one of us."

"Why'd you move here, you little shit?" cried Leila Wyche. "Why make our lives miserable?"

"The Devil's spawn," crowed Ethel Tanner, Reverend Ben Tanner's wife.

The crowd seemed to move as one, inching ever closer to Manders and the young arsonist. A spark was all that was needed to turn these normally placid people into a frenzied mob that would only be sated by Lonnie Burkett's blood. Manders had to act now before they were beyond reason.

"Hold it folks!" he said above the din. "We got us here a suspect
... and only that. It's been hell on all of us, but I'm not about to let you
take the law into your own hands. And I don't want to be arresting any
of you for obstructing justice. Now let us pass."

While he'd been talking to all of the forty or so that had gathered,
his eyes were fixed on Samuel Crum whose paper mill had gone in
flames four days earlier. At 6'4" and 250 pounds, Crum had it in his
power to ease tensions or turn the crowd rabid. Crum stared at Manders,
his face contorted in rage, fists balled so tight his knuckles were deathly
pale. Crum looked at the man who'd been his friend since grade school,
cursed to himself and shook his head in acknowledgment. As Manders
moved towards him, the boy by his side, Crum let him pass.

"You should have arrested him a month ago," Crum said as he
passed. "Could have saved us all heartbreak and grief."

"Knew it was him all along!" another shouted.

The sheriff ignored the catcalls that continued as he made his way
to his office. He understood their rage only too well. Arson in a
close-knit community like Elkins brought out the worst in everyone.
Petty grudges became grounds for suspicion; friends, even relatives,
looked at one another differently. Anyone could be the cause of the
terror that filled them as they awaited the next inevitable fire. And
Lonnie Burkett had been a suspect from the very beginning; albeit for
no sound reason.

Nepotism was an established practice, born out of necessity and
inertia, in Elkins as few left and fewer yet moved into the community
of two hundred souls, give or take. A Dillard had been the town's mayor
long as anyone could remember; a Lawson had run the weekly
newspaper since it had opened; farmers passed their property to their
children and most stores were owned by the descendants of those who
had founded them. A Manders had been sheriff for three generations.

The Burketts, on the other hand, had moved in only a year before.
Ethel Stinson had been a spinster. When she died and left her
ramshackle cabin to some distant cousin, no one expected them to accept
the meager inheritance. Less than a week later, however, Lonnie
Burkett had moved in with his invalid father. The old man, a Korean
War veteran, received a paltry disability check once a month. Lonnie
did odd jobs to bring in additional money, mainly to feed the five dogs
the old man kept for company.

In a town where gossip traveled like a tornado, where all were an extended family of sorts, the Burketts stood out like a fox in a henhouse. When the fires began even Manders cast his eye on Lonnie. It was more comforting than to consider it might be a valued friend or neighbor. Suspecting and proving, however, were two entirely different propositions and Manders wasn't about to arrest the young man on conjecture alone. Proof hadn't surfaced until just three days before, too late to save Samuel Crum's paper mill, which employed four members of his family and 16 others – all now joining at least eight others on the unemployment line. Manders still couldn't believe his daughter, Shelly, of all people had cracked the case.

He turned Burkett over to Alvin Lukins for booking. A Lukins had been deputy near as long as a Manders had been sheriff; none particularly bright, energetic or ambitious. Second banana, without the ultimate responsibility, had suited them just fine. Looked as though pretty soon a Lukins *would* become sheriff after all, Manders thought ruefully.

He suddenly felt lightheaded and was forced to sit down; the stress of the past nine weeks finally catching up. *No sense in kidding yourself*, he thought. It wasn't merely stress. His health had been in steady decline since the accident that had claimed his wife, Amanda, two years before. A few too many drinks; the temperature dipping without either of them noticing; the road icing up; the jeep skidding and sliding . . . striking a tree. Amanda dead and he in a coma for nearly a week with a severe concussion. He'd been back to work in less than a month, passing the fatigue and shortness of breath, that descended upon him like a suffocating blanket, as aftereffects of the accident.

He'd been scared shitless, however, when he'd found himself driving aimlessly miles from town with no idea where he was going or, glancing at his watch, how three hours had slipped by. After the third such episode, he'd grudgingly gone to see his doctor. He'd been sent to a specialist in Philly for three days for tests.

Doc Fletcher had been blunt as always with his diagnosis, upon his return.

"There's nothing wrong with you that retirement won't cure."

"What the hell is that supposed to mean? I'm fifty-one. My father stayed on the job til he was near seventy and the same with his father before him."

"Neither of them slammed into a tree at forty miles per hour."

"That what them big-city doctors told you?"

"No. Them big-city doctors told me what you *didn't* have. No tumor, which is what I'd feared. In layman terms, when you hit that tree your brain bounced back and forth in your skull like a marble in a pinball machine. There was some permanent damage. Nothing life threatening *if* you start taking it easy. But, with the stress of your job . . ." He shrugged his shoulders.

" . . . the fatigue and the headaches . . ." Manders tried to finish for him but couldn't.

" . . . and the blackouts will continue and worsen. One day you'll be driving, go into one of your funks and instead of hitting a tree, you'll hit some kid or drive over a cliff."

"The timing's not right," Manders said.

"Never is," Fletcher said. "Look, Ev, in a year, Danny will be out of the Army. Let him take over. Hell, we all get old. I've been thinking of doing the same myself. Paul will finish his residency in six months. I figure it'll take all of two or three months before folks will want to be seeing him and not his old fart of a father."

"I'll think on it." He saw Fletcher eyeing him suspiciously. "Really, I will."

"For now cut back just a wee-bit. Let that deputy of yours – the Lukins kid – earn his pay. I'm serious, Ev. You got a lot of good years ahead of you. You'll have grandchildren pretty soon and you'll have the time to spend with them you didn't have for Danny and Shelly. Push yourself though . . ." He didn't need to finish the sentence.

Manders bolted as the door slammed. He glanced at the clock. He'd been asleep for two hours. Or had he blacked out again? He wondered. He eyed his daughter as she came across the room with two trays stacked on top of each other.

"Here's the salad you asked for. All right if I take Lonnie his supper?" She looked at him warily. "Are you okay?"

"Just dozed off for a minute there. You kinda caught me by surprise. Sure, you take the kid his supper." He paused and almost as an afterthought added, "You done real good, Shelly. I'm proud of you."

The girl smiled and left her father to his salad.

Damned right, I did good, Shelly thought as she passed three vacant cells; cells that remained unoccupied save for a few drunks who fought it out Friday or Saturday night. The fourth cell was Lonnie's. Shelly wondered at what she had ever seen in the man, though truth be told, she couldn't afford to be choosy. He was 5'7", the same as she, but wafer thin where she was "full bodied," her father's euphemism for hefty. Though twenty-three, he had a boyish face with acne still playing havoc with his complexion. His lips were thin, his nose pinched, his cheeks gaunt. What amazed her was the contrast between his thick straight blond hair and his utterly hairless face; not only no facial hair, but no eyebrows nor eyelashes. In one of God's cruel jokes she had too much of what he had too little. Her face was chubby; not even her father could soften the description. Her nose was broad, her lips full – possibly even sensuous, if she'd lost a bit of weight from the rest of her face. She too had a full head of hair – jet black, but cropped short. Unfortunately, there was more than a trace of facial hair; full eyebrows, long lashes and a hint of a mustache. Plain, dour; certainly not repulsive but no one who could be choosy about accepting a date.

The two locked eyes for a moment; his pale gray penetrating, probing but devoid of emotion; hers a fiery blue that spoke of hidden passions and desires.

She silently slid the tray under the bars and turned to leave.

"Shelly, for the love of God, please help me," he said, his voice a whine that now grated on her nerves. "Someone's framed me. I ain't set no fires. You of all people *know* I couldn't do such a thing. Will you help me, please?" The last came out *pleeeease*.

She smiled and she could see a glimmer of hope rise within him.

"Save it for the judge, shithead." She turned, her coarse husky laughter filling the corridor. *Help him*, she thought to herself. *You little shit, if it wasn't for me you wouldn't be here.*

The need to pin the blame on Lonnie Burkett had sprung from her father's decision to retire. Yes, she'd seen he'd become a shell of himself after her mother's death, but she thought he'd respond by throwing himself into his work with even greater intensity, if that were possible. And, while he'd been shaken to the core by Danny's death, five months before, retirement was the last thing she expected. Yet, three months ago, after he pushed his half-eaten supper away, he announced his intentions.

"I'm planning on retiring, Shelly. Doc Fletcher's been on me about it for well over a year now and it's time I listened. I'd hoped Danny would take over . . ." The sentence went unfinished.

While she knew he didn't love her any less, Danny was his son and it was he who would pass on the Manders name. No, he didn't love her any less, but she was a girl. It had taken every ounce of her persuasion to allow her to work at the jail when Danny had joined the Army. Her father hadn't even given her an official position. She wasn't a deputy, though she patrolled the town at night when her father wasn't feeling up to it. Usually she did the grunge work; got meals for the few prisoners who visited their cells, ran errands, answered the phone and kept the office clean.

Her father had told her on more than one occasion how he looked forward to the patter of countless grandchildren; young'uns that would spring from *her* womb. That was her role in life. But Danny had fucked things up by stepping on a land mine in the Persian Gulf in the closing hours of the triumphant Desert Storm. Even with his death, Shelly was certain her father would somehow rebound and remain sheriff until he was in his late-sixties, as had been the case for three generations.

"Who'll take your place?" she asked.

"Al Lukins, I reckon. He's adequate and he's got more ambition than his father."

"But a Manders has always been sheriff."

"There's nothing I can do about that now, is there? I'm too old to marry again, have a son, and wait for him to grow up. No, Lukins it'll have to be."

"What about me?"

"You can't be serious." He saw the hurt he'd inflicted, as she fought the tears that threatened to betray her emotions. "I mean, even if I could train you, this town isn't ready to accept a woman as sheriff. You know it as well as I do."

With the announcement his appetite seemed to return and he attacked his dinner with renewed vigor.

Shelly remained silent. No amount of talk, she knew, could change his mind. If she was to replace him she'd have to prove it by her deeds.

The opportunity presented itself a little over a month later.

◆   ◆

Shelly had been seeing Lonnie Burkett on the sly for two months. He'd been filling in as a cashier at Darwin's Diner; Ruth Darwin's appendix had ruptured, Lonnie had been between jobs – a perfect match. Shelly would come over each day to order breakfast for her father, Al Lukins, and the occasional drunk who'd spent the night in jail. Lonnie had a quick wit and didn't feel intimidated that she was the sheriff's daughter. He was no hunk, but being no prize catch herself she found herself soon flirting with him. The only problem was her father would never approve of their dating. Lonnie was an outsider. Worse, he had no steady job, no ambition and no skills that could allow him to become part of the fabric of the community. When he'd asked her out her first impulse was to reject his overture. But she hadn't had more than two or three dates since her high school graduation over two years before and it wasn't as if he were a leper or an ex-con. She relented, but she'd have to meet him in Flourtown, six miles away where no one from Elkins was likely to be.

She was surprised how at ease she felt with him. She sensed he was as new at this as she was and they stumbled along together. He didn't hold her hand until their third date; didn't try to kiss her until the fifth. When he unsuccessfully tried to unhook her bra the eleventh time they went out she cracked up and he followed suit. She helped him and his whisking ever so gently across her nipples brought out passions she had long kept bottled within her. She gave herself fully to him a week later. She wasn't in love – not yet; maybe never, but she couldn't remember being happier.

Then the shit hit the fan. First, her father with his talk of retirement, then the fire at O'Connnor's Service Station and then her period . . . her little friend who stopped visiting.

There'd been fires in Elkins; not many, but it wasn't as if she'd never witnessed one. But this was somehow different. A farmhouse burns down; another is built. Hell, even when there'd been a fire at the high school, they just closed one wing and moved classes to the church. But O'Connor's was totaled and with two other service stations in town, Sean O'Connnor decided to take the insurance money and retire. It left two full-time employees out of work.

Tom Kerrigan, head of the volunteer fire department, had spent two years in Camden learning all about fires, accidental ones and those of suspicious origin, not that he'd have much use for the latter in Elkins. No sooner had he returned to Elkins than his father had stepped aside. He naturally took charge, as Kerrigans had for five generations.

Inspecting the fire sight, it wasn't difficult to see what had happened. An old stuffed chair Sean O'Connor had brought in to ease his aching back was burned to a crisp. While Sean had been picking up a months supply of oil, filters, hoses, and the like, his son, John had dozed in the big chair, a cigarette dangling from his mouth. Clearly an accident. John would get a job at one of the other stations. Sean still had connections. But neither Fred Hogan nor Jim Barrett had been so fortunate.

Shelly had been passing the station, around 11:30 a week later; she and Lonnie having returned from Flourtown, each going their own separate way. Shelly spotted movement at the vacant station, parked a block away and approached on foot. Sitting on the floor of what had been one of the bays where cars were repaired was Fred Hogan, a beer in hand. Shelly relaxed at the sight. She'd feared vandals and didn't have a weapon as she wasn't officially a deputy.

"Watcha doing here at this time of night, Fred?" Shelly asked, visibly relieved.

"Ain't working, that's for sure," Fred said, his words slurred. Shelly saw five or six empty beer cans scattered near Hogan. Even sitting, Fred Hogan was an imposing figure. He'd been a semi-professional boxer she remembered her father telling her. Now, in his mid-forties, his massive chest strained at a T-shirt. She recalled a story how he and Jim Barrett had won a bet with the grease monkeys at one of Elkins' other stations as to who could change a tire faster. The other pair used a hydraulic jack; Fred merely lifted his side of the car while Barrett changed the tire. He'd been a fixture at O'Connor's, just as his father had worked for O'Connor's old man before him.

"No luck at the other stations?" Shelly asked, though she knew the answer.

"Hell no. Everyone's real sympathetic and such, but sympathy don't pay the bills."

"Wish there was something I could do to help," Shelly said, feeling uncomfortable at the turn the conversation had taken.

"Hollow words, child," Hogan said, laughing bitterly. "If I asked you to speak to your daddy . . . which I ain't, mind you, would you do that for me?"

Shelly was silent.

"See what I mean?" he said. "Everyone got good intentions, all say the right things, but words don't pay the bills. Spare the *Wish I Could Help*, because talk is all it is."

"What you going to do?"

"Just sit her for awhile. No harm in that. There's nothing for me to take, even if I was a mind to."

"I mean, what are you going to do for a job?"

"You got me there, girl." He was silent, lost in his thoughts. Then, "Just gonna sit here awhile, drink me some beers. Nothing to fear from me, Miz Manders."

Shelly left the man to his thoughts. A fire had always been some abstract notion to her. A building burned down; another took its place. She'd never thought of it in terms of the lives it impacted upon. O'Connor had his insurance to tide him over, but what would become of Fred Hogan and Jim Barrett?

She went across the street to Elkins Diner. Though Fred Hogan had been oblivious to the elements, she was chilled by the wind and needed some coffee. She was surprised to see Jack Davenport, the owner, at the counter.

"Where's Wendy?" Shelly asked. She had gone to school with Wendy Phillips, who'd been working at the diner since graduation.

"Had to cut back her hours," Davenport replied curtly. He was a burly bear of a man, coarse black hair sprouting from his body like grass grown wild. Unlike Fred Hogan, he'd let himself go to flab, a double chin and gut that obscured his belt making him look ten years older than his forty-seven years.

"She sick? Pregnant?"

"No, nothing lucky like that. Just don't have the business to keep her on."

"The food's not that bad," she said with a smile.

He returned the smile, but there was little life in it. "It's the fire at O'Connor's," he said. "I got a lot of business from Sean. Kinda took it for granted. He and his son were regulars, along with Fred Hogan and Jim Barrett. And being on the outskirt of town, customers would come here for a bite while their cars were being worked on. Business is off thirty, forty percent since the fire. I can't afford to keep Wendy a full eight hours. I feel bad, but part-time's better than no time. Just look at Fred out there."

"See what you mean," Shelly replied. "You ain't gonna close, are you?"

"Nah, but it'll be a struggle. More hours for less money."

Shelly was about to say, *Wish there was something I could do to help*, but remembered Fred Hogan's reaction and reconsidered. It was like asking someone, *How ya doing?* You didn't expect an answer. Just seemed the proper thing to say. She drank her coffee in silence, said goodbye and went her way.

All that week she felt like shit in the mornings and fatigued by mid-afternoon. It coincided with her period failing to appear on time. She bought a self-pregnancy test kit in Flourtown and her worst fears were confirmed. Pregnant. Expecting. With child.

She broke the news to Lonnie after they'd made love in the backseat of his car, parked off a little used road halfway between Elkins and Flourtown. She'd considered telling him before his fevered gropings, but suspected he wouldn't be in the mood after and wasn't about to give up one of life's pleasures. Naked, laying across his stomach, both smoking a cigarette, she told him. She felt his body tense. There was a prolonged silence. Then he seemed to relax.

"So what you gonna do?" he finally asked.

"Do?" She didn't understand. "Have a baby, silly."

"Shelly, folks in Elkins don't have babies without getting married . . . and I don't intend to get married, leastways not right now *and* not with a gun pointed at my head."

"Nobody's pointing a gun at your head. Don't you love me?"

"You know I do. But your father's not gonna take too kindly to our getting married, baby or no baby."

"He'll come around. I'm sure he will."

"That's beside the point. I do love you and in time, hell, I might be the one pushing to get married, but now's not the time."

"I'm sorry, Lonnie, but this baby ain't about to go away."

"Why not?"

"What?" She was bewildered.

"What about an abortion?"

"Hush your mouth. I could never . . .''

"Don't give me that *I could never* crap. Think about it, girl. Think about what's best . . . best for us. I ain't got no job or steady income. My Pa's not in the best of health and I've got to support him. Once you have the baby you won't be fit for working. Hell, your father won't allow you to work even if you wanted to. How are we gonna make ends meet? Look, honey," he said, his fingers brushing her nipples in a way that never ceased to arouse her. She thought of pushing him away, but it felt so good, she couldn't. "I don't like the idea of an abortion any more than you do. But I don't see anyway around it."

"Doc Fletcher would never . . ."

"Not here in Elkins, girl. Shit, you really *aren't* thinking straight. Have it here and you might as well take an ad out in the paper. Not even Flourtown. But, I heard some talk that in Maple Grove there's a doctor who, you know . . ."

"What if I said no? What if I said I wanted this baby? Would you marry me?"

He stopped brushing his fingers across her breast. "Shelly, I won't be bullied into marrying you. When the time's right we'll both know. But don't force me into a corner."

"And if I refuse to have an abortion?"

"You made damn sure nobody knows we're going together, seeing as I'm such as outcast and all."

"You'll deny it's yours?" she asked incredulously.

He sat up and his pale gray eyes pierced through her. "It's simple. Get an abortion or we're history."

She was about to argue further, but saw he was adamant. She reluctantly agreed. For his part, Lonnie insisted on paying half the cost of the abortion. With the matter settled, they made love again.

Shelly didn't have the abortion. Never had the slightest intention to terminate the pregnancy. She wouldn't show for two months, maybe three if she dressed properly and by then things would sort themselves out.

A week later, Lauder's Market went up in flames; just after midnight, so fortunately, no one was injured. This time, though, Tom Kerrigan found evidence of arson.

"How do you know?" asked Ev Manders.

"We have an erratic pattern here, Sheriff," Kerrigan explained patiently. "A flammable substance was placed in three different locations. No way this was accidental."

Word spread quickly.

"An arsonist in Elkins? Rubbish," said Rhea Stone, who worked in the pharmacy across the street.

Shelly had bought some Tylenol, the morning sickness still ravaging her body, and continued to browse through the drugstore when the conversation turned to the fire.

"Who'd do such a thing?" asked Clive Justice, waiting for his hemorrhoids medication prescription to be filled.

"That's two fires in less than a month," chimed in Winston Stone, Rhea's father and the store's owner.

"The other was an accident," said Clive. "Young Kerrigan said so, didn't he?"

"A bit wet behind the ears, if you ask me," was Winston's response. "How can he be sure that the other wasn't arson, too."

"I still can't believe it," Rhea protested again. "It's not like there's a bunch of strangers lurking about town. If it *was* arson, it had to be someone we all know. One of us!" She shuddered at the thought.

Five days later, Shelly dropped by again, around four, just as Winston was closing up.

"Closing early today, Mr. Stone? Something special planned at home?"

"No, Shelly, closing early cause no sense staying open with business so slow."

"I don't understand."

"I never knew how much business Lauder's generated. Folks would drop off prescriptions, then go shopping. With Lauder's closed, folks are driving out to Flourtown for their weekly groceries. Seems they're getting their prescriptions filled there, too."

"But isn't Mr. Lauder planning to rebuild?"

"Sure, but it'll take time. In the meantime my business has been halved. Same with Jake Atkins's dry cleaning business. He's open just four days a week. Had to lay off a presser. We all have to cut costs to the bone. Best tell your Pa to find the bastard who's starting these fires. Lots of anger in town, what with layoffs and money drying up."

Six days later the Victory Theater burned down. Unlike Ed Lauder, Curt Jenkins had no plans to rebuild. Though a lifelong resident of Elkins, he decided to move as soon as the insurance money arrived. Three employees lost their jobs.

Tom Kerrigan's finding of arson was a foregone conclusion.

"Is it the same person?" Manders asked.

"Looks like it," said Kerrigan. "Same flammable material, same pattern."

"Still think O'Connor's was an accident?"

"Think so, but then again, I might've been a bit hasty. Fact is, though, we know for certain at least two were arson . . . and I'd wager set by the same person. Any suspects?"

"Not a one," Manders answered, resignation in his voice.

With folks going to the drive-in, a bit more than halfway between Elkins and Flourtown, businesses around the Victory began to suffer.

Shelly stopped by Earl Wheeler's Ice Cream Crib and found the usually affable Earl in a foul, closemouthed mood. He was a short, dark-complexioned man in his mid-fifties, with thinning brown hair. Shelly remembered the many times he'd given her a double scoop of chocolate marshmallow ice cream even though she'd only asked for one. Seems he did the same for any of the neighborhood kids who were polite, did well in school, or whose parents might be down on their luck. Today it was Shelly who broached the subject of his discontent.

"How's business been since the fire, Mr. Wheeler?"

"What business? I made a tidy profit with the Victory the only theater in town. Did well even though I'd give doubles for the price of one to some of my favorites." There was a hint of a smile beneath his troubled face. Fleeting. There for a moment, then gone. "Kids would come in beforehand and return after each show. Guys brought their dates. Cheaper than going for a bite to eat. Now . . ." He shrugged. "Sometimes hours go by without a customer. I'm not smack in the center of town so I don't get the casual stroller. You have to go out of your way and not many are that hungry for ice cream."

"What will you do?"

"Might have to sell. There's an abandoned building near the drive-in. I can take out a loan, do some renovating and maybe open up there. Take at least six months, though, and mean some lean times. I let Jaspar Peabody go today. Worked part-time while in high school, full-time the past two years. No longer enough work for one, much less two right now."

Shelly heard rumblings and grumblings wherever she went in town. Cavanaugh's Bar was one of the few establishments to profit from the fires. She went in for a beer after work one day and it was like a reunion – Fred Hogan, Jim Barrett and Jaspar Peabody drowning their troubles with beer and talk. She remained on the periphery and listened.

"Thinking of moving on," Jim Barrett said. "Lived here my whole life, but there's just no work to be found. Hear there's an Exxon station opening in Maple Grove. Me and Fred, we're going over tomorrow to see about a job."

"What bugs me," Jaspar said, "is Ev Manders seems to be sitting on his ass doing nothing."

"What do you expect him to do?" asked Fred Hogan. "He's spoken to all of us, and to people who lived in the areas of the fires. Hell, hear tell he even checked into the insurance of those whose buildings caught fire."

"I can't help but think he would've caught the bastard if he had his mind on his job." Peabody wasn't about to let the matter drop.

"What's that supposed to mean?" asked Barrett, who'd gone to school with Ev Manders.

"Shit, it's common knowledge he ain't been the same since Danny died. I just wonder if he's got his heart in his job. Know what I mean."

"Don't want to hear you talkin' trash about Ev Manders," Barrett said, poking his finger at Jaspar's chest. "Known him all my life and no matter how much he be grievin' about Danny, he's doing his best."

"Quit poking me, Jim," Peabody said and slapped Barrett's hand away.

"Don't be telling me what to do." He was in Jaspar's face now, his stale breath pouring over the younger, shorter man.

Sam Cavanaugh intervened before it went any further. Shelly never ceased to marvel how the man sensed just when the tension had reached its peak. He'd be serving someone on the other side of the room, yet materialize with a baseball bat out of nowhere before an argument threatened to break out into a brawl.

"You two stop jawin' at one 'nother right now or you'll be doing your drinking somewhere else."

It wasn't a threat to be taken lightly, as Cavanaugh's was the only place to go if you wanted to whet your whistle. And if you got warned off, Sam would never take you back, even if you came groveling and bearing gifts.

Jaspar Peabody glared at Cavanaugh, then at Barrett, and back to Cavanaugh again. "Shit. Ain't worth the trouble." He took his beer, went to the other side of the bar and engaged some others in conversation.

Fred Hogan brought Barrett a fresh beer, patted him on the back and soon it seemed the incident was forgotten.

Shelly sensed it was only a matter of time before baseless accusations started flying and fights would be the norm rather than the exception.

The fire at Sam Crum's paper mill therefore was incendiary in more ways than one. While only a dozen or so had felt the impact of the other fires, the paper mill was the lifeblood of the community and, one way or another, everyone was affected.

Crum had beefed up security after the fire at the Victory but after two-and-a-half weeks without any new fire, the evening patrols became lax. Crum, who'd visit every night between midnight and 1:00 a.m., firing on sight any guard not totally vigilant, skipped a night with a case of the flu and another shortly after when his in-laws dropped over unexpectedly. With their guard down, the arsonist somehow got in, started the fire, and slipped out in the confusion unnoticed.

Crum was in Ev Manders office the next day and minced no words.

"Do you want to see this town go under, Ev?"

"What are you talking about?"

"Wake up, man. I know you've been preoccupied and I'm sorry as hell to lay the blame at your feet, but without the mill I don't know how long we can hold this place together."

"You're not planning on moving out, are you?"

"Course not, but we're talking six months, maybe a year to rebuild what with the insurance investigators and all. Do you think my employees can live off their savings that long? And the ripple effect could be ruinous."

"Ripple effect?" Crum was one of the few in Elkins who'd gone to college, which was why the mill had grown and prospered since he'd taken over after his father's death. But he tended to talk in riddles as far as Ev was concerned.

"Twenty men without jobs means twenty families who'll be pinching pennies, which means other businesses will suffer and they'll become frugal. Stores will close, families will leave to find work elsewhere. Like dominoes falling, man."

"Sam, I've been doing everything in my power."

"Maybe that's not enough. Maybe we need someone with experience in arson."

Manders bristled at the suggestion. "Be my guest. Hire a stranger who doesn't know squat about this town. Have him waste two or three weeks duplicating everything I've already done. By that time you'll have another fire or two . . . more of your damn ripples."

"Ev, I'm at my wits end. Maybe you're right, but you've got to find this bastard . . . and soon, or we'll have to consider other options." With that he stormed out.

Shelly had heard it all. Her father's office hardly offered much privacy and both Crum and her father had been yelling at one another. The time was right, she decided, to tell her father her suspicions. She knocked and entered without waiting for a response. Her father looked terrible; his face blotchy and puffy, sweat dotted his forehead.

"Papa, I've been asking around and I think I've found someone with a motive to start the fires."

Manders smiled wanly, but didn't respond.

"Humor me, please, Papa. If I'm wrong you'll have wasted half-an-hour. But can you not afford to hear me out?"

He looked at her, *really* looked at her as a person for the first time in weeks – months, hell, maybe years, she thought.

"Okay, Shelly. Everyone else has given me their theory. Why not you?"

She told him. He listened, becoming increasingly interested as she progressed. When she was done he left without a word to verify her story. Brought in Lonnie Burkett three days later and waited for the trial that he hoped would vindicate him.

It didn't hurt that in the six weeks leading up to the trial there were no more fires. Certainly didn't help Lonnie Burkett in the eyes of the rest of the town.

The trial was held in Maple Grove, with a local lawyer defending the youth. The evidence was damning. Ed Lauder on the stand:

"Yes, sir, Lonnie worked for me for a short time. Stocked shelves, swept the floor . . . everything but work the register. I came up short a couple cartons of cigarettes. He denied everything, of course, but I fired him and told him to steer clear."

Lonnie had also worked at the Victory. Curt Jenkins told of an argument he'd had with Burkett:

"I usually paid by check, but as Lonnie was taking the place of a sick employee, well, I gave him cash. He accused me of shorting him. Cursed me out and, truth be, I wasn't too civil to him. He left in a huff."

Samuel Crum's testimony was equally devastating.

"I added extra security after the Victory Theater burned down. I hired Lonnie. He worked steady for a few nights, asked for a day off, worked two more then wanted another off. Fed me a line about his father needing him. I came by a bit early one night – two days before the fire – and caught him taking an unscheduled break with one of those Walkman radios stuck to his head. Fired him on the spot."

Ev Manders told how he'd questioned the victims and pieced together the story. He'd wanted Shelly to take the stand; get the credit she deserved, but she'd convinced him otherwise. He'd make a far more impressive witness, she told him.

"Did Mr. Burkett have an alibi, Sheriff?" the prosecuting attorney asked.

"Only that he was with his father."

"Did his father confirm his whereabouts at the time of the fires?"

"His father went to bed at nine without fail. Slept like a log, were his words. Lonnie was there when he went to bed, but he admitted his son could have left and returned without his knowledge."

"Did you find anything to physically connect him with the crimes?"

"I'd searched his home and car once before and found nothing. Being new in town, he'd been a suspect from the start. After I'd spoke with Samuel Crum and the others, I got a warrant and searched again. Under the driver's seat of his car was some broken glass and a damp rag . . . smelled of gasoline."

"Did you confront him with the evidence?"

"Yes, sir. He said he had no idea how it had gotten there."

The night before Lonnie was to take the stand, Shelly brought him his dinner and was about to leave.

"I need your help, Shelly," he said.

"I can't help you, Lonnie." She now regretted her outburst the first night he'd been arrested. No gain in antagonizing him, she thought. But she'd kept her distance just the same.

"We were together the night of each of those fires. Couldn't you testify to that?"

"We always got back before eleven. I don't know what you did after we separated."

"You know I couldn't do what they're saying."

"Do I?"

"You can't think I'm guilty."

"I don't know what to think. I wonder if I ever really knew you. I was infatuated, thought I was in love. Now . . . I'm confused."

"I could tell them we were together, that you were with me when the fires started."

"No, you won't. It will mean you lied and your father lied to protect you. Anyways, I went straight home whenever I left you. My father, *the sheriff*, will testify to that. Don't make things worse on yourself. I'm really sorry, Lonnie. I wish there was something I could do to help."

Lonnie stuck with his original story and was found guilty two days later. The judge wanted to toss him in prison and throw away the key.

"With your callous disregard for a community that welcomed you, you have ruined many a life. Elkins may never recover. Fortunately for you, we live in a civilized society and I am bound by the laws of this state. I thereby sentence you to the maximum of eight years in prison."

Shelly was sympathetic when she brought him his dinner that night. In two days he'd be transferred to a State facility.

"Eight years in prison for something I didn't do," he said, wiping his eyes.

"More like four years, if you behave yourself," she told him.

"Four years, eight years, it don't matter. I'm innocent!"

"I'm sorry, Lonnie, but . . ."

"No, Shelly, you're not sorry. Not one damn bit. Your father told me something today that got me to thinking. You know what?" He looked at her as if seeing her for the first time.

"Okay, I'll bite, what did he say?"

"He bragged how *you* cracked the case. His daughter, the next sheriff of Elkins. Told me all about it. Only one problem. If I didn't start the fires, your crack detective work means it had to be you."

"Come off it, Lonnie."

"Look, lover, you were the only one who knew all my secrets. Odd how all the fires, except O'Connor's, were set right after I'd a run-in with the owner. And who knew? You're clever, I'll give you that. You framed me good."

"You think anyone will believe you?"

"Maybe not. But, it will cast a cloud over you. Enough of a cloud so you can kiss being sheriff goodbye."

"What do you want from me, Lonnie?" she asked, resigned.

"I don't want to go to prison. You'll help me escape . . . tomorrow. I figure it's the least you can do."

"And if you're caught?"

"All I want is a chance to get away. If I'm caught, at least I tried. Diming on you won't help. You'll have to trust me, won't you lover?"

The next night a figure slipped past Al Lukins, dozing in the front office, and approached Lonnie's cell.

Lonnie blanched at the sight.

"Specting someone else, Lonnie?" Ev Manders said, a smile playing at the corners of his mouth.

"No . . . no, sir. Just, uh, surprised to see you here so late."

Manders unlocked the door to the cell.

"Don't be screwing with me, son. Shelly told me everything. *Everything*." He stretched out the last word for emphasis.

"She told you *she* set the fires?" Lonnie asked, his face clouded with bewilderment and a hint of terror.

"Everything. The baby. Your demand she get an abortion. Her starting the fires." There wasn't the slightest trace of emotion in the brief recital.

"What's going to happen to her?" Lonnie asked, clearly relieved.

"Happen to her? Don't quite catch your drift, son."

"You'll have to let me go, now that she'd confessed . . ."

"She told me everything," Manders interrupted. "That doesn't change the matters none, though."

"But . . ."

"Listen now, boy, and listen good. You don't belong here . . . in Elkins, that is, and never did. Shelly did what she had to do . . . leastways what she thought she had to do. And, damn it, boy, I'm proud of her. Both you and I painted her in a corner and she found a way out. What's going to happen to her, you ask? She's going to be the new sheriff of Elkins, that's what . . . with my blessing."

"What about me?" Lonnie gripped the bars of the cell.

"I aim to keep Shelly's promise. Took some convincing on her part, but we don't want your fool allegations causing a fuss, now do we?"

"You'll let me go?"

"Out the back door," he pointed. "And I go home. Chances are Al Lukins'll sleep for another few hours and probably won't check on you when he does wake up. You should be well on your way before anyone's the wiser. And pissed as I'll act with me chasing after you, don't think you have much to worry about. Now, come on, time's wasting."

At the door, he stopped him for a second. "Shelly wanted me to tell you something, Lonnie."

"That she still loves me?" Lonnie asked.

"Hardly. That she didn't get that abortion. She wouldn't have been able to hide it much longer, anyway. I'd been on her for eating like a pig and gaining weight. She just thought you should know. You'd best be going now."

Lonnie stepped into the darkness of the alley, heard the door close, and was grabbed roughly from behind.

"Going someplace, boy?"

He stared into the eyes of Samuel Crum. Next to him were Fred Hogan, Jim Barrett, Jasper Peabody, and half-a-dozen others. Standing to the rear of the group was Shelly, a smug look of triumph on her face. Crum slapped a piece of tape across his mouth.

"Eight years ain't near enough for what you've done to us. Even the judge said so."

"Not even eight," Barrett hissed. "Shelly told us you'd get out in four. Don't see no justice in that. No sir, no justice at all."

Lonnie strained to speak.

"Shelly was real upset you got off with a slap on the wrist," said Fred Hogan. "She's one of us. Told us she'd arrange for you to escape so we could dispense a proper sentence. Smart girl, that Shelly."

Hogan hit Lonnie in the mid-section and he went down. Kicked him in the nuts and then made room for another. Each, in turn, administered justice. When Crum, the last to go, was finished, Lonnie Burkett was an unrecognizable bloody pulp.

They left him for the dogs and other scavengers.

A robust looking Ev Manders knocked on the door of the Sheriff's private office. With him was three-year-old Everett, Jr., who looked very much like his mother except for pale green eyes that probed the answers to his endless string of questions.

"How's the sheriff doing, today?" Ev greeted his daughter when she opened the door.

"A hard day, Papa," she said with a smile. "Ethel Tanner's been in again complaining Leila Wyche has no control over her dog. Seems he's gotten her little Bitsy pregnant . . . for the third time. Wants me to do something about it. And what have you been up to?"

"We been fishing with Doc Fletcher. Gonna go up to the Victory this afternoon for the reopening. One of them *Ninja Turtle* movies little Ev's been talking about all week. Why not take off and join us?"

Shelly looked offended. "Don't recall *you* ever taking the afternoon off. I've got big shoes to fill. There are still some waiting for me to foul up."

"They'll be old and gray before that happens," Ev laughed. "I worry about you, though. Don't want you missing the best years of your life going after dogs in heat."

"It's a tough job, Papa, but someone's gotta do it."

ALMOST NEVER

Edward Lee

crunch

Katie took another step, then froze, listened.

crunch

Just a tiny sound, from the trees behind her. Perhaps she'd imagined it; Grandpa always said she had a big imagination. But then — a rustle? Did she hear a voice? Katie's heart fluttered.

crunch, crunch

She broke briskly down the narrow, tree-lined trail, taking long strides over fallen branches and gnarled roots. Around her, the woods seemed too still, too quiet. The moon, just rising, dappled her little face in white light. The grocery bag under her arm felt like a satchel of dead weight.

Those two men, she realized. She'd noticed them several times, following her in the store. Now, the faster she walked, the more aware she became of the soft, quick crunching behind her . . .

And the more certain: that someone was following her. Someone was . . . stalking her.

"Someone's been following me, Grandpa." The flimsy screen door snapped shut. Katie rose on her tiptoes to set the bag of groceries on the counter.

"What's that honey?" Grandpa wheeled forward, keen at the sudden question. "You say someone's been—"

"Two men. I've seen them in the grocery store a few times, and I think they've been following me down the trail." Her confused little face turned to the old man. "Why would two grownups want to follow me?"

Grandpa's aged visage seemed to twitch; his knuckly hands tightened on the rungs of the wheelchair. *Blast it*, he thought. *Two men. Jesus.* He and his granddaughter didn't bother anyone. Why couldn't people leave them alone? "You just steer clear of them, honey," he said. "From now on, I'll do the shopping. You just stay here where it's safe."

"Grandpa!" she scoffed. "You can't get to the store in your wheelchair. The trail's not big enough."

"I'll get on all right, don't you worry. I'm not as useless as people might think," Grandpa said. "What you got to understand, honey, and it's a sad thing, but, see, there're a lot of bad people in this world, evil people." He gulped thickly at the thought. "People who'd want to do bad things to a little girl like you."

Katie began to put the groceries away, oblivious to her innocence. "What kind of things, Grandpa?"

"Never you mind about that." God, what a question! How could he explain something like that to a little girl? *There shouldn't be no need to explain*, he retorted himself. *'Cos such things just shouldn't be.* "You just do like your granddad tells ya. I'll be able to get this blasted chair down the trail. Might take awhile, but I'll manage. Old duff like me could use the exercise."

"*Grandpa.*" Katie stretched the word. "That's dumb. I can get there in ten minutes."

"I don't want no more said about it, you hear me, miss?" No, he could never explain. Never. Child molesters, pedophiles. *Creatures*, he thought. They were out there, everywhere. His disgust seemed to percolate in his head, like pitch bubbling. He watched Katie bend to place the steaks and nonesuch in the refrigerator. She seemed radiant in her naiveté, springy and slim in the simple avocado dress and flipflops. She was a lone flower in a vast, parasitic field. Bright white-blond hair hung long and straight to the middle of her back, several strands of which swayed before her unblemished face. The old man's heart felt squashed, in the sure knowledge that it was her innocence that made her such easy prey for all the evil in the world.

◆   ◆

"We shoulda nabbed her tonight," Binny said, peering forward through low branches. "Why piss away time? The sooner we get her upstate, the sooner we get our scratch."

Cementhead, Rocco concluded. "I told you, it's supposed to rain tonight. That's a *dirt* road we're parked on back there. The van'd leave treadmarks. And you left your damn gloves on the console, as usual."

Binny shrugged, as though the observation were of no significance whatsoever. "So what? We're gonna torch the place. What I need gloves for?"

Rocco was no crime tech but he wasn't stupid. In the joint, you hear about the latest. "They got lasers now, man, and special lights, and some new resin stuff that can lift prints ten years old off charred wood and metal. Our mitts are both on file and you know it. We'd be boy-pussy before we could even blink." Rocco had already done a nickel in the cut; an abduction rap would put him away for twenty, easy. Binny must've lost half his brain the last time he took a shit. *No way I'm going back to the Concrete Ramada on account of this numbskull.*

"Yeah, talk about a cake walk," Binny assessed, ignoring his partner's cautions. They'd staked the place out good a couple of times already, and had the routine down pat. Just about every night at seven sharp the kid would take the trail around the woods to the Safeway, pick up groceries, and walk back. A cute little girl, real young, like eight or nine. *The old guy in the chair must have some real dogshit for brains letting a kid that age walk the woods at night*, Rocco thought. *Some people just didn't get it, did they?*

Rocco had run up some high markers at the wrong place. He'd taken five large from shylocks to win back his dump, and hit a losing streak. The shylocks had been Vinchetti's men. They gave him a choice, since he was from the neighborhood and only had one stint on his rap sheet. "You can feed the fish, or you can work for Vinchetti." Rocco didn't like water. They'd set him up with Binny, to run errands for Vinchetti's lieutenant in Maryland, and to "make grabs." They'd pulled a dozen so far. Malls seemed best, and the safest, but this . . . Even Rocco had to agree. A cake walk. They couldn't ask for an easier grab. *Almost too easy,* he thought, hunkering down beside Binny, who roved the lit windows with a small pair of Bushnell's. The squat little house sat way back in the woods, off one of the old county logging tracks. No car, no outside lights, no neighbors. From what they could make of the place, there wasn't even a telephone, and it was just the old guy and little girl. Probably the usual story; the kids' folks croak in a car wreck, or maybe mom leaves town with the plumber, and dad takes a bullet in the Gulf thing, so now the geezer's taking care of the kid. And the kid . . .

Rocco's belly squirmed.

"Would you gander that little peach, man," Binny remarked. The scumbag actually licked his lips. "Vinchetti'll pay double for that kind of soft stuff."

"Why?"

"She's blond. The Yaks pay *big money* for blond kids that aren't beat."

Yaks referred to the Japanese mob, and *beat*, in the business, meant that the kid wasn't over twelve. He'd seen some of the shit himself once or twice; sometimes they helped Vinchetti's crew set up when they made a delivery. Rocco had about puked. He was no saint, sure — a pinch, a fence, he'd even run skag in the 70's — but this shit drew the line. Rocco, after all, was born Catholic.

"I was thinking of getting out," he said.

Binny shot him a funky look. "Getting out of what?"

"This whole gig, man. I don't like it. I mean, we're talking about *kids*, for Christ's sake."

"You ain't getting out of nothing." Binny went back to the binoculars. "Your marker's clean only for as long as you grab for Vinchetti, so don't be stupid. You walk out on him, paisan, and they'll find you the next day in some apartment project laundry room looking like a platter of cold cuts."

Rocco frowned. This was probably true. He'd never met Vinchetti — aka Vinnie The Eye, on account of he had an eye for short stuff. Vinchetti ran the kiddie porn circuit all along the east coast. What they did was they grabbed kids and used them for videos, then they'd sell the kids to their dope honchos overseas, the Japs, the Burmese. They'd flick the kids on 1/4-inch masters, then dupe the masters and send them out to their lab maildrops for mass-reproduction. The feds called it "The Undergound," and it was a big market. Lot of times, Rocco couldn't sleep. He'd seen the kids' faces, the terror in their eyes, the innocence. He couldn't bear to think of what went on in their heads while Vinchetti's crew set up the cameras and the lights . . .

"Kids," he muttered. "Christ. Kids."

"Shut up, man," Binny sniped. "You're starting to sound like a stool. If we don't do it, someone else will — fact of fucking life. Besides, we'll bag five grand a pop on this little nookie." Binny looked up, grinning in the dark. "*Five grand.* That's righteous bucks if you ask me. Shit, we'd be on the street taking down candy stores if Vinchetti hadn't dropped this gig in our laps. And you remember the last guy who tried to book on him? They picked him up in Jersey, autopsied the guy alive in a Red Roof Inn. Then they cut off the fucker's face and fed-exed it to his mother . . ."

Rocco's mouth went dry. That would be some party. *Thank God my mother's dead*, he thought.

Binny rambled on, "Plus I gotta feeling we're gonna bag more than five large on this one. The old fucker gives the kid cash whenever she goes to the store. You ever see her stop at the bank? He's probably one of those old-fashioned putzes who doesn't believe in banks. Keeps his life's savings in a gym bag under the bed or some shit. We're gonna be walking with some green here, paisan"

Rocco felt distant, barely hearing the words. All he could see just then, and all he could think about . . . were the kids . . .

"And I say we take them out tonight, right now."

Rocco ground his teeth. "No way they're sending me up on a kiddie porn bust. I told you, it's gonna rain. We'll leave evidence all over the place."

Binny opened his mouth to complain further, when suddenly the sky broke. A moment later, it was teeming.

"Okay, man," Binny gave in. "So we do it tomorrow night, then. No ifs, and or buts. Got it?"

"Grandpa?" Katie leaned over, gently nudged the old man. "Hey, Grandpa?" He sat sound asleep in the chair, his head lolled to one side. Katie didn't have the heart to wake him; he was old, he needed his rest. Yesterday, he'd forbidden her to go shopping, but . . . *I'll go*, she decided. *He can't go. In the chair? It'll take hours!*

Grandpa kept his money behind the kitchen baseboard; Katie plucked out a twenty dollar bill and replaced the board. A long time ago, he'd turned his money into T-bills, whatever they were, and once a year a special cab came out to the house and took him to town where he cashed in some interest. Katie wasn't sure what interest was, either, not that it mattered. Grandpa was a good man, and he always made sure there was enough money for things.

It was already dark when she embarked, dressed in her Smurfs shirt, flipflops, and spangled pants. It would be getting cold in a month or so, and Katie worried about that. Grandpa had some problem where his hands hurt in the cold. With that, and the chair, he had enough problems. The least Katie could do was go to the store.

She moved briskly down the narrow trail through the woods. An owl hooted; moonlight shimmered in the trees. As she quickened her pace, her fine blond hair rose behind her like and aura.

Her big eyes fixed ahead. She remembered what Grandpa said, about how there were some people who would want to do bad things to a little girl like her. Katie didn't understand what those things could be, but that only distressed her more deeply. *Why can't everybody be good?* she wondered. She and Grandpa never did bad things. *Why would people want to do bad things to us?*

At the grocery store, her heart quickened as she wandered the aisles. She always checked for the things that were on sale. A special on ground beef. Window cleaner two for the price of one. And laundry detergent. She chose the store brand because it was a quarter cheaper than Tide. She knew she was hurrying. She felt antsy and weird in the express line. She wanted to get out of there, and back to the house before Grandpa woke up.

On the way back she failed to notice the big white windowless van parked just off the utility road. She felt watched all the way back down the trail. She knew she hadn't imagined those two men. Several times when she'd been shopping, they'd followed her around the store, always stopping, they'd followed her around the store, always stopping and turning when she'd looked back. *But they weren't there tonight*, she happily realized. Nor did she hear any sounds behind her as she walked the trail. Katie suddenly smiled. *They must be gone!* Yes, the two men must've gone away, gone to follow someone else.

Katie's smile widened. She skipped back to the house, happily toting her bag of groceries.

"Blast it, Katie!" Grandpa railed, leaning forward in the chair. "I told you not to go to the store! I told you—"

"Don't worry, Grandpa," Katie cut in.

"Don't worry! How am I supposed to not worry with that pair of weird ones followin' you around?"

Katie closed the door and began to put away the groceries. "You were asleep, Grandpa. I didn't want to wake you up. And besides, those two men are gone."

Grandpa's stern visage laxed a bit, and he eased back into the chair. "You mean they weren't followin' you tonight?"

"Nope," Katie was happy to inform. "And they weren't at the store either. They're gone."

Grandpa considered this: "Well. Hmm. Maybe they are, but you still shoulda woke me up. Can't be too careful, not these days."

Katie's young face beamed at her grandfather. "Don't worry, Grandpa. I told you. Those men are gone. I'm sure of it."

"Yeah, I'm sure of it," Binny acknowledged, focusing the binoculars from their low lookout in the trees. "It's a gas stove, all right. Makes the place easier to torch."

Rocco's face felt like a mask of wood. He had the timer ready to go, a simple rig yet an ever-reliable one — a metal-case watch with a plastic face strapped around a six-volt drycell battery. You tape the positive lead to the watch closing, and the negative to a thin nail melted through the plastic face. A piece of Jetex had been tied between the leads. When the minute hand made contact with the nail (the watch had no second hand) the circuit was made, the Jetex burned off at eight-hundred degrees, and *BOOM!*

Rocco, however, wasn't thinking of pyrotechnics at this precise moment. He'd dreamed again last night, of the bleak faces of the children, of their vacant thousand-yard stares. *This is some bad shit*, he very simply thought. In a queer moment of vertigo, he looked at the back of Binny's head. *God, it would be so easy*. Rocco packed a Smith Model 49 in a clip holster under his shirt. It would be so easy to slip that hammerless snubnose baby out and pop Binny a nice .38 semijacket right in his sick skull . . .

And in the next moment, Rocco found that his right hand had moved to the revolver's slim grip.

"I called Vinchetti's crew and told them about the girl." Binny never took his eyes off the binocs. "Guaranteed them we'd have her in

Jersey by morning. This time tomorrow night, we'll be partying hearty, paisan, with green in our pockets."

Rocco's fingers trailed off his piece. *Vinchetti*. Rocco knew he'd have to be very careful. Popping Binny right here would be suicide. He'd never beat Vinchetti's hawks without a plan. He needed papers, and cash. There was a printer he knew in Davidsonville who did good work; for a couple of grand he'd set Rocco up with a phony driver's license, SS number, birth cert, and an MVA record that would wash right up to a fed-level check. Good fake ID was the only way he'd get away from Vinchetti. There was only one option: *Just one more job. I'll do this one last job, take the cash, get my paper. Then I'll pop this evil fucker and disappear for good.* There was no other way. To buy good paper, he'd have to do this job on the old man and the girl first.

"Aw, God," Binny remarked. "Check it out."

Rocco took the glasses and focused up. The old man was sitting in the lit kitchen, at the table. "Big deal. He's eating dinner."

"No, no, man," Binny corrected. His breath was hot on Rocco's neck as he leaned over. "The bathroom. Tell me that ain't the sweetest stuff you ever saw. Vinchetti's gonna love us. That right there is pure angel food cake, partner."

You fuckin' slime, Rocco thought when he moved the binoculars. The kid stood buck naked, her blond hair tied up as she stepped out of the tub. She began to towel herself off under the bright light.

"Yeah, man." Binny grinned. "I could eat that myself."

Rocco reserved comment, electing instead to think, *I can't wait to take you down, Binny.* It provided a glorious fantasy. *Once I get my papers, I'm gonna put your sick brains all over the floor.*

Binny chuckled. "Let's hit it."

They emerged from the trees, breaking off. Rocco's head pounded with each step. His last job, sure — but that didn't do the kid any good. She'd be meat on Vinchetti's porno slab, and they'd have to kill the old man. *Just don't think about it*, he commanded himself. It was the lesser of two evil, that was the only way he could look at it. The back window popped open with just one press of the crowbar. Rocco climbed in. A bedroom. Dark, but the door was open, and down the hall he could see the kitchen light, and the old man at the table.

Rocco set down the timer to free his hands; he moved into the hall. The kid was still in the bathroom — the light glowed under the door.

Binny already had a cord around the old man's neck by the time Rocco made it into the kitchen.

A pitiful sight. Binny grinned as the old man squirmed in the chair, gagging. "Let him talk," Rocco complained.

"Just havin' a little fun first."

The old man's crabbed hands roved to and fro like a drunk conductor; his thin chest heaved. Just as the aged face began to turn blue, Binny loosened the garrot.

"Blasted bastards!" the old man wheezed, hacking and bringing his arthritic fingers to his throat.

Binny grinned down. "Get to work, Roc. Me and Grandpa here have some talking to do."

"Get the hell out of my house, the both of you!" gargled Grandpa. "Ya got no right!"

"Sure we do, Gramps." Binny tightened the garrot a bit. "We know you got cash stashed in this cozy little dump of yours." A little tighter. "So how about it, Gramps? Where's the money?"

Jaundiced eyes bulged in their sockets; the wizened mouth struggled. "Let him talk!" Rocco yelled. "You're killing him!"

"Relax." Again, Binny loosened the cord. The old man slumped, sucking air and pointing to the floor. Eventually he was able to croak, "Baseboard. By the stove. Take it."

Binny knelt and pried out the board. "Christ, Roc! It's the fuckin' motherlode!" He slid out bands of bills, twenties and fifties. "There must be ten or fifteen grand here, man!"

"Closer to twenty," the old man said, waving a worm-veined hand. "Take it and get out of here. Leave us be."

"Oh, we will, Gramps." Binny chuckled and rose. "After we're done killing your tired ass. Huh, Roc?"

Rocco smirked, then suddenly jerked around. Feet pounded. A little blur swirled and at once small hands were dragging at him. The little girl jumped up onto Rocco's back and yanked at his hair, shrieking, "Leave my grandpa alone!"

Binny laughed. Rocco turned in hunched circles, trying to keep the kid's fingers out of his eyes. When he flipped her to the floor, she sprang right back up and socked her little foot square into his groin. Rocco went down.

"Look at this!" Binny laughed. "One of Vinchetti's bulldogs is getting his ass whipped by a little kid!"

Rocco tried to wrestle the girl down, but she slipped out of his grasp like a greased lizard. *Shit*, Rocco thought. The girl banged through the door to the basement and scampered down.

Rocco got up, sputtering. At least there were no windows in the basement. No way the kid could get out.

"Go get her, killer," Binny mocked, then got back behind the old man, who futilely whipped his hands around.

"Ya blasted punks!" he rasped. "Don't you hurt that little girl, I'm warnin' ya! Why goddamn it all, if I wasn't in this blasted chair—"

"But you *are* in the chair, Gramps, you *are* in the chair," Binny ripped off that great old Bette Davis line.

Now the old man pleaded, his fine white hair sticking up as his face strained in the most desperate despair. "I'm beggin' ya not to do this. I got more money in the bank. I'll give it to ya, all of it. Just leave us alone . . ."

"This'll do just fine, pops," Binny said. "See, we gotta deliver that sweet little girl of yours upstate tonight, so our friends can take some pretty pictures of her. And that means it's time for you to say goodnight."

The old man lurched, then hacked. Binny deftly brought the blade of his Gerber Mark IV straight across the throat. Blood gushed, pumping. The old man hitched twice in the chair, gargled a final invective, then died.

Rocco felt enslimed. *Look at us*, he thought. *Two backalley thugs fucking up little kids' lives and killing old men in wheelchairs. Christ almighty.*

"Don't just stand there, man," Binny complained, scooping up the banded cash off the floor. "Go get the girl. I'll get the joint ready to torch."

"Timer's in the back room," Rocco said. His heart felt sunken as he slid out the flask of Roche Pharmaceutical chloroform. "I'll bring her up now."

"Fuckin'-A. And be careful. That little hellfire's probably down there waiting for you with a pitchfork."

Or maybe a gun, Rocco mused. He almost wished it. He almost wished the kid would blow both their asses away.

"Get a move on!"

Rocco descended the creaky wood steps. Light wobbled from a suspended bulb. The little girl sat sobbing in the corner, her face long

with despair and glazed by tears. Rocco poured some chloroform into
his handkerchief.

What could he say? What could he tell this innocent little child?
The chloroform wafted up, sickly sweet. "Come on, kid. You gotta
come with us."

"You're the two men who've been following me," she sobbed.

"Yeah," Rocco said.

"But why?"

Why? The question haunted him. "I don't know why, kid. It's just
the way things are sometimes."

The tears streamed. Strands of fine blond hair stuck to her face.
"Grandpa said you wanted to do bad things to me. We haven't done
bad things to *you*. Why do you want to do bad things to us?"

Rocco gulped. He stared at her as her wet face peered up, her little
feet tucked under her legs as she crouched in terror and confusion. She
wore a long flannel nightgown with rabbits on it. *Rabbits*, Rocco
thought. *Bunny rabbits. She's just a little innocent kid, and I'm gonna
deliver her to a bunch of child pornographers tonight. What kind of a
monster am I?*

But he had no recourse, did he? The spector of Vinchetti's
hatchetman loomed behind him, a dark surging shape.

"I'm sorry, kid. I really am. But I got no choice."

Rocco moved forward, leaning down, and reached for the girl.

Binny rolled the dead old man out of the way, into the corner, then
bagged the rest of the cash. What a fuckin' haul! Not only would they
walk with decent scratch for the kid, but there was this in the baseboard.
I could use a beer, he thought. *Yeah, a cold tall one. All this hard work
makes a guy thirsty.* But when he opened the fridge all he found were
some steaks and hamburger. Not a can of Bud to be found.

Rocco, he thought next, walking to the back bedroom. It was a sour
thought. The guy was losing his edge, and this wasn't good. *A job like
this, you don't bring your conscience.* What was the big deal? It was
like anything. When somebody wanted something, you got it for them,
so long as the money was right. Supply and demand. That was the
American Way, wasn't it?

He came back to the kitchen with the timer. *Yeah, piece of fucking
cake.* "Hey, Roc!" he yelled. "Sometime this year, huh?" *Christ.* The
gas range looked ancient. He figured they'd set the timer for a couple
of hours, give the dump plenty of time to fill up. So what if he started

a forest fire? That wasn't his problem. Smoky the Fucking Bear could worry about that.

What the fuck? he thought. He'd turned on the gas knobs, but no pilots came on, and no tell-tale hiss. He put his ear to the burner. Nothing. Then he slid the range out to take a peek.

The gas lines weren't even hooked up. *This thing hasn't been used in years.* And that didn't make a lick of sense, did it? A busted range and fridge full of meat. He noticed no hotplates, no microwaves. What the hell did they cook their meat on?

This was a good question, not that it really mattered. What did matter, though, a moment later when he turned to the corner, was this: The wheelchair was empty.

"You better not," the little girl sobbed just as Rocco stooped to press the handkerchief to her mouth.

Rocco paused. What could she mean by that? "Look, kid," he began. "I don't like this anymore than y—" but then his words were severed, cut off cleanly as a knife through yarn. Cut off by the wavering, high-pitched scream which exploded next from upstairs:

"HOLY JESUS CHRIST GET THE FUCK AWAY FROM ME!"

Rocco dropped the rag and shucked his five-shot snub. His heart hammered as he raced up the stairs. Binny continued to scream, loud and hard as a truck horn, when Rocco three-pointed into the kitchen. The first thing he saw made his eyes bulge. The old man's wheelchair with no old man in it. No way the guy could've lived. Binny'd cut his throat clear to the bone.

And the second thing he saw . . .

Binny flailed frenetically on the floor beneath a dark form. It was not a dog which vigorously yanked out his partner's lower g.i. tract; it was a wolf. A *big* wolf.

Rocco emptied his bladder while he simultaneously emptied the Smith snub into the animal's side. Binny flinched, blood bubbling from his mouth. The huge animal paused only a moment at the shots, ripped off Binny's face, then turned. Its great angular head rose, lips peeling back to show rows of crooked teeth the size of masonry nails. Jet black eyes bore into Rocco's stare. The eyes seemed mocking, even amused. Then the creature lunged.

Rocco missed having his throat bitten out by all of half an inch. He jerked back into the basement entrance, pulled the door closed, and fell head over heel to the bottom of the steps.

The little girl was standing now, her arms crossed over the rabbit-printed nightgown. "See?" she said defiantly. "I told you."

Rocco's head spun. Upstairs, he could hear the wolf return to its meal, bones crunching like potato chips. The image of the little girl bobbed back and forth like something floating.

"Your grandfather's a—"

"He's been that way a long time," the girl said. "But he's always been good. You should've been good, too."

Rocco stared at her. Upstairs, the crunching went on and on.

"Nobody has to be bad. It's better to be good," the little girl philosophized. "I'm the same way. Just little animals and things." She pointed to the corner of the basement, to little piles of animals that looked dried as husks.

"Never people," she said. Then her face seemed to flutter, as if adrift in an intricate confusion. He couldn't get up. He couldn't even look away from the big, glittering eyes.

"You're just like your grandfather," Rocco croaked.

"No, I'm not," the little girl said. *Did she smile?* "I'm a lot worse."

She moved forward very slowly . . .

The twin incisors glinted.

Rocco began to scream as the girl began to suck.

BLOODLINE

Roman A. Ranieri

I don't take crap from anybody. I never could. That's why I'm not with the Bureau anymore. That's why I'm a private investigator in Altoona, Pennsylvania, population 57,078. I probably would've gone pretty far in the Bureau if I would've played their games, but I never kissed butt, and I never let my superiors take the credit for my work.

I guess you could say I'm making a decent living. I've got an apartment in a clean blue-collar neighborhood, and last year, I stashed away enough cash for a down-payment on a new Ford Mustang. I really shouldn't complain. There's plenty of people around who are worse off then me. It's just that it gets to me sometimes. I know I'm too good to be wasting my time taking photographs of sleazy people in sleazy motel rooms so that their even sleazier spouses can drain them dry in divorce court. I guess that's why I acted like a jerk when Joan McNally walked into my office and offered me a job.

"What can I do for you?" I asked.

"I need help," she answered softly. "It's about my husband."

"One of your girlfriends saw him in an out-of-the-way restaurant with his secretary," I sighed wearily, "so you want me to follow him around for a week or two, and get some embarrassing pictures for you to throw in his face in court. Right?"

The woman looked as if I had just slapped her. "No," she replied, beginning to cry. "My husband was killed two nights ago, and I wanted you to find out what really happened."

I quickly stood and came around the desk. She was blindly rummaging through her handbag for a pack of tissues as I gently laid my hand on her shoulder. "I'm really sorry, ma'am," I said, feeling terrible. "That was a rude and stupid thing to say. Please forgive me. Just tell me how I can help you and I'll do it."

It took a few moments for her to regain her composure, then she began, "My husband was a police officer. He'd been assigned to plain-clothes duty for the past six months. Two nights ago he was working with a decoy unit down at the old train yard. He told me that several street people had been attacked down there and the decoy unit was going to try to lure out whoever was responsible."

"What happened?"

"Captain Polk said someone attacked Bob with a knife. He managed to fire a few shots before he was stabbed. When the other officers reached him, my husband and the assailant were both dead." She began to sob again. I remained silent and waited until she was able to continue. "That's the story Captain Polk told me, but I don't believe it."

"Why not?" I asked.

"Because they won't let me see my husband's body," she said, gazing at me with red, swollen eyes.

"I don't think that's such a bad idea. It would be a very disturbing sight, especially if they've performed an autopsy."

"I'm a registered nurse, Mr. Stark. I've worked the emergency room many times. I've probably seen more damage to the human body than you have. I think the police are covering up something about the way my husband died, and I want you to find out what it is."

"Well, I'll look into it for you, but I really don't think the police are hiding anything. It sounds like they're just trying to save you from further pain."

"I appreciate your honesty, Mr. Stark, but I still want you to look into it. How much is your fee?"

"Let's not worry about my fee now. I'm not going to charge you anything if there's nothing for me to find out."

"At least you have an open mind. The other investigator I spoke with wouldn't even let me finish my story," she said.

"You mean I wasn't your first choice?" I asked, smiling.

"You are now."

✦   ✦

After lunch I went to see my friend, Sergeant Cook. He and I had a lot in common. He was a damned good detective who should've made captain by now, but he just wouldn't play the department politics game. I knew I'd get some straight answers from him.

"Sorry, Tony. I can't help you."

"What's the big deal?" I asked. "Why can't I see the report on McNally's death?"

"Because it's confidential. There are certain facts in the report that the department doesn't want made public while the investigation is still in progress."

"But I'm not a reporter, Paul. You know you can trust me."

"I do trust you, Tony, but this order came straight from the commissioner. No one who's not directly involved with the investigation gets to see the report. Period."

"Well, at least tell me what you know. What was the cause of death?"

"Get yourself a copy of yesterday's paper. Everything that's been made public so far is in there."

"Thanks, Paul. You've been a big help," I said sarcastically.

Next, I decided to go see George, the assistant coroner. I knew he'd tell me the truth; he owed me a favor. I figured my luck had gotten better when I found him alone in his office.

"How've you been, George?" I asked, flashing my friendliest smile.

"Just fine, Tony. Did you really come here just to see me, or do you want something?"

"Actually, both reasons. I wanted to see how your diet was coming along, and I need to see the autopsy report on Officer Robert McNally."

"No way! I'd get fired in a minute for showing you that report."

"Come on, George. You can trust me. Why the big cover-up? What really happened that night?"

"Sorry, buddy. I just can't tell you anything."

"But you know I can keep my mouth shut. I didn't tell your wife about you and that nurse over at Mercy Hospital, did I?"

"You promised you'd never mention that again," he whispered, his face flushing red.

"I know I did, but I'm backed into a corner here. Nobody'll tell me a damned thing about what happened that night, and I'm getting pretty sick of this run-around."

George stared at me while he slowly calmed down, then spoke, "Who's your client?" he asked.

"You know I can't tell you that."

"Either *you* trust *me* enough to tell me who hired you, or you can get the hell out of here."

"Okay," I sighed. "I'm working for Mrs. McNally."

"All right. I'll let you see the report for *her* sake, but if you'd been working for anyone else, I'd have told you to go to hell."

He took a ring of keys from his pocket and unlocked the file drawer of his desk. A moment later he handed me a large manila folder. As I opened the folder, the first thing I saw was a photograph of Robert McNally's dead body. My jaw dropped open in shock. "This was not done by a knife," I said, staring at a picture of a man with his neck and chest torn open.

"No. It wasn't," George whispered. "He was killed by a coyote."

"A coyote?" I repeated, dumbfounded.

"Come with me."

I followed George out of his office and into the hall. I was halfway down the white-tiled corridor before I realized I still had the open folder in my hands. I shuddered as I took one last glance at the horribly mutilated body, then closed the folder and carried it in my left hand. We came to the end of the hall. George stopped at a set of double doors, unlocked them, and led me inside. Before he could turn on the lights, I knew where we were. There was the powerful scent of disinfectant, but it still smelled the revoltingly familiar stench which could never be completely washed away from this room. It was the odor of death. We were in the *Holding Room*. A nice, inoffensive name for the place where the corpses were stored until autopsies were completed, then they were returned here until the undertakers came for them.

George pulled open a drawer and lifted the white sheet for me. I thought the photograph had prepared me for what I was going to see, but I nearly lost my lunch. I had never seen such savagely inflicted wounds.

"If you were him," George said. "Would you want your wife to see *you* like that?"

I gulped down a few lungfuls of air before answering. "No, I wouldn't."

He lowered the sheet and closed the drawer, then reached down to the bottom drawer in the same row. I flinched as I saw the occupant of this compartment. It was the coyote.

I tentatively leaned down for a closer inspection. It certainly was a mean-looking son-of-a-bitch.

"Notice anything unusual?" George asked.

"I see that this thing took six bullets from a large caliber handgun and still managed to tear up McNally before it died. That seems pretty damned unusual."

"Look at the size of it. That thing's three times larger than a coyote is supposed to get."

I glanced down at the animal with renewed interest. "Do you have any idea how it could've gotten this big?"

"No. And neither did the so-called expert they brought in from the Pittsburgh zoo."

"What happens next?"

"Tomorrow it gets shipped to the zoo for dissection."

"How do you think the damned thing got here? I thought coyotes were only out west?"

"They originated in the western states, but now they've spread from coast to coast, as far north as Alaska, and as far south as Costa Rica. That's what the guy from the zoo told me."

"That's amazing. Have there been any coyote attacks anywhere else?"

"The police are still checking into that, but the zoo guy said that normally a coyote would never attack a human unless it was cornered, wounded, or starving."

"Well, this one certainly wasn't starving. What did the guy say about its size?"

"He was shocked – said he'd never heard of a coyote growing this large before."

"Okay, George. Thanks for showing me all this. I really appreciate it."

"I'm trusting you to keep your mouth shut about what you've just seen. Don't let me down."

I was about to walk out of the room when a thought suddenly came back to me. "In your office you said that if I hadn't been working for

Mrs. McNally, you wouldn't have shown me anything. Who did you *think* I might be working for?"

"I thought Benjamin Williamson might have hired you. He's called here a half-dozen times demanding that we send him a copy of the report on this case. The old bastard's tried everything from threats to bribery, so far."

"Why would he be that concerned about a police matter?"

"I don't know. He said that as chairman of the city commissioners, it was his business to know about any danger to the public. I told him I only take orders from the police commissioner, then I hung up on him. That old bastard thinks he owns the city."

"He owns a damned big chunk of it," I said, turning to leave.

I decided to do a little research before visiting Williamson. When I got to the library, the first thing I did was read everything I could find about coyotes. I learned that their expansion across North America was mainly due to their extraordinary survival instincts and their amazing adaptability. Although they are extremely capable hunters; they themselves have several enemies — wolves, golden eagles, pumas, and especially man. But the most important thing I learned was that coyotes were wary of humans and that attacks on people were very rare. I wondered if McNally had inadvertently cornered the coyote and made a mental note to examine the scene tomorrow morning.

I then went to the microfilm room to check the newspaper archives for any reports of previous coyote attacks in the area. After four eye-straining hours I had found twenty-three wild animal attacks in the past one hundred and fifteen years. As I compared the reports, I noticed a disturbing pattern. All of the victims up to 1955 had been blacks or other minorities; after 1955 the victims were drifters and bums. It was almost as if the animals were deliberately choosing victims whose deaths would cause the least amount of concern among the general population.

A bizarre theory began to form in my mind.

It was almost dusk when I arrived at the front gate of the Williamson estate. The huge mansion certainly was impressive. It towered above the surrounding pines like a man-made mountain. It had been built by Colonel David Williamson in 1785, and the local history book from the library had said Colonel Williamson had amassed his fortune through extremely unscrupulous fur trading with the Indians. I got out of my car and pressed the button on the intercom bolted to the gate.

"Who is it?" asked an electronically-distorted voice.

"My name is Anthony Stark. I'm a private investigator. I'd like to speak with Benjamin Williamson."

"Mr. Williamson doesn't see anyone without an appointment. Call his office tomorrow morning."

"Tell him it concerns Officer McNally's death."

A moment later there was a click and the hum of an electric motor as the gate began to slide open. I got back in my car and steered along the crumbling driveway to the house. I was climbing the moss-covered steps when the front door swung open, exposing a huge guy who looked like a cross between a human and a gorilla.

"You'll have to leave your gun with me," the thing growled.

"Who said I carry a gun?"

"Mr. Williamson has a list of everyone in the area with a license."

"What if I don't want to give it to you?"

"Then you don't see Mr. Williamson."

I sighed as I reached for the Taurus PT-99AF in its holster behind my right hip. I handed it to him, then held my coat open with both hands. He methodically checked my chest, sides, back, and arms. He was about to reach for my left thigh when I stopped him.

"You touch my leg and I'll knock out your teeth, then feed them to you one at a time."

He stared at me for a few moments, then straightened and headed down the hall. I smiled as I followed him. My dad always said if you could convince the other guy that you would definitely hurt him, then most of the time you wouldn't have to fight him. Not only had I just gained a valuable psychological edge, but I had also kept the ape from finding the Walther PPK strapped to my left ankle. I had gotten into the habit of carrying two guns when I was with the FBI; now it was common practice for most undercover officers.

As I entered the den, Benjamin Williamson was seated on a sofa facing my direction. He was a man of medium height and build, with short, white hair and a white mustache. He looked to be between seventy to seventy-five years of age.

"Have a seat, Mr. Stark," he said, motioning to the armchair near the fireplace. "That will be all for now, Darrell," he said to the ape.

"Darrell?" I mimicked. I had learned long ago that when you're in the presence of a potential enemy, act as formidable as possible.

"What information do you have for me?" Williamson asked, lighting a cigarette.

"I wanted to ask you a few questions before I went to the police, Mr. Williamson."

He looked up and placed the cigarette in a marble ashtray on the arm of the sofa. "About what?"

"About coyotes."

He shifted uneasily. "What about them?"

"I have a theory that your family has been breeding a huge species of coyote for over a hundred years, and that periodically they are let loose to thin out the number of undesirables in this city."

Williamson threw back his head and roared with laughter. I felt my face flush with anger as I stood up. "Let's see if the police think my theory is as funny as you do." I started to leave.

"Your theory is so preposterous because you assume that these occurrences are intentional. I assure you they are not, Mr. Stark. Please sit back down."

Curiosity won out over anger. I sat.

"Back in 1782 my ancestor, Colonel David Williamson, was responsible for the massacre of some ninety Christian Indians, most of them defenseless women and children, at Gnadenhutten, Ohio. The Chiefs of the Delawares vowed to take revenge for the slaughter. They managed to defeat the American militia at the Battle of Upper Sandusky, but Colonel Williamson somehow escaped. The Indians captured his commanding officer, Colonel William Crawford, and burned him to death for the massacre.

"When the Chiefs realized their mistake, they summoned their greatest shaman, Wangomen, to cast a spell upon Colonel Williamson. But Wangomen was not content to place his curse on the Colonel alone, he decided to curse all of the Williamson descendants as well."

"Do you really expect me to believe that kind of crap?" I asked, trying to sound sarcastic. I didn't want to believe him, but the chill tracking across my spine and the hair on the nape of my neck told me I did.

He continued as if he hadn't heard me.

"At certain times — unpredictable times — during a Williamson's life, he or she transforms into the form of a large coyote. Even more remarkable is that the animal completely retains the intelligence of the person it was before. The only way for the coyote to return to its previous form is to take a human life.

"Don't confuse this with the legend of werewolves," he said, freezing me with his stare. "This has nothing to do with the moon, or any other natural cycle we've been able to discover. Unless of course it's based on some Indian calendar long since forgotten."

"Then that dead coyote I saw this afternoon—"

"Yes. *That* was my son, David. Can you imagine how I feel, Mr. Stark. Knowing that I can't even give him a proper burial. That the body will be dissected and picked apart until there is nothing left of it."

"Then his attack on Officer McNally was a mistake."

"Of course. An error in judgment. David had no idea he was a policeman. He thought he was attacking an ordinary bum. Just as you've said yourself, we've never killed indiscriminately. We only took those whose lives were worthless."

"Who in the hell are you to decide whose life is worthless?" I spat, shifting in my seat. "I don't know if anyone will believe me, but I intend to see that your history of murder does not repeat itself."

"What a fool you are, Stark. Did you really think I would let you live after telling you all this? Although we never discovered a way to prevent the transformation from happening, we *did* find that we could induce it to occur."

Benjamin Williamson smiled at me and began to change. His face elongated into a canine muzzle and coarse, gray fur sprouted from his skin. I jerked my left leg up rather than bending to reach my ankle, knowing that to take my eyes off this creature would mean certain death.

My thumb was flicking the Walther's safety when the half-formed coyote lunged at me. I raised my left arm to block the deadly, slavering jaws as my first shot hit the animal in the chest. I screamed as the sharp teeth sank into my forearm, and my mind flashed an image of McNally's mangled corpse. Hadn't the officer emptied his gun into the coyote that killed him?

But I knew I had an advantage that McNally hadn't enjoyed. My gun was loaded with jacketed hollow points, bullets designed to explode into small fragments upon impact. Police officers were only permitted to use standard full metal jacket ammunition.

I used my captive left arm to push back the coyote's head, at the same time bringing my other hand up under its jaw. I fired the remaining seven bullets through its brain, each impact spraying me with bits of gore. The final bullet blew out a large chunk of its skull and the creature pitched backwards and collapsed a few feet away from me.

I don't know how long I stood there staring down at the beast, or what I was expecting to happen. I already knew that since Willliamson had been killed as a coyote, he would remain in that form.

I pulled off my necktie and used it as a tourniquet, tying it just below my left elbow. I then exchanged the Walther's empty magazine for the full one in the pouch strapped to my right ankle and went looking for Darrell. When I couldn't find him, I decided he must have taken off when he heard the gunshots; I guess you can't buy loyalty. I retrieved my Taurus from the table beside the front door and walked out to my car.

I drove straight to a doctor I knew who wouldn't ask any questions and had him stitch up my arm. The next morning I went to see Joan McNally and told her that her husband had been killed in the line of duty just the way she had been told. I couldn't see how telling her the truth would've made things easier for her. That is, *if* she would've even believed any of it.

I don't really expect anyone to believe all of this, but I wanted to put it down on paper anyway. I've done some checking, and there's a hell of a lot of Williamsons in the state of Pennsylvania. Only God knows how many of them are descendants of Colonel David Williamson. Not that it matters whether there's ten or a hundred. I intend to find them all.

I had the doc give me shots for rabies, tetanus, and anything else he could think of, but I still keep wondering if the saliva from Williamson's bite could have infected me. That's why I have to find them all — why I have to wipe out the bloodline — so that I won't become part of it.

FOUR-IN-HAND

William Relling, Jr.

"You know what I think?" Tony Summers said to me the day we found the strangler's fourth victim. He was slapping the flipper button with his right hand, twisting his backside hard at the same time — Body English — seeing the silver ball ricochet off a lighted bumper, not looking at me as he spoke. "I think we're going at this all wrong."

I was watching the counter on the pinball machine light up his score — he was Player #1 — and listening to the machine's buzzing and jangling; not saying anything myself, just waiting for him to talk. Tony was always like that; being his partner for eight months had taught me that whenever he had something important to say, he would always take his time to preface whatever it was. He liked to let you in on things his own way at his own pace, and it could get pretty damned annoying sometimes. But that was Tony. Most of the time, when things were good, he was terrific to be around: a crack-up, a real card. But when things weren't so good . . . well, you either lived with the way he was or you didn't.

"We keep thinking whoever's doing these murders doesn't have any motive," he was saying. "But it just occurred to me what he's been up to all along."

Suddenly the machine chunked, his points registering a free game.

"How 'bout that, Tony," I said. "You won."

✦   ✦

We went from the pinball machine into a booth that was against the wall opposite the front entrance to the dim saloon. It was late in the afternoon, but the saloon was one of those places that's always dark no matter what time of the day or night. We might as well have been in a cave, like a couple of vampire bats hiding from the sun.

Each of us had a bottle of beer before him — for Tony it was already his fifth one, and we'd been in the place not quite an hour. I was only on number two, and my bottle was still half full.

I could tell just by looking at him that whatever he had on his mind, it was weighing him down. Which should've come as no surprise to me, considering what he and I had been through the past couple of weeks: Trying to catch up with the phantom killer who the media had just the day before taken to calling the "Streetside Strangler."

The first victim was a young woman, a teller at a savings-and-loan downtown; her body had been found in an alley a few blocks from the place where she worked. The second was an older man, a plumber; he'd been left behind the wheel of his own truck, parked on the street in front of his shop. The third was another man, a gas station attendant whose boss found him in a stall in the station's men's room.

The last one had been just this morning — and it was one that struck a little too close to home. She was a computer operator who worked for the police department, and she'd been found in her apartment by her roommate, a stewardess who had just gotten back from an out-of-town assignment. Four victims: two male, two female; three white, one black; ranging in age from nineteen to forty-five. They each lived in different parts of the city, and none of the victims had ever met any of the others, not even a chance encounter. There wasn't a single common thread, nothing to connect the victims to each other. Nothing at all.

Except for the black knit necktie that had been used to strangle each of them.

It was our case. Mine and Tony's.

At four-thirty that afternoon, after we had come from the morgue, where we watched the autopsy on Victim #4, our boss, Captain Ramsey, called Tony and me into his office, where he laid into us. Not that we weren't expecting it; it'd been nearly three weeks since the first strangling, and the captain was getting antsy because not one lead nor any of the dozen nutcase phone calls confessing to the murders had panned out. We were at a dead end; we knew it and the captain knew it. But he chewed us out anyway, for half an hour.

Tony didn't take it well. As we came out of the captain's office, he steered me by my elbow, out of the homicide squad room, past our desks. Whispering to me, "We gotta get out of here." I knew it wouldn't do any good to argue; in spite of all the work that we were skipping out on, Tony was in no mood to stick around.

I looked down at my watch. It was after six.

Tony signaled the bartender for another beer, then looked over at me. I drained the rest of my bottle and nodded. He called out to the bartender, "Make it two!" The bartender waved back.

I watched Tony reach into his pocket for a pack of cigarettes, pull one out, tap it on the table, light it and draw in a deep breath of smoke. He exhaled a heavy sigh, then looked over at me again. The corners of his mouth turned up into a thin smile.

"Waiting me out," he said. "You know me pretty good."

The bartender came over with fresh beers and took away our empties. Tony waited until the guy was out of earshot, then lifted his beer and took a long swallow.

I waited.

"We been lookin' for the connection," he said at last. "Tryin' to figure out what our victims got in common, right? It looks like there isn't a thing. Random killings. Different sexes. Different ages. We find their bodies in different places, all over town. Where's the connection?"

"You tell me," I said.

He nodded slowly, still not entirely sure that he'd made up his mind whether to do that or not. Then he said in a low voice, "What've we got? A bank teller, a plumber, a kid who works in a gas station, a computer operator. Again, what's the connection?"

I sipped my beer. "It's your theory, pal."

His thin smile reappeared. Then he asked me, out of the blue, "Did you know the last one?" He mentioned the name of the victim we'd found this morning. "Did you ever have to deal with her, ever have her run a record check or anything for you?"

I shook my head no.

"You're lucky," he said. "She was a real cunt, man. I'm talkin' cunt with a capital C. Like it was a major favor to have her do something for you – something that was part of her job anyway, but still she had to give you grief about it." He swallowed the rest of his beer, then gestured to the bartender again. "I can think of a dozen people off the top of my head who'd like to've strangled her. She was that miserable a human being."

"So?"

He frowned, then said, "So think about it. Bank teller, plumber, filling station man. And her." He was looking at me, waiting for an answer.

I shrugged.

"You're not tryin'," he said.

I said impatiently, "Then why don't you tell me—"

Just as the bartender set another bottle in front of Tony. The guy looked at me and I shook my head. He went away.

Tony was watching the bartender move back to the other side of the bar and resume a conversation he'd been having with a pair of young ladies — they looked like secretaries who had just gotten off from work. Still looking at them, Tony said to me, "You ever notice what's really wrong with the way things are today? I mean *really* notice?"

I didn't say anything.

"You go into a supermarket," he said. "You see a kid stacking cereal boxes, you ask him, 'Excuse me, but where do you keep the stewed tomatoes?' 'I don't know' he says, 'ask the manager.' And he says, 'He's not here today.'"

Tony stubbed out his cigarette. "Or say you're in a department store. You ever notice how the sales help, they don't find the customers anymore, it's the customers who have to go find help? You got to look for somebody who's hiding in a corner or a woman who's walking real slow down an aisle or somebody who's trying to stay out of sight behind a counter. Or maybe three or four people together, and they're all laughin' and havin' a good time, and you walk up to 'em and say, 'Can somebody help me, please?' and what you get is, 'Sorry, we don't work in this section.'"

He had reached into his coat for another cigarette, and seemed to be having trouble remembering which pocket he'd put the pack into. He found the pack at last, but had to put the cigarette to his lips slowly to keep it under control. I took his lighter from him and lit the cigarette, and he nodded thanks. I noticed that his eyes had started to glaze over, and I thought to myself: *That's enough for you m'lad . . .*

"It's a fucking epidemic," he was saying. Then he was leaning over the table, resting his arms. He motioned for me to come closer. I could smell the stale beer and burnt tobacco on his breath.

He said, "What if you got somebody who's had it up to here?" The edge of the hand that was holding the cigarette sloshed across his throat. "Somebody who's so sick and tired of being treated like a piece of crap by people who are s'posed to be serving *him*."

"Him?" I said.

"Or her. Man, woman, doesn't matter. Maybe it's somebody whose job it is to be nice to people all day himself. Maybe another salesman or something, or somebody who runs a complaint department and works damn hard and just sees everybody else getting away with being ignorant slobs all the time. I don't know, maybe somebody who had to spend all day listening to other people's problems . . . like a priest or a shrink or—"

"Or a cop?" I said.

His eyes locked on mine. "Yeah," he said. "Sure. A cop. Why not?"

I saw him looking over to the bartender once more, and I caught his arm as he raised it to signal. "Forget it," I said. "It's time you and I went home—"

"What do you think pushes him over the edge?" he went on, ignoring me. "He goes to the bank 'cause somebody there's screwed up his statement or something. And after he stands in line for half an hour, the teller treats him like it's his fault that on account of their screwing up his deposit he's bounced a couple hundred dollars worth of checks, and it's tough luck, but he's gonna have to pay the ten or twelve or fifteen dollar service charge on each one anyway. That's one. Then say a couple days later, the guy's bathtub backs up and the plumber gives him a hard time about it, like he's the reason why all his pipes are corroded. That's two. Then the guy pulls into a gas station and maybe asks the kid to check under the hood, and the kid says, 'Who me?' 'Yes, you, dammit, it's supposed to be a goddamn *service* station . . .'"

He caught himself when he noticed that everybody in the place was looking in the direction of our table. He had gotten very loud.

"C'mon," I said, pushing myself up. I dropped some money on the table, then bent to help my partner to his feet. "We're getting out of here."

The alley was dark. It was also deserted except for the two of us, and I could make out his lumbering figure ahead of me, staggering as he walked to our car. All the while I was running through my mind what he'd said to me in the saloon.

As well as what he didn't say.

I was thinking to myself: *What is it that you're really telling me? That he could sympathize? Or that maybe he was confessing to me he knew who the killer really was . . .?*

Or what?

I wanted to ask him, very badly.

I considered asking him as I came up from behind while he was fumbling with his keys, trying to open the passenger's side door. But I decided not to as I looped my necktie around his throat. I couldn't risk it, because there were still too many people who needed taking care of.

But I was also remembering what Tony had said that afternoon in the squad room as we were leaving. He'd said, "Let's you and me go tie one on."

I pulled the loop tight, smiling to myself. Thinking: *That Tony, he sure is a card.*

Tie one on. I like that. I like that a lot.

THE CUTTY BLACK SOW

Thomas F. Monteleone

Twelve-year-old Jamie stood with his parents and his little sister, Gloria, around Great-Grandmother McEvan's bed while a cold autumn wind rumbled the shutters and whistled through the seams of their old house. Rain tapped on the windowpanes like tiny fingers, slapped against the shingles like sheets of clothes-line.

Great-Grandma was a tiny bird of a woman at the age of 103. She had always looked the same to Jamie: silver-blue hair in a bun, thin pointy face, dark sparrow eyes, and long, spider-leg fingers. But she had always been a strong old woman. She had never been to a doctor in her life, and she had birthed eight children. Lost five, and raised the rest as best she could.

Now she lay in the warmly lit bedroom, her eyes closed, mouth half-open, breath wheezing in and out of her like a cold wind.

"She's not going to make it, is she, Dad?" asked Jamie with the matter-of-factness of a twelve-year-old.

"Jamie! Stop that!" said his mother.

His father sighed, touched her arm. "No, he's right, Hon. He's just saying out loud what we've all been thinking . . ."

"Is she going to die?" asked nine-year-old Gloria with a touch of awe in her voice. "Is she really going to *die* right here in our house?"

"We don't know that for sure, sweetheart," said Mother. She looked at her husband. "Should we call Dr. Linton?"

"I don't think there's much use in doing that. You remember what she said . . ."

Jamie noted that no one was actually crying, but everybody was fighting their feelings. They were all witnessing something they had known was coming for awhile now. He was thinking about the idea of death and dying, and how it changed people into such bad imitations of themselves. His great-grandmother had always been so lively and active. She had entertained him and Gloria with stories of her native Scotland and the Highlands she loved so dearly.

Now there would be no more stories.

The sheets rustled as the old woman stirred. Jamie saw her eyelids flutter as she gathered the strength to look at him and the others around her bed. "What day is it?" she asked.

"Thursday," said Jamie's father, without thinking.

A pause, then: "No . . ." Great-Gran's voice was hoarse and low. "What date?"

"Oh . . ." said his mother. "It's the thirtieth."

Another pause, a wheezing of breath, then: "Of October?"

"Yes, Great-Gran," said Jamie, keeping his own voice low and soft.

"All Hallow's Even," said the old woman. There was a different tone in her voice, an inflection which could have been awe or respect, or even fear.

"What? What did she say?" asked Jamie's mother.

"I'm not sure," said his father. "Grandma, what was that you said?"

"All Hallow's Even. I'm going to die. On All Hallow's Even."

"Jim, what's she talking about?"

"Halloween," said Jamie's father. "Tomorrow's Halloween. That's what they called it in Scotland."

"But why . . . I mean, what does she mean?" Jamie's mother held his father's arm tightly.

"I don't know . . ." His father looked at his watch. Outside a gust of wind whispered against the house. "Eleven-thirty. It'll be the thirty-first soon . . ."

Jamie's mother leaned over the bed, tried to talk to Great-Gran, but the old woman's eyes had closed and her breathing had returned to its former shallowness. Turning back to her husband, Jamie's mother looked distressed.

"I think we'd better call Dr. Linton."

His father nodded, sighed. "All right, I'll call him. You kids, it's time to get off to bed."

✦   ✦

Hours later, Jamie lay in his bed in the darkness. The storm still buffeted the house and the trees around it. He could not fall asleep, was not even feeling tired. He'd been awake when Dr. Linton arrived, wet and blustery in the downstairs foyer. The tall, white-haired doctor had looked in on Great-Gran, then returned downstairs to confer with Jamie's parents. The boy listened to Dr. Linton's words: ". . . and I'd say there's nothing much more you can do to make her more comfortable. She's lapsed into a coma. Might hang on for weeks — or, she might not make it till morning."

The words stung Jamie as he lay in his dark bed. Great-Gran dying was one of those terribly impossible things to imagine. She'd *always* been a part of his life. Rocked him as a baby, fed him his bottles, bathed him, and always the stories about Scotland. To think of her as *gone* was like knowing when you woke up in the morning your right arm would be missing. Unthinkable. And yet, true. She might not last the night.

He didn't know how long he lay in bed without sleeping. Long enough for the storm to quiet and his parents to finally retire to their bedroom. Long enough for the heavy clouds to part and let the moonlight creep through his window. Jamie wanted to fall asleep, but he could not.

More time passed. In the silent house, he could hear every creak and groan of old wood, every tic of cooling radiator pipes.

And then a new sound: Great-Gran was talking.

She sounded so bright and clear that he imagined she must have arisen from her coma. A spark of hope was ignited in him, and he slipped noiselessly from the bed to creep into her room at the end of the hall. The door was open and the room stalked by tall shadows of old furniture, cast by the feeble glow of the night-light.

Silently, Jamie approached the bed. If anything, the old woman looked worse than before and she spoke as though in a trance.

But her words were soft and clear: ". . . *and down we would go to Balquhidder with the other children to gather for the fires. A-beggin' from the folk, and we would say 'Give us a peat t'barn the witches, good missus!' Pile it high, we would! With straw, furze and peat . . . what a beautiful Samhnagan it would be!"*

Jamie felt a chill race down his back. He thought of calling his parents, but they would only make him go back to bed. Yet he sensed an urgency in the old woman's voice.

Then he thought of his tape recorder, and moving quickly, silently, he retrieved it from his room. Turning it on, he captured the trance-like ramblings of the old woman.

" . . . and the fire would burn through the night on All Hallow's Even, and we would dance about it, we would! The fire that kept away the Cutty Black Sow! Kept it away from any soul who died on that witches' night! Till the heap had turned to bright red coals. And we would gather up the coals and ash in the form of a circle. Then into that circle we would put stones — one marked for each member of our families. The stones were our souls! And as long as they stayed inside the circle of Samhnagan, ole Cutty Black could not harm us! And in the mornin' everyone would run to the cool ashen circle — to make sure that not a stone was disturbed or missin.' For if it was, the soul that stood for that missin' stone would be took away by the Cutty Black Sow!"

Jamie listened as the old woman rambled. It was some memory, a bit of remembered childhood. He tried to speak to her, to ask her what she meant, but she continued on to the end, the last words only a whisper.

He waited for her to continue, but there was nothing more. Great-Gran's breathing became ragged, catching in her hollow chest, then wheezing out as if released by a cruel fist. Suddenly her body became rigid, then a tremor passed once through her bones. Jamie watched as her drawn little body rose under the bedcovers for an instant, then fell slack, her head lolling to the far side of the pillow.

He could not see her face, yet he knew she was gone. There was a coolness in the room that had been absent before. He felt utterly alone in a vast darkness despite the pale glow of the night-light.

Slowly, Jamie thumbed off the Sony recorder as his gaze drifted to an old Westclock on Great-Gran's bureau. 4:35 in the morning. She'd been right: she *did* die on Halloween.

He padded silently back to his room, replaced his cassette recorder on a shelf by his bed, then woke his parents. He told them he had heard Great-Gran making strange noises, and that he was afraid to go see her. His father moved quickly from the bed and down the hall. A few minutes later he returned to announce quietly that she was gone.

The time had come when they would cry. Jamie's mother held him while they both sobbed, and she whispered that everything would be all right.

But he was thinking about the recording he'd made — and he was not sure if what his mother said was altogether true.

Halloween came early that year because nobody went back to sleep. They sat in the kitchen having a very early breakfast while the sunrise burned through the autumn trees in the backyard. Then, while Jamie dressed for school, his father made lots of phone calls, and his mother cried openly a few more times. Gloria was still asleep as Jamie sat in his room and replayed the tape he'd made. To hear Great-Gran's voice, knowing she was gone, gave him a strange feeling. It struck him that he was listening to those "last words" everybody talks about.

Listening to her words for the second time, he realized the old woman was fearful of dying *on Halloween*. She was telling him something — something important. Her people had always protected anybody who dies on that day. Protected them from the Cutty Black Sow — whatever *that* was . . .

Jamie stuffed the Sony into his backpack, along with his school books, and returned to the kitchen. His mother poured him another glass of orange juice.

"Your father's not going to work today," she said.

"He can drive you and Gloria to school."

She paused as though suddenly remembering something important. "Oh, God — she's still asleep. I've got to wake her and tell her . . ."

His mother left the kitchen, leaving Jamie alone with his thoughts. He could hear his father's muffled voice as he spoke on the phone. Other than that, it was quiet. He thought about Great-Gran, wondering if she'd *known* he was listening to her last night, if she'd been talking about that stuff with the stones for a reason.

Jamie couldn't get the story out of his mind as he and Gloria rode into town with his father. The bonfire and the stones and the Cutty Black Sow.

At school he waited until study hall just after lunch, then transcribed the recording into his math notebook. When it was written out, he was able to study words more carefully, and he became even more convinced that Great-Gran had been giving him a message.

Jamie asked Miss Hall, the school librarian, for books about Scotland and Scottish folklore. Usually quiet and dour, Miss Hall volunteered that she was Scottish on her mother's side, and it was good to see young people interested in their heritage.

With her help, Jamie figured out a lot of what Great-Gran had been talking about. A *Samhnagan* was a ritual bonfire, burned on Halloween night to protect the people from the forces of Evil, and to save the souls of any who died on the Witches' Day. There was nothing about the "Cutty Black Sow," but Miss Hall told him that she would be happy to look it up when she went home that evening. Jamie thanked her and gave her his phone number, making the librarian promise to call if she discovered anything.

On his way home on the bus, Jamie planned his evening. He knew what he had to do for his great-grandmother. Gloria kept interrupting his thoughts and, finally, he knew he'd have to talk to her.

"Do you think we'll still be able to trick-or-treat tonight?"

"Gee, I don't know, Gloria. I wasn't really thinking about it. I guess I figured we'd go, but I might have to do something else."

"Oh yeah? Like what?"

He considered telling her what he intended. Sometimes Gloria could be trusted with secrets, but often times not.

"You wouldn't understand," he said after a pause. "Something Great-Gran wanted me to do. For her."

Gloria's eyes flashed. He had her hooked now. "But she's dead now . . ."

"She asked me last night — right before she died. It was like a . . . a last request."

"Really?" Gloria's voice flirted with true awe.

"Yeah, but this is a *secret*, you understand?"

"Sure I do! I can keep a secret."

Jamie grinned. "Yeah. Sometimes. Now listen, if I tell you about this, you have to *swear* you won't tell anybody — not even Mom or Dad, okay?"

"Gee, what're you gonna *do* anyway?"

"You swear?"

She nodded with great seriousness. "I swear."

"All right," said Jamie. "Last night . . ."

When the bus dropped them off at the house, Jamie's mother informed them that The Undertaker had picked up Great-Gran. Jamie went into the backyard and sat on a swing. To his right was a barbecue pit and outdoor fireplace. If he was going to build a fire, that was the place. The yard was enclosed by tall oak and poplar trees, and a cool wind sifted through the brown and orange and yellow leaves, shaking them loose and bringing them down all around him. It was pretty, but he found it also very sad.

The back door slammed and Gloria ran down to the swing-set. "I just talked to Mommy, and she said we can still go trick-or-treating!"

"Okay."

"They're going to be at the funeral home, but she said I can go out as long as *you* stay with me. Then we gotta go to Mrs. Stamrick's house when we're done. They'll pick us up there when they get home, okay?"

"Yeah," he said absently. "That'll be fine. But we'll have to make that bonfire first."

"What?"

"C'mon. Gloria. Get real. I just told you about that."

"That didn't make much sense to me." She grimaced.

"Well. It did to me. And I gotta make that fire for Great-Gran. She wanted me to."

After dinner that night, Jamie's parents left for the funeral home. He went out to the backyard, down toward the wood which bordered the property, and began gathering up sticks and branches from a big deadfall left from last winter's storms. He also gathered up five stones about the size of baseballs. As he began arranging the wood in his father's barbecue pit, he heard Gloria coming down the back steps. She was dressed in her trick-or-treat costume — a skeleton in a hooded robe.

"Getting it ready?" Gloria asked as she watched.

"What do you think, stupid?"

"I'm not stupid. I was just asking."

With matches he lit the wood; it took several attempts to get the heavier branches burning, but soon the fire licked and cracked with a small, contained fury. It warmed their faces and cast a hot orange glow on the surrounding trees. Jamie piled on more wood from the deadfall, and the blaze became a small inferno, roaring as it sucked up the cool autumn air.

"It's going good now," said Gloria, entranced by the everchanging shapes and glowing coals. Jamie finally pulled an El Marko from his jacket pocket and an old rag he'd taken from his father's workroom in the basement. He wiped the stones as clean as possible, then marked each one with an initial.

"What're you doing now?" asked Gloria.

"I have to fix the stones. One for each of us in the family. See that G? That's for you. And these are for Mom and Dad, and me and Great-Gran. Now, we have to throw them into the middle, like this." Jamie tossed Great-Gran's stone into the center of the coals. Then he tossed all the others in, one by one, with a small amount of ceremony. "There, it's done."

"Why'd you have to do that, Jamie?"

"Because. That's the way they always did it. To protect us all—"

"Protect us?" Gloria giggled beneath her skull-mask. "From what?"

"I'm not sure . . . from the Cutty Black Sow, I guess."

"What's *that*?"

"I don't know," said Jamie. "I couldn't find out."

The only sound was the wind in the tree-tops and occasional pop of a coal cooling down.

"Hey," said his sister. "Are we gonna go trick-or-treating. Or what?"

"Oh yeah, I guess we can go now," he said.

"Finally!" Gloria turned toward the house. "I'll be right back — gotta get my shopping bag!"

Then they went trick-or-treating and when they returned from a tour of the neighborhood streets, it was almost totally dark. Jamie guided her back to their house and Gloria reminded him that they were to go to Mrs. Stamrick's place.

"In a minute. I want to go check on the fire."

"Aw, Jamie, I'm tired . . ."

"Look, it'll only take a minute. Come on, you got what you wanted, didn't you?"

"Oh, all right." She followed him as Jamie took a flashlight from the garage and moved close to the barbecue pit. Only a few orange embers belied the location of the small bonfire. He played the light over the ashes, searching for the five stones in the debris.

"What're you doing?"

"Just checking to see that everything's okay." He counted the stones as the beam of light touched them: three . . . four . . . where was the last one? From the looks of the ashes and embers, the wood had collapsed, then spilled toward the edge of the firebrick. He directed the beam down to the patio and found the fifth stone, amidst a scattering of ash. It had fallen from the fire, and he remembered his Great-Gran's words: "*no stone should be missing or disturbed* . . ." He bent low and saw in the flashlight beam that it was the stone with a just-legible "J" on its face.

His stone. His soul?

It would be best if he left it as it lay — undisturbed.

"Hey, look," said Gloria. "One of 'em fell out!"

Before he could say anything, his sister, costumed as a miniature Grim Reaper, swooped down beside him and grabbed for the stone.

"No, Gloria! Don't touch it!"

But her fingers had already encircled it, had begun to pick it up. In that instant, Jamie felt a jolt of energy spike through him. His heart accelerated from a burst of adrenaline, and suddenly Gloria screamed.

Pulling her hand back, she let go of the stone in the same motion. It was flung into the darkness and Jamie could hear it thump upon the lawn somewhere to his right.

"It burned my hand!" sobbed Gloria. "It was still hot!"

"I told you not to touch it! Oh, jeez, Gloria, you really shouldn't have touched it! I've got to find it!"

"Let's go to Mrs. Stamrick's. Come on!"

"No, wait! I've got to find that stone."

"What for? It's just an old rock. You can get it in the morning."

"No, it might be too late then." *It might be too late already*, he thought.

Despite Gloria's protests, she helped scan the lawn for the missing stone. She must have heard the urgency and fear in Jamie's voice because she even got down on her hands and knees to grope about in the grass.

When they found the stone, it was still hot, but cool enough to pick up. Jamie carefully returned it to the spot where he had first disturbed it, and hoped that nothing would be wrong. After all, Gloria hadn't meant to touch it. Perhaps it would be all right since it was not yet morning.

He and Gloria went to Mrs. Stamrick's house two blocks away, and she welcomed them with affectionate hugs and kisses and mugs of hot chocolate. She spoke in saccharine tones and made a fuss over them.

Outside the clapboard house, the winds began gusting. Jamie listened to it whistle through the gutters and downspouts as he sat in Mrs. Stamrick's parlor watching a situation comedy on TV. Gloria was busy pouring her loot into a large mixing bowl on the floor; Mrs. Stamrick oohed and aahed appropriately as his sister scooped up especially fine prizes from the night's haul.

Jamie sipped his cocoa and watched TV without actually paying attention. At one point he thought he heard something tapping on the windowpane, even though the others did not seem to notice. When he took his empty mug into the kitchen to place it in the sink, he heard another sound.

A thumping. Outside.

Something was padding across the wood floor of Mrs. Stamrick's back porch. It was rapid and relentless, as though some heavy-footed dog, a large dog, was pacing back and forth beyond the kitchen door.

Slowly, Jamie moved to the door, but could not bring himself to draw up the shade and peer out. The thumping footsteps continued and at one point he thought he heard another sound — a rough exhalation, a combination of a growl and a snort.

Moving quickly out of the kitchen, he told Mrs. Stamrick that it sounded like there was a big dog on her back porch. She walked past him into the kitchen, raised the shade and looked out. Seeing nothing, she opened the door, admitting a cool blast of face-slapping wind — the only thing that was out there.

"It must have wandered off," she said. "Nothing's out there now."

Jamie nodded and forced a silly grin, then let her lead him back into the parlor.

✦   ✦

While Gloria was dozing off on the couch, Jamie tried to get absorbed in a cop-show drama. But he couldn't concentrate on anything except the sounds of other things he couldn't always identify.

When his father arrived to pick them up, Jamie could not recall ever being so glad to see him. He picked up his sister's treat-bag as his father carried the sleeping Gloria out to the car where their mother waited. As Jamie walked down the driveway toward the safety of the big station wagon, he listened for the sounds, searched the shadows and the shrubbery that lurked beyond the splash of Mrs. Stamrick's porch light.

He sensed there was something out there, could almost feel the burning gaze of unseen eyes, the hot stinging breath of an unknown thing so very close to him.

In the car, he exchanged small-talk with his parents. It was best if he tried to act as normal as possible. But his mother turned to look at him at one point, and he wondered if she sensed — as mothers often can — that something was not right with him.

As soon as the car stopped in the driveway, he jumped out and moved quickly to the back door, waiting for his father with the keys. A single yellow bug-light cast a sickening pall over everything, but it also sparked feelings of safety and warmth.

Finally, they were all inside the house. While his father carried Gloria off to bed, his mother checked the Code-A-Phone; its green light signaled calls waiting. Jamie hung up his coat in the closet. In the other room he could hear his mother as she played back the tape from the phone answering machine — mostly messages of condolence from friends and relatives. He was about to go down the hall to the stairs when he heard a loud thumping noise outside the kitchen window.

He fought down the urge to run blindly to his mother and wrap his arms around her. The sound of her voice breaking the silence almost made him cry out.

"Jamie," his mother called. "There's a message for you here."

As casually as possible, he moved to the table where his mother rewound the tape and played it.

". . . Hello, Jamie. This is Miss Hall. I found what you were looking for in some of my books at home. I guess you're out trick-or-treating, so you can call me back till 11:00, if you want. Bye now . . ."

His mother glanced at the kitchen clock as she stopped the tape. "It's only ten o'clock. Are you going to call her?"

"Nah, it's getting late. I'll just see her Monday. I guess."

His mother smiled as she returned to the rest of the messages, and Jamie moved quickly up the stairs to his room. He said goodnight to his father, undressed, and slipped under his sheet and quilt.

It was at least a half-hour after his parents had also gone to bed when Jamie heard more of the strange sounds, the thumping footfalls of something in the yard beneath his window. His room faced the rear of the house, his window overlooking the roof of the back porch. Broken moonlight splintered the darkness as he slipped from the covers and forced himself to look out.

The jutting slant of the roof obscured his line of sight, and for a moment, he saw nothing unfamiliar. Then, for an instant, one of the shadows moved, seemed to step back into the deeper darkness of the yard.

Looking beyond it, Jamie was surprised to see the still-glowing embers of his bonfire at the end of the yard. From this distance, they were nothing more than points of deep orange, but he would have thought they'd be dead now. The rising wind must have stirred up the last coals.

Again came the faint sounds of something moving with a heavy-footed gait. And the distant, snorting breath he had heard once before.

Jamie was trembling as he moved away from the window, and it became suddenly important that he speak with Miss Hall. He moved quietly downstairs to the kitchen phone, and looked up her number in the phone book.

Miss Hall answered on the fifth ring.

"Miss Hall, it's Jamie . . . I'm not sure what time it is, I hope I'm not calling too late . . ." His voice sounded unsteady.

Miss Hall chuckled. "Well, almost, but not quite. Jamie, what did you need this information for? It struck me as somewhat odd that—"

"Oh, just for a project I was doing. About Halloween and all." There was a pause, and when the librarian did not reply he rushed on: "You said you found it for me . . ."

"Yes, I did." There was a sound of papers being shifted about. "Yes, here . . . in Scotland and Wales, there was a belief that bonfires protected people from demons and witches."

"Yeah, I already found that stuff," he forced himself to speak in hushed tones. "What about the . . . the . . ."

"Oh yes, the Cutty Black Sow." Miss Hall cleared her throat. "You see, it was a common belief back then that demons could assume the shape of animals. And it was believed that on Halloween these demons took the shape of a pig – a large black-haired creature that walked on its hind legs. Its hair was supposed to be bristly and closely cut. The Cropped Black Sow or The Cutty Black Sow was what they called him."

Jamie felt stunned for a moment, and he tried to speak but no words would come out.

"Jamie, are you there?"

"Yes! Oh . . . oh, well, thank you, Miss Hall. Thanks a lot. That's just what I needed to . . . finish my project."

"Well, I'm glad I could be of help, Jamie. It must be pretty important for you to be working on it this late."

There came the sound of footfalls again. This time, they seemed so loud in Jamie's ears that he almost felt the house move from the impact.

"Yeah, its pretty important . . . I guess. Listen, I'd better go, Miss Hall. Thanks a lot."

He hung up the phone before she could reply, and moved quickly back to his room. He didn't want to wake up his parents, or tell them he was scared, but he didn't know *what* to do. The thumping grew louder and it was now intermixed with snuffling, snorting sounds.

The kinds of sounds a pig would make.

Jamie looked out his window. The yard seemed darker than before, but the embers of the fire in the distance seemed brighter . . .

. . . until he realized that the embers were not brighter, but closer. And that the two fiercely glowing orbs were not coals at all . . .

They were eyes.

Backing away, he heard scraping sounds. Rough, abrasive, crunching sounds, as though something was scrambling for purchase on the side of the porch, something trying to climb up, towards his window.

The sounds were very loud now. The old wood of the house groaned as it was splintered. It was so loud! Why didn't his parents hear it, too! Jamie jumped into his bed, grasping at the covers the way he had as a child when he had been afraid of some terrible night-thing.

Something scraped across the windowpane as ember-eyes appeared beyond the glass . . .

He must have cried out, although he didn't realize it, because he heard his father's voice calling him. Relief flooded through him as he heard his father's hand on the door knob.

"Jamie, are you all right?"

The door swung open, and he could see his father's silhouette against the bright light of the hall beyond. Quickly he glanced back to the window, and the burning eyes were gone. He felt silly as he tried to speak.

"Dad! Yeah, its okay . . . just a bad dream, I guess."

His father said nothing as he walked into the room, drawing close to the bed. In the darkness, he sat on the bed and drew his son close to him. Jamie relaxed in the comforting embrace, and put his arms around his father.

He was about to tell Dad how scared he had been, when his hands touched the back of the neck of the thing which held him, when he felt the close-cut, bristly hair . . .

THE LIAR'S MOUTH

Darrell Schweitzer

"Graham! Graham Wentworth! Good old Graham Cracker! I bet it's been a long time since anybody called you that. Hey — !"

He didn't ask. He didn't say, "Why don't you sit with me?" He merely grabbed me by the wrist and yanked me down into that booth in Marcello's Diner, suburban Philadelphia's most exclusive all-nite greasy spoon.

He leaned over, staring into my face, holding both of my hands down on the formica tabletop, the expression on his own face a weird combination of delight, quivering hints of what might have been grief, and undoubted confusion.

"Harry Crandall?" I tugged. He let go of my hands and sat back. He looked awful, his face sagging like a half-melted wax mask, already pooling into a wattle under his chin, enough crow's feet around his eyes to account for an annual migration, and his once famous explosion of brilliantly red hair reduced to a fringe, almost white, a matted, shoulder-length tangle. Every detail was unsavory: the top of his head liver-spotted, something I would have thought impossible at his — our — age, his three-day beard like pig-bristles, his green trenchcoat worn and filthy, his breath vile.

"Graham, old buddy, it's — "

"You look terrible, Harry," I said, but I couldn't deny that it was he. I knew this man. We had gone to college together, Villanova University, class of 1974. He could be no more than forty or forty-one.

I thought of a cartoon I'd seen once —

"Yeah," he said, "I can't think who drew it. Not Gahan Wilson. Somebody else." He pressed his fingers to his temples, as if concentrating intensely. My unease increased as I noticed that both hands were heavily bandaged, and the bandages did not look fresh, or clean. "I . . . think it was in *Playboy*. A bunch of seedy middle-aged bums hanging around a campus during Homecoming, and one asks another, 'Was it something about the year, or is there something wrong with *us*?' Well, is there, Graham? What do you think? How do you like my mind-reading act?"

"I'm impressed, Harry," I said flatly.

"Great minds move in similar gutter, Mein Cracker."

"You seem the worse for wear, Harry."

He said nothing as the waitress came over. I ordered hot tea, something I could probably nurse along for quite a while before I'd have to leave. I wasn't hungry, but I didn't have anywhere to go just then. The weather outside was a matter of wind and sleet and freezing slush. But there was also something I couldn't focus on, something I had to do or had done, a gray spot in my consciousness where the details hadn't been filled in yet. I must have shared some of Harry's own confusion.

After a long pause, he said, "*I* may look like hell, but *you* look great. Are you sure you didn't get your portrait done by the same guy who did Dorian Gray's? I mean, have you changed a bit since you were twenty? I can only envy your hairline. You *have* a hairline, and it's in *the same goddamn place!*" He laughed at that as if it were terribly funny, hugging himself, bending over until his head dropped below the table. Then he sat up straight. "Just checking to see if you're still wearing twenty-eight-inch-waist bellbottoms."

"I sent them to the laundry sometime in the Eighties, Harry. They should be back by the turn of the century."

He laughed again, louder, braying. People turned and stared.

"Please . . . " I whispered. "What do you *want*?"

"What do I *want*?" he whispered back, leaning conspiratorially over the table. "Well — "

The waitress came with my tea. Harry sat up and we both waited in silence until she was gone.

"I want — " His voice changed abruptly, almost broke. He was holding back tears. "I want to see an old friend one last time before — Let's just say I want to get maudlin. You know. Try all my tricks again to see if they still work. I — "

He twirled the salt and pepper shakers on the tabletop as if he were playing a shell game, but with only two shells. He lined them up and indicated that I should choose.

"Okay, which one is it?"

The solution, I knew from long experience, was that whichever one I would pick would be wrong, "it" being whatever he decided on *after* I had made my choice, a premise he would then defend with mock-Hegelian dialectic of no greater stupefying absurdity than the real thing. ("Everything I say is correct. That includes this definition.")

That had actually been funny once, long ago, back when Harry Crandall was a noted and vastly entertaining "character" on campus, the brilliant scion of a rich Main Line family of whom great things were expected. Harry was going to be a great writer, or a movie star, or at least win a Nobel Prize —

"Yeah, yeah, so I've seen better days. Even my jokes have seen better days. Whatever have I been doing with myself all this time? You haven't seen little old *moi* since graduation." He tapped his dirty fingers on the tabletop as if he were playing a piano, faster and faster, and he spoke the same way, in a machine-gun patter, filled with pain and jokes and something he couldn't quite get into words. I felt ever more squeamish as the bandages on his hands seemed about to come loose.

"What?" he said. "What? Sailing the world? Hobnobbing with the Kennedys? Abducted by aliens? Expanding my imaginative and visionary potential through creative chemistry? Ah, *gotcha!* You *believed* that one, didn't you? But it's no more true than any of the others, or that I've become a great writer or movie star or whatever. No, Graham, what I've been doing is *telling lies*, and that includes this one, and I'm very good at it. Let me demonstrate. Suppose I told you, yeah, Harry's the scion of a *mucho richo* Main-Line-cum-Philadelphia family who should have had all the advantages, but he fucking near *choked* on the silver spoon he was born with in his mouth because his Papa was a sadistic lunatic who beat Mama to death with a golf club while little Harry was cowering inside the closet *with the light on* and the blood oozed under the door just like that scene in *The Leopard Man* and it all came back to him one night when he saw the movie on TV, resulting in a nervous breakdown which lasted for fifteen years? Eh? You're almost ready to believe that. Suppose I add that Marquis de Daddy raped little Harry at least once a week from the time he was eleven, and used to handcuff him naked to the overhead pipes in the basement and beat

him with whips until the blood made pretty patterns all over the walls?
Well? How about that too?"

Very calmly, I finished my tea and started to get up from the table.

Quick as a striking snake, he grabbed me by the arm and yanked
me down again.

I spoke in a low, steady voice. "I have to be *going*, Harry. I have
a class tomorrow and I have to prepare. I teach at Penn, you know —"

"Of course I know, Graham, because *thee and me*, are one and the
same, and when we look into the mirrors of our souls, we see one
another." He smiled broadly, viciously. His teeth were green and black.
"That's how I know you'll never teach another day's class again.
Beware the Ides of March, old chum."

Now I was angry. I could have hit him. But we were in public.

He assumed a phoney accent. "A bit of *nastiness* last night in the
English department. Names were mentioned. Yours among them. And
that girl on the phone this evening, threatening to tell *everything* — "

"How the *fuck* did you know — ?"

He started drumming the tabletop again, faster and faster. "Maybe
I don't. Maybe I'm not even here. Maybe I am, myself, one more lie,
the product of a diseased mind. Maybe I'm the Ghost of Christmas past,
or Mephistopheles, here to trick you into damnation. Or I might be your
conscience, an airy nothing given form and habitation after your wife
deserted you and you beat your mistress to death. How can you ever be
sure? But we're off the track anyway. The subject at hand is Daddy
and the buggery and the whips and — well, your old friend pops up out
of nowhere and tells you *such a story*. What *can* you do about it?"

I sat back and closed my eyes.

"Not very much, Harry."

"Ex*act*ly!" he poked my chest with his finger. I opened my eyes.
He was grinning again, virtually beaming in triumph.

"Exactly what?"

The smile faded. "You're entirely too credulous, Harry. Here I tell
you this monstrous slander about my father, who was a good and gentle
man, and you're ready to believe me. You don't even wonder how the
kid hid all the whip-marks in the locker room during gym class. Besides
which, a child that severely abused ought to be bugfuck crazy — "

"How do I know he's *not*?"

I was beginning to feel genuinely ill. I did *not* want to continue
this conversation. I looked up for the waitress and she came over, but

before I could ask for the check, Harry chimed in, "Won't you bring my friend here some of that wonderful blueberry pie, Love?"

As soon as she was gone, he turned back to me.

"The point you are still trying to evade, Graham, my dear friend, is that you *can't* deny a story like that to someone's face. It's too agonizingly intimate, too *awful*. I *may* be lying, but if there is the tiniest scintilla of a possibility that I am *not*, you can't risk the psychological damage you might do by saying you don't believe me. I've *got* you by the conscience, which is even worse than by the balls."

"Then we can't really believe anything — "

"*What is truth*? Pilate was wrong to ask. The only comfort we can hope for is the comfort of uncertainty, that existential gray fog which allows us to deny *everything* we want to, the good, and most especially, the bad. Maybe my father didn't abuse me. Maybe you didn't murder your mistress. Maybe we're not even here having this conversation, but you are, instead, in a farmhouse in Bucks County, seated alone at the kitchen table, writing this out as a piece of fiction. There is no pain that way, Graham. No death. Just lies. More lies. Lies forever. *Nothing* is more all-powerful than a lie, artfully told. Don't you agree?"

I don't know if I was trying to be cruel or kind when I attempted to snap him out of it by saying, "How did you hurt your hands, Harry?"

He held both of them up for a few seconds, in silence, long enough for me to notice what was unmistakably a dried trickle of blood on his left wrist.

"Yes," he said finally, "*I* hurt them because only my hands can destroy my lies. They jabber like two relentless mouths and they speak the *truth*." He jerked his head from side to side, oddly, like a bird. "Truth is a cancer, Graham. The problem is that I can't get it all *out*."

His expression had become that of a small child desperately begging for help, but he *had* me, just as he said he had, pinned to the wall by the power of his lying. I couldn't say or do anything.

He produced a steak knife from somewhere. "I keep trying to finish the job," he said, and, to my immense disgust, started picking under the left-hand bandage with it.

"Harry! Jesus Christ!"

He pointed the already bloody knife at me and said, "Have you considered that you are confined in close quarters with an obvious lunatic and *he's got something sharp*?"

I was about ready to scream for help or even jump through the window, but just then a crowd of noisy college students waving pennants and blasting on plastic horns poured into the diner, brushing against me, shouting, tossing hats back and forth. In the confusion, Harry Crandall vanished like some apparition. I even leaned down to see if he was hiding under the table, but he was gone.

I caught the waitress's eye. She hurried over with my pie and a second cup of tea.

"Sorry, Sir, but the rush — "

"Miss, did you see where my friend went?"

"Who? I didn't see anybody." She left the check and hurried to take care of the college kids.

I drank and ate slowly, but then nearly barfed everything back up when I saw what Harry had left on the tabletop besides a few greasy fingerprints.

It was a tooth.

Meanwhile, the "bit of nastiness" in the English Department breaks out in a dozen directions at once. It is great scandal-sheet stuff: Assistant Prof sleeps with beautiful, sadistically misnomered Grad Assistant Angelica, gets her pregnant (so she says), tries to deny everything. Un-angelic lady forthwith claims messy abortion, medical bills, psychological problems requiring expensive and ongoing therapy; blackmails Prof for cash he doesn't have. That she also hints she can "prove" he stole most of his celebrated treatise, *Invention and Evasion: Strategies of the Recursive Narrative* from her thesis (abandoned on his advice) is a mere sideline entertainment once the fun *really* gets rolling and the price goes ever on and on; "not while I can see you squirm, you fucker," quoth she in language more basic than you'd expect from a Literature graduate student, *sans* poetic allusions, *sans* textual apparatus, *sans* even an Abandon All Hope, Ye Who Enter Here, *sans* everything save considerable income on her part when she begins selling examination papers and even grades with the cheerless cooperation of the aforementioned squirming fucker.

Who eventually balks. Who hovers on the threshold of getting caught about the time Angelica goes to the newspapers, having first called up the Assistant Professor's wife to tell her the entire, "true" story.

Which, from swerve of shore to bend of bay, brings us by commodiously vicious recirculation to Marcello's Diner and environs, where we find our Graham violator d'amores wandering aimlessly in the freezing rain, the Damned Spirit having spoken the truth.

I never taught another day's class again.

But wait, there's more. My wife threw me out. I can't see my two little girls, and that tears me up worse than anything.

And more: That night, after disappearing from the diner, friend Harry rematerialized on a bench at the Wayne train station, a five minute walk away, and there slit his throat from ear to ear.

And the cream of the jest: His will was in perfect order. Though he was obviously of unsound mind, there were no heirs to contest it. Harry's parents were dead. He had never married.

He left me his house, or "refuge," as he kept calling it in the will, fully furnished and paid for.

I had nowhere else to go. I moved in.

The future was clear enough. I was going to spend the rest of my life seeing lawyers or going to court, with maybe a few vacation stretches in jail. Career, respect, family, all down the toilet.

I almost couldn't bring myself to care anymore, but for the girls, Goneril ("Gonny") and Cordelia ("Cordie") — their pictures in my wallet — that's all I have left.

But action numbs pain. We keep busy, rushing frantically through life in an attempt to forget that we're dying. I set myself to work, first, with my rapidly diminishing funds, acquiring a junk station wagon from a newspaper ad — it ran, sort of, and I couldn't think as far ahead as inspection. Since my wife hadn't changed the locks on the doors, I managed a little raid while she was out and the girls were at school, huffing and puffing up and down stairs, carrying books, clothes, files, my computer, the trappings of a professional life I didn't ever expect to resume. I took them in order to surround myself with familiar things. Out of habit, I guess.

Lies. All Lies.

It's hard for me to remember the sequence of events sometimes. At the core of our existence lurks the indeterminate mystery, for which no words are adequate.

Angelica disappeared, either on, before, or after that night in the diner with Harry. Snap fingers. Gone. Hadn't been seen since — whenever. Since she made those phone calls. The police and I had several long, chilly conversations, which concluded nothing. A bit of nastiness.

I am getting ahead of myself now. Or behind. Not sure. I only remember a stone-gray January afternoon, snow whirling, parting before the windshield like curtains as I drove for hours across a hushed landscape, listening only to the sounds of the tires and the engine, my thoughts themselves, stone-gray and featureless. I followed the map Harry had left for me, feeling like a rat in a maze, directed by experimenters beyond my comprehension to some end I could never hope to guess.

At least there might be a bite of cheese when I got there.

Highway, exit, little road, country lane, gravel path. When I finally emerged from the long, tree-lined driveway it was like coming out of a tunnel. I let the car roll to a stop, axle deep in snow. The storm was worse now, the first serious blizzard Pennsylvania had seen in decades. Trees creaked and swayed in the wind.

And the house before me was dark, a huge, dilapidated pile of stone and wood, its architecture a mishmash of everything from Colonial Farmhouse to Haunted Victorian Gothic, overgrown with vines, many of the windows broken.

"*Velcome to my house*," I said aloud. "*Enter freely and of your own will. I am . . . Dracula.*"

I just sat there, leaning my head against the steering wheel, uncertain whether to laugh or cry, listening to the silence, as the evening darkened. Eventually I went inside, carrying only a single suitcase. The rest could wait for later.

Of course the electricity was out. But the phone was ringing. I groped for it, found the receiver, and made no reply as my wife Lorraine, furious, swore she would have me arrested, while in the background my younger daughter, Cordelia, screamed, "Daddy! Come home, Daddy!" her mother shut her up angrily, then went on for a while with her tirade, before I sighed and hung up. The phone went on ringing for several minutes again before she gave up.

So, how come the phone worked and the lights didn't? How had she known I was here? I guess it makes some sort of sense, but I never bothered to figure it out.

I flicked on the tiny flashlight on my keychain and started exploring. It was cold enough that I could see my own breath, inside. Before long I discovered the kitchen, and since I hadn't eaten all day, unthinkingly opened the refrigerator. Of course no light went on. There was nothing inside but dust, a bottle of extremely suspect milk, and a set of mechanical teeth.

When I picked up the teeth, I notice the index card under them. It was a note:

> Graham —
>   I knew you would understand. Eventually.
>   — Your friend.

It wasn't signed, but I had no doubt of its authorship. I crumpled up the card and threw it away, then wound up the mechanical teeth and left them chattering as I closed the refrigerator door.

So this was where Harry Crandall had lived. Hardly the lap of luxury.

I found some candles in a drawer in the kitchen and used one of them instead of the flashlight, drifting, I am sure, like a ghost from room to room, noting how many of the rooms were empty, how many more contained old, broken furniture or just boxes.

I started up the back stairs and almost tripped over something that gave me a genuine fright: a golf club, bent at about a forty-degree angle. I couldn't bring myself to touch it, and just kicked it down the stairs, into the all-encompassing darkness.

I explored the second floor, and the third, as night closed over the house. The wind howled outside. A branch cracked. Snow buffetted the roof with a dull thud.

Still I wandered, pretending I was an archaeologist here to reconstruct the lives long gone from tiny shards of evidence. No, just one life, that of Harry Crandall. But there was no trace of him here, no evidence that any place in the house had been recently "alive" in the sense that a kitchen, family room, or den is alive when you're there all the time, working, eating, watching TV, not always cleaning up after yourself. More than once I opened doors to cold blasts of air and found rooms where the windows were gone and snow lay plastered on the floor and furniture. Once, for a terrible instant, I thought I'd found a corpse frozen in a bed, but it was just a misshapen mattress and a trick of the light.

I wondered if Harry had ever lived here at all, or if this might be some kind of perverse and posthumous joke.

But then, up in the tower — for this was the sort of house that had a tower — I came upon what may have been a bedroom, for all there was no bed in it, only a few blankets thrown over a mattress on the floor, and several half-burned candles set in empty beer bottles. Newspaper lay scattered about, and there were a few books, all of them, I saw as I crouched down and examined them one by one by the light of my single candle, on morbid or even hideous subjects. *The Aesthetics of Putrefaction* by Jeffrey Quilt. *A History of Torture* by Daniel Mannix. A Dover reprint of *Regnum Congo*, with its famous pictures of the cannibal butcher shop. And several about Nazis, one large photographic volume still open on the mattress, filled with skeletal, almost rubbery-looking bodies from Auschwitz. Next to that, *Jack the Ripper from A to Z.*

No, there were no books. It was only in a dream that I found them in Harry's room and dumped them into a cardboard box in the hall, then lit several of his candles and chanced to look up and see manacles — or maybe handcuffs — dangling overhead.

That *must* have been part of the dream — the mind lying to itself — for I surely would never have slept in such a room, huddling on Harry's mattress with my winter coat and gloves on, curled up in an almost fetal position beneath his blankets, staring at a candle burning down into one of the beer bottles. The flame flickered in a sudden draught, then went out. I shivered in the dark and even considered the possibility of freezing to death, but there was no place else for me to go. To sleep, perchance to dream. Aye, there's the rub. The dream began, or had already begun long before I was aware of it; and I lay there, in what could well have been my grave, listening to the wind, to the trees creaking outside, to the house itself shifting and groaning and speaking to itself in a myriad of subtle voices, whispering, *Look, look who's here. It's old Harry's friend.*

And after a while there was a new noise, inside the house, like mice scampering at first, then something louder. Footsteps, a man's heavy shoes clomping slowly from room to room. Doors opening. The sound of the wind changed whenever he opened the door to a room where the windows were broken out, and the cold and snow rushed into the body of the house, a new, whistling voice added to the chorus.

The voices. Harry's, droning on and on about lies, monstrous lies so enormous you were unable to deny them; and another, echoing everything he said, repeating, shifting, twisting his words around, growing ever more shrill, a woman's voice, distinct in its screaming obscenities intended, not for Harry, but for me: *"You think I'm going to let you off the hook, fuck face? Never! Never! Never!"* It was Angelica all right, faithless, blackmailing, mysteriously missing Angelica.

The heavy footsteps followed her soft, light ones, the other chasing her up the stairs, to the second floor, then the third. I sat on the mattress, in my dream, in absolute darkness, my knees drawn up to my chin, blankets wrapped around me, listening, merely puzzled by the realization that she seemed to be barefoot, in this weather.

"I know where you are, fuck-face — "

Then her voice was suddenly muffled, as if she'd been gagged, and silence followed.

A minute or so later, Harry came into the room and crouched down beside the mattress. I couldn't see him, of course. But I didn't have to, any more than I had to say, "But you're dead," or he had to reply, "That's only another lie." We were beyond all that now.

He snapped his fingers and the tip of his index finger sparked into flame. He used it to light a candle, then made a fist, and there was only the candle, flickering in the draught.

He didn't say anything at all.

I watched by uncertain candlelight as he unwrapped the dirty gauze on his left hand, and I saw that in the middle of his palm was not the bloody, oozing wound I expected, but something far worse, a living mouth, alive in its own right, the full lips slightly parted, the tongue wandering over the teeth lasciviously.

"Hello, Professor."

I swallowed hard and said, "Hello Angelica."

"I bet you thought you were rid of me once and for all."

"Why . . . do you say that."

"Because I am the truth and the way and the light, to coin a phrase, Professor. You can't cut the truth out and throw it away, no matter how hard you try. I'm still here."

"Harry? What is this? Harry? Stop this, please."

"He can't hear you, fuck-face. Harry's dead."

"What do you *want*? Haven't you done *enough*?"

"No, I have not. I want you to stop lying, just for once."

"I . . . can't."

"Then you'll have to come and see the truth if you won't say it."

Harry's hand closed over my wrist. He pulled me to my feet, patiently but firmly, and we two walked in silence down the front stairs, out of the tower, to the third floor, then the second, where we crossed the breadth of the house. He paused once before a room, as if remembering something, but I could neither see nor remember anything. I only heard the muted voices of the wind and the branches and the house's timbers and the light rattle of the vines against the windows. Harry's hand was cold and dry and hard, like a thing of wood.

It was because this was all a dream, because this really wasn't happening, that I didn't struggle at all as we made our way down the basement stairs; nor did I find the golf club once more, inexplicably in my hands; and it was never necessary for me to swing it frantically until it connected with something which *yielded* to the blow, as if I'd cracked a hard shell and driven the head into something soft and pulpy. No, it was all a dream. Remember? I didn't stumble the rest of the way down the stairs, nearly breaking my neck, the golf club banging against steps and walls.

None of that happened.

And I most definitely did *not* hear Angelica's voice calling me gently, seductively out of the further darkness, from what I somehow knew was an older, dirt-floored cellar room beyond a worm-eaten door. That room was in the oldest part of the house, late 17th century, before the later architectural encrustations, the hidden, secret heart of this place, the core; filled with ghosts, so the story went, of people who'd died in the winter and been buried there because the ground was frozen outside. But those were just old stories and lies and it was all a dream anyway.

Angelica wasn't calling me.

Not when I awoke, disoriented and frightened, unable to explain even to myself how I had come to be lying at the bottom of the basement steps with the golf club — now bent almost in half — still in my hand. I threw it away in disgust, concluded misadventure, and hurried back up. From behind me, a frigid draught blew, smelling of earth.

Upstairs, through the snow-plastered windows, I saw that it was dawn. I was exhausted, cold, hungry, but somehow it seemed appropriate to stay awake and active, to avoid going to sleep again, lest the dream resume. I busied myself unloading my goods from the car, wading knee-deep in snow.

The phone rang. I ignored it.

I couldn't use the computer without power, of course, so I sat down at the kitchen table by candlelight, shivering in coat and scarf and hat, a blanket in my lap, fumbling to manipulate a ballpoint pen through heavy gloves, and I wrote, like some impoverished scholarly character in a 19th century novel, this lurid fabulation which purports to explain — but actually obscures — my circumstances; an imaginative exercise recounting a bizarre dream *which began well before the story does*, well before that strikingly well-wrought scene with Harry Crandall in the diner, a scene which, I just now confess, never happened in real life at all, but which I mischievously interpolated into the text.

So I am only dreaming that I am writing this, and the text only exists within a dream.

For I am that bugaboo of modern literary criticism, that theoretical impossibility, the unreliable narrator, whose recursive ravings make no sense at all, folding back on themselves to create a series of irresolvable paradoxes.

I am lying. Everything I say is by definition false, including this definition. Lies. If I tell enough of them, I can escape pain, responsibility. I can fade into that comforting gray fog of uncertainty.

The phone's ringing.

God, my hand hurts. Maybe I burned it on one of the candles.

Someone pounds on the window, someone else at the door. Many people now, more cars pulling up, lights flashing, whirling.

A fist hammers the door.

"*Open up, Mister Wentworth. This is the police.*"

Angelica, did you make just one more phone call I didn't know about, in my dream? Did you tell them where — ?

Glass shatters. A hand reaches in.

No, no. All wrong. My story doesn't end that way. Here, let me make up a better ending.

Amid the noise and confusion, I rise calmly from the kitchen table, leaving blanket and manuscript behind, and go down into the basement, into that earthen-floored room beyond the rotting wooden door (which hangs open). High up the wall, just enough light trickles in through a tiny window to reveal a heap of dirt, a shovel, and Angelica, *sitting up in her half-finished grave*, naked, her face a bloody horror where her head was smashed in with the golf club.

"Hello there, Professor, dear love," she says. "I always knew we'd get back together again in the end, somehow. Give me a kiss."

"Shut up!" I scream. "Shut up, bitch. Shut up!" I gag her with my right hand, wrestling with the corpse, and my hand is burning as if acid has been poured into it. I tear my glove off, and can only gape in nauseous horror at the *mouth* which opens in the flesh of my hand, speaking with Angelica's voice, cataloging all my sins.

The booted policemen come clumping down the basement stairs and they find me like that, in a necrophilic embrace with a naked, frozen corpse, staring with some unbreakable fascination at my own right hand.

That's a pretty good ending, but it's as fictional as any other. I never knew anyone named Harry Crandall. I didn't kill Angelica with the golf club. I've told so many monstrous lies that you wouldn't be able to believe me if I admitted that I did.

I dreamed of her just one more time. She was there, with me in the intimate darkness, her whole head a bloody lump, and where her face used to be, a huge, outstretched hand, the reddened fingers waving gently like the tentacles of a sea anemone; and there, in the middle of the palm, the liar's mouth, whispering slanders, impossibilities, horrors.

I reached up to silence her, and the mouth came away into my hand. For an instant I held it in my cupped hand, like a butterfly resting there. Then it fused into my flesh.

I have to get rid of it. Here's how. I shall tie my forearm off, like so, to prevent myself from bleeding to death afterward. Of course we are not in Bucks County at all — that was all a story I made up — but on the Main Line, in Wayne, in front of Marcello's Diner. What I intend to do is merely toddle over to the train station, lie down by the tracks with my wrist on the rail, and when the next train comes by, well, there will be some pain, but then I'll be free, and I won't have to tell lies anymore.

SHATTERED SILVER

James Kisner

Ginger:

She floated across the small screen, her body flowing into the movements of her partner. The music swelled, and they danced like two angels in a celestial embrace. Strands of feathers fluttered from her dress, swirling through the dream-like haze, drifting to the floor and seeming to disappear.

The twelve-year-old boy was entranced.

He lay in bed watching the black-and-white images on the 21" screen, not only seeing but feeling the movie, tuning into the 1935 ambiance the film represented, as if it were his own era.

The boy smiled as the dance ended, and Fred Astaire offered a breathless Ginger Rogers a cigarette.

The boy didn't belong in 1959; he belonged *there*, in the simple past when all the people were beautiful, and they sang and danced and made jokes and had a good time in magnificent settings. Everything was so pure back then. No one smelled bad. No one ate too much. No one belched or farted.

He had the sound turned down low, so he wouldn't waken anyone. He wasn't supposed to be watching television. He was supposed to be sleeping. But he couldn't miss an Astaire-Rogers movie. Not ever. No matter what the consequences. Their world was so wonderful, so different from his own, where he had to sleep in a room that was supposed to be a dining room and apprehensively watch TV in the middle of the night to escape the realities of his day.

"I told you to go to sleep tonight, Billy," his father's voice boomed, shattering the boy's mood.

"I had to see it."

His father stood in the doorway to his bedroom, which adjoined Billy's room with no hallway separating them. He wore only a T-shirt and briefs, and his black hair was mussed. He didn't seem angry or surprised.

He rubbed his eyes and glanced at the television. Its screen provided the only light in the room making his father appear black-and-white as well.

"*Top Hat*," he said.

Billy nodded, trembling. Usually, his father would go over and shut the TV off without saying a word, then stumble back to bed, grumbling about his son's tendency to stay up too late watching old movies.

"You've seen that a dozen times."

"I . . . I like it."

His father sat in a chair in the corner. He took a cigarette from the pack of *Old Golds* on the end table and lit it. "Turn the sound up."

Billy could barely conceal his glee. He was going to get to watch the movie — and his father was going to watch it with him! He scrambled down to the end of the bed and reached over to the TV, which sat atop his dresser, and kicked the volume up. Irving Berlin's music filled the room.

His father said nothing further for a while. He just sat and watched the movie with Billy, smoking cigarettes, his dark gray eyes seeming to reflect the same wonder Billy's eyes held. Every now and then he would turn his head and gaze at his son, then shift his attention back to the movie quickly. He was pondering something apparently, getting ready to make a statement.

Billy tried not to notice. He was too happy to care. He wondered if somehow his father understood why he *had* to see these movies.

Ginger and Fred whirled across a vast terrace in a fairytale set that was supposed to be Venice

"I know what you're thinking," Billy's father said at last.

"What?" Billy answered, annoyed. He loved this number. Interrupting it was almost criminal.

"You're thinking just what I thought when I saw this movie when I was a kid your age."

Billy turned and stared at his father expectantly. Did his father possess a sensibility he never guessed existed? Had *he* once been entranced by the fantasy of it?

"You're thinking," his father said, pointing at the television, "about what it would be like to get in *her* pants. I know you're old enough to think about girls that way, so don't tell me it ain't so."

A shock ran up Billy's spine; it was as if his father had told him there was no Santa Claus and no God in the same breath and that the world was going to end tomorrow.

"We all used to go down to the Welles Theater and watch Ginger dance on the big screen. And then afterwards, we'd talk about what a nice little box she must have. That's what you're thinking. How you'd like to get into that box."

Billy shook his head

"I'm sure it's a pretty one, even now, after twenty-five years. I sure wouldn't mind a taste of it."

Billy started to tremble. He didn't know what to say.

"Turn that off and go to sleep as soon as it's over," his father said, yawning and standing from the chair. "But this is the last time I'm letting you stay up. A boy your age needs sleep to grow." He shuffled back to his bedroom, shutting the door behind him.

Billy could barely watch the rest of the movie. His mind had been turned inside-out. He couldn't believe what his father had said. It was the cruelest revelation Billy would ever face in his life.

Ginger Rogers had a box?

The first one:

The Indianapolis police detectives were sickened by the mess in the woman's room. The naked victim, a pretty young woman with striking features, had been killed, gutted, and, as the coroner would tell them later, raped repeatedly. Everything below her breasts and above her knees was a tangle of glistening, bloody gore. It was the work of a savage killer.

"Jesus H. Christ," one of the detectives remarked, gagging.

When the photographers were finished, the body was lifted from the bed and they found a picture lying there.

The big gray-haired detective, John Stone, picked the picture up by the corner to avoid smudging possible fingerprints. It was a Polaroid of a naked woman who resembled an old movie star, one whose face he recognized, but whose name he didn't recall. It looked strange, as if it had been copied from a book. He turned the photo over and there was writing on the back.

"Joan," was all it said.

Joan:

Billy browsed through the used bookstore, looking for goodies. His mind was a maze of flickering images unable to focus on anything, unable to remember exactly what he was searching for.

He saw a battered paperback of *The American Way of Death*, and he suddenly remembered the day his father died, the year before. At that time he'd had to become a man on his own, thrust into the hostile universe which humanity tenanted only by the tolerance of a benign but careless creator. At thirty-six, Billy still hadn't been ready for the world. He was undereducated, too frail for physical labor, and barely able to interact with people. He also felt he was ugly, though that was not entirely true. His face was merely plain.

But he had gone through the motions, found a job, set up his life in proper order. The job had been given to him out of pity, but he didn't care. He would need the money to keep up the house his father had left him. The insurance money took care of the mortgage, but it hadn't left much for him to maintain the crumbling old house, where in the past few years, only he and his father had lived. His stepmother had died a decade before the old man.

One good thing had come from his father's death; he could now do whatever he wanted, whenever he wanted. So he had taken up where he had left off some twenty years ago, beginning to collect again. Which was why, he recalled at last, he was in the used bookstore.

He pushed the image of his father's death from his mind and concentrated on his browsing. He came to the section he was looking for. He ran his fingers over the tops of the books, scattering the layer of dust as he searched through the old movie books. One of them had an intriguing title: *Hollywood Babylon*. The book seemed to jump into his hands.

He flipped it open randomly and saw a black-and-white picture of a nude woman with a dark black tuft of hair between her legs. She leered at the camera. Her hair was bobbed and curled, and her eyes were familiar. He skipped to the next page and read, "Overleaf: frame blow-up from one of Joan Crawford's alleged porno movies."

He shuddered with excitement. He went through more pages, saw more jarring images of movie stars. It was a wonderful book! He tucked it under his arm and hurried to the cashier to pay for it, before someone took it away from him. Outside, he jumped in the '68 Buick, his other inheritance from his father, and drove home quickly.

That night he went through the book page by page, staring at the lurid, revealing photographs, not bothering to read the text. He didn't stop until four o'clock in the morning. He would have finished sooner, but he had to pause repeatedly to take pictures.

He didn't have to worry about his father interrupting him now.

The second one:

"She was a church-going woman," the landlady said. "She never had any men up to her room."

"She didn't date at all?" John Stone asked skeptically, jotting something down in his notebook.

"If she did, it had to be someone at church," the old woman said with conviction. "There *never* was a man in her room."

John thanked the woman and turned away to his partner as she shut the door. "She sure had someone in her room last night," John told him. "Just like that case from last year. You remember that, don't you?"

"Jesus, how could I forget? But this was worse. You think it's the same guy?"

Stone nodded. "And he left a picture under this one too." He took a photo from his pocket and studied it. It showed a platinum blonde standing in the woods, dressed in a see-through garment that accentuated her breasts and pubic hair. This was also a Polaroid taken from a book or magazine. On the back it was identified as "Jean." Dried blood marked the photo's bottom left corner.

"Jean Harlow," Stone said, finally recognizing the face.

"I don't understand."

"Christ," the big detective said. "The murdered woman — she looked like Jean Harlow — sort of."

"And the one from last year?"

"Joan Crawford," Stone recalled. "That was the connection we couldn't find last time. If we compare that photo with her face, I'll bet we'll see a resemblance."

"We don't have any other clues," his partner said. "No prints. No trail of blood. Nothing incriminating left behind. How does that photograph help us?"

"I don't have any goddamn idea."

Jean:

By the time he was fourteen, Billy had collected a stack of *Playboy* magazines, some nudist colony books and some lesser-known men's magazines in which the women weren't particularly pretty but rather sexy in a crude way. *Playboy* was running a series on "The History of Sex in the Cinema," which fascinated him. He was sure he had all the issues with the series articles now.

Late at night when he was sure his father and his stepmother were asleep, he would get the magazines out from his secret hiding place at the back of the closet and page through them with one hand, fondling himself with the other.

His greatest arousal came from the pictures of nude movie stars which some archivist had unearthed and which were now being reprinted. He especially loved the candid nude shot of Jean Harlow, which he clipped out and put in his secret envelope.

He didn't care for the pictures of current movie actresses, though. They were all whores anyhow. *Anyone* could see them half-naked in their movies.

He had learned a lot about old movie stars since his father told him about Ginger Rogers. That knowledge had stung at first, but now he reveled in it.

Then he had found his father's secret cache of eight-pagers: the underground comics of the 30's and 40's in which movie stars were depicted in various sexual acts. The comic strips somehow made the concept his father had whispered more real. He had covertly taken his father's comics and traced certain sections of them, finding in this act a kind of fulfillment.

One night, Billy fell asleep while loving his magazines, and his father found him the next morning, sprawled face-down in a mass of clippings.

His father was very angry. "Billy, you're not old enough for this trash."

"It's not trash," Billy said defiantly. "It's my collection."

"Pictures of naked women ain't a collection. It's dirty."

"No, it's not!"

His father grunted and started gathering up the magazines, pushing them off into the box Billy kept them in.

"What are you doing?"

"Getting rid of this trash."

"No!" Billy, who was slight and timid, nevertheless jumped on his father, trying to stop him. His father swatted him away.

"I'm burning this shit right now!"

"NO!" Billy screamed, tasting blood. His lip was split.

The old man carried the box away. As soon as he closed the door, Billy rushed to the bed and gathered up the clippings his father had overlooked and stuffed them in the secret envelope. He hid the envelope behind the dresser.

A few minutes later, his father returned.

"Where's the rest of it?"

"That's all there is."

"You're lying. There were some cut-out pictures on the bed."

"I'm not."

"You little shit." His father beat him for the next twenty minutes, but Billy wouldn't tell.

After his father left the room, Billy threw himself on the bed and sobbed. He realized now that he had been betrayed by the old movie stars. They were whores just like the new ones: they got him into trouble.

He took his clippings from their hiding place and pounded them with his pocket knife, shredding them beyond recognition. He missed once, nicked himself with the blade and blood dripped on the mangled paper.

Billy stared at the blood a long time.

The third one:

Two years had passed. Detective John Stone had given up trying to solve the "movie-star lookalike murders" as he called them in his mind. There had been only two, both frustrating cases. How could a man who killed so recklessly leave behind no clues at all?

Perhaps the murderer had moved on to another place. Or something had happened to him. Stone hoped.

Then he was called out to a house on the east side. A woman with olive skin lay mutilated in her own living room. They had to use her driver's license to piece together what she looked like, because her head was missing. The license identified her as Carla Ramirez. She was a Hispanic woman with beautiful features that could not be diminished, even by the license bureau's camera.

Underneath her was a Polaroid photo of Carmen Miranda, dancing with Cesar Romero. The camera had caught Carmen with her skirt bellowing out, showing everything underneath. But there was nothing under there but Carmen herself.

Stone stared at the dark pubic hair so obviously displayed. It made him feel strange to see this on an older movie star. It wasn't quite right. It undermined the fantasy of the classic movies of the silver screen.

Then, suddenly, he realized what the photos meant.

The killer was saying the same thing, only in a sick and twisted way. He couldn't face the reality of the old movie stars being as sexual or as real as anyone else. The killer wanted to hold on to his dreams by destroying what represented the contradiction of those dreams.

Quite an insight, Stone reflected, knowing instinctively it was true. But understanding a killer didn't stop him. He might not kill again for years. Or he might kill again tomorrow night.

This would be another tough case to crack. As before, there were no prints anywhere and no clues left behind, not even a hair from the killer's head. Without even checking, Stone knew the photo would be clean too. All the others had been. It would all end up in the file of unsolved cases, another frustration to gnaw at the detective's mind for years to come.

Stone wondered what the murderer had done with the head and the other parts he had taken from the previous two victims.

Carmen:

Billy was ecstatic. He had found a new book, *Hollywood Babylon II*. It cost a lot of money but it was loaded with pictures that spoke to his obsession, even better ones than he had found in the first *Babylon* book. One showed Carmen Miranda's box. He stared at it a long time, letting the reality of it sink slowly into his mind.

Carmen Miranda's pubic hair. He was seeing it for real.

He got out his Polaroid camera and made several copies of the picture. He stuffed one in his pocket and headed off to work.

Others:

Detective Stone studied the special file he had created, as he often did during idle moments. Five women, all of whom vaguely resembled movie stars of the past, all savagely raped and murdered. Each murder more violent than the previous one. The latest one, six months ago, had been completely dismembered. As in every other case, parts of her had been missing.

She had resembled Hedy Lamarr.

What really bothered Stone was that he couldn't think of a way to even warn potential victims. What would he say to them — if you resemble an old movie star you're a target? All these women were too young to even know about the old movie stars they seemed to represent to the killer.

There was yet another bothersome aspect of the killings. The resemblance wasn't always that close. The killer's imagination made the woman look like the stars he thought they were.

Stone sighed. If only there were a pattern. But the killings were spaced at very odd intervals. He had checked into every possibility for when they occurred, including astrology.

But there was no connection. The time of year varied, the weather varied, and whether the moon was full or not made no difference to this guy.

A psychologist had told Stone that the killer was obsessed, as if that explained everything.

Stone was obsessed too. He wanted the kinky bastard in a bad way.

Another Joan:

Billy felt restless after his work shift and went down to the all-night adult bookstore on Shadeland. Here he had bought many things over the years since it opened, including a videotape which purported to show movie stars in porno movies, but which he thought was faked, and various rubber goods that he used regularly on himself. Most of all, he bought magazines.

One of them was called *Celebrity Skin*. At first it had printed only photographs of current movie stars, but then it started a feature about stars from the past. He thumbed through the current issue and found two pictures of Joan Blondell in the nude. She was so beautiful.

He bought the magazine and got in his car to drive home. As he drove, he reflected on the stark reality of women. A tear came to his eye as the picture of Joan Blondell flashed into his mind. She was just like the others, and he hadn't expected that of her, of all people.

Her smile was pretty, though.

He remembered the last time he had tried to pick up a woman for a regular date. It turned out badly as it always did. Ordinary everyday women were turned off by him, and he was turned off by them. He wondered why he made the effort, especially since he could manufacture movies in his mind that came out the way he wanted them and featured movie stars of his own choosing. Maybe he tried because of the intermittent guilt that rose in him occasionally, or the feeling he sometimes had that his stern father watched him from beyond the grave.

His father would say his indulgences were not right.

He pulled up in front of the house and walked up to the front door, unlocked it and entered. It was dark in the house, but as soon as he switched on a light, he felt perfectly safe. He liked being alone here.

Before settling down to enjoy the magazine, he got some ice cream from the deep-freeze. He almost opened the box that had the head in it by mistake and laughed to himself. Someday he would figure out what to do with that thing. He never realized the head wouldn't stay the same, even if frozen. It no longer looked like Carmen Miranda at all.

The other parts he had collected hadn't preserved well, either. He couldn't even play with them anymore. He would have to dispose of them eventually, he supposed. Maybe he would throw them in the White River.

At least the books and magazines were substantial. And he could make as many copies of them as he wished.

One too many:

The smell of blood in the room was so fresh. Stone was certain the killer couldn't be very far away. A neighbor had called in to report the screams, and Stone had been close to the house when the dispatcher radioed his car. He sent out his men immediately to search the area.

As usual, several parts of the woman were missing; the killer had to be carrying them in something big.

This was the first time he had any hope.

He lifted the body and found the photograph he expected. Another Joan. Joan Blondell, the perky, wise-cracking femme who always played second lead to the real star. Her naked breasts were big and full — just like the breasts of the corpse on the floor.

Stone had learned a lot about the old movies since the first case. He had bought books on the history of films and stayed up late to see the old movies on television. He thought if he knew more about old movies, he'd have a better chance at nailing the killer. Stone didn't know if his understanding had increased that much, but he had certainly learned to enjoy the older movies.

As long as he didn't think about the reality of the people in them.

Billy ducked in the alley as the squad car played its spotlight along the street. When he hurried into the shadows, he almost dropped the bowling bag stuffed with pieces of flesh he was carrying. He wished now he hadn't parked so far away.

But they couldn't find him if he was careful. They couldn't stop him. He had confidence in himself. He wasn't an ordinary man, now. He was Robert Montgomery successfully eluding the fumbling police, who were no doubt led by Jimmy Gleason or Donald MacBride. They never caught anybody unless they had the help of a private eye, and there were no detectives around.

After the car continued down the street, Billy reluctantly deposited the bag between two trash cans and walked out of the alley. Despite the danger of discovery, he kept his scalpel and the knife with him, keeping them tucked in his belt under the jacket he wore. He couldn't give them up.

He hated to leave his souvenirs behind — he wanted them for his collection — but he knew the policemen would not let him live his life the way he wanted if they caught him. They would be much more forbidding than his father had ever been.

He whistled warily in the darkness, until he finally came upon his car. He opened the door, got in and drove away into the night.

He felt unsatisfied at a deep level, though, and he hated returning home empty-handed. It spoiled the evening and made all his searching of the past few weeks mean nothing. He had never felt so frustrated.

On impulse, he turned at the next corner and walked up the street where he stopped at an all-night restaurant.

He found himself inordinately hungry, ordered a big meal and ate it slowly, while watching the women coming and going. Most of them had escorts. Or they were ugly. None of them really looked like Joan

Blondell. Nor did any of them fit the scenario in his mind, the movie he played so often — a movie just like one from the thirties, with wise-cracking dames and even wittier men and funky old music with lots of saxophones in it.

Only the female stars in this movie were all naked.

He often played movies in his mind. They could go on and on trapped inside his head. They all ended the same way: with the death of the female star, but he could never imagine that part very well. He had to act out the ending on his own, and then it became very real for him.

The waitress, a plumpish woman of about thirty-five, leaned over to refill his coffee, and he couldn't help seeing deep into her cleavage.

"Thank you, Joan," Billy said, really noticing her for the first time. Now, he was not clumsy Billy, with no ability whatsoever with the women; he was Clark Gable, whom no woman could turn down.

"My name ain't Joan, honey."

"I'm sorry," Billy hastened to say.

"It's Sheila."

"You just reminded me of a movie star named Joan, that's all."

Sheila flashed him a suspicious look. "Are you shitting me? A movie star? I ain't heard that come-on in years."

"Sorry. Forget it." He sipped the steaming coffee. "But it's true. I know all about movie stars, and I wouldn't say that if I didn't mean it."

"Don't . . ."

"You *know* you're built like one."

Sheila blushed. "Let me know if you need anything else," she said and hurried away.

Billy smiled. He restarted the movie in his mind, putting in a character named Sheila, a perky, wise-cracking dame played by Joan Blondell.

✦   ✦

"What do you mean you lost him?"

"We didn't lose him. We just couldn't find anyone, Sergeant Stone."

"Christ, he would have to be slippery too. Why the hell don't I get a break?" Stone sat on the edge of the bed, cursed and lit a cigarette. "All these years and not one goddamn clue or lead I can use."

A uniformed officer rushed into the room. "Hey, we found something in an alley. A bowling bag."

"So what?"

"Wait until you see what's in it."

Stone put the bag on the floor between his legs and unzipped it. Bingo! Various body parts lay in a bloody heap inside. He zipped it shut immediately, just barely managing to control a gag impulse.

"Hot damn! Get this down to the lab. It's got to be covered with the guy's prints." He looked heavenward. "Thank you, God."

"I don't think I ever heard of Joan Blondell," Sheila said, as Billy helped her off with her coat.

"She was an actress back in the 1930's," Billy explained. "A very pretty one who always made jokes and . . . well, she was very special. If you saw any of her old movies, you'd see what I mean."

Billy was playing this one very carefully. As soon as he removed Sheila's coat and draped it across the chair, it seemed the world became black-and-white in his eyes. Sheila turned and became Joan Blondell. Billy became William Powell and was suddenly as glib and debonair as the actor. He liked being William Powell even better than Clark Gable.

The film unreeling in his head was beginning. There was a Warner Brothers logo and their fanfare music, then the title zoomed into focus near the center of the screen.

It was a murder mystery with a twist, directed by Mervyn Leroy.

"You look very pretty tonight, Sheila," Billy said. He sat down in the nearest chair and eyed her lovingly.

"No, I don't," Sheila protested coyly. "I'm all hot and sweaty, and I smell like grease from the restaurant."

"Not to me, you don't. You smell like lavender. You smell like life. You're a very attractive woman. I can't help saying that."

"You got a hell of a line, all right," Sheila said, touching him lightly on the face. "It ain't bad, though. Would you like a beer, honey?"

Billy heard: *"Would you like a cocktail, darling?"*

"Certainly, my dear."

Sheila laughed, showing bright white teeth. Even in black-and-white, he could see that her eyes were bright blue and her hair naturally blonde. "No one ever called me 'dear.' You're a real character, ain't you?"

"We're all characters in the drama of life."

The twist would startle the audience . . .

Sheila brought him a cold Budweiser and set it on the table next to his chair. "I'll be back in a minute, 'dear.' I want to freshen up."

Billy heard: *"Do you mind if I slip into something more comfortable?"*

"Don't keep me waiting too long," he replied. After she left, he stroked his non-existent mustache, then sipped his beer and waited.

Detective Stone was driving home for the night . . . feeling good. Finding that bag would crack the case; he was certain of that. It had to. He'd catch the sick bastard and make sure he'd get the death penalty, one way or another.

Secretly, he wished he could catch the mother in the act. Then he could just blow him away and not have to agonize through a trial that might result in the killer landing in the nuthouse for a couple years — or, even worse, might let him go free.

He could see the guy's head exploding when he pumped a couple shots from his Magnum into it. He'd be a worse mess than any of his victims.

Stone would also take great pleasure in blowing the guy's balls off.

Saxophone-laced jazz swelled in the background. He held Sheila close, dancing with her slowly. She smelled fresh from the bath and wore only a robe. The press of her fabulously firm breasts was arousing him already.

And Sheila could feel the press of his arousal.

"You're a fast one, ain't you?" Sheila said in his ear.

Billy heard: *"Is that a pickle in your pocket, or are you just glad to see me?"*

"Don't worry, my dear. I will take my time."

... The twist was that William Powell wasn't the hero in this movie; he was the villain.

Audiences would be shocked.

Stone called the station from his house. He was right. The bowling bag was covered with prints. They'd run them through the computers, and send them off to the FBI, the CIA, and every other acronym they could think of. The guy had to have a record somewhere.

Stone crawled into bed, cuddling close to his wife, luxuriating in the warmth of her body. He slept soundly.

The first time she helped him. The second time, it was rape. The third time, after he showed her the Polaroids, it was forcible entry.

Then he reached for the knife and scalpel he had tucked away under the pillow next to her head.

He had to hurry. Any minute, Warren William — as Perry Mason — might burst through the door and catch him in the act. The cops were fools, but the private dicks always caught the criminals.

But he knew even Perry Mason couldn't catch him. Not until the final reel. And Billy's film never came to a final reel.

Suddenly, as he dragged the knife across Sheila's throat, the world became Technicolor.

After he finished, he walked calmly into the bathroom and took a shower, scrubbing off the blood as he always did. He hummed as he washed, feeling very satisfied now. The evening wasn't a waste after all.

Later, he went home with his souvenirs in a white plastic trash bag.

The Penultimate Reel:

Detective Stone couldn't believe it. The killer had struck twice in one night and slipped away both times.

Stone was sick at heart about the second one, because he felt somehow responsible. He cursed his men's inefficiency, but mostly he cursed himself.

But at least he had the bastard's fingerprints now.

Later, he discovered the prints were on file nowhere. The killer hadn't been in the service. He hadn't registered a gun. He hadn't ever been arrested.

It was almost as if he did not exist.

Stone pounded the top of his desk furiously. Then he sobbed quietly, his arms hiding his face. Something deep inside him revealed the stark truth of the matter: he would never catch the man.

How could you catch someone who didn't exist?

The Final Reel:

Billy squinted through the square hole at the giant black-and-white images shifting on the theater screen. He glanced at the other projector, making sure it was ready for the changeover. He sat back on his stool, and casually scraped brown-red dirt from underneath his fingernails with the scalpel he always carried in his shirt pocket.

He loved his job. Being a projectionist in the city's only revival theater didn't pay much, but he did get to see all his favorite stars on the big screen, larger than life, as they were supposed to be seen. He had been working there for years, and the magic never wore thin, renewed every night when he threaded the projectors.

Tonight the theater was showing *42nd Street* with Warner Baxter, Dick Powell, Ruby Keeler, and a very young Ginger Rogers. It was one of his all-time favorites. He could barely resist caressing the film as it ran through the projector, as if he could somehow touch the life buried in the frames on the celluloid and be revitalized by it.

After the last showing that evening, he stood in the alley next to the theater. He leaned against the building, as Warner Baxter had at the end of the movie, watching and listening as the people filed out of the theater. He scanned the faces of the women closely, searching for the stars of the movie.

Ruby Keeler, Ginger Rogers, Una Merkel.

Then the world became black-and-white, and he remembered what his father had revealed to him.

Ginger Rogers had a box.

He sighed as he stood in the shadows watching the parade of women passing by.

Ginger Rogers. Joan Crawford. Jean Harlow. Hedy Lamarr. Ann Sheridan. Joan Blondell. Gloria Stuart. Carmen Miranda. Alice Faye. Myrna Loy. Claudette Colbert. Greta Garbo.

Their silvery images danced in his mind, their skirts hiked up, displaying what lay underneath.

They all had boxes.

He was going to get into them, one by one. Because he loved them. And no one would ever stop him.

The final reel was his alone to play out.

YSEX

Steven Spruill

"Are you the detective who was in charge of the Hangman investigation?"

"Yes." Detective Sergeant Sharon McKenna chose not to quarrel with the word "was." But she felt the familiar simmering anger, the sour ache in her stomach. She put the phone in the crook of her neck and shook out two quelacid tablets. "Who's calling, please?" Chewing the tablets, grimacing at the chalky taste.

"Oh, I'm sorry. Are you eating lunch?" His voice was low and hoarse, as though he wanted to disguise it.

"Please identify yourself, sir."

"I'm . . . I'm . . . ? It doesn't matter."

She heard confusion in his voice. Didn't he know? "Do you have information?" she asked.

"I can tell you that I've started again."

She felt a stab in her stomach. The room contracted around her. She nudged her desk against the back of Gabe's, sending his top middle drawer into his stomach. Without looking up from his reports, he picked up the extension. McKenna felt a pain in her jaws and realized she was clenching her teeth. She drew a calming breath. The case was dead, no new leads for almost a year. Probably just a confessor — nothing to get excited about.

"Are you listening?" the voice on the phone growled.

"Yes."

"Good. If you go to sub-level ten, northeast octant, you'll find her hanging from a service pipe just like all the others."

Gabe looked up at her now; he winced and she realized how her face must look. "Wouldn't you like to tell me who you are?"

"Yes. But I can't."

"Why can't you? I'd really like to know. So would lots of other people. You could be famous." Carefully, keeping the disgust and anger from her voice.

"Do you think so, Detective McKenna?"

Son of a he-dog! "Of course."

"Maybe I will. When I've had my fill. This last one was the best. I'll give you a clue, Detective; I vidded it. I vidded them all. That way I can enjoy them over and over."

McKenna could not trust herself to speak. Chances are the man was just a wanna-be, but he disgusted her all the same.

"Goodbye, Detective." The line went dead.

She replaced the receiver gently, aware of Gabe's gaze on her. "Pay phone," Gabe said. "One-fiftieth, southeast octant. He'll be long gone. I've radioed some blues to it. They can interview people around the phone, maybe get a description. Or should I hold them up until we've checked?"

"No, let'em do it. Let's go."

Gabe grabbed his red skullcap and followed her out the door. She was conscious of his silence as they caught the emergency pedline to the drop shaft. He took the serial killings personally too, she knew: the Hangman, and the other bastard before him — the Cross Killer. But he didn't hate it as much as she did, he *couldn't*.

Her eye recorded a couple of kids poaching the emergency line ahead, unaware of the cops behind them. Gabe squeezed the siren on his belt, two whoops, and the kids dived off, bolting like scared deer. A foodorama whipped by, brilliant yellow marquees blurring together. The smell of pizza and hot pretzels spiked up McKenna's nose. Her stomach reacted with a queasy lurch. *I'm too young for an ulcer*, she told herself determinedly.

All I really need is to catch the Hangman.

And the Cross Killer.

McKenna realized she was grinding her teeth. Two serial killers, still free. They had stopped, that was the most important thing. But

God how she wanted to catch them, close the files that mocked her day after day.

Why did they stop? That was the question.

McKenna saw that they were almost to the northeast dropshaft. Gabe had already grabbed the exitstrap. She snagged another and lifted her feet until the strap had curved off the line and coasted to a stop at the end of its rail. "Police," she said, pushing through a crowd waiting for the drop, trying to ignore the resulting angry mutters. The door opened. About twenty people were already inside. "Sorry, folks. Police emergency. Everybody out."

A big, red-faced man in front balked. "I wanna see your badge, femmie."

"See this, scrot," Gabe snapped, showing his taser. The man blanched and hurried out of the shaft with the others.

When the door closed, McKenna said, "You shouldn't have done that."

Gabe grinned. "I know." He unlocked the access and punched the speed drop. McKenna felt suddenly light, her stomach squirming around her rib cage, looking for a way to her throat as the drop plunged down a hundred levels through the citytower.

"It's just," Gabe said, "that you don't need some jackass in your face right now."

She felt a surge of warmth for him. She didn't want him thinking he had to protect her — but he'd be that way with a y-partner too. Most of the guys at the precinct wanted to wash her back; Gabe watched it. And I'll watch yours, partner, she thought. That way we'll make it to retirement.

The door slid back at sub-ten and she led the way into a concrete corridor that dripped cold water and stank of mold. The lights were dim, the passage empty, power and water conduits thick as swamp roots overhead. She hurried ahead of Gabe, keeping to the outside curvature of the corridor, feeling the immense weight of the citytower pressing down on her.

She saw the body — nude, female, hanging from a pipe — and felt a snarl forming on her face.

"Shit," Gabe said behind her.

Then they got closer and she saw the fixed, rigid way it dangled, the wrong angles of the legs and feet. Not even rigor could do that.

"A mannequin!" Gabe exclaimed.

She felt an immense weight lifting from her shoulders. It *hadn't* started again. This was just some craze with a puke sense of humor.

"Okay," she said. "Let's get a lab unit down here. Maybe this walking dildo left us some prints."

Her relief began to fade. Not a real woman, no. It hadn't started again.

But the Hangman was still out there.

The Hangman and the Cross Killer, *and she wanted them.*

II

Going in, Cutler felt sick with shame. What if someone from the office saw him? Some friend of Hannah or the kids? He tried to swallow and his throat clenched.

Just a few more steps. He was off the concourse now — if somebody'd seen him, they'd assume he was going into the pharmacy. Cutler located the other door, at the end of the short entry hall. As he bypassed the pharmacy entrance, he forced his shoulders straight, trying to walk with dignity. The door to Ysex was opaque, a falsely pristine white. No letters on it, just an address number. They'd made it easy as possible for you to slip in, unnoticed—

Except by yourself.

Cutler felt the shame again, heat prickling to his face. The door swept aside for him, closing the moment he was through. He felt a small relief, as though he'd run a gauntlet, ducking a dozen blows. He focused on the room: hanging plants, innocuous art prints, a muted Mozart sonata flowing from some hidden speakers. He felt a mild surprise. This was nothing like the spartan government clinic he'd expected.

"May I help you, sir?"

A woman! Embarrassment flooded Cutler, then annoyance. They shouldn't have put a woman in here. Didn't they know anything? Cutler turned and saw her, half hidden behind the desk in a front corner of the room. Devious, placing her off to the side like that. They knew that men like him — *perverts* like him — might not step through the entry if they saw the woman first.

She said: "I'm May Allegra, Dr. Tremoyne's secretary."

He took off his skullcap respectfully and made himself look her in the eye. "Andrew Cutler, here to see Dr. Tremoyne." He saw that she was very pretty — a dark pixie haircut above luminous, green eyes, pert nose, a finely molded mouth, red and glossy.

The mouth smiled warmly. "Yes. Please come with me."

Half addled with embarrassment, he nevertheless got an impression of girlish breasts and a slim waist. Her plaid, flaring skirt swirled seductively as she walked. He followed her down the hallway, feeling in his hands what it would be like to bunch that wool plaid, slide it up along her thighs. The old guilt knifed through him: Why did he always have to see that part of a woman first? Allegra had a charming inner glow, a sense of humor, he could tell. She was more, so much more, than a thing, and yet his first response was to covet her. Would he ever be free of it?

Allegra led him into a low-lit office. Dark oak, the aroma of leather and pipe tobacco. A man about forty stood, offering his hand. Allegra introduced them, her voice clear and silvery.

Tremoyne indicated a low slung chair in front of his desk. Cutler sat, feeling the chair mold itself to his back and neck. Allegra seated herself beside Tremoyne's desk. Alarm swept Cutler. What was this? Surely Tremoyne couldn't dream of having a woman present during the session!

"Tell me about yourself, Mr. Cutler."

Cutler centered his attention on the doctor, trying to shut the beautiful secretary out. He said: "I'm associate director of planning for Novasol Chemicals. I'm thirty, been married seven years, two sons. I live at level one-sixty, the Northeast octant . . ." the words ran out.

Dr. Tremoyne nodded encouragement, his eyes sharp with interest, as though Cutler were the only person in the universe. A handsome man, Cutler thought. I wonder if he has a thing going with Allegra.

"Why have you come to Ysex, Mr. Cutler?"

Cutler felt himself choking up. He glanced at May Allegra. How to say it without being rude? "Doctor, I'm afraid it would be easier for me if we could excuse your secretary."

Tremoyne nodded soberly. "Of course."

Allegra rose and left the room without a word. Cutler felt guilty. "I hope I haven't offended her."

"That's not possible."

Cutler felt confusion, and then a jolt of realization. "You mean she's . . ."

"An x-sim, yes."

Cutler was astonished. "My God, it's incredible! I was expecting something fairly realistic, of course, but I had no idea sim technology was this advanced. The ones you see on the concourses —"

"Are clearly identifiable as machines," Tremoyne said, as though he had been through this a hundred times. No doubt he had. "In normal circumstances it is important for citizens to know they are dealing with machines. Here, the illusion must be perfect."

"It is. I thought she was real."

Tremoyne waved a finger in mild astonishment. "Oh, she's very real, Mr. Cutler. But she's a machine. She feels nothing, thinks nothing. She and the other x-sims here do only what they are programmed to do."

Cutler saw the purpose of Allegra's flawless little opening charade and was impressed. He had reacted to her in every way as he would a real woman. The whole point of the Ysex clinics.

Tremoyne said: "Knowing what you do about her would you want her back in here during our session?"

"Absolutely not."

"Good. I think we'll be able to help you. Now, let me rephrase my question about why you've come to Ysex: Exactly what would you like to do to a woman?"

Cutler felt a stab of nausea, a heavy pressure in his chest. How could he do this? The secret must stay hidden. But this stranger wanted him to push it out, reveal the slick, squirming snake that had hidden so long inside of him. "I . . ." Sweat sprang up on his face. He blotted it with his handkerchief. "Sorry. This is rather difficult."

"Why is that?"

Cutler looked at him in surprise. "Because I'm ashamed, damn it. I've been ashamed all my life, from the moment I first really looked at a girl and wanted . . ." Cutler felt his throat closing, refusing to release the words. He felt the old, weary resentment at his shame. "Doctor, I'd give anything to not to need to be here. I never asked to be the way I am. I wish I knew . . . *why*."

Tremoyne looked at him with a mixture of pity and something else. Cutler could not quite read. Exasperation? "We'll delve into how you became what you are in later sessions, Mr. Cutler. But today I want to get started on the basic Ysex therapy as quickly as possible."

Cutler felt his breath shorten in anticipation. He thought of May Allegra. Her body yielding to him, accepting him.

"So what would you like to do to a woman?"

Cutler hunched forward, taking a deep breath. "I . . . I would like to take a woman while she's unconscious."

"I'm sorry, I didn't quite hear."

Cutler repeated it, his face hot with embarrassment.

"But it's more than that, isn't it?"

Cutler nodded.

"How does this woman become unconscious?"

Cutler told him, every word in agony.

Tremoyne nodded serenely, as if they were talking abut the weather. He said: "And, after all these years of fighting it, you're afraid you're losing. You're afraid you might do it. That's why you've finally come in."

"Yes," Cutler whispered. "Help me."

III

Cutler stood in the open doorway. It looked like an office on the outside ring of the citytower. The tall trid-windows beyond May Allegra portrayed a night sky riddled with stars. Allegra sat with her back to him, her silky voice murmuring into the word processor. Cutler felt feverish with need. The fantasy filled his mind: *she's a secretary, working late, everyone else gone. She doesn't know I'm here.* He felt himself swell, hard as steel inside his pants. He could smell the sweetish odor of ether in the rag clutched in his hand. Realism, Dr. Tremoyne had said. Everything about it must be as real as possible. Another surprise, Tremoyne having real anesthesia in the clinic — *has he seen other men like me?* Cutler was half dazed by the incredible thought. Other men came to Ysex, of course, but he had never imagined that some of them might have his exact same perversion, that he might not be locked up all alone in the squalid little prison of his fantasy.

He suddenly realized something else: Despite the large array of x-sims the doctor had shown him, Tremoyne had known he would choose Allegra. Back when he'd first asked Tremoyne to excuse Allegra, she'd gone straight to the programming room instead of back to her secretary's desk. Cutler was amazed that someone could guess so much about him in the first five minutes. It was oddly reassuring, actually. He felt safe with Tremoyne. He knew that the minute he stepped into the room, Dr. Tremoyne would be monitoring his every move with hidden vidlenses, and yet it didn't bother him as much as he had expected. What was it Tremoyne had said, "You've already shown yourself to me by what you've said. I know your fantasy now and you mustn't be afraid to act it out fully. That is what I want you to do. That is what will heal you. Remember as you go into the room, that I approve of everything you are doing. Then put me from your mind You take care of your end and I'll take care of mine."

Cutler felt his heart booming inside his chest. His vision narrowed down to May Allegra's back, the sound of her voice, so real. He crept forward, raising the rag. *Christ Oh God!* He slipped it over her nose and mouth. She gave a little cry, bucking up from her chair, half falling back against him, soft buttock against his straining hardness, her hands on his wrists, struggling, little muffled cries.

"No, please!" he heard someone shout and realized it was him.

She sagged against him, still clutching his hands, now grappling feebly. "Please, please," he gasped. He could see her chest rise and fall, feel her earlobe against his wrist. Her hands dropped to her sides. She fell limp against him. He thought he was going to explode. He felt a rush of fierce exultation.

He lowered her gently to the floor, then ran back to the door, locking it. He returned, looking down at her face reposed. The upper lip curled open, revealing a pearly edge of teeth. Beneath it he could see the tip of her tongue.

Tenderly he undressed her. First the skirt, then the blouse, bra spilling small, perfect breasts to his hands. He noted with surprise that the nipples were erect. He nuzzled them gently and was stricken with an involuntary image of Hannah, aroused. *No! He must never think of Hannah this way!*

He blocked his wife out, fumbling at Allegra's panties, breathlessly amazed to find a tan line, a small tidy belly button. He tore his own clothes off, never taking his eyes from the waiting lushness of her body. He could look at her without fear, take his time, thrill to every curve, every soft, secret place.

He knelt, trembling with need.

When he was finished, he gazed down at her, half dazed with release. Gradually, the absolute stillness of her body penetrated to deeper levels inside him, triggering alarms. She looked so real. What if, somehow, she *was* real?

He scrambled forward and lifted one of her feet, looking at the heel. Yes, there was the mark, molded into the flesh: x-sim. He sagged back, relieved and exhausted.

Depression and shame began to settle over him. The construct on the floor was not alive, had never been alive. What he had just done was all right, approved even. Because of it, the loathsome desire was more fully purged than it had ever been — defused, Dr. Tremoyne's word. He should feel good about that. But all he really wanted right now was to leave this place, regain his dignity, go about his life for as long as possible free of the maddening need and the shame and fear that went with it.

I don't want to do this again, he thought fiercely. I don't want to want it, ever again.

But he knew that he would.

IV

Cold with fury, McKenna looked down at the woman's body. What final twitch of contempt had caused her murderer to leave her naked? Or maybe it wasn't contempt but a sick pride, the killer wanting to make it clear that it was a *sex* killing. If he had not left the clothes off, there would have been no other obvious sign.

Beast!

McKenna fought to get hold of her rage. A wind sprang up, chilling her, agitating the dark, exquisitely pruned shrubs of the maze into a skeletal rattle. Down the lane, almost hidden around a corner of the maze, the pathologist and two orderlies waited like jackals to complete the indignity of the kill.

She was glad that Gabe was down with the flu. Otherwise, he'd be wracking his brain for ways to make her feel better right now. She did not want to feel better.

The Hangman, the Cross Killer, and now this.

A fierce determination filled McKenna. *This one I'm going to catch.*

She bent close to the corpse's mouth, sniffing the sickly sweet smell around her cheeks and nose. Ether. Probably what killed her — there was no other mark on the body. A pretty woman, with her pixie haircut, her girlish figure, now so forlorn and empty. McKenna took the i.d. from the woman's handbag and turned it over in her hand. Mandy

Redfern. Secretary for Public Works. Address in level 162, the efficiency sector. Mandy's face looked out at her with a pretty, hopeful smile that said "please like me." Good photo for an ident-card. McKenna felt a twinge of envy. Mine always looks like I'm on thorazine, she thought. But there was no envying Mandy Redfern now. She had looked *too* good, to the wrong man.

Strange, that lack of any mark, no bruise on the throat, no biting, cutting, hitting. No signs of forcible rape.

Had he entered her after she was dead?

McKenna shuddered. She pulled the sheet over the still, alabaster body. Standing, she turned her back and glared up over the wall of the maze of Meridian Alpha. The mammoth citytower seemed to lean forward over her, pushing her back on her heels in a dizzy instant of vertigo. Suddenly she hated the city that thrust like a phallus a thousand meters into the soft pink dawn. McKenna motioned the pathologist forward with a curt jerk of her hand. She threaded her way out of the maze, stalking through the edge of the parkland toward the portal of Meridian Alpha. Now she must walk another maze, the repellant, twisted mind of the man who did this. The fury began to build again inside her.

I'll nail the son of a he-dog, Mandy. For both of us.

V

"I think it's time you stopped avoiding," Tremoyne said.

Cutler looked at him, mystified. "What do you mean?"

"This is our fourth session together. You're making progress, being very candid — in every area but one. Unfortunately, that is the most important one." Tremoyne tamped his pipe and puffed. A ghostly djin of smoke writhed up between them, dissipating with a smell of hot hickory.

Cutler searched his mind, baffled. What was he holding back? He was trying to tell everything, each excruciating detail, searching out with Tremoyne what had caused — and what now maintained — his perverted drive. And the sessions with the Allegra-sim were going very well. He was beginning to feel the first positive effects of the "fantasy reshaping," just as Tremoyne had promised. He was now able to go in and take the sim without first being aroused by her struggles as he anesthetized her. Now he pretended that he came upon her sleeping.

He was still able to get it up that way, the arousal almost as great. Maybe, in time, he could be reshaped all the way to a cure. It would be wonderful not to have to be afraid any more, terrified that he might hurt a woman.

"Mr. Cutler, how do you feel about women?"

"I like them."

"But they don't like you very much, do they?"

Cutler tried to understand what Tremoyne was getting at. "Not in my fantasies, no. Not when it comes to sex, as I've told you. But in real life, I think women *do* like me. I get along very well with women."

"Really." The word came out flat with skepticism.

"I know it's strange. But I like women better than most men. They're more interesting and complex. More humane. I like talking with them, learning how they feel, what they're afraid of, what they want. If they do like me, maybe that's why — they can tell I'm interested in more than trying them on." And that *is* the truth, Cutler thought with consternation. So why in God's name can't I get rid of the other? He gave a bitter laugh. "Ironic, right?"

"Bullshit."

Cutler felt a mild shock, then hurt. "What?"

"You want their bodies."

"Yes, of course. I admit that. Nothing in this world is more desirable to me than a beautiful woman. And most women are attractive in some way, even if they aren't—"

"You want their bodies, but they won't let you have them. They find the thought of sex with you loathsome. Admit it, Mr. Cutler, deep down inside, you're angry as hell at women. *That's* why you want to knock them out and take them. That's why, deep inside, you want to *kill* them."

Cutler began to feel annoyed. *Loathsome*, his own word, yes, but he didn't like having it used against him. "I never wanted to kill a woman. What I *do* want is bad enough. And I realize, logically speaking that most women aren't revolted by sex. For God's sake, Hannah wants it more often than I—"

"But you still *feel*, deep down inside, that the women you meet would find the thought of sex with you disgusting."

Cutler's throat ached. "Yes. But I don't blame them."

Tremoyne looked grave. "Mr. Cutler. Your denial is dangerous in the extreme. If you persist in keeping an absolute lid on your anger, it will continue to dictate your behavior. It could even make you do things of which you are unaware. Terrible things."

Cutler felt fear plunging in his stomach. He closed his eyes, fighting it. "No," he said. "I'm sorry Dr. Tremoyne, but I can't accept that. I've lived with this from the day I woke up to sex. I've despised myself for it, but I've never lied to myself about it. I didn't come in here because I was afraid I'd do something I wouldn't even be aware of, but because I was thinking it, sometimes even planning it."

Tremoyne sat forward, his face earnest. "Listen to me, Cutler. You think you'd always be aware of what you were doing, no matter how horrible it was. But I've never treated a schizoid who didn't feel the same way — at first."

"I'm not a schizoid."

Tremoyne sighed and sat back. "Bitches," he said. "I want you to say it. Women are bitches."

Cutler felt a disbelieving smile twisting his face.

"Say it."

"Women are bitches," Cutler whispered.

"Damn it, man, let some feeling into it! Women are bitches! COLD, WITHHOLDING BITCHES!"

Cutler said it; all he could feel was disgust at himself. Tremoyne must be right, he *was* evading, refusing to face up to his real feelings. How could he expect to be cured, when he couldn't even be honest with himself? Maybe he *was* schizoid, one half not knowing what the other half was doing. The thought struck dread into Cutler. He felt the old fear resurging inside him, the sick fear, the worst fear of all — fear of himself. He tried to fight it. After all, even if he could not be cured, he had the clinic now. He could always come here, use the x-sims whenever he had the urge to hurt a woman.

He could. But would he?

VI

McKenna inspected herself in the mirror, wondering about the Rag Killer, as she'd begun to think of him. Would he feel his deadly lust for the image in her mirror? A cold shiver went through her. Yeah, probably. If she wasn't at least sort of pretty, why did the guys at the precinct keep trying to hit on her? I've got a regular nose, she thought, and my eyes are pretty. She flipped at the short hair, barely an inch down her forehead, thinking with another chill of the pixie cut of both women who'd been murdered. Number two, Gloria Dennard: short hair, and turned up nose, just like mine. Shorter than average, like me.

But not strong like me.

McKenna flexed her biceps at the mirror. Could she fight off a man who clapped an ether-soaked rag over her nose? Roger cubed, she thought savagely. Heel up into the balls, elbow in the solar plexus. Or clap his ears.

McKenna blinked in surprise as Sheba jumped up on her dressing table and stretched her front legs, tail arching up, angling to have her ears scratched. McKenna obliged, stroking the cat's soft fur. "You're a born killer," she said. "Give me some ideas."

Sheba purred, looking civilized and innocent.

The killer probably looked that way too.

McKenna turned away from the mirror, slipping into the mylar jumpsuit, buckling on the weapons-belt. Okay, so the Rag Killer likes his victims pretty. What does that tell us about him, McKenna? Some of the psycho slimebags want good looks in their victims and others could care less. Maybe when any woman will do, the anger's the thing — the desire to dominate and humiliate any human female. And when the looks of the victim matter, maybe the main goal is stealing sex. That would fit with the Rag Killer not inflicting pain or damage. Cosmetic damage, that is. McKenna remembered the famous quote of Satchel Paige about airplanes: "They can kill you, but they can't hurt you."

But you couldn't hurt a person worse than killing them.

McKenna felt a heavy weight of frustration: Two serial murders, no leads. If she couldn't do something quickly there'd be another killing within days. Once the press got it, the headlines would terrorize every woman in Meridian Alpha.

So are you going to let this one get away too?

The mocking inner voice stung McKenna to fury; she slapped the dressing table, scattering make-up and launching Sheba halfway across the room. McKenna stomped to the kitchenette, taking her coffee from the slot, letting its rich aroma fill her nose. She gazed out her trid-window at the grand canyon sunrise. In tune with Meridian Alpha time, a molten dawn was inching down the western face of the canyon, warm and soothing. It looked just like yesterday's sunrise, though she'd only used up a few months of the three-year cycle.

Suddenly her mind rejected the illusion. The real Grand Canyon is two thousand miles away, she thought. The only thing really beyond that window is the wall of the next efficiency. She turned away, dejected, wishing she could as easily strip away the killer's protective illusion.

He looks normal, she thought, maybe even attractive. His distaste for gore might indicate a sense of aesthetics. He's probably a professional — anesthetics are controlled substances readily available only to physicians, pharmacists, and the like.

Aesthetic and anesthetic. The words blurred together, taunting her with their elusive meanings. A sick despair spread throughout her. She couldn't shake the dread feeling that the Rag Killer was shaping up a lot like the other two. Six women for the Cross Killer, five for the Hangman; would the Rag Killer stop at four?

What am I thinking? she wondered, surprised. That the Rag Killer might actually be the same man as the other two? She turned the possibility over in her mind without enthusiasm. The Hangman's M.O. *was* similar: Neither man mutilated his victims. Both killed by cutting off air. Both left the victims nude.

But there were still too many differences. Serial sex killers usually stuck closely to their M.O. because it was what gave them their kicks. But throughout history, there had always been exceptions. Henry Lee Lucas made a point of changing M.O.'s. So did Brecknaur. Could the Rag Killer be the Hangman be the Cross Killer?

If so, what made her think she could catch him this time when she hadn't before?

McKenna realized she was just tormenting herself again about the open files. Forget them! she told herself fiercely. They're history. They got away. Moved to another citytower, got religion, fell down a drop shaft, were cured . . .

McKenna's mind focused. Cured?

She remembered this morning's synpape, and felt a dawning excitement as she realized where her mind had really been leading her. She paced from the trid-window to the computer console and called up the synpape, scrolling until she found the article she'd glanced over earlier: "First Study on Ysex Clinics Completed." She scanned the article again: Longitudinal study, begun three years ago when the clinics were first established; post-prison subjects only — no voluntary clients included. And there it was — the impressive finding: Sex crimes had been committed by only 9% of Ysex assignees with prior sex convictions, compared to a recidivism rate of almost 80% in released prisoners for the six years prior to the establishment of Ysex clinics.

McKenna felt a curdling skepticism. Hard to believe slime like that could be "cured." Ysex was government; this was probably just some bureaucrats massaging data to make themselves look good.

Didn't matter. The point was, Ysex could be the break she'd overlooked until now — a way to find the killer. Sure, the identities and records of Ysex "clients" were strictly confidential, even from the courts and police. But what was to stop her from "interviewing" the head of the clinic? "Doctor, what sort of man would kill with anesthesia?" Watch the doctor's face, see if she'd struck a nerve. If the killer was a Ysex client, and the doctor was a decent human being, he might let something slip, no matter what the rules.

And she might get a line on the other two at the same time. The thought gave her a savage pleasure. *Is that why you stopped, you bastards? Because you were "cured?" Do you think you're safe now? You're not. Not as long as I live.*

VII

Dr. Tremoyne's secretary, May Allegra, showed McKenna into his office right on time. McKenna was struck by the woman's similarity to both victims: short, pretty — even the same haircut. She put that from her mind and studied Tremoyne, trying to figure out whether to use the soft or the hard approach. He was a big, tidy man with kindly wrinkles around his eyes.

Try soft first, and if that doesn't work, hard.

She gave him the rundown: two killings, victims similar, M.O. the same. Then, on impulse, she went for broke, asking him if anyone at the clinic was being treated for urges to anesthetize women.

Tremoyne hesitated. She thought she detected a flicker of dismay in his eyes. "Now Miss McKenna, you know I can't answer that. If it ever became known that we had cooperated with the police, no man would ever come here again. I'd like to help you catch your killer, but I'm more concerned about stopping ten others like him from ever doing such a thing."

Irritated at being called "Miss," McKenna said: "I'm not convinced you stop anyone, Mr. Tremoyne."

"Doctor."

"Sorry, I didn't realize we're using correct titles today." So much for the soft approach, she thought with resignation. "Doctor, isn't it just possible that your nice, pliant little x-sims incite men to new fantasies, open new worlds of perversion to them that they can go out and try on real women?"

Tremoyne looked pained. "That is the tired argument of the ages. Images of whatever kind — pictorial, mental, or three-dimensional as here at Ysex — do not cause fantasies, they arise from them. More importantly, the statistics about our cure rate don't lie: In this morning's synpape—"

"Yeah, I read it." McKenna felt her anger boiling close to the surface. She kept her voice calm. "I guess I just don't care for your assumptions, Tremoyne: Serial murderers — Rape-killers — are *sick*. We've got to *cure* them. You can't help it, you're a doctor and it's how you think. But if the courts believe your claims, they'll buy in. Rapists and sex murderers will start getting minimal sentences followed by a cozy stop-off here to practice their brutality on your sex dolls and get their *cure*. Me, I'm a cop; I see the *symptoms* of their goddamned *disease*. Those symptoms don't remind me much of the measles."

Tremoyne steepled his fingers. "And I suppose you think the proper cure is that 'ruptor on your belt."

McKenna suppressed a sigh. This was getting them nowhere. Suddenly she noticed the faint orange glow on the doctor's white coat and realized that Tremoyne's desk terminal was on. He'd been working when she came in. Were the client files in there? God, if she could just sneak a look! She tried to plot a distraction, but could think of nothing that wasn't too obvious.

Tremoyne said: "Officer McKenna, not all the men who come in here are remanded by prisons. Regular, law-abiding men walk in here everyday, not to abuse sex dolls but because they need help. Most of them are afraid they might do something bad. They've done the bad thing in their mind over and over, usually while masturbating. But this fantasy fulfillment is inadequate, leaving them obsessed. The gap between what they imagine, and what they think the actual act would be like draws them like a flame draws a moth. I fill that gap. And then, session by session, I gradually shape the experience backward toward normalcy."

McKenna gave a cynical grunt.

Tremoyne shook his head. "Sergeant, we have a man here right now with brutal rape fantasies. He selected an x-sim of the physical type he fantasizes. I programmed the sim to respond just as he desires, with cries for help, struggles, screams. That, in itself, satisfied the man and made him much less dangerous to real women."

McKenna imagined the similacrum of a woman, pleading, screaming, while a man beat her. It turned her stomach. She felt a sudden, deep hostility toward Tremoyne. A doctor, or a master pornographist?

"But I did not stop there," Tremoyne went on. "As you may or may not be aware, there is a neuroelectric net in the mouth and genital tissues of the x-sims. It will tune itself to the male organ, and can be set to greatly increase or decrease the pleasure of the orgasm. For months I have been shaping the man away from his brutality. Each time his approach is less violent, his climax is better. He is changing, and he's not even aware of it—"

The phone on Tremoyne's desk chimed. He picked it up and listened, a slight frown forming on his face. "I see. Yes, I'll be right there." He replaced the receiver and gave McKenna an apologetic look. "A slight mechanical problem in one of the sims. Shouldn't take more than ten minutes. If you'd care to wait?"

"Thank you, Doctor," McKenna said and held her breath.

He rose and exited in a hurry . . .

Leaving his computer on.

McKenna looked prayerfully at the ceiling. "Thank you, *God*." She hurried around to Tremoyne's console. The operating system was government standard. She could run it in her sleep. She read a few lines and realized with a thrill that she was inside the central file of Ysex. Her heart began to race. It couldn't be this easy!

She tapped a search command into Tremoyne's console: *Find: ether.*

The screen scrolled for a moment and then stopped. Terrific — the middle of a client file! She scrolled up to the top and read the name: Andrew F. Cutler, Associate Director, blah, blah. Eagerly she scanned Tremoyne's psychological profile of Cutler: He is the youngest of four children and the only boy. His parents were both physicians. He remembers trying, out of sexual curiosity, to sneak looks at his older sisters. On these occasions, the sisters would shriek and scold him severely, calling him a dirty brat, a pervert, and other names. These experiences preconditioned Cutler as he reached puberty to believe all girls would be repelled by his sexual interest in them. Thus, from the first floods of adolescence, Cutler's normal sexual desire met the dam of this belief in the unlikelihood of release, causing frustration and anguish.

When Cutler was twelve, a key event hardened these emerging beliefs about sex into a specific fantasy obsession: Cutler was with his family visiting the home-apt of friends who had a daughter about his age. He and the girl were playing alone in the den, when Cutler screwed up his nerve and suggested they trade looks at each other. The girl went along at first, but when he tried to see down her panties, she pushed him and began to scream. Terrified, he clapped a hand over her mouth, also inadvertently pinching off air to her nose. She struggled briefly, then passed out. Cutler was torn between terror and a powerful arousal. He sneaked looks at the girl. Then, when she began to wake up, he arranged her clothes properly. She did not remember what had happened, and Cutler told her she'd fainted. Thus escaping any consequences other than his own shame.

This experience strongly shaped the fantasies that have continued to afflict Cutler through his adulthood: If the woman is unconscious, she will not suffer the repugnance of having him touch her. Her body would accept him fully, and she would feel nothing; he need have no fear of rejection.

McKenna shuddered. She read on: Even as a child, Cutler knew that knocking a girl out was wrong. He suffered — and continues to suffer — immense guilt and shame over his recurring fantasy. He is terrified of his impulses and feels dirty and perverted. Ironically, he was a very nice looking boy and is now a handsome man. In adulthood he has come to intellectually understand that the prettiest girl in his high school would probably have been quite happy to have sex with him. But that knowledge is far too late and too cerebral to uproot the fantasy burned into his psyche through the magnifying lens of his first sexual awakenings.

McKenna sniffed in scorn at Tremoyne's florid metaphor. But she realized that she was fascinated, too, in a dread way. She did not want to be. Who cared why this Cutler did what he did? All she wanted was to stop him.

But she read on anyway, nerves on edge, listening for the sound of Tremoyne's return: Cutler cannot see a pretty woman without normal

male arousal paired with abnormal hopelessness. This triggers the
fantasy of anesthetizing a woman with ether and enjoying her at his
leisure. It should be noted that Cutler has access to his firm's drugs,
including anesthesias.

All right! McKenna thought.

Cutler has entered Ysex because he feared he might actually act out
his fantasy. Arousal testing for other sexual fantasies is negative.
Cutler is horrified at the thought of typical rape, with the woman
struggling and protesting. He also claims that he has never imagined
killing a woman. This latter claim is doubtful. Cutler is probably filled
with dangerous, buried rage at women, which he will not admit—

McKenna felt a sudden crawl of nerve at her neck, conscious of the
open door behind her. Tremoyne would be back any second. She
scrolled ahead, checking the dates of Cutler's therapy sessions. Both
murders occurred the day of sessions. McKenna felt a grim satisfaction.
Just as I thought! Ysex doesn't "defuse," it infuses. It eggs them on!

She heard a sound behind her and hurried back to her chair,
suppressing her exaltation. As Tremoyne walked in, she realized she'd
left the computer in Cutler's file. Her heart sank. Tremoyne would
know.

"Sorry about the interruption," he said. He flipped the screen off
as he sat, never looking at it. His avoidance of the screen seemed
deliberate; had he arranged the phone call, deliberately left her alone
with the computer up and running? Had he *wanted* her to find Cutler's
file?

Suddenly she liked Tremoyne a lot better.

VIII

McKenna waited on the concourse for Cutler to come out from his
Ysex appointment. She held a shopping bag in one hand — a prop, filled
with lots of nothing. She watched the late shoppers wind their way from
the stores along the concourse to the drop and lift shafts, paying
particular attention to the women. Maybe tonight would be the night.
Cutler would finish his session, see one of these women and follow her.

And then I follow him.

She looked at her watch, impatient. Cutler wasn't due out quite
yet. Two weeks of stakeout and it was getting old. Five appointments,
nothing. But there was no other way. The information on Cutler she'd

stolen from Tremoyne's computer was worth exactly nothing in a court of law — except, possibly, her badge.

She had to catch him in the act.

She hoped it would be her not Gabe, who about now would be positioning himself outside Cutler's home-apt on one-sixty. She felt a little guilt at wanting to edge her partner out, but dismissed it, knowing Gabe would understand. You're all mine, Cutler, she thought fiercely.

And after I've got you, maybe I'll go after Ysex.

The thought of closing down the clinic, with its hidden chambers of vicious fantasy appealed to her. She did not want anything that even looked like a woman taking abuse from some animalistic man, encouraging him, making him think it was all right. The hell with the statistics, there was a moral issue here: The cure was worse than the disease—

There! Cutler coming out of the clinic — a few minutes early. McKenna felt a burgeoning excitement. It might mean something — that his little scene with the x-sim had disappointed him, left him wanting more.

He hurried along the concourse, blue V-suit and skullcap flashing in the store lights. She made herself stay a good distance behind, her heart quickening as she saw that he, too, seemed to be following someone — a woman, her arms full of packages.

McKenna closed some of the distance, concerned. She must stay far enough back to avoid scaring Cutler off, but stick close enough to save the woman if he attacked. The woman had not volunteered as bait, and there was no way McKenna was going to let him hurt her. She felt the blood singing in her ears. *Try it, woman hater. Feel how a woman hates back!*

There! The woman was turning into an access alley, taking a shortcut. Guilt leapt up in McKenna. She should have pushed harder with the synpapes, driven home the message that going into alleys wasn't safe . . .

Yes, and then the women of Meridian Alpha — all of them and not just the few who might be killed — would lose a part of their freedom. McKenna felt a bitter resentment at the killer, all the other women killers through time. How neatly they fit into the politics of male power. How easy it was to use them as boogeymen to keep women in line. A woman should not have to fear to walk where any man could walk.

McKenna grunted in disgust. Why was she thinking about politics? She was a cop. Her job was to nail the boogeyman.

Hurrying to close up with Cutler, she saw him follow the woman into the alley. His hand dipped into his pocket as he disappeared. McKenna broke into a run, filled with urgency and a perverse hope. This would be the place, he would do it now.

She burst into the alley five seconds behind him, too fast, seeing the woman step through into the light at the other end as she felt the rag close over her own nose. The awful, sweet stench of ether filled McKenna's head. Panic slammed through her. She fought it, closing her throat against the urge to gulp that first instinctive breath, groping for her 'ruptor as his arm clamped around her waist, pinning the weapon to her body.

She kicked back and up with her heel, but he had his knees together, stopping the blow. The panic surged back, he was going to get her, he'd suckered her into his trap and she'd gone for it—

But how did Cutler know she was following him?

Faint sparks circled before her eyes. She was desperate to breathe. If she didn't, anoxia would do what the ether could not. She cupped her palms and clapped up and back at his ears, striking solidly, hearing a gasp of pain. His grip loosened. She lifted her feet, letting her weight pull her free, dropping and rolling, tugging her 'ruptor out as she gulped air, seeing his dim shape running back for the opening of the alley. She fired, hoping, but knowing he was almost out of range of the stun beam. He stumbled and fell, rolling onto his back, lying still, moaning.

She hurried to him, gasping, and planted a foot on his chest, aiming her 'ruptor at his forehead. A savage glee filled her. He stopped straining and lay back, his face dropping into the bar of light from the concourse.

McKenna grunted in shock. "Tremoyne!"

"Congratulations, Miss McKenna." Even through the hoarseness of his stun-slackened vocal cords, she could hear his hatred. She took a step to the wall, found the emergency lighting switch. The alley lit in a harsh, orange glow. She recognized Cutler's jacket.

"You tried to set up your own client."

"I was protecting him. I've seen you following the poor, sorry bastard. So tonight I took his cap and coat and left ahead of him, so you'd follow me instead."

"How noble. Except that you deliberately left your computer open in the first place, or I'd never have known Cutler existed." McKenna's skin crawled. "I walk into your office and, just like that, you decide it would be a kick to snuff me. So quick, Tremoyne. So mindless. You began planning it right then, didn't you? Dangle your own patient as bait, sucker me into being your next victim." In her mind, McKenna saw her own face on Mandy Redfern's naked, empty body; the pathologist coming for her, Tremoyne going on with his life. Fury rose in her in a choking wave. She flipped the 'ruptor to "kill."

Tremoyne's face paled. "Easy, sergeant."

"You've done this before — stolen the fantasies of your clients. The Cross Killer, the Hangman."

Tremoyne said nothing, but the truth was in his face, a cunning smirk that infuriated her. And then the awful reality began to sink in — of what was going to happen in the days to come: "You've killed thirteen women," she said. "And if I take you in, they'll call you *sick*. You'll draw short time, then a *cure* in a Ysex clinic. But it won't cure you. You've had everything right there all along and it hasn't mattered a damn. It isn't enough for you. You want the real thing."

McKenna aimed the 'ruptor at Tremoyne's heart.

"No," he gasped. "Don't. You're wrong — I could be cured. It was just that I couldn't treat myself. I should have gone to another clinic, I see that no—"

"Bullshit. You'll get out and kill more women, not because you're sick, because you're *evil*."

Tremoyne's eyes bulged. "You're a law officer, you can't just execute me in cold blood."

McKenna sighted down the barrel at him, possessed by a savage rage. Just squeeze the trigger, one bolt into his heart . . . Her hands began to shake. A wave of sickness rose in her. I can't do it, she realized. Frustrated, she flipped the 'ruptor back to stun—

Just as Tremoyne struck, kicking her wrist, a crushing blow. The 'ruptor sailed away as Tremoyne leapt up. Part of her mind realized with horror that the stunner must have barely have gotten him, and then his fist exploded against her chin. The alley spun, the walls flipping crazily in the orange glare. Then it steadied up and she realized dimly that she was on the floor, Tremoyne straddling her. She tried to fight, but he had her securely pinned, her arms trapped under his knees. In the phosphor bronze light, his eyes looked red, feral. He clamped the damp rag over her nose and mouth; the cloying stench of ether filled her lungs. *I'm going to die*, she realized. She bucked against him with everything she had, cursing, feeling herself weaken, her body sliding away from her. A galling disgust filled her.

Then Tremoyne's eyes changed from lust to surprise. McKenna felt the rag slide from her face as Tremoyne groaned and pitched off to the side. She heard herself sobbing as she pushed and shoved Tremoyne's slack body the rest of the way off her. She struggled to her knees and gulped huge lungfuls of sweet air. Full awareness returned in a rush; she saw a man standing over Tremoynes' prone form.

"Cutler!"

He didn't seem to hear her. Slowly he pointed her 'ruptor at Tremoyne's chest, flipping the stun off. A look of loathing transfixed his face. *No!* McKenna thought, but her voice refused to say it. The 'ruptor bucked in Cutler's hands; Tremoyne jerked once then settled. His heels rattled briefly. She smelled the stench of burned meat, then saw the blackened, cauterized hole where his heart had been.

She tried to get to her feet, faltering, holding out her hand to Cutler for help. He turned away. She glimpsed the bulge at the crotch of his pants, his face, twisted in shame. It aroused him, she realized. He saw Tremoyne overpowering me and it turned him on. McKenna was surprised to find that it did not disgust her. Instead, she felt sorry for him. She pulled herself up the wall and leaned against it. "What are you doing here?" she said.

Cutler still wouldn't look at her. "You know me?"

Suddenly, *she* felt ashamed. "I've seen your Ysex file," she said.

A low, tortured groan escaped Cutler.

She did not tell the rest — that she had been following him for weeks. She gazed at him, feeling the pity again, trying to understand what else she felt.

"After my session," Cutler said, "I couldn't find my cap and coat. I thought someone must have just stolen it, so I ran out into the concourse. I saw Dr. Tremoyne and followed him. I saw him come in here, then you. When I got here, you had the 'ruptor on him. I stayed outside, but I could hear what you said to each other. Why didn't you kill him?"

"I wanted to," McKenna said. "I couldn't. I'm glad you did."

"But you're going to arrest me."

"I have no choice."

He nodded. "If you could let me go now, you could have shot him in the first place. I admire your honor. People like you are the hope of us all." For the first time, Cutler looked directly in her eyes. "You were wrong about one thing you said to him, though. He didn't kill women because he was evil. He was evil because he killed women."

McKenna looked at Cutler's pants and saw that the bulge was gone. "When you saw him killing me, you were aroused, weren't you?"

Cutler looked away. "Yes."

"But you shot him anyway."

He looked at her again; his shamed expression faded, replaced by dawning comprehension. "You're right. It excited me, but I never even thought of letting him do it."

"And yet you felt guilty."

"I think maybe I'm stuck with that for as long as I live."

Her sadness for him deepened. His actions were above reproach, heroic, even. And yet the thing in his mind that hurt no one but himself would torment him always.

McKenna said, "I'll do everything I can for you. With luck, there will be no prison."

He met her gaze. "Thank you, Detective McKenna."

"Thank *you*, Mr. Cutler."

MONGREL

Steve Vernon

"Nine of them. Imagine that. That were a good sized litter, for sure."

The old nigger woman has been talking incessantly, as was her wont, but I do not listen to her words. She is like the wind in the trees, rousing the leaves into their mocking dances. I do not choose to hear her, do not listen to what she says. Instead I listen for a softer sound. A scuttling, a crawling, perhaps beneath my own porch. Beneath my very feet.

"She were a spaniel, pure and clean, all soft and feathery and shiny as the sun."

I sit down heavily, feeling the boards sagging beneath my weight. A small dark creature, disturbed by my sudden impact, wriggles before me. I bring my fist down upon it, killing it instantly. With some distaste, I wipe my hand upon the footworn plank. I should have had them ripped up long ago. Rotten underneath, no doubt. Perhaps the whole damned foundation ought to be gutted. Perhaps the whole damned house . . .

"The father were supposed to be a spaniel too, but something else must have gotten there first."

Damned old nigger. Did she know? How could she? We had told no one. But did she know? I stared in helpless fascination at the movings of her mouth, toothless, roped with saliva. Was there mockery hidden behind her wizened black features?

"Every one of them pups crawled out of their momma, black as sin, not an ounce of gold in them anywhere. Yessir, something had surely gotten there first. Goddamned mongrels!"

The last two words are spat, and they hit me like a gutshot. I feel the blood leaving my face, crawling below the skin, into the hidden places. A tremor in my voice threatens to betray me, as I excuse myself from the one-sided conversation. An all too familiar hitching tugs at my throat.

Inside, I splash whiskey in my glass, and water on my face. Neither helps, and I must sit for a while in my favorite chair, sobbing helplessly, beating my fist upon the arm, feeling the wood hidden beneath the fabric resisting my blows.

Why did she do it? When did it happen? So many questions. My mind is a drowning sailor, hungering for answers to cling to, as I drift dangerously close to the brink of insanity. I need facts to hang onto, something that makes sense. Did she do it willingly? In our bed? Or in the cellar . . .

She has yet to answer a single one of my repeated questions. Instead she has taken refuge in the nursery, hiding behind a darkening wall of silence. I should pack my bags, should leave this accursed house, yet my family has lived here for so many years. And despite her silence, I still believe that she is genuinely remorseful. I have loved her for such a long time. Surely I could forgive her this one transgression.

I could, but then there is the child. I should have killed it at birth, but there had been so much to do, so little time to think. If only the doctor could have made it here in time. But thank god he didn't. When he did arrive I sent him away. I had seen to it all. I staunched the bleeding. I buried the afterbirth. Not a trace remained. But if only I had buried the child as well. Wrung its neck, and buried it. Instead I had chosen to place it in her arms. To make her hold it, although at first she couldn't bear to touch the thing. I had wanted to shame her, to teach her a lesson. I had wanted to hurt her. To make her see clearly the dark skinned little bastard she had borne.

That had been a mistake, for before the week was out she had grown to care for it. It was her child, after all. And now, three weeks later, I felt sure that she loved it, and that feeling frightened me all the more.

Of course I dismissed the servants immediately, that very night, sending them off without a word of explanation. Did one of them find out, and pass my shame amongst the town folk? Amongst their own kind? Far better had I shot them all, goddamned niggers. Before the war I could have. Things had been better back then, but times have changed.

I rise for another glass of whiskey, and walk with it about the house, carefully avoiding the hallway to the nursery. Dust everywhere. How quickly a place falls to ruin, without any servants. I peer out between the heavy curtains for a moment, then reclose them. I stand beneath the so dark eyes of my grandfather's portrait, looming over the unlit fireplace. I finger the grotesqueries, carved upon the mantle. And then I find myself at the cellar door.

I had boarded it up the same night she had given birth, and I had shunned it for these past three weeks. Now I stare at it, fascinated by its sheer massiveness. It was a heavy thing, black and solid. Swamp oak by the looks of it, banded in cold iron. I press my cheek against the timbers, feeling the roughened splinters hiding in the grain. I listen for a moment, holding my breath. I hear nothing; an oppressive, bludgeoning silence that nearly deafens me. For a long time I wait there, listening to the murmerings of my imagination, the whisperings of my thoughts, telling me what I must do.

I go to the servant's quarters, and from the toolchest I retrieve a heavy prybar. Returning to the cellar door I begin to remove the boards that are nailed there, one by one. It is hot, noisy work. Beads of sweat crawl down my brow, as the groans of the protesting nails echo into the cellar. Once the task is complete I pause. I take several long breaths. And then I open the door. The hinges are ancient, and thirsty for oil. They complain loudly. Once open, the doorway is shrouded in darkness, like the open maw of a hungry dragon. I listen for another moment, almost sure that I can hear something moving down below.

Quickly I go to my desk, and withdraw my pistol. It had been father's pistol once, in the war, and had been sent back along with the rest of his belongings. I load four shells into the chamber. Four should be all I need.

I walk down the hallway to the nursery. I can hear the baby wailing, hungry as usual. My footsteps are heavy and slow. I feel much like a condemned man upon his final walk to the gallows. The hallway is dark, I have kept it darkened for the last three weeks, and the shadows flicker like living things upon the wall.

I shiver slightly, there is a nip in the air. It will be a cool October. I stop just short of the nursery, and for a third and final time I listen.

The babe continues its lament, and underscoring its squalls I hear the dry, husked out sobbing of my wife. Steeling myself for what I will see, I enter.

Inside I see my wife, rocking slowly, holding the child. It is gnawing at her breast. I think she sees me, she may even have smiled, but I am not sure. Without looking I fire two shots, one into my wife, and one into the child. I do not miss.

Gently I place her upon the floor. She seems at peace, almost happy. I wrap a small blanket about her, so as to cover the teeth marks upon her bosom.

I pick up the child, if child it ever was. Its blood is blackish red, and foul smelling. The body seems strangely heavy. The creeping black bristles that crawl up its tiny twisted spine, rasp against my arms. I carry him to the cellar door, still open, and fling him down the stairs. He lands like an overripe melon.

"We don't want your bastard in this house!" I shout.

I return to the nursery, and sit upon the rocker, still sticky from my wife's blood. I wish for another whiskey, but there is no time. I sit, I rock, pistol in lap, awaiting the slow sluggish footsteps of the proud father, the jealous lover. In the so dark window I stare at the blackened reflection of myself, staring back at me.

One bullet for him, one bullet for me. I pray god one will be enough.

THE WINDS WITHIN

Ronald Kelly

Idle hands are the devil's workshop, so goes the saying.

Particularly in my case.

During the day, they perform the menial tasks of the normal psyche. But at night, the cold comes. It snakes its way back into my head, coating my brain with ice. My mind is trapped beneath the frigid surface; screaming, demanding relief. It is then that my hands grow uninhibited and become engines of mischief and destruction.

As the hour grows late and the temperature plunges, they take on a life of their own. They move through the frosty darkness like fleshen moths drawn to a flame. Searching for warmth.

And the winds within howl.

"Dammit!" grumbled Lieutenant Ken Lowery as the beeper on his belt went off. He washed down a mouthful of raspberry danish with strong black coffee, then reached down and snapped off the monotonous alarm of the portable pager. "I knew it was going to be a pain in the neck when the department passed these things out. Makes me feel like I'm a doctor instead of a cop."

Lowery's partner, Sergeant Ed Taylor, sat across from him in the coffee shop booth. He nibbled on a cream-filled donut, looking tanned and rested from his recent vacation in Florida. "I hope it's not anything serious," said Taylor. "I don't think I could stomach bullet holes and

brains my first day back on the job. Not after I've spent the last week
in Disney World, rubbing elbows with Mickey Mouse and Goofy."

Lowery stood up and stared at the man with mock pity. "Oh, the
tragic and unfair woes of a homicide detective."

"Okay, okay," chuckled Taylor. "Just make the damned call, will
you?"

The police lieutenant went to the front counter and asked to use the
business phone. He talked to the police dispatcher for a moment, then
returned to the booth, looking more than a little pale.

"What's up?" asked Taylor. "Did they give us a bad one?"

Lowery nodded. "You know that case I was telling you about
earlier? The one I was assigned to while you were on vacation?"

"The mutilation murder?"

"One and the same. Except that it's two and the same now."

Taylor felt his veneer of tranquility begin to melt away. The
lingering effects of the Magic Kingdom and Epcot Center faded in
dreadful anticipation of blood and body bags. "Another one? Where?"

"The same apartment building," said Lowery. "1145 Courtland
Street."

"Well, I'm finished," said Taylor. He crammed the last bite of
donut into his mouth. "Let's go."

"Welcome back to the real world, pal," said Lowery as they
climbed into their unmarked Chrysler and headed for the south side of
the city.

The apartment building on 1145 Courtland Street was one of
Atlanta's older buildings, built around the turn of the century. It was
unremarkable in many ways. It was five stories tall, constructed of red
brick and concrete, and its lower walls were marred with four-letter
graffiti and adolescent depictions of exaggerated genitalia. The one
thing about the structure that did stand out were the twin fire escapes of
rusty wrought-iron that zig-zagged their way along the northern and
southern walls from top to bottom. The outdated additions gave it the
appearance of a New York tenement house, rather than anything
traditionally Southern.

There were a couple of patrol cars parked out front, as well as the
coroner's maroon station wagon. "Looks like the gang is all here,"
observed Lowery. He parked the car and the two got out. "The

dispatcher said this one was on the ground floor. The first murder was on the fourth floor. The victim was an arc-welder by the name of Joe Killian. And, believe me, it was a hell of a mess."

"I'll check out the case photos when we get back to the office," Taylor said. He followed his partner up the steps and past a few curious tenants in the drab hallway. The apartment building was nothing more than a low-rent dive; a place where people down on their luck — but not enough to resort to the housing projects or homeless shelters — paid by the week to keep out of the cold streets. And it was plenty cold that month. It was only mid-December, but already the temperature had dipped below freezing several times.

They located the scene of the crime in one of the rear ground floor apartments. The detectives nodded to the patrolman at the door — who looked as if he had just stepped into the cramped apartment. Tom Blakely from the forensic department was dusting for prints in the living room, which was furnished with only a threadbare couch, a La-Z-Boy recliner, and a 25-inch Magnavox.

"The ME is in the bedroom with the stiff," Blakely told them, not bothering to look up from his work.

Lowery and Taylor walked into the back room. The coroner, Stuart Walsh, was standing next to the bloodstained bed, staring down at the body of the victim, while Jennifer Burk, the department's crime photographer, was snapping the shutter with no apparent emotion on her pretty face.

"Morning, gentlemen," said Walsh with a Georgia drawl. He eyed Taylor's tanned, but uneasy face. "So, how was the weather down in Orlando, Ed?"

"Warm and sunny," the sergeant said absently. He felt the donuts and coffee boil in his stomach. "Who do we have here?"

"The landlord of this fine establishment," said the medical examiner. "Mr. Phil Jarrett. White male, fifty-seven years of age."

"Who found him?"

"According to the officer in the hallway, a tenant stopped by to pay his rent early this morning. He knocked repeatedly, but got no answer, and found the door securely locked. He then went around the side of the building, stepped onto the fire escape, and peeked in the bedroom window over yonder. That's when he discovered Mr. Jarrett in his present state."

Lowery stared at the body of the middle-aged man. "Just like the other guy?"

"Yep. Exactly the same. The same organs were taken before the throat was slashed from ear to ear, just like Killian."

"Organs?" asked Taylor.

The coroner bent down and, with a rubber-gloved hand, showed the detective the extent of the damage. "Pretty nasty, huh?"

"I'll say," said Taylor. He turned away for a moment. He felt nauseous at the sight of mutilation, even though he had been on Homicide detail for nearly ten years. "Why would someone do something like that?"

Walsh shrugged. "I reckon that's what we're here for." The coroner turned to Lieutenant Lowery. "Did you ever find any leads after the Killian body was found?" he asked.

"Nope," said the detective. "Haven't had much of a chance. The Killian murder was only last Friday, you know. I only interviewed the landlord here. He didn't have anything useful to say. Looks like that's still the case."

Ed Taylor regained his composure and studied the body again. It was clad only in a V-necked undershirt and a pair of Fruit of the Loom boxer shorts, both saturated with gore. He stared at the ugly wounds, then glanced at his partner. "Did you interview any of the tenants, Ken?"

"Not yet," said Lowery. "But that would be the best place to start." The detective looked over at the lady photographer, who had finished taking the crime photos. "Could you have some prints for us later today, Jenny?"

Burk lit a cigarette and blew some smoke through her nostrils. "I'll have some glossy 8x10's on your desk by noon," she promised, then glanced around the grungy bedroom with disgust. "This guy was a real scum-sucker. Look at what he put on his walls."

The detectives had been so interested in Jarrett's corpse that they had neglected to notice the obscene collage that papered the walls of the landlord's bedroom. Pictures from hundreds of hardcore magazines had been clipped and pasted to the sheetrock. A collection of big-breasted and spread-eagled women of all sizes and races graced the walls from floor to ceiling, as well as a number of young boys and girls who were far under the legal age.

"Yeah," agreed Lowery. He spotted a naked child that bore an uncomfortable resemblance to his own six-year-old daughter. "Looks like the pervert deserved what he got. Kind of makes it a shame to book this bastard's killer. We ought to pin a freaking medal on their chest instead."

"We've got to find the guilty party first," said Taylor. "And we're not going to do that standing around here chewing the fat."

"Then let's get to work." Lieutenant Lowery clapped Walsh on the shoulder.

"Send us your report when you get through with the post mortem, okay, Doc?"

"Will do," said the coroner. "And good luck with the investigation."

"Thanks," said Taylor. He glanced at the mutilated body of Phil Jarrett and shook his head. "Hell of a contrast to Snow White and the Seven Dwarfs."

"Like I said before," Lowery told him, "welcome home."

"Pardon me, ma'am, but we'd like to ask you a few questions concerning your former landlord, Mr. Jarrett," Lowery said. He flipped open his wallet and displayed his shield.

The occupant of Apartment 2-B glared at them through the crack of the door for a moment, eyeing them with a mixture of suspicion and contempt. Then the door slammed, followed by the rattle of a chain being disengaged. "Come on in," said the woman. "But let's hurry this up, okay? I've gotta be at work in fifteen minutes."

Lowery and Taylor stepped inside, first studying the tenant, Melba Cox, and then her apartment. The woman herself was husky and unattractive, sporting a butch haircut and a hard definition to her muscles that hinted of regular weight training. The furnishings of her apartment reflected her masculine frame of mind. There was no sign of femininity in the decor. An imitation leather couch and chairs sat around the front room, and the walls were covered with Harley-Davidson posters. The coffee table was littered with stray cigarette butts, empty beer cans, and a ton of militant feminist literature. Lowery and Taylor exchanged a knowing glance. Cox was either a devout women's libber or dyed-in-the-wool lesbian. A combination of both, more than likely.

"Really nothing much to say about the guy, is there?" asked the woman. "He's dead, ain't he?"

"Yes, ma'am," said Taylor. "We just wanted to know if you have any idea who would kill Mr. Jarrett? Did he have any enemies?"

"Oh, he had plenty of enemies," declared Cox. "Me included. Jarrett was a real prick. Always hiking the rent, never fixing a damned thing around here, and always making lewd remarks to the women in the building. He tried to put the make on me once and I just about castrated the sonofabitch with a swift kick south of the belt buckle."

"What about the other victim? Killian?"

Melba Cox frowned. "Didn't know him very well, but he was a sexist pig, just like Jarrett was. Just like all men are."

"Have you seen or heard anything out of the ordinary lately?" Taylor asked. "Arguments between Jarrett and a tenant, maybe? Any suspicious characters hanging around the building?"

"Nope. I try to keep my nose out of other people's business, and hope that they'll do the same." She glanced at a Budweiser beer clock that hung over the sofa, then scowled at the two detectives. "I gotta go now. Unless the Atlanta PD wants to reimburse me for docked pay, that is."

"We've got to be going ourselves," said Lowery as they stepped into the hallway. He handed her one of his cards. "We would appreciate it if you would give us a call if you happen to think of anything else that might help us."

Melba Cox glared at the card for a second, then stuffed it into the hip pocket of her jeans. "Don't hold your breath," she grumbled, then headed down the stairs, dressed in an insulated jacket and heavy, steel-toed work-boots, and toting a large metal lunchbox.

"Wonderful woman," said Taylor.

"Yeah," replied Lowery. "She'd make a great den mother for the Hell's Angels." His lean face turned thoughtful. "She might just be the kind of bull dyke who would hold a grudge against a guy like Jarrett too. And maybe even do something about it."

"Won't you gentlemen come in?" asked Dwight Rollins, the tenant of Apartment 3-D. "Don't mind old Conrad there. He won't bite you."

Lowery and Taylor looked at each other, then entered the third floor apartment. The first thing that struck them about Rollins was that he was blind. The elderly, silver-haired man was dressed casually in slacks and a wool sweater, giving him the appearance of a retired college professor. But the effect was altered by the black-lensed glasses and white cane. The dog that laid on the floor was the typical seeing-eye dog; a black and tan German shepard.

"We didn't mean to disturb you, Mr. Rollins," said Lowery, "but we wanted to ask you a few questions concerning the recent deaths of Phil Jarrett and Joe Killian."

Rollins felt his way across the room and sat in an armchair. "Terrible thing that happened to those fellows, just terrible. Not that I'm surprised. This certainly isn't one of Atlanta's most crime-free neighborhoods, you know. Some young hoodlum broke into my bedroom six months ago. The bastard slugged me with a blackjack while I was still asleep and stole my tape player and all my audio books. Now why would someone stoop so low as to steal from a blind man?"

"There are a lot of bad apples out there, sir," said Taylor. "Some would mug their own grandmother for a hit of crack. About Jarrett and Killian . . . what sort of impression did you have of them?"

"Killian was nice enough. He was a welder. I could tell that by the smell of scorched metal that hung around him all the time. I never said much to the gentleman, though. Just an occasional 'hello' in the hallway." The old man frowned sourly at the thought of his landlord. "Jarrett was a hard man to deal with sometimes. He could be downright dishonest. He tried to cheat me out of rent money several times, telling me that a ten was a five, or a twenty was a ten. I'd never let him hornswaggle me, though. The bank where I cash my disability checks always braille marks the bills for me. Of course, I really couldn't say much about Jarrett's treachery. A blind man has a hard enough time making it on his own, without making an enemy of the one who provides a roof over his head."

"Have you seen . . ." Embarrassed, Lowery corrected himself. "Have you heard anything out of the ordinary lately? Strangers? Maybe an argument between Jarrett and one of the other tenants?"

"There's always some bad blood in a place like this, but nothing any worse than usual." The old man's face grew somber. "I have had the feeling that somebody's been prowling around the building, though. I've heard strange footsteps in the hallway outside. Several times I've felt like someone was standing on the other side of my door, just staring at it, as if trying to see me through the wood." He reached down to where he knew the dog laid and scratched the animal behind the ears. "You've sensed it too, haven't you, Conrad?"

The German shepard answered with a nervous whine and rested its head on its paws.

"Well, we won't keep you any longer, Mr. Rollins," said Taylor. He caught himself before he could hand the man one of his cards, giving Rollins the number vocally instead. "Please give us a call if you think of anything else that could help."

"I surely will," said Dwight Rollins. "Do you think the murderer lives here in this building?"

"We can't say for sure, sir. It's a possibility, though."

"Lord, what's this world coming to?" muttered Rollins. "Well, at least I've got good locks on my door. Somebody would have to be a hell of a Houdini to get past three deadbolts."

The two detectives said nothing in reply. They thought it best not to upset the old man by telling him that, strangely enough, the apartment doors of both Jarrett and Killian had been securely locked from the inside, both before and after the times of their murders.

"Who the hell is it?" growled a sleepy voice from inside Apartment 4-A.

"Atlanta police department, sir," called Lowery through the door. "We were wondering if we could talk to you for a few minutes."

"Is it real important?" asked the tenant, Mike Porter. "If you're selling tickets to the freaking policeman's ball, I'm gonna be mighty pissed off!"

"There's been another murder in the building, Mr. Porter," said Taylor. "We'd like to talk to you about it."

The click of deadbolts and the rattle of chains sounded from the other side, then the door opened. A muscular fellow with dirty blond hair and an ugly scar down one side of his face peered out at them. "Somebody else got fragged?" he asked groggily. "Who was it this time?"

"The landlord," said Lowery. "Mr. Jarrett."

"Well, I'll be damned," grunted Porter. He yawned and motioned for them to come inside. "You fellas will have to excuse me, but I work the graveyard shift. I catch my shut-eye in the daytime."

"We just need to know a few things," Taylor told him. "Like what your impression of the two victims was and if you've noticed anything peculiar around the building lately."

"Well, old Jarrett was a first-class asshole. That's about all I can tell you about him. The other fella, Killian, was an okay guy. Had a few beers and swapped a few war stories with the man. He was a die-hard Marine, just like yours truly."

Taylor walked over to a bulletin board that was set on the wall between the living room and the kitchenette. A number of items were pinned to the cork surface; a couple of purple hearts, an infantry insignia patch, and a few black and white photos of combat soldiers. "You were in Vietnam?" he asked.

"Yes sir," Porter said proudly. He shuffled to the refrigerator and took a Miller tall-boy from the lower shelf. "The Central Highlands from 1968 to '69. Just when things were starting to get interesting over there." He plopped down on a puke green couch and popped the top on his beer can.

"What about things here in the building?" asked Lowery. "Any fights or arguments between the tenants or with the landlord? Maybe someone hanging around that you didn't recognize?"

"It hasn't been crazier than usual. I'm not surprised that it's happening, what with all the crack dealers and gangs in this part of town." Porter grinned broadly. "They just better not screw around with old Sergeant Rock here." He stuck his hand between the cushions of the couch and withdrew a Ka-Bar combat knife. "If they do, I'll gut 'em from gullet to crotch."

The two detectives left their number and exited the apartment. As they headed up the stairs to the fifth floor, Taylor turned to his partner. "Did you notice anything strange back there in Porter's apartment?"

"Other than that wicked knife and the crazy look in the grunt's eyes?" replied Lowery. "Not really. Did you?"

Taylor nodded. "Those pictures on the bulletin board. One of them showed Porter wearing something other than his dog tags."

"And what was that?"

"A necklace . . . made out of human ears."

"Interesting," said Lowery, recalling the mutilation of the two victims. "Very interesting."

"What do ya'll want," glared the tenant of Apartment 5-C. The skinny black woman balanced a squawling baby on her hip as she stared at the two detectives standing in the hallway.

"We'd like to talk to you about the recent murders here in the building, ma'am," Lowery said. "Can we come in for a moment?"

"Yeah, I guess so," she said. "Just watch that you don't go stepping on a young'un."

Lowery and Taylor walked in and were surprised to see four other kids, ranging from eighteen months to five years old, playing on the dirty carpeting of the living room floor. Three looked to be as dark-skinned as their mother, while one was obviously a half-breed, from the lightness of its complexion and the color of its hair.

When they asked Yolanda Armstrong about the landlord, she scowled in contempt. "That bastard got just what he deserved, if you ask me. He was white trash, that's what he was. Wasn't about to take responsibility for things that were rightly his own."

"Pardon me?" asked Taylor, trying to clarify what she was talking about.

"The one beside the TV there, that's his. I came up short on the rent a couple of summers ago and Jarrett took it out in trade. Tried to get him to wear a rubber, but he was all liquored up and horny."

Lowery's face reddened slightly in embarrassment. "Uh, no need to go into your personal life, ma'am. All we need to know is if you noticed anything strange going on in the building lately. Strangers in the hallway, or arguments you might have happened to overhear."

"Lordy mercy!" exclaimed the woman. "If I was to pay attention to every bit of trouble that's gone on in this building, I would've gone plumb crazy by now. Half the people in this place are junkies and drunks, and the other half are losers and lunatics. You'd just as well take your pick of the litter. Anybody in this here building could've killed both of those men."

"Including yourself?" asked Taylor.

"Don't you go accusing me!" warned Yolanda Armstrong shaking a bony, black finger in his face. "True, I've been wronged more than most. But I'm too damned busy trying to put food in my babies' mouths to go getting even with every man who treated me badly. I just take my lumps and hope they don't come knocking on my door again."

After the two detectives had left, they called on the rest of the tenants who were there at that time of day, then headed back downstairs. It was nearly twelve-thirty when they climbed into their car and headed for a rib joint over on Peachtree Street. "So, what do you think?" asked Taylor. "Think we have a suspect somewhere in that bunch?"

"Maybe," said Lowery. "Or our killer might be a neighborhood boy. A pusher or a pimp that Jarrett and Killian might have wronged in the past."

"Or we could have something a little more sinister on our hands. Maybe a serial killer."

"Let's not go jumping to conclusions just yet," Lowery told his partner. "This is just a couple of murders in a sleazy apartment building in South Atlanta, not some Thomas Harris novel. We'll grab a bite to eat, then head back to the office and check out the crime photos and Walsh's autopsy report. Later this evening we'll come back here and interview the tenants we missed the first time around."

"Sounds good to me," said Taylor. "I just hope we come up with something concrete pretty soon. I have a bad feeling that this could turn into a full-scale slaughter before it's over and done with."

"Yeah," agreed Lowery. "I'm afraid you might be right about that."

The warmth has gone and the chill of the winter twilight invades me once again, freezing the madness into my brain. My hands shudder and shake. They clench and unclench, yearning for the spurt of hot blood and the soft pliancy of moist tissue between their fingertips. The damnable winds must be stopped! They must be driven away. And only death can provide that blessed relief.

But I must be careful. The first was easy enough, and so was the second, but only because no one expected it to happen again so soon. The next time might very well be the last. But it simply must be done. There is no denying that. Even if there are suspicious eyes and alert ears on guard throughout the building, I must let my hands do the work that they are so adept at. I must allow them to hunt out the warmth necessary to unthaw my frozen sanity.

Oh, that infernal howling! The howling of those hellish winds!

Lowery and Taylor were going over the coroner's report and the 8x10's of the two victims, when a call came in from Doctor Walsh. Lowery answered and listened to the medical examiner for a moment. Then he hung up the phone and grabbed his coat from the back of the chair. "Do you still have those binoculars in your desk drawer, Ed?" he asked hurriedly.

Taylor recognized the gleam of excitement in his partner's eyes. "Sure," he said. "What's up? Did Walsh come up with something important?"

"Yep. He found some incriminating evidence on both of the bodies."

"What did he find?" pressed Taylor. He retrieved the binoculars from his desk and grabbed his own coat.

"I'll fill you in on the way," said Lowery with a grim smile. "Let's just say that I think our killer is going to strike again, sooner than we think. And I have a pretty good idea who it is."

The blanketed form was so sound asleep that it didn't hear the metallic taps of light footsteps on the fire escape. Neither did it hear the rasp of the bedroom window sliding upward, giving entrance to a dark figure with the glint of honed steel in hand.

The snoring tenant knew nothing of the intruder, until she felt the weight of the body pressing on her chest and the edge of a knife blade pressed against the column of her throat. She laid perfectly still, afraid to move, waiting for the fatal slash to come. But the action was delayed. Instead, she felt a hand creep along her flesh, the fingers clenching and unclenching, searching through the darkness. Suddenly, she recalled the rumors that had been going around the building that day. Rumors of the organs that had been forcefully taken from Phil Jarrett and Joe Killian.

Then, suddenly, the room was full of a noise and commotion. She heard footsteps coming from the direction of the open window, as well as the sound of cursing. Abruptly, the weight of her attacker was pulled off of her, along with the sharpness of the deadly blade.

Melba Cox reached over and turned on the lamp beside her bed.

The two detectives who had visited her earlier that morning were standing in the room. The one named Taylor was beside the window, holding a snubnose .38 in his hand. The other, Lowery, was pressing the attacker face first down on the hardwood boards of the bedroom floor. As Melba climbed shakily out of bed, she watched as the detective cuffed the killer's hands.

"Are you all right, ma'am?" asked Taylor, holstering his gun and walking over to her. She saw that he had a pair of binoculars hanging around his neck.

"I think so," she muttered. She pressed a hand to her throat, but found no blood there.

Then the face of the sobbing intruder twisted into view and the woman got a glimpse of who her assailant had been. "You!" she gasped. "I would've never figured you to be the one!"

The wail of sirens echoed from uptown, heading swiftly along Courtland Street. A frigid winter wind whistled through the iron railings of the fire escape and whipped through the open window. The blustery chill caused Melba Cox and the two policemen to shiver, but it made the captured murderer howl in intense agony, as if the icy breeze was cutting past flesh and bone, and flaying the tortured soul underneath.

It was two o'clock in the morning when Ken Lowery and Ed Taylor stood in the main hallway of their precinct, drinking hot coffee in silence. They dreaded the thought of entering the interrogation room and confronting the murderer and mutilator of Jarrett and Killian. The suspect had stopped his cries of torment when brought into the warmth of the police station. That was probably what had spooked the homicide detectives the most. Those awful screams blaming the winter winds on the madness that had taken the lives of two human beings.

"Well, I guess we'd better get it over with," said Lowery, crumpling his styrofoam cup and tossing it into a wastebasket.

"I reckon so," said Taylor. He thought of the suspect and shuddered. He secretly wished that he had taken two weeks of his vacation time instead of only one. Then he would have been fast asleep in an Orlando hotel room, rather than confronting a psychopath in the early hours of the morning.

They opened the door and stepped inside. The suspect was sitting at a barren table at the center of the room. Fingers that had once performed horrible mutilation by brute strength alone, now rested peacefully on the formica surface. The cold December winds had been sealed away by the insulated walls of the police station, returning the killer to a sense of serenity. It was a serenity that was oddly frightening in comparison to the tormented screams that had filled the car during the brief ride back to the precinct.

"You can go now, officer," Taylor told the patrolman who had been keeping an eye on the suspect.

"Thanks," nodded the cop, looking relieved. "This one really gives me the creeps."

After the officer had left, Lieutenant Lowery and Sergeant Taylor took seats on the opposite side of the table and quietly stared at the suspect for a moment.

"What put you onto me?" the killer asked. "How did I slip up?"

"The coroner found some strange hair samples on the bodies of Jarrett and Killian," Lowery told him. "Dog hair. And you were the only one in the building who was allowed to keep an animal."

Dwight Rollins smiled and nodded. "Unknowingly betrayed by my best friend," he said, then bent down and patted the German shepard on the head. "I don't blame you, though, Conrad. I should have brushed off my clothes before I went out."

The dog whimpered and licked at its master's shoes. Lowery and Taylor had brought the dog along, hoping that it would calm the old man down. But only the warmth of the interrogation room had quelled the imaginary storm that raged in the blind man's mind.

"Can we ask why, Mr. Rollins?" questioned Lowery. "Why did you do such a terrible thing?"

Rollins calmly reached up and removed his dark glasses. "*This* is why."

"Good Lord," gasped Taylor, grimacing at the sight of the man's eyeless sockets.

"It happened when I was a child," explained Rollins. "I was running like youngsters do, not really watching where I was going. I tripped and fell face down onto a rake that was buried in the autumn leaves. The tines skewered both my eyes and blinded me for life. I used to have glass eyes, you know, during happier and more prosperous days. But hard times fell upon me and I had to pawn them to buy groceries. I had no idea what a horrible mistake that was."

"And why was that?" asked Lowery. He tried to lower his gaze, but the gaping black pits in the man's face commanded his attention, filling him with a morbid fascination.

"I could have never forseen the horror of the winds," he said. "They've tormented me during these first days of winter. They squeezed past my glasses and swirled through my empty eyesockets, turning them into cold caves. And do you know what lurked in the damp darkness of those old caves, gentlemen? Demons. Winter demons who encased my brain in ice and drove me toward insanity. I would have become a raving lunatic, if it hadn't been for my hands." He brought his wrinkled hands to his lips and kissed them tenderly. "They saved me. They found the means to seal away the winds . . . if only for a short time."

Taylor felt goosebumps prickle the flesh of his arms. "You mean the stolen organs? The eyes of Jarrett and Killian?"

"Yes. They blocked out the winds. But they didn't last for very long. They would soon loose their warmth and feel like cold jelly in my head." A mischievous grin crossed Rollin's cadaverous face, giving him the unnerving appearance of a leering skull. "You know, I was wearing them when you gentlemen came to call."

"Wearing them?" asked Lowery with unease. "You don't mean—"

"Yes," replied Rollins. "Jarrett's eyes. I was wearing them when you came to my apartment yesterday morning." The old man put his glasses back on. "And you didn't even know it."

An awkward silence hung in the room for a moment, then Taylor spoke. "You'll be transferred to the psychiatric section of the city jail across town. A couple of officers will take you there later this morning. You'll remain in custody until your arraignment, after which you'll likely be sent to the state mental hospital. There you'll be evaluated to see if you're psychologically fit to stand trial."

"Very well," said Rollins passively. "But I do hope that the cell they put me in is well heated."

"We'll make sure that it is," promised Lieutenant Lowery. "I'm afraid that you won't be able to take your dog with you, though. It's against police policy, even given your handicap. But we'll see to it that Conrad gets sent to a good home. Maybe we can find some blind kid who needs a trained guide dog."

"That would be nice," said Rollins. "But couldn't he just ride to the jail with me? That wouldn't hurt, would it?"

"No," allowed Lowery. "I suppose we could bend the rules just this once."

"God bless you," said the old man. He leaned down and hugged his dog lovingly.

After calling for an officer to watch the confessed murderer and leaving instructions for those who would transport Rollins to the main jail, Ken Lowery and Ed Taylor left the station hoping to get a few hours sleep that morning. As they walked through the precinct parking lot, a stiff winter breeze engulfed them, ruffling their clothing and making them squint against the blast of icy air.

Before reaching their cars, each man put himself in the shoes of Dwight Rollins. They wondered how they might have reacted if the cold winds had swirled inside their own heads, and if they might not have grown just as mad as the elderly blind man under the same circumstances.

It is cold here in the police van. The officers who are driving me to my incarceration claim that the heater is broken and tell me to quit complaining, so I do. I sit here silently, enduring the creeping pangs of winter, hoping that I can make it to the jailhouse before a fine blanket of frost infects convolutions of my aged brain and once again drives me toward madness.

A mile. Two miles. How far away is the comforting warmth of my designated cell? It is dark in here in the back of the van. Dark and as cold as a tomb. My hands jitter, rattling the cuffs around my wrists. I try to restrain them as they resume their wandering. Through the shadows they search for the warmth that I must have.

My friend. My dearest friend in the world . . . I am so very sorry. But it shall be over soon enough, I promise you that. You must remain faithful, my dear Conrad. You must serve me in death, just as you have in life.

You must help me block out the winds. Those horrible winds within.

CRYING WOLF

Rick Hautala

1

The summer sun had started to fade, stretching long, blue shadows across the lawn. Billy Lewis was sitting on the front steps of his house, staring earnestly at Sarah Cummings, who was straddling her bicycle and leaning over her handlebars on the walkway in front of him. Billy was eleven-years-old, so there was nothing provocative about Sarah's stance; it just made him feel a bit uncomfortable.

"You're just like that kid in the story who was always crying wolf, you know that?" Sarah said. "I'll bet this is just another one of your stupid stories." She huffed and blew her breath up over her face, making her bangs jostle.

"It ain't," Billy said. "You gotta believe me. I saw lights up there in the Laymon house for the past three nights in a row. Honest to God!"

Against her will, Sarah shivered. Although she couldn't see the Laymon house from Billy's front yard, she knew all about the decrepit, old place. Built at the end of the dirt road that wound through the woods and past the swamp behind Billy's house, the house looked at least a hundred years old. No one had lived in it for . . . well, at least as long as Sarah could remember. The few times she had asked her mother about it, her mother had simply commanded her to stay out of the place. "It's dangerous in there," she had said, her voice edged with exasperation. "You never know when a floor or something will give way and cave in on you. Just stay out of there!"

Warnings like that from just about every parent in Hilton, Maine, hadn't stopped just about every kid in town from entering the Laymon house at least once in their life. Most of them made their entries during the day, usually with several friends for mutual support; and just about all of them came away disappointed. There was no dust-covered furniture, no heavy curtains that shifted eerily in the wind, no ghostly shapes in the dark corners. It was just an empty house with faded, peeling wallpaper and exposed lath where the plaster walls had crumbled away. The windows had practically no glass at all left in them, and the rocks that had done the damage were scattered over the floor like boulders in a New England field. Oh, yeah, — sure there were probably rats in the walls, and there certainly was a terrible smell wafting up from down in the dank cellar; but that was to be expected. The Laymon house was nothing but an old, abandoned house – scary and spooky only to overactive imaginations, and certainly not haunted — not *really*!

Over the years, a few kids *had* dared to enter the house at night. More often than not it was part of some silly initiation rite for some gang or other. No one, to Sarah's knowledge, had ever spent an entire night there, but then again, she was only twelve years old. She had heard stories from her older sister, and had no intention of going there — even on a sunny day like this!

"Well, I think you're just trying to scare me," Sarah said. "This is just like the time you had me and everyone else convinced there was a ghost out at Cedar Pond Cemetery. A bunch of us went out there, and you had rigged up a sheet with a flashlight under it, hanging from a tree."

"That was just a Halloween trick — a little early," Billy said, glancing down at the ground. Still sitting, he leaned forward, his elbows on his knees.

"And how about the time you got my brother, Johnny, and Curt all convinced there was a werewolf in the woods behind the Canal Street school? Remember that?"

Billy shrugged coyly, focusing more intently on the ground.

"You convinced a whole bunch of guys to stay out in the woods all night looking for it, and what did you get? Johnny came home with a cold that almost turned into pneumonia. And he got grounded for two weeks after he got better 'cause he lied to my folks about sleeping out in your back yard that night."

"Well . . ." Billy said, almost whining. "There was something out there in the woods. I heard it — and both Johnny and Curt heard it, too!"

"And I'll just bet you're making this one up, too," Sarah said sharply. Her grip on her handlebars tightened, and she cast a fearful look behind her. "And even if there *is* someone out there, how come you're always so sure it's that killer that escaped from Thomaston?"

"It's *gotta* be him," Billy said, his eyes wide and glistening. "If any of the guys were staying out there, don't you think we would've heard about it?"

"Then how come you haven't told Johnny and Curt about it?" Sarah asked pointedly. "*They're* your best friends."

"They wouldn't believe me," Billy said. "'Specially not after the werewolf thing."

"But you expect *me* to believe you?"

Billy shrugged and said nothing.

"Well . . ." Sarah said. "I don't!" She shifted her foot on the bicycle pedal, making ready to ride away.

"Wait!" Billy barked, so suddenly Sarah let out a surprised squeal.

"What is it?" she asked, exasperated.

"Look, how often do I ask a favor from you?" Billy said.

Sarah shrugged, thinking that more often than not Billy, like her brother Johnny, made it a point of honor to ignore her — and irritate the shit out of her when possible.

"You've gotta believe me, Sarah. I'm positive that killer's out there, and I—"

"Then why don't you just go to the police and tell them instead of me?" Sarah asked. She kept gnawing at her lower lip, and Billy took this as a sign that he was getting to her.

"Because they'd believe me even less than you do," Billy said. "I want to go out there tonight and peek in the cellar windows. Just to make sure. But I need someone else there to see, too, so they can back me up when I go to the cops."

Sarah shook her head and scratched the side of her neck. She could still feel the sprinkling of goosebumps that had arisen when Billy had first mentioned the Laymon house. Another, deeper shiver ran up her back now as she stared blankly at the long shadows on the ground.

"Make a unanimous phone call to the police, then," she said.

"You mean anonymous."

"Whatever!"   Sarah's frustration was rising higher as she
see-sawed between skepticism and belief.

"You ain't chicken-shit, are you?" Billy asked.

Sarah was about to say that she *was* chicken-shit, and she didn't
care if Billy or Johnny or anyone else knew it; but something made her
hold her tongue. She just stared at Billy.

"I figure," Billy went on, "if we keep this just between you and me,
then we're gonna be the town heroes for helping catch this guy. I'll bet
we even get our picture in the newspaper — maybe even get on T.V.
and meet the governor and stuff!"

"Who'd *want* to meet the governor?" Sarah asked.

She knew Billy was throwing this stuff out just to tempt her. He
was laying down a line of honey to draw her in; and she knew she should
follow through on her first impulse – tell Billy to take a hike to the moon
before she biked away. She should forget all about him and his
hair-brained story about an escaped murderer living out at the Laymon
house. Why would a convicted killer go there in the first place? How
would he even have known about it? This was just another case of Billy
trying to sucker people in with another one of his wild stories.

But, just like her dad was always telling her, there's always another
side to everything. Granted, the escaped killer might not be living out
there . . . there might not be *anyone* out there; but what if there was? If
there *was*, then, like Billy said, she would be a hero. And if nothing
else, *that* would certainly slap Johnny into place, the fact that she was
counted in, and he wasn't.

"So . . . uh, what are you gonna do?" Sarah asked. She swung off
her bike, laid it gently down on the ground, and came over to sit on the
steps beside Billy.

"Can you get out tonight and meet me behind my house around
. . . say, eleven o'clock?" Billy asked. His voice had a conspiratorial
hush, and she didn't like the way he wouldn't look her straight in the
eyes.

Gnawing at her lip again, Sarah nodded. "It might take some doing,
but I think I can manage it."

"Good," Billy said. "Wear dark clothes, and bring a flashlight.
And make sure no one sees you leave!"

2

The night was filled with the chirping sound of crickets. Overhead, stars sprinkled the sky like powder. A crescent moon rode low in the east. The ground beneath Sarah's feet was lost in darkness as she cut across the neighbor's yards between her house and Billy's. She didn't dare chance walking down the road where a neighbor driving by or glancing out a window might see her. She was wearing a thin jacket against the chill, and, in her hand, she gripped a flashlight she had taken from the glove compartment of her father's truck. Summertall grass whisked at her legs, soaking her cuffs with dew and sending a thin chill up to her knees.

All of the lights were off at Billy's house as she approached it from the side. A faint current of fear raced through her as she looked at the silent, dark house. Her parents had stayed up a little later than usual, and she knew she was at least fifteen minutes late.

. . . What if Billy had given up on her coming and had already gone back to bed?

. . . Or what if he decided to go out to the Laymon house alone?

. . . Or — most likely, she thought — what if he was off hiding somewhere in the trees behind the house, just waiting to give her a scare, pretending he was the escaped convict?

"Psst! Hey, Billy!" she whispered, looking back and forth along the length of the dark house. "You out here?"

The sound of the crickets went on undisturbed. From where she stood, she knew, if she turned around and looked, she might be able to see the Laymon house through the trees. If she turned around, she thought, maybe she *would* see a light in the cellar window.

But as much as she wanted to look, she just couldn't bring herself to do it. If this *was* one of Billy's half-assed jokes, he might already be up there at the old house, shining a light in the window to lure her. And now that she thought about it, maybe her rotten little brother Johnny was in on this, too. Come to think of it, he had gone off to bed tonight without too much complaint; none of his usual fussing about wanting to stay up to watch Carson or Letterman.

"Damn you, Billy! Where the hell are you?" she muttered, stamping her foot angrily on the ground.

"Huh? What's the matter?"

Coming so suddenly out of the darkness, his voice sounded less than an inch from her ear. Stifling a scream, Sarah wheeled around just as Billy was walking toward her around the side of the house.

"You scared the crap out of me!" Sarah said, her voice ragged from her repressed shout.

"Keep it down," Billy whispered, signaling her with a wave of his hand and then pointing upward. "My parents' bedroom window is right there."

Without another word, Billy turned and started walking across the back yard, keeping to the shadows of the trees cast by the thin moonlight. Within seconds he was lost from sight; but before following him, Sarah had to stand there a while longer, waiting for her heart to stop racing.

"You coming or not?" Billy whispered from the shadows. She could hear him but not see him.

For an instant, Sarah considered saying, *No, I'm not coming! This whole thing is ridiculous!*

Any way she looked at it, she was foolish to be following Billy to the Laymon house — or *anywhere* — at night. If the killer really was there, then they would both be in serious trouble. If he wasn't there. . . well, just to deny Billy the satisfaction of scaring her, she was determined to steel her nerves against the inevitable surprise he probably had planned for her. Knowing Billy and his practical jokes, he probably had one heck of a surprise planned for her. Finally deciding that she had come too far now to turn back, she took off in the direction Billy had taken across the yard and through the stand of trees that skirted the dirt road leading up to the Laymon house.

In the dark, she tripped and stumbled in Billy's wake as they felt more than they saw their way through the woods. Wind rustled the leaves overhead, the sound — as much as Sarah tried to resist the idea — reminding her of dry, hard bones clicking together.

"Did you see the light out there again tonight?" she asked at one point when he stooped to let her catch up with him.

In the dark, she saw him nod. "Yeah, just before I snuck out of the house I saw it blink on and off a couple of times. Sorta like he was signaling someone or something." He peered through the darkness to where he could see the looming black bulk of the house through the night-dark puffs of foliage. The abandoned house was no more than a dark smudge against the black stain of the night.

"You're just trying to scare me, that's all," Sarah said, angry at herself for letting her teeth chatter as she said it.

"We'll see. We'll see," Billy replied. "Come on. I figure we can swing around and come up on the back of the house. That'll probably be the safest, and we can avoid the swampy ground."

They fought their way through a thicket of briars that bordered the swamp. Both of them got their feet wet, and their sneakers made soft, sucking sounds as they left the cover of the trees and crept, shoulder to shoulder, up the grass-choked slope behind the Laymon house.

Sarah's heartbeat sounded all the louder in her ears and she couldn't repress a shiver as they crouched at the crest of the hill and stared at the deserted house. She had never been this close to it, looming up against the night sky. The peaked roof glinted like metal in the moonlight, and the blank, glassless windows gaped like yawning mouths. Everything about the house was silent, dark, and dead. Her conviction that Billy was setting her up grew all the stronger.

"I figure we can try the cellar window nearest us," Billy whispered as he pointed toward the foundation steeped in shadow. "I think it was that one where I saw the light."

"Don't you know?"

Billy grunted. "It's hard to tell. All we gotta do is check."

"I don't think I want to go any closer," Sarah whispered. It surprised her that, although she usually didn't even like Billy, she found a strong measure of reassurance just being close to him. "There's noth—"

Before she could finish, as if on cue, a light came on, illuminating the cellar window from the inside. A distorted rectangle of sickly yellow light spilled out onto the ground, showing in sharp detail the tangle of grass and weeds that grew there. The window was skimmed too thickly with dirt for either Billy or Sarah to see inside clearly.

"We've *got* to get closer," Billy whispered harshly, sounding almost desperate. He shifted forward, preparing to scramble the rest of the way to the house, but he was checked by Sarah's hand tugging at his sleeve.

"You don't have to," she said, keeping her voice low, forcing herself not to let it quaver. "I know *exactly* what you're up to!" Turning toward the house, she rose to her feet and, cupping her hands to her mouth, shouted, "Okay, Johnny — and Curt, too, no doubt! You can come out now! Game's over!"

Suddenly, from behind, something hit her in the back of her knees. Her legs gave out, and she twisted as she went down, crumpling to the ground. Billy's weight came down hard on her stomach and chest. The air was forced out of her lungs in a single burning gasp. She wanted to scream and shout, but all she could manage was a breathless moan.

"What . . . are you crazy?" Billy hissed, his mouth close to her ear.

Sarah struggled to get out from under him, but he worked his arms and legs to keep her pinned flat to the ground.

"You—just—get—off—me—right—now!" she sputtered. Try as she might, she couldn't dislodge him by wiggling.

"You'd just better hope to Christ he didn't hear you," Billy said. He had his head cocked up and was anxiously scanning the house. The dull glow from the window washed over his face, giving it a ghostly cast.

"You didn't fool me for a minute," Sarah managed to say now that Billy had shifted his weight a little, and she was able to draw a breath. "I know darn well that my brother's in there, shining that light just so you can try to scare me. Well, Billy Lewis — it just won't work this time!"

"Ahh, but I think it *will* work," a man's voice said, coming to her like a boom of thunder from the surrounding darkness. Sarah had no idea of the direction. "I think you will be scared . . . a whole lot!"

Still unable to see, Sarah listened as steady footsteps approached them from the side of the house. When she looked up, she saw the huge bulk of a man towering above her. He was almost featureless, no more than an inky silhouette against the starry sky as he stood there with his hands on his hips, looking down at her.

"I want to thank you for bringing her to me, Billy-boy," the man said, followed by a hollow laugh. "Now, be a good boy 'n help me get her into the cellar. That way, you'll get to see what I like to do with people like her."

3

Sarah couldn't believe any of this was happening, but it was real; she knew that when she felt the man's strong hands slide under her and heave her up onto his shoulder as if she were a sack of grain. Her throat closed off; nothing more than a feeble squeak would come out as he carried her around to the back of the house. With each step, his shoulder bumped into her like a soft fist in the stomach, taking her breath away. Pinpricks of light spun like comets in front of her eyes. The night song of crickets roared like the ocean in her ears.

Before heading down the cellar stairs, the man paused and turned to look back at Billy. "So, Billy-boy, this is your lucky night tonight, huh?" he said. Down inside the cellar, Sarah could see the faint light of a single candle washing the floor and walls like a coat of cheap paint.

Billy said nothing; he simply followed when the man started down into the dank cellar.

A choking, musty smell tinged with something else, possibly the smell of sewage, nearly gagged Sarah as her mind, like a transmission that had lost all of its teeth, kept whining, louder and louder. No matter how fast it revved, it just wouldn't catch and hold onto anything.

Who is this man? And what is he doing? she wondered frantically. If the point was to scare me — all right, he and Billy have done it. The joke's over and done! They'll be letting me go home now, I'll bet. But then why is he taking me down into the cellar.

These and other questions roared through her mind like a funnel of wind. There were no answers, but Sarah knew it was going beyond a joke; she knew she was in serious trouble when the man unslung her from his shoulder and dropped her roughly to the floor. She hit hard; a jolt of pain as bright as lightning ran up her spine. Her chest ached, and she still couldn't get enough air into her lungs to scream as she watched the man stand back from her, fold his arms across his chest, and smile menacingly. The faint sounds of other footsteps on the cellar steps made her look around, but her heart sank when she saw Billy.

"Just what — are you trying — trying to do?" Sarah said between gasps. Her question was directed not at the man but to Billy, who was lurking in the dark corner by the cellar door. It was the man, however, who answered her.

"We're not *trying* to do anything, missy," he said. His voice was low, booming like a cannon in the distance. "We've already done it, haven't we, Billy-boy? You see, Billy-boy, here, has been helping me out the last few days . . . ever since I blew into town after breaking out."

"You mean . . ."

Knowing what the rest of her question was, the man chuckled and nodded. "You must've read about me in the paper, or maybe seen me on the T.V."

Sarah's eyes felt as though they were bulging six inches out of her face as she stared up at Billy. He was still cringing in the shadowed corner. The feeble light of the candle made his shadow dance and weave. She couldn't begin to accept that Billy had set her up for something like this, and her blood ran cold when she began to imagine what might happen next.

"You didn't happen to bring that food you promised, did you, Billy-boy?" the man asked. He never once took his eyes off Sarah as he spoke.

"No, I . . . uh, I couldn't bring it when I was coming out with her," he replied, his voice sounding thin and weak. "I mean, she would've suspected something was up."

"I been gettin' kinda hungry, Billy-boy," the man replied. He shot Billy a quick, angry glance, then turned back to Sarah, who was pressing herself back against the stone wall.

"Then again," the man went on, "I always was a business before pleasure kind of guy." With that, he reached behind his back and quickly snapped his hand out in front of him. Held tightly in his right hand was a thick-bladed knife, at least six inches long. The blade glinted wickedly in the candle light as the man turned it back and forth admiringly.

"You . . .? What are . . . you?" Sarah sputtered. Her mind was nothing more than a black blur as she stared, horrified, at the gleaming knife.

This is going too far! her mind screamed. *This man isn't kidding! This isn't just some practical joke. He means it!*

"Billy . . .?" she said, no more than a whimper.

"Billy-boy ain't gonna help you, little girl," the man said. He took one slow step toward her, the knife weaving in front of him in a lazy figure-eight. "Oh, no! Billy-boy's the one who brought you up to me. He's the one who said he wouldn't mind if I carved you up. Ain't that right, Billy-boy?"

Wide-eyed and trembling, Billy nodded in agreement.

"You see, little girl?" the man said. "Billy-boy found me living out here, 'n — well, my first recourse was to waste him. I couldn't very well have him blabbing about the escaped convict living up here in this deserted house, now, could I? But before I gutted him, we started talking; 'n before long, he and I had worked out a little deal. Ain't that so, Billy-boy? He'd bring me food so I could hole up here until I figured where to go next, but what was in it for ole' Billy-boy, here? Then, just yesterday, we struck on our little deal."

"I can't believe you're doing this to me!" Sarah yelled at Billy. Hot tears stung her eyes, but she forced herself not to cry. Her chest still felt like it was bound with steel bands, but the horror of her situation now fueled her anger.

"Oh, Billy-boy ain't gonna do a thing . . . 'cept watch," the man said, taking another step closer. "When we got to talking about what I was put in jail for, he told me he'd just like to see what it looks like when someone dies. You see — that was our deal. He'd bring someone out here, and I'd put on a little show for him. Right, Billy-boy?"

Before Billy could respond, the man laughed a deep, watery laugh and came closer to Sarah, leaning down so the knife blade was level with her face, no more than three inches away.

Sarah's hands and feet scrambled wildly on the floor, but the solid granite blocks prevented any further retreat. It took several seconds for her brain to register that her right hand was wrist deep in some gritty-feeling stuff, either sand or crumbled mortar; but once she realized it, she acted quickly. Grabbing as big a handful as she could, she screamed and flung it straight into the man's face.

In the split second the man staggered back in surprise, bellowing his rage as he tried to clean his eyes, Sarah coiled her legs and jumped to her feet. She was running full speed for the cellar stairs when she heard the man shout behind her. It sounded like he was right behind her, inches away.

"*Stop her! Goddamn yah! Stop her!*"

In a blur, Sarah saw Billy jump out to intercept her. She felt his hand snag the loose flap of her jacket. With a shriek, she turned and swung out, hard, at his hand, but he held on tightly as she lurched forward, dragging him toward the cellar stairway.

"*Don't let her get away, you son-of-a-bitch!*" the man yelled.

Sarah could hear him stumbling toward her, and all she could think about was that gleaming knife blade slicing cleanly through her throat. Panic whined in her ears like a power drill and fueled her efforts to get away. She was just starting to think all was lost, she wasn't going to make it, when she heard the harsh whisper of tearing cloth. The backward pulling pressure on her jacket suddenly released, and she stumbled forward. Her shins slammed into the bottom step, but she quickly regained her balance and leaped up the stairs and out into the night. Not waiting to see how close her pursuers were, she clenched her fists into tight balls and ran straight down the dirt road toward home, screaming as loud as she could.

4

"You let her get away, Billy-boy!" the man snarled as he watched Sarah disappear up the stairs and into the night. His eyes were still stinging from the grit she had thrown at him, and he repeatedly wiped at them with his shirt sleeve. He moved over to where Billy was standing by the cellar wall.

"I . . . I'm sorry," Billy said, helplessly dangling in one hand the piece he had torn from Sarah's jacket.

"Do you realize how much of a problem this is going to cause me?"

Billy wasn't able to keep eye contact with the man, so he looked down at his scuffed, dew-soaked sneakers. "I really am sorry," he muttered. "She was moving too fast."

The man walked over to the cellar doorway. With a sudden sinking feeling in his gut, Billy realized that he had positioned himself between him and the stairs.

"This blows it all for me as far as *I* can see, Billy-boy," the man hissed. "We had a nice set-up here, and now, sure as shit, she's gonna have the cops down on this place in a matter of minutes."

Billy took a shuddering breath, wishing he could edge his way over to the doorway that led to freedom.

"I'm sorry I didn't get that food to you," Billy said. His voice was so tightly constricted, he sounded more like a girl.

"Ohh, I wouldn't worry 'bout that," the man said.

Billy couldn't help but notice that the man hadn't put his knife away. Shouldn't he start gathering his few things so he can make good his escape before the police show up? he wondered.

"I'm just sorry you didn't get to see what you came for," the man said. He shook his head sadly. The anger had left his voice; his words now were as smooth as honey. Coming up close to Billy, he placed his hand gently, almost lovingly on Billy's shoulder. Then the fingertips started to dig into his shoulder . . . at first, just enough to hurt, then unrelentingly.

"'Course, we can take care of that before I have to take off, now can't we, Billy-boy?"

With that, he snagged Billy by the wrist and roughly jerked him around so his arm was pinned up between his shoulder blades. A jolt of pain ran up to the base of Billy's skull, but that was nothing compared to the fear that suddenly surged through his body when he fully realized what was about to happen.

"Now, I know you could see this a damn-site better if we had a mirror or something," the man whispered. His breath was hot on the back of Billy's neck. From the corner of his eyes, Billy saw the six-inch blade come from around in front of him.

"But we'll just have to make do, won't we? Now, lookey here, Billy-boy," the man hissed. "This is what you came for . . . this is what it looks like."

With a quick, tearing slice, the blade tore through Billy's shirt and drove into his stomach. Surprisingly, Billy felt no pain at first, just numbed shock as he watched the man's clenched fist push the knife against the rubbery resistance of his stomach muscles. Blood gushed out of the wound and over the man's hand, and then — at last — Billy's brain registered the pain, silver splinters that exploded through his body.

When Billy's legs started to tremble and give way beneath him, the man jerked him roughly back up. The knife was buried to the hilt in Billy's stomach as the man tugged on it, opening the wound even wider. Guts spilled onto the cellar floor, uncoiling like heavy, wet ropes.

"Now don't go passin' out on me, Billy-boy," the man rasped close to his ear. "I don't have much time, and you've *gotta* see what you came here to see."

ANIMAL RITES

Jay R. Bonansinga

Stirring awake, Daddy Norbert found himself tied to a moldy Lazy Boy in the tool shed out back of the garage. Head felt like a rusty nail had been driven into it. Something sticky was digging into his belly. Would have rubbed his puss-bleary eyes, but he found his big calloused mitts hog-tied to the springs beneath him.

"Whylmmmphrump—?" Daddy's query was sabotaged by stupid lips.

"Good!" The voice popped out of the shadows like a firecracker. "You're comin' awake."

"—lllliihhsh—?" Although Daddy's mouth was still asleep, his eyes were sharpening, beginning to make out a faint figure before him.

"Takes it a spell to wear off," the voice said.

Daddy Norbert blinked. "Lizzy . . . ? That you?"

"Yessir."

"The hell is going on?!"

Stone silence.

Daddy Norbert blinked some more, and started putting things together. His teenage step-daughter Lizabeth must have slipped him a mickey back at the house and dragged him out here to the tool shed. Girl was seriously wrong in the head. Been that way ever since her mama died. Getting skinnier and skinnier, messin' with that faggoty colored boy up to Little Rock. Now the girl must've gone stark raving screwy. Crouching in the shadows across from Daddy, fiddling with something that sounded like a tin cup with a nail in it. Girl was crazy as a cross-eyed loon.

"Almost ready," the voice finally said. "Just hold your horses."

"What in the wide friggin' world of sports is going on?!"

"Be still."

"What did you slip me, girl?"

"Called Tranxene. It's temporary, so just shut up and sit still for a minute."

"Don't you sass me!"

Skinny little bitch didn't even react, just kept on working with that rattling box of metal. Daddy's eyes were adjusting to the dark. He could see strips of old duct tape wrapped around his massive girth. Something leather was holding his head in place like blinders on a plough horse. Smelled like wet dog fur. Daddy swallowed hard. "Lizzy—why you doin' this?"

"It's a secret."

"Whattya mean, secret?"

"You'll see."

"I'm sorry," he told her all of a sudden. His bowels were beginning to burn, his mouth going dry as wheat meal. It was dawning on him, this girl could very easily hurt him. Maybe hurt him a lot. "I'm sorry for what I did to you and your mama. You hear me? I'm tellin' ya how sorry I am."

No answer.

"Lizzy—?"

She switched on the light.

The sudden glare of an old aluminum scoop light exploded across the shed. Blinking fitfully, Daddy saw the shriveled carcasses splayed across his work bench to his left. His future projects. Parts of a rabbit, a young fox, the hind end of a bobcat. Rusty traps were arrayed across the walls. Behind him, mounted on a shim of hardwood, a deer looked on, its lifeless eyes glimmering.

Daddy looked down at Lizzy and drew in a sudden breath.

She was on the floor, securing one of Daddy's favorite guns, a custom Roberts rifle, into a weird contraption of metal and wood. Looked like a spring loaded skeet shooter. The rattling sound that Daddy had heard must've been the bullet. Lizzy was loading a .219 Zipper into the gun's chamber. The Zipper was Daddy's favorite brand.

A 90-grain heavy power compression load, the bullet would take down an adult Elk bull at two-hundred yards.

The barrel of the rifle had a bead drawn right smack dab on Daddy.

"Now hold on, child—!" Daddy Norbert started breathing hard, fighting his restraints, electric current shooting up his spine. Fear made his sphincter contract. "Y-y-y-y-y-y-y-y-y-y-you ain't gonna shoot me—just simmer down now!"

"There," Lizzy said softly to herself, finishing the load as though she had just put a cake in the oven. She stood up and gazed at Daddy emotionlessly, her eyes rimmed in dark circles. She looked like a person who had just come home from a funeral. Drained and wrung out. She was holding a jury-rigged triggering device—the pull-string from an old push mower. It was tethered to the Roberts. Underneath Lizzy's sleeveless blouse, a tank top had the letters P.E.T.A. imprinted on it. People for the Ethical Treatment of Animals. Daddy had never seen that before.

"Taste it?" she calmly asked him. "The fear?"

"Let-let-let-let-l-l-let go of that thing," Daddy stammered, "we can talk this out."

"Like the deer?" She bored her gaze into him. "You talk things over with the deer?"

"Ww-w-w-w-wait-wait-wait-wait—! Just tell me w-w-w-w-w-w-w-what you want me to do? You want me to say I'm sorry? I'm sorry! Awright? I'm sorry, I'm sorry, I'm sorry!"

Lizzy didn't answer. Instead, she closed her eyes, bowed her head, and began mouthing a secret litany. Daddy Norbert started to say something else, but he stopped abruptly when he saw the objects in her other hand. Lizzy was grasping a handful of objects twined together with string. Sprigs of herbs or weeds or some other kind of nonsense that her Jamaican boyfriend had probably given her. Strands of hair, human hair maybe. A silk ribbon, a book-mark from Lizzy's old Concordance bible, and some other strands of unidentifiable fabric. But none of it currently seemed as important, or made as much of an impression on Daddy Norbert, as the tiny black objects hanging from the bottom of the thing.

The broken beads of her dead mother's rosary.

"Hold the phone—!" Daddy Norbert barked at her. "You ain't mad about no deer! You're still steamed about your goddamned ma! For God's sake, it ain't my fault she up and died! Already told you a million times, I'm sorry I hit her! You'd think I planted the goddamn cancer in her goddamn cervix myself! It weren't my fault! Now—Lizzy, just—stop it! STOP IT RIGHT NOW!"

Lizzy kept gazing at him.

"YOU SKINNY LITTLE HALF-PINT, PUT THAT GUN AWAY 'FORE I GIVE YOU ANOTHER WHOOPIN'!!"

Lizzy gripped the cable and smiled. Her face was a rictus of pain. "This is for you, great white hunter," she uttered. It sounded rehearsed.

Then she pulled the cable.

"AAAAAAAHHHHHHHHHHHHHHH—!!"

Eyes slamming shut, Daddy Norbert winced. Matter of fact, he winced so hard a little squirt of shit spurted from his anus. He thought he heard the pop. The sharp blast of the hammer hitting the pin, and the bones shattering in his face. But he must've imagined it. Actually, he felt nothing. Just the warmth in the seat of his pants and the painful throb of his heart.

He opened his eyes.

At first, he figured the gun must've misfired. There was a thin veil of smoke rising in the light, and Daddy thought he smelled the oily aroma of gunpowder. Lizzy was backing toward the door, her gaze still riveted to the man. What the hell was going on? Why was she looking at him like that?

"For you . . . " she whispered as she slipped through the door and into the cool Arkansas night.

"What the—?"

Daddy looked down at the gun and studied it for another moment. The black hole of its barrel was staring at him, the smoke diffusing, the silence like a block of ice over Daddy's head. Daddy blinked again and suddenly there were tears in his eyes. All at once, he realized just how lucky he really was. "I'll be a sonofabitch," he muttered, grinning to himself in spite of his frayed nerves. "Twenty-three years in the woods, and not one dud, and tonight the god damned thing decides to misfire!"

He began to giggle.

"I'll be a swivel-hipped sonofabitch! Goddamned misfire! GOD DAMNED   MISS-FUCKING-FIRE!! WHOOPTY-DO-AND-FUCK-ME-BLUE!!" Daddy laughed and laughed and laughed, and then he looked down at the gun.

His laughter died.

Something had appeared in the mouth of the barrel. Something round. Just barely poking out, the light shining off it like a tiny planet. At first, Daddy wondered if it was an obstruction, an odd fragment of metal that had gotten wedged in there after a misfire during his last hunting trip. The thing looked familiar, the blue steel gleam winking in the dim light.

The .219 calibre Zipper.

"Holy fuckin' shit," Daddy uttered, staring at the bullet peeking out of the barrel. He'd heard stories of freak misfires, bullets getting lodged in barrels and such. But he never really believed them. Always figured it was whiskey talk, nothing more. Grin widening, he closed his eyes. "Sweet Jesus, Lord in heaven, I realize I ain't been to church in a month of Sundays, but I wanna thank y'all just the same."

A chill breeze wafted in through the half-ajar door, and it cooled the beads of sweat on Daddy's forehead. He opened his eyes, grinning like an idiot. He could smell the surrounding farms, the sorghum, manure and wet hay. The odors never smelled so good to Daddy Norbert. He was alive, and that was all that mattered. Next step was to figure out how to get out of this fucking chair. Glancing down at the rifle, he took one last gander at the bullet.

His smile faded.

The bullet had moved, just a tad. Matter of fact, if Daddy Norbert was any less familiar with the shape of the Zipper's casing, he might have not even noticed. But there it was, poking out of the barrel, one, maybe two additional inches of casing. Daddy swallowed air. Maybe it was just a trick of the light, op'kil illusion or whatever you call it. He studied the muzzle of the Roberts and felt his heart flip-flop in his chest.

The bullet was halfway out the barrel.

"Gotta have that damn thing checked." He chuckled softly. "Ain't that a kick."

Daddy stared at the rifle. If he didn't know better, he could have sworn the bullet had moved some more. Moved with the subtle steadiness of a clock. 'Course, that was impossible. That was damn near mad-hatter crazy. He took a breath and tried to rip his arms free. The rope held tight. His fingers were going numb, and he could feel the mess in his pants, burning his butt crack, stinking to high heaven.

"Wait'll I get my hands on that skinny little—!"

All at once, Daddy Norbert noticed the bullet was protruding nearly all the way out of the barrel now. Defying gravity. He blinked, and he blinked, and he blinked some more, and he still saw it. With his very own watery eyes. The Zipper was sticking almost clean out of the muzzle. Daddy wondered if a strange pocket of air had gotten trapped in the muzzle behind it . . . or something like that. Didn't really matter though, because the bullet was going to clear the lip of the barrel any second now and fall to the floor.

Except it didn't fall.

"What the fuck—?"

Daddy gawked. Damn bullet hung in midair in front of the muzzle like a moth in aspic. No visible means of support. And Daddy got to thinking all of a sudden, thinking about Lizzy and that shit she was holding in her hand a minute ago and how she had that screwy look in her eye. Something cold and hard started turning in Daddy's gut. Chills rolled up his back, and the tiny hairs stood at attention along the back of his neck. The duct tape was digging into his belly. His head throbbed against its restraint. The worst part wasn't the fact that the bullet was frozen in space, which was pretty goddamned impossible if you thought about it for a second. Wasn't even the fact that it seemed to be slowly yet steadily inching forward.

The worst part was that it was heading straight for Daddy Norbert.

He frowned. The bullet was out of the muzzle by several inches now, moving through the space between the gun and Daddy with the inexorable slowness of a sundial. It looked like a tiny grey stain in the air. Impossible. Goddamned impossible, but here it came. A two-hundred calibre magic trick. Maybe six feet, seven at the most, between the bullet and Daddy. At this rate, it would take the bullet at least ten minutes to reach him. Then what? Stupid thing would probably bump Daddy's nose and plummet to the floor like some second-rate levitation trick, like some throw-off from the Amazing El Moldo. "Piece of shit parlor trick!" Daddy giggled again, his voice stretched thin. "Can't scare me with some cheap dime store gag!"

The bullet continued coming.

A scalding tear of sweat ran down Daddy Norbert's forehead and pooled in his eye. It burned. Daddy blinked, and cursed, and strained against the leather head restraints. He shook furiously against the tape. It was no use. Lizzy had done a bang up job on the bondage.

Daddy's laughter sputtered and died.

"This ain't possible," he uttered, suddenly stricken, his gaze glued to the bullet.

Daddy Norbert had never really believed in magic before. Growing up dirt poor in the Ozark Mountains, he'd certainly run across his share of hokum. One old gal who lived behind the Norberts' pig farm was rumored to be a witch, but Daddy never believed it. Occasionally there'd be a gypsy clan who'd pass through the neighboring town. Some said it was gypsies that brought the drought of '49 to Pinkneyville. But Daddy never bought any of that hoodoo shit. Daddy Norbert was a simple hillbilly boy who grew up into a simple hillbilly man. Never got much of an education. Stayed out of trouble most of his adult life. Sure, he slapped his women around a little bit; he wasn't proud of it. But Jesus God, did he deserve this?

The bullet kept coming, crossing the halfway mark now, hanging in the air just as horrible as you please.

Something snapped inside Daddy Norbert, as sure as a guillotine in his brain. Fear. It stole his breath and flowed cool through his veins. Stung his eyes. Made his fists clench up like vices until blood started soaking the ropes. He'd been up against many a rough scrape in his day. Tangled with the Mueller boys down to Quincy. Got caught cheating at Anaconda on a river boat casino. Fought three cops on the side of the road once, got away with a single broken rib and a chipped tooth. But this was different, way over the edge; because all of a sudden Daddy realized this was what his own daddy used to call bad juju.

The bullet crept closer.

"Okay, okay, okay, okay—" Daddy started breathing deeply, trying to settle down, trying to convince himself it was all a trick, and that everything was going to be okay . . . but there was that shiny grey stain in the air coming right at him. And the leather binding holding his head in place. And the terrible certainty that Lizzy and her colored buck had planned this thing especially for Daddy. And that the bullet's destination was somewhere in the vicinity of Daddy Norbert's forehead, just above his left eye. *"Okay, okay, okay, okay, calm down, okay, get it together, calm down, calm down—"*

Daddy Norbert blinked.

Something sparked around the armature of the bullet. Sudden veins of light, erupting outward like the afterimage of a photographer's bulb. Faint lines mapping the darkness. A ghostly image curling around the zipper like a heat ray mirage cured in whiskey-misted eyes (*years ago, drooling drunk, his rough hands on pale flesh, wedging himself inside*

*a young girl's thighs, forcing himself into her, again and again, the
sound of her smothered cries)*

"Wwwwhhha—?!"

Daddy slammed his eyes closed.

The realization was like a claw hammer to his forehead. *Visions.*
He remembered his grandmammy having visions of the end of the
world, talking to Jesus in her sleep, and all of a sudden Daddy Norbert
realized this was one of those kinds of visions. Daddy Norbert was
having a vision of the end of the world. He was a sinner, he had done
wretched things and now this was his very own reckoning day.

"Our father—who, who, who, who—art in heaven—hallowed by
thy name, they, they, they—*SHIT*—!!"

Eyes popping open, Daddy saw that the bullet was less than two
feet away now. So close, Daddy could see the serial number on its
collar. He tried to swallow, but his spit was long gone. Throat like a
lime pit. Piss spurting out of him. He didn't deserve this kind of hellish
fate. Simple hillbilly, never got an education, never meant no harm, he
just didn't deserve this. He began to cry. *"GET IT OVER WITH! JUST
DO IT! FINISH IT!!"* His voice was like old metal tearing apart. *"GET
IT OVER WITH!!"*

Twelve inches to go.

Another vision bloomed from the metal jacket. Veins of electric
lightning threading out in all directions, coalescing into images, stormy
images, apocalyptic images bombarding Daddy Norbert (*the snap of a
belt on a woman's thick rear end, across the backs of her arms, drawing
red streaks and welts . . . the red rain falling on parched ground, the
locusts and the seven wax seals pealing away in the wind . . . the
strangled cries of his wife, begging for mercy, mercy, no mercy*) until
he shook the memories off like gasoline on his face and cried so hard
his snot ran across his lips in salty stringers. He prayed, and he bawled,
and he begged God to come deliver him from this terrible trick.

Six inches now.

Daddy watched the bullet inching toward his forehead, his body
convulsing with the fear and the tears and the shaking. The tape held
him steady, the leather braced his head. Five inches. Four. Three.
"Our-father-who-art-in-h-h-h-h-h-h-h-h-h-h-h-heaven—ha lllllllll-
hah-hahhhh—!" The sudden flare of blinding light strangled off his
voice.

He slammed his eyes shut and jerked backward with the force of the vision.

This time, the image was brutally clear.

(*daddy was naked, hunched in a thicket of weeds in the forest, breathing hard, trapped . . . he could smell his own spoor, the warmth of his fur and the tympany of his heart . . . his hooves were split and bleeding in the leaves . . . his antlers ached, and he could see the glint of something shiny through the trees across from him, the barrel of a well-seasoned Roberts rifle sticking out of the brush . . . then the flash of a shell exploding*)

At that moment, in the harsh light of the lonely tool shed, the cool metal tip of the bullet softly kissed Daddy Norbert's forehead just above the left eye . . .

. . . and kept coming . . .

. . . beginning Daddy Norbert's official, albeit long overdue, education.

EASY'S LAST STAND

Nancy A. Collins

"I want to fuck my mother; isn't that naughty of me?"

"I really can't say, Floyd, until you give me your credit card number and its expiration date."

"Tell me it's naughty! Tell me it's bad: the worst thing in the world! The worst thing you've ever heard!"

"Floyd—"

"I won't give you the number if you don't tell me it's dirty."

Sandra rolled her eyes. If it was up to her, she'd hang up on the little perv. She'd never seen Floyd before in her life. Never would. She pictured him as a middle-aged CPA in Sans-A-Belts slacks, leather oxfords and the wrong color tie. It was also certain he had a platinum AmEx card, and that's what really mattered.

The Gaboochi Brothers, her employers, liked to eavesdrop on the line now and again, to make sure everyone observed proper procedure. It wouldn't do to have the girls insulting the customers. Or giving away too much for free. She could tell from Floyd's shallow, nasal breathing that he was whacking off, but she didn't dare cut the line before getting his card number.

"Yeah, it's the most horrible thing I've ever heard," she lied. This seemed to be what Floyd wanted to hear, as the sound of one hand clapping rapidly increased and he moaned something under his breath.

"Now, about that card number . . . "

click.

Sandra swore into the mouthpiece of her headset. She should have known better. Why give the cow your AmEx number when you can get the milk for free? Usually she was better at spotting the jerk-offs, as she liked to call them; the guys interested in getting their rocks off before you could snag their credit card numbers.

She'd been working for Easy's Hot Talk for three months, long enough to give her seniority in the call room and gain a boost in pay. $5.50 a hour. Not bad for work that consisted largely of sitting on your ass talking on the phone. Granted, you had to talk to some really sick puppies but, as Gloria was fond of saying, 'you knew the job was dangerous when you took it, Fred'.

Easy's Hot Talk was a phone sex joint. Well, not really. Actually, the women harnessed to the state-of-the-art telemarketing headgear and multi-line telephone banks weren't hired to help lonely, faceless men achieve long-distance sexual fulfillment, although the classified ads salted in the back of skin mags like HOT MILK, BIG BAD MAMAS, CATFIGHT QUARTERLY, and GIRLS WITH CUNT LIPS THE SIZE OF SADDLEBAGS, certainly gave that impression:

Hi! I'm Easy! I've got a HOT, NASTY TONGUE and I want to make U cum! I know what men like and I've got what men want! I'll make you EXPLODE with PLEASURE! Call now for WILD UNTAMED phone sex! Call anytime! I'm ALWAYS there for YOU! 1-900-468-8255 (HOT-TALK)

The come-on hooked them but good; hundreds of hot and horny readers called the 900 number, the vast majority of them at night. Instead of the oozing, cooing sex-doll shown cradling a telephone receiver at an inappropriate angle for conversation, the callers got an operator with a prepared speech designed to be mildly titillating without being actually obscene. Each "Hot Talker" was under orders to sell the caller a list of "secret phone numbers" for a nominal fee (charged to their credit cards, of course) along with "candid photos" of 'Easy' frolicking with her friends.

The phone numbers "sold" to the callers were really pre-recorded tapes of Gloria reading letters from PENTHOUSE HOT TALK. To top it off, the callers were billed three dollars a minute, including for time spent on hold.

It was a blatant rip-off and the Gaboochi Brothers made money hand over fist. The operation had been around since the late Seventies, but with the increase of herpes, penicillin-resistant gonorrhea, and AIDS, business was booming like never before.

Barnum was right; there *is* one born every minute. But Sandra wondered how, since it seemed half of America was into one-handed telephone conversations.

She decided it was time for a brief respite from the perverts of America's heartland and removed her head-set. Gloria frowned at her from the foot of the huge table. Sandra mouthed the words *gotta pee* and made her way to the hall.

Easy's Hot Talk was located in a nondescript one-story single-family dwelling that had been converted, for all practical purposes, into a twenty-four hour answering service. The house was just beyond the city limits, in an unincorporated section that was a no-man's land of third-hand auto dealerships, after hour pool-halls, and tail-gate flea markets. The Gaboochi Brothers' prize operation wasn't illegal, but it didn't exactly have a Better Business Bureau sign hanging in the front window.

Sandra glanced back into the call-room; cigarette smoke hung over the table like mosquito netting. Most of the women chain-smoked while on duty, Sandra included. Non-smokers tended to quit after a couple of days. If any of the poor sweaty-handed bastards who surrendered their Visa, MasterCard and AmEx numbers (the Gaboochis didn't accept Discover) could see who was answering the phone for Easy (she of the silicone injections and artfully spread labia) they'd never get it up again.

She'd talked to enough desperate college students and terminally aroused hicks to know most of them thought they were going to talk to the woman pictured in the ad, or one of her so-called "personal friends," when they called. In reality no one, not even the Gaboochi Brothers, knew who 'Easy' was. She was some bimbo who posed nude for a semi-pro photographer sometime during the Seventies and had signed a model's release.

The operators fielding Easy's eager suitors were mostly housewives and retirees. Sandra, at twenty-seven, was one of the youngest women working the phones. Doris, grandmother of three, calmly knitted a sweater for her husband while reciting her spiel into the throat mike while Muriel chatted incessantly between calls about her ex-husbands. Nora snapped her wad of Dentine while she fiddled with her bouffant wig. Then there was Gloria, the Head Honcho.

If anyone could be said to dominate the call-room, it was her. Gloria weighed close to five hundred pounds, sat on two folding chairs, and sounded like Marilyn Monroe in heat. She'd been with the Gaboochi Brothers for a few years and rewarded with a promotion to night manager.

When Sandra had answered the ambiguously phrased ad for a "telephone sales woman", the first thing Gloria told her was: "We got three rules here: we don't take calls from minors; we don't take calls from women; and we don't take calls from guys with numbers on the Hot Card list." It seemed like a simple enough philosophy.

Gloria ran the show from eight in the evening to two in the morning, the heaviest calling period, and she didn't tolerate goofing off on her shift. Despite her insistance on treating Easy's Hot Talk like a legitimate business, Sandra and the others liked her. Gloria, unlike the day manager, wasn't scared of the Gaboochis and wasn't above making jokes at their expense. She would also send one of the girls out for doughnuts or pizza if the mood struck her, something frowned on during the day when the Gaboochis might stop by in person to check on business.

The bathroom door opened and ZuZu stepped out, tugging on her leather miniskirt. Of the entire group, the only one that looked like a pin-up girl was ZuZu, if you ignored the yin-yang tatooed on her skull (bisected by a magenta mohawk) and the collection of gold rings piercing her ears, nose, belly-button and labia.

"Hey, Sandy! Howzit going, girlchick?"

"Got the weekend off to catch your gig!" ZuZu fronted her own all-female thrash band, ZuZu's Petals. That weekend they were opening for the Butthole Surfers at the local hardcore venue. ZuZu claimed the only reason she worked for 'pigs like the Gaboochis' was to raise the cash for a Stratocaster. She'd been there almost a year.

"Awright! Better get back to the yoke before Big Mama starts losing her cool! Catch you later, Sandy."

As she washed her hands at the sink, Sandra froze as a shadow flickered across the frosted window pane. She hurried from the bathroom and back into the call-room. Gloria looked up when she entered and frowned even deeper than before, causing chain reactions in her chins.

"We got company, Gloria."

"Shit. You sure?"

"Pretty sure. He was standing outside the bathroom window."

Gloria grunted and pressed her strangely small hands against the tabletop, levering her vast bulk onto her elephantine legs. Not only was Gloria fat, she was big too, towering a head taller than Sandra. The metal folding chairs seemed to groan in relief as she stood up. Sandra stepped back, momentarily overwhelmed by the body heat radiating from the other woman. Gloria seemed to sweat all the time, even in the winter.

"Better wake up Carl, then. I'll call the Brothers."

Technically, Carl was one of the Gaboochis, but in the same way Gummo was one of the Marx Bothers. Carl was the youngest Gaboochi and by far the least motivated of the family; he slept in one of the rooms during the night-shift and his job was to chase off unwanted visitors. It was an undemanding job, it kept Carl out of trouble, and it theoretically involved him in the family business. The Hot Talkers didn't resent Carl's prescence; unlike his elder siblings, Carl was occasionally useful. Jealous boyfriends and outraged husbands were fairly common, as were the occasional lust-struck callers hungry to meet Easy in the flesh. While the Gaboochis didn't advertise their comings and goings, the location of Easy's Hot Talk was something of an open secret.

Usually the sight of Carl, baseball bat in hand, was enough to chase off any would-be trouble makers. Sandra banged on a door marked "General Manager".

"Carl! Wake up, damn it! We got a prowler!"

There was some muttering and after a couple of seconds Carl Gaboochi opened the door, revealing the "General Manager's" office to be a mess of stale beer cans, empty bologna wrappers, and dog-eared Louis L'Amour paperbacks. He wore a pair of grungy blue jeans and a smelly Harley Davidson t-shirt.

"Wuzzit?"

"Gloria told me to tell you to check the perimeter. Someone's sneaking around outside."

Carl seemed to wake up a little more. "Izzit that dumb-ass motherfucker again?" he yawned, showing the gap where his front teeth used to be. A couple of weeks ago the boyfriend of one of the new girls decided to try and save her from eternal damnation by dragging her, kicking and screaming, out of the house. Carl had been forced to separate the boyfriend's cowboy hat from his skull the hard way.

"I don't think so. Charlene quit a couple of days ago."

"Get back t'work. I'll take care of it." Carl reached behind the door to his office and retrieved a Louisville Slugger with a taped handle.

Damn it, can't a guy sleep in peace around here? Carl mused as he unlocked the front door. As if it wasn't bad enough his jerk-wad brothers had him babysitting a gaggle of old biddies . . . He stifled another yawn and scratched himself. Still, it was better than bouncing at the after-hours joint.

He stepped onto the lawn, the dew wet under his feet, squinting into the darkness. A couple hundred yards from the front door was the old highway. The traffic was light and infrequent after ten o'clock.

"Anybody out here?" Carl bellowed in his best mean-ass redneck voice. "If y'are, y'all better git 'fore I find you!"

Carl walked around the corner towards the rear of the house, swinging his Louisville Slugger with each stride. He wasn't really expecting to find anyone in the bushes. Usually one look at him brandishing his bat, was all it took to scare off the little rubber-dicks. Mostly they were high school kids who somehow got it into their thick heads the place was some kind of bordello.

There was the sound of a heel slipping on gravel behind him and Carl spun in time to see the hunting knife, then it was too late to see anything else.

✦   ✦

Gloria took the call.

"Hi, I'm Easy!" she said, trying to make the prepared speech as suggestive as possible. She'd recited the same damn spiel so many times since she'd first come to work for the Gaboochi Brothers that it'd become something of a mantra for her. *Hi, I'm Easy! Hi, I'm Easy! Hi, I'm Easy!* She often went to bed with those three words looped into her thoughts.

"Hello, Easy. It's me." There was something about the caller's voice that made her pause. "I've been waiting to talk to you for a long time."

"Is that so? Well, I want to talk to you *too.* 'If you're interested in women who know what you want . . . '"

"Cut the sales pitch, bitch." The voice on the other end of the phone grew hard, sharp thorns. "I'm wise to the game you're playing."

Oh-oh. Dissatisfied customer.

"You thought I was stupid, didn't you? Thought I wouldn't catch on to the shit you were trying to pull on me, huh? I bet you don't even *remember* me, do you? You don't even remember me asking you if I'd get to talk to you or some fucking machine. You said I'd get to talk to *you*. To someone *real*. You lied to me, bitch!" The voice grew shriller, biting her ear with needle-point teeth. "You're a slut, just like the others." The caller's voice suddenly was cold and flat, like a metal wall. "So be it. But you should have known better. You know I don't scare that easy." He chuckled at some private joke.

"What do you mean?" Gloria let the sugar-and-spice coating slip.

"I dealt with your boyfriend. Or was he your pimp?"

"What are you talking about?"

"Why don't you look on the back porch?"

Dead air.

Gloria stared at the telephone for a few seconds before slipping her head-set off. She could see Sandra and Doris staring at her.

"Sandy, where's Carl?"

"He went to check out the prowler. Why?"

Doris paused in her knitting. "What's the matter, Gloria?"

"Nothing. Just a crank call, that's all."

"Oh. I *hate* those." Doris clucked as she continued her knitting. "People can be so rude and thoughtless."

"Excuse me a minute, ladies. Nature calls." Gloria heaved herself out of her chairs and waddled out of the phone room. She tried not to move any faster than usual. It wouldn't do to call attention to herself.

You're a slut, just like all the others.

There was probably nothing to the call; nothing to worry about. Easy got "her" fair share of threats and weird calls, at least two or three a week, but so far there'd been nothing to them.

Instead of heading toward the bathroom, Gloria doglegged into the kitchen. A Mr.Coffee machine and a microwave oven sat on the counter, alongside cardboard boxes full of plain brown envelopes stuffed with xeroxed nude photos and advertisements for french ticklers, full-sized love-dolls and other rubber goods. The Gaboochi Brothers made most of their money in the mail-order sex-aid business and selling their ever-growing mailing lists to like-minded entrepeneurs for a nickel an address.

Gloria prided herself on being tough-minded. By the time she'd graduated from high school she knew a woman of her size didn't stand much of a chance in a society that valued physical beauty. She'd been denied any number of jobs, even though her credentials were impeccable, simply because she didn't fit in with the company's "look". The diplomas and degrees didn't amount to shit. She tried dieting, even going so far as to seriously consider having her mouth wired shut, but nothing did any good.

Working for the Gaboochi Brothers, helping sustain Easy's fictional life, was the closest she'd ever come to getting any real respect. The Brothers treated their employees indifferently, but Gloria had coerced them into acknowledging her business know-how enough to let her run the show as she saw fit.

Just like all the others.

Gloria was wheezing, sweat running down her face and plastering her bangs to her forehead, by the time she reached the back door. Her ankles ached from moving her bulk the fifty or so feet from the call-room. She fumbled with the deadbolts and tried not to think about what the mystery caller meant by 'the others'.

Carl lay sprawled across the bare planks of the back porch, gutted like a fish. Gloria stared at the sticky blackness radiating from his mangled body like a reverse-negative halo. The porch smelled like a butcher shop.

I won't scream. I won't scream.

"Gloria . . . ?"

It's him. It's gotta be. No one else could have done that to Carl.

She slammed the door shut, leaning against it as she fumbled with the deadbolts and burglar chains. The newspaper headlines swam behind her eyelids, taunting her.

They called him the Judge because his victims were prostitutes and each had been found with a moral pronouncement carved into their lifeless flesh. He'd claimed six victims in the last fourteen months.

"Gloria? What's the matter?" Sandra was standing in the kitchen doorway.

"What are you doing away from your station?" Gloria snapped, hoping to shift the younger woman's attention away from her nervousness.

"It's the phone line—"

"What about it?"

"It's been disconnected."

The lights went out.

✦   ✦

"What th' fuck's goin on here? First th' phones go dead, now the electricity cuts out!" ZuZu pulled off her head-set and tossed it onto the table. The other women in the room were asking the same questions, all of them talking at once. ZuZu snorted in disgust; they sounded like a bunch of damn hens clucking away in the dark.

"Where's Gloria?"

"She said something about going to th' john just before the lights went out," Muriel explained. "Geez, I wish Albert was here. He was my third husband. Wasn't much in bed, but he sure was handy 'round the house! That man could change a fuse faster'n you could say 'Jack Robinson'!"

ZuZu rolled her eyes. She could see the fat lady falling down in the confusion of the black-out and not being able to get back up again, like one of those giant turtles. No doubt Muriel could find a corresponding anecdote from one of her disastrous marriages for *that*, too.

"Maybe there's a tornado warning out," Doris mused aloud in her patented June Cleaver voice. "It's that time of year, you know."

ZuZu pushed herself away from her station. "Probably some drunk bozo piled his car into a transformer somewhere up the line. I'm gonna go get my lunch outta th' fridge before it starts to defrost. Anybody else want something outta th' kitchen?"

"Stay put, ZuZu! I don't want any of you ladies wandering around in the dark!"

Gloria filled the doorway, a plastic flashlight gripped in her left hand. She shifted to one side to allow Sandra to squeeze into the room, her arms loaded with what looked to be second-hand sporting equipment.

"What th' hell's goin on here?" drawled Nora, her mouth still working the ever-present cud of Dentine.

"We got us a problem, ladies."

"No shit, Sherlock."

Gloria shot ZuZu a look that made her feel like she was back in second grade.

Sandra's face was wan in the light cast by the flashlight. "She's not kidding, Zu. We're in deep shit. Carl's dead."

There was a moment of silence, then everybody started talking at the same time. Gloria waved at them to be quiet.

"Carl's dead! It's true! Some sicko laid him open like a catfish!"

"But who'd do a thing like that?" gasped Muriel.

"I'm not sure, but I think it's the Judge."

Doris looked perplexed, her knitting forgotten. "But I thought he only killed, you know, women of ill repute. Why would he want to hurt *us*?"

"Some guys have a real broad definition of what constitutes bein' a whore, honey," sighed ZuZu.

"I'm afraid ZuZu's right. Just before the lights went out, I got a call from whoever it is who killed Carl. I guess he was using a car phone. Anyway, it's pretty obvious he's got a grudge against Easy."

"What are we gonna do? We can't protect ourselves against a crazy man!" Nora whimpered. "I wish my man Gus was here! He'd know what to do—"

"Bullshit! If Gus was here he'd be passed out under the table by now!" ZuZu spat.

"How *dare* you talk about Gus that way!" Nora's bouffant wiggled with rage. "You no-count whore! *You're* the one he ought to be goin' after! Not us!"

"Ladies—Ladies, please!" Gloria held up her hands for silence. "Look, I know you're all scared! So am I! But I *did* put a call into the Brothers about the prowler before the phone line was cut. They'll try and call back, sooner or later. You know those guys! But until help arrives, we've got to make sure this loony-toon doesn't hurt anyone else, right?"

"Fuckin' A!"

"That's m'girl, Zu!" Gloria grinned. "Sandy found this stuff in Carl's office. See what you can find to protect yourself."

There was barely enough light for everyone to see the half-assed arsenal spread across the tabletop; one cracked baseball bat, a field hockey stick with green plastic tape wrapped around the handle, a fishing reel and a badly rusted tire-tool.

"I realize it's not very promising, but anything's better than defending ourselves with our bare hands," Gloria said. "Look, I don't know what this crackpot's going to do or how he's going to do it, but I'm willing to bet he doesn't know how many of us are actually here."

Nora frowned at the weathered bat she held in her neatly manicured hands. "But he's already killed Carl. If he can do that, what difference does it make how many of us there are?"

Gloria slammed her fist against the table. "Sweet Jesus, woman! Just because he killed Carl doesn't mean we have to stand around and wait for him to slit our throats like a bunch of damn sheep! Yeah, he killed Carl! Carl was bigger and stronger than any three of us put together, but Carl was *stupid*, Nora! That's how the Judge got the drop on him! Besides, you want to be found stark naked with your guts hanging around your knees and the word 'slut' carved on your backside for the whole world to see?"

The Judge wormed his way through the attic, searching for what he knew must be there. In the dim light spilling past the ventilation grid he'd forced open, he could make out the collapsible stairway that opened into the house downstairs. He grinned, ignoring the dust swirling in his nostrils. He would not sneeze or cough. Those were affectations for mere mortals, not avenging angels of the Lord. Or was he working for Satan? The Judge occasionally forgot exactly whose greater glory he was striving to promote.

It was probably the Lord's this time out, so that meant he was an avenging angel.

The Judge's real name was Oscar Rudolph Welcome. He was forty-seven years old. He had been married for three months during the Seventies, before his grandmother had the union annulled. He'd been many things during his adult life: part-time real estate agent; part-time postal employee; part-time clerk in the family business. But what he really excelled at was being a full-time psychotic. He was *very* good at that.

He had been born illegitimate back before being a "single parent" was considered a viable alternative lifestyle. His mother worked at the U.S.O. and, apparently, believed in doing her bit to make sure America's brave lads wanted for nothing. She dumped her unwelcome Welcome at the gate of the family estate and was never heard from again, although Oscar's grandmother delighted in reporting all kinds of mischief her prodigal daughter was involved in.

She once told Oscar that she'd received "irrefutable proof" that his mother had been tied into the Rosenberg scandal and that she'd gotten the information from a special radio she kept hidden under her pillow. Oscar believed everything his grandmother said. After all, she was a saint. And his mother was a slut, therefore, capable of any treachery imaginable.

Sluts were not to be trusted. Sluts will betray without a moment's thought. Sluts grow bored and ruin your life just to amuse themselves. Sluts want nothing but money. Sluts will take all you have and laugh in your face. They think they are so smart. Like that slut-of-sluts, Easy.

He could see her lolling about on a pile of red satin pillows, dressed in a filmy peignoir, stuffing her cherry-red mouth full of bon-bons as she bilked foolish, lust-crazed men of their credit card numbers. The vision was so sharp, so *real* he could smell the scent of masticated chocolate on her breath as she screamed.

The Judge closed his eyes and punched his crotch, rebuking his traitorous flesh. But even the memory of his grandmother screaming *"What's this? What's this!!??!"*, grabbing his tumescent penis in her dry, wrinkled hands, could not banish the longings inside him. Only the smell of blood and the sensation of flesh parting beneath his knife would douse the fire in his veins.

And only one person's blood would do.

Easy was the one. Easy must die.

He came in through the attic trap-door, riding the collapsible stairway like a magic carpet. It was dark, but there was no way anyone living could ignore the squeal of rusty springs and the slam of the stairwell folding back on itself as the Judge made his entrance. Not that it mattered. The Judge *wanted* Easy to hear. Wanted her to know that he had penetrated, in the first of many senses, her inner sanctum. He wanted her to know that he had come to collect the wages of sin. And he expected what was due him.

The Judge wrinkled his nose, sniffing the bordello's air. Funny. The place reeked of sweat and stale cigarette smoke, mixed with the odor of spilled coffee grounds. The Judge had never really been inside a whore house before, but he'd always imagined they smelled more of sex and cheap French perfume. This place smelled like a secretarial pool.

Moving into a darkened doorway, he brushed against what seemed to be a kitchen counter-top, knocking a cardboard box onto the floor. The Judge stared at the material spread across the warped linoleum. Blurry xeroxes of naked young girls, their ill-defined labia spread in an approximation of wanton invitation, leered up at him.

What's this?!? What's this?!? His grandmother's voice vibrated against his inner-ear like a dentist's drill-bit.

Shadows moved in the shadows, jerking the Judge's attention from the filth spread at his feet. He pounced and pulled the slut from her hiding place.

Stupid! Stupid slut! Didn't she know it was useless to hide from the All-Seeing Eyes of The Lord's Divine Punisher? He held the struggling slut by her hair. She stopped trying to free herself when he showed her the knife.

"Repent, slut!"

"Young man, I am *not* a slut!"

The Judge frowned and stared harder at his captive. She was in her sixties and dressed conservatively. She looked almost grandmotherly. The kill-lust dimmed. The Judge blinked in confusion. He hadn't expected this.

"Let go of me!" Doris snapped. And, to her surprise, the Judge obeyed. The huge knife held inches from her nose wavered, then disappeared. The Judge looked like a sleepwalker stirred from his dream.

"Granny?"

Doris stabbed her knitting needle into the killer's right shoulder.

The Judge shrieked, nearly dropping his knife, as he clawed at the needle piercing his shoulder.

Sluts can not be trusted! Sluts betray! Remember that, boy! Have I ever lied to you? shrieked his grandmother.

Tears of anger and shame spilled down the Judge's twisted face. The false-grandmother was trying to make her escape through the back door, clawing frantically at the locks. He would not be fooled again! Ignoring the pain shooting through his wounded shoulder, the Judge advanced on his victim.

There was a high-pitched whirring sound, like the drone of a mosquito, and something bit the Judge's left ear.

"Doris! Run for it!"

Muriel reeled in and was rewarded by the sight of the man with the knife twirling about on the end of the line, slapping at his ear like a flea-ridden hound. After all those years, the co-ed fishing trips her second husband, Ray, had insisted on had finally paid off! Muriel felt strangely proud of herself: when Ray was around she never caught anything more exotic than crappie or bluegill; but now she had a real-live psycho-killer on the end of her hook!

The Judge flailed at the taut fishing line with his knife, trying to free himself before the hook completely bisected his ear. Blood was already running down the side of his face. That it was *his* blood enraged him all the more.

Doris darted past the snarling murderer and her fly-casting savior. Muriel dropped the rod and reel and hurried after her, leaving the Judge to claw at the hook buried in his ear.

He didn't know who these women were, but they weren't Easy. The Judge had expected there to be one, maybe two, women in the house, but he hadn't expected them to be waiting in ambush. And the two women—he shook his head; no, not women, *sluts*—he'd seen were hardly the big-titted, mush-brained whores he'd fantasized about. Unwanted thoughts kept intruding on his kill-lust, making his head hurt even more.

Ignoring the throbbing pain in his mangled ear, the Judge edged his way back into the hall. He stared at the three doors, two on the left, one on the right. Wary of another surprise attack, he tested the knob on the right-hand door. It was unlocked.

"Psst! Buddy! Why don't you try Door Number Two?"

The Judge turned on his heel in time to see a grinning savage with a ring in her nose swing a field hockey stick at his head.

"Take *that*, you sexist motherfucker!"

He was blinded by the fireworks going off inside his head, but still struck out at the crazed she-demon. He heard her cry out and felt her blood on his fingers. The Judge smiled. After a bad start, things were finally turning out the way they should!

When the fireworks died away, he found himself alone in the hallway. The field hockey stick lay abandoned on the floor. The bathroom door stood open. So that's where the she-demon had been hiding . . . The Judge touched his forehead gingerly. The pain from the contusion fed his righteous anger. He would cut the ring from the scheming hell-slut's nose and skin the tattoos from her supple flesh. They would make wonderful souvenirs.

He grimaced as blood and sweat trickled into his eyes. Fuck stalking. They knew he was here. He knew they knew he was here. It was time to announce his intentions.

"Easy!"

Silence.

"I know you can hear me, bitch! I know you're here!" he bellowed. "I've come for you, like I said I would! I'm going to make you a deal, Easy! I'm here for you! I'm not interested in the others! You're the one I want! If you surrender to me, I'll leave the others alone! I promise!"

It was a lie, of course. He had no intention of letting any of them go. Especially the slut with the ring in her nose. But everyone knows how stupid sluts are. There would be much blood tonight. Blood enough to wash himself clean of sin in the eyes of both the Lord and his grandmother.

"Easy! Answer me, bitch!"

The third door on the left opened, and the Judge made out a shadow lurking on the threshold.

"You looking for me?"

It was *her*. There was no mistaking that voice: smooth as fine brandy; smokey as a late-night cabaret; sleek as a silk kimono. Before him stood the author of his torment. The Whore of Babylon who had lured him into sullying his soul and his flesh with her promises of carnal gratifation; the reason behind his phone bill averaging in the high triple-digits. His knife was hard and ready to taste her blood; ready to fuck her the only way he knew how.

"*Easy*." He breathed her name as if it was both benediction and curse.

"Yeah, I'm Easy," she said, stepping into the hall. "What's it to you, asshole?"

The Judge stared in horror at the massive woman blocking the door. Vast rolls of flab hung from her upper arms, chin, waist and hips. Her face was slick with sweat and flushed the color of raw meat. Her breathing was ragged, as if she'd just climbed a flight of stairs. The knife between the Judge's legs shrivelled.

"Y-you're not Easy!" he whimpered.

"Oh, but I *am*! And I want you out of my house!" Easy's voice coming out of the fat lady's mouth was disconcerting. Oscar Welcome was suddenly aware of the huge bruise over his left eye and the throbbing pain in his right shoulder. He wished the Judge would come back. When the Judge was in charge, pain didn't hurt like it usually did.

"But you *can't* be Easy!" Oscar shook his head, trying to clear it of the confusion. He felt the tears building in his eyes. The fat lady took another step towards him. She towered over him, threatening suffocation with her neolithic breasts. "Easy's supposed to be beautiful, and you're fat and ugly!"

"That's it. I've had all I'm gonna take outta you!" Gloria lunged forward, grabbing the Judge's knife-hand. "It's bad enough being terrorized by some sicko, but I'll be damned if I'm gonna stand here and let you call me names!"

Oscar struck instinctively at his attacker. He felt the knife sink into her flesh up to the hilt and heard the giant slut grunt in surprise and pain, but it just wasn't the same. There was no pleasure to be found in the tearing of her flesh. Not without the Judge to guide his hand.

Oscar struggled to free the knife, but it wouldn't come out. The false-Easy rolled her piggy little eyes, whether in pain or pleasure it was hard to tell, and clasped Oscar to her ample bosom, bearing him to the floor.

Oscar's last thought, before Gloria fell on him, was that it wasn't supposed to end like this.

✦   ✦

Gloria came to in the hospital. The nurses lashed two of the beds together so she could rest easier. The first thing she saw was ZuZu, her right arm in a sling, grinning down at her.

"Hey! Boss-lady! You feelin' okay?"

"Not really."

Sandra bobbed into view behind ZuZu. "You're a hero, Gloria! You killed the Judge!"

"Killed—?"

"Yeah! You squashed him like a bug!" ZuZu elaborated with a ripe raspberry. "Guy was some kind of nutcase! They went to his house and found his granny's corpse rotting in the bedroom! Just like *Psycho*! I'm writing a song about it!"

"That's nice . . . I think. I'm glad you weren't hurt. That was a damn foolish—and brave—stunt you pulled, young lady."

ZuZu blushed and shrugged her left shoulder. "Look who's talking! I'll have to lay off playing the guitar for a week or two, but the Doc says I should have a nice scar!"

"Sandy—what happened? The last thing I remember that bastard stuck a knife into my chest. I was sure I'd had it."

"The doctors said your fat kept the knife from getting anywhere near your heart. If you looked like Easy, you'd be dead by now."

"What about the others?"

"Everybody's okay. Doris ran all the way to the juke joint down the highway and called the cops! Did you know she competes in the Senior Olympics? That old girl's really something! Muriel's got herself all excited about one of the paramedics—she says it's the Real Thing Part Five. The only person who got hurt, besides ZuZu, was Nora. Her no-good white trash live-in, Gus, finally found out what she was doing and blacked her eye. He said it wasn't 'fit work for no lady'."

"What about the Gaboochi Brothers?"

"They won't talk to the press. Something about the family being in mourning. But they sent you flowers." Sandra hoisted a pot of african violets. "See?"

Gloria sighed and rolled her eyes. "I'm more interested in whether we still have jobs."

"Why shouldn't we?"

"Can't you two figure it out for yourself? When it gets out that the Hot Talkers are really a bunch of housewives and Easy is actually a refugee from a sideshow—what do you think's gonna happen?"

"There goes my Strat!"

Gloria looked away, trying to control the emotion in her voice. "Easy's dead. That bastard killed her as sure as if he really *had* stuck a knife in her!" She eyed the i.v. drip running into her arm. "And here I am, flat on my back without health insurance!"

"You're taking this too hard, Gloria! So what if Easy's dead? So what if you're out of a job? It sucked to begin with!"

"It's easy for *you* to talk like that, Sandy. You're young—you're *thin*."

"And you're rich. Or will be."

"What do you mean?"

Sandra held up a thick sheaf of legal-sized paper. "See this? It's a *contract*, Gloria! A *movie* contract! This guy from Universal Pictures was in here earlier, when you were still out of it. They want to make a movie about what happened!" She handed the contract to Gloria, who squinted at it suspicously.

"You're kidding! ZuZu, tell me she's kidding!"

ZuZu grinned even wider than before. "It's true, boss-lady! We've *all* got contracts! Even Nora! Boy, is Gus gonna be pissed off when she tells him to pack his bags!"

Gloria stared at the contract, but she was no longer hearing what her friends were chattering about. From what little she was able to understand of the contract, it was obvious the studio sharpies thought they could get the rights to Easy's last stand on the cheap.

"Has anyone signed anything yet?"

"Huh? Uh, no—I don't think so."

"Good. We need to show a unified front on this, if we want to get the best of this deal! Sandy, get on the phone to Doris, Nora and Muriel. Tell 'em to hold off until I've had some time to scope out the deal!"

"Aye-aye!" Sandy hurried out of the room.

"ZuZu, be a dear and see if you can't hunt me up a little something to eat. I think better when I'm eating."

ZuZu tilted her head to one side. With her colorful mohawk, she looked like a quizzical cockatoo. "Mind lettin' me in on the game plan, boss?"

Gloria grinned, visions of a Universal Studios office with her name on the door and a handsome male secretary answering the phone taking on a certain clarity behind her eyes.

"Let's just say Hollywood producers aren't the only ones who know a thing or two about exploitation."

A CHRISTMAS STORY

James S. Dorr

He wasn't dreaming of reindeer and sugarplums. At least not yet. But as Timmy Hunter lay in his bed, still half awake, he did think about the new fallen snow, ideal for the runners of Santa's sled when it came down to land. He thought about the crisp night air, and about how Santa would be bundled up against the cold. About how, with so many homes to visit, so many more presents to be delivered before Christmas morning, Santa would be tired when he got there.

Tired and hungry.

◆   ◆

Downstairs, Timmy's mother, Annet, was finishing decorating the tree. She turned to her friend, Charles.

"Darling," she said. "How's the eggnog coming? Did you leave some unspiked like I asked you?"

"Just about finished," Charles replied. He straightened the red, fir-trimmed cap on his head, then looked at her sternly. "The unspiked for you?"

Annet giggled. "Only if I've been a good little girl, Santa. What do you think?"

Charles laughed as well as he poured out two cups with rich, sweet rum in them. He handed one to the slim, dark-haired woman who reached out to take it, then put it down on the table behind her. "First things first, Santa," Annet said, smiling.

He set down his own drink and pulled her to him, his lips meeting hers, as she, in turn, steered him toward the soft fleece rug in front of the fireplace. "Not too loud, darling," she said between kisses. She guided his hand to the back of her skirt. "One time, before . . . before Robert died, Timmy actually came downstairs thinking he'd heard the real Santa Claus and . . ."

Charles held her to him. "You're sure you're okay, Annet? I mean, I know it's been more than a year since the accident, but some memories stay on. They *should* stay on. They . . ."

Annet touched her finger to Charles' lips. "Shhh, darling," she said. "Of course I loved Robert, but I love you too, now. And Timmy likes you. The really sad memory — you'll think this is silly — but Timmy's so young. The really sad thing was, what with the funeral expenses and all, I couldn't afford to get Timmy the presents he'd wanted that Christmas. And you know what?" She giggled the way she had before. "I tried to explain to Timmy, about the money, but he was too young to understand. Instead, he blamed Santa."

Charles reached to straighten his cap again, then glanced to his right, to the jumble of brightly wrapped packages heaped underneath the tree. "Well," he whispered, "I hope *this* Santa will have helped make it up to him this year."

"Yes, I think so, darling," Annet said. She pressed against him and nuzzled his neck, then pulled him down with her onto the rug. "But what about *me*?"

"It was a lousy Christmas for Timmy," Annet said, after they'd readjusted their clothes and were sipping eggnog on the couch. "All I could wrap for him was a scarf and some shirts and things — the kind of things kids know they'll get anyway — and one or two cheap toys. I was really afraid he'd lost his belief in Santa that year. Still, kids bounce back. This year he wrote his letter to Santa Claus as usual. You know, you've seen it. And then, tonight, just before bedtime, he shooed me out of the kitchen the same way he's always done to make Santa's sandwich."

"Santa's sandwich?" Charles asked.

"Yeah," she said. She started to snuggle closer to Charles, then glanced at her watch and stood up instead.

"Oh, my gosh," she said. "It's almost time for you to leave, and I'll need you to help me. Anyway, you know how, when you were a kid, you maybe left out milk and cookies for Santa? So he could have a snack on his rounds? And then, Christmas morning, you'd always check to make sure some of the milk had been drunk and the cookies eaten?"

"Yeah," Charles said. He put his red Santa Claus cap back on. "Of course, later on, we realized it was always Dad who . . ."

"Shhh," Annet said. "Timmy doesn't know yet that you're going to be his new daddy. I thought tomorrow night, when you come over to have dinner with us, we'd make the announcement . . ."

"I *love* you, Annet," he said in her ear, then held her and kissed her. "But you're right. It is late. What are you going to want me to do?"

"Well, we do a sort of variant here. It started because neither Robert or I cared for milk — you know how it is when you get older. So I'll get you a glass from the kitchen and I'll want you to pour the unspiked eggnog into it, then take a big drink, so it makes a stain on the glass like milk does, then put it on the mantelpiece."

"Okay," Charles said. He waited until she came back from the kitchen, a milk glass in one hand and a sloppily put together sandwich on a paper plate in the other. He took the glass and filled it with eggnog straight from the carton, then went to the fireplace and took a big drink.

"How am I doing?" he asked with a wink, as he set the half empty glass down on the mantel.

"Wonderful, darling," Annet said. "But now comes the tough part." She handed him the plate with the sandwich. "You see, after we'd convinced Timmy that Santa would probably prefer to have eggnog instead of just milk, he got his own idea. He figured, instead of store bought cookies, Santa would rather have something he'd made for him all by himself. So" — Annet giggled — "that's why I'll need you to take a big bite of this perfectly *awful* peanut butter and jelly sandwich."

Charles gave the sandwich a dubious look. "You know something, Annet. Maybe I could just tear off a corner . . ."

Annet laughed. "It has to be a *real* bite. He'll check it. That's why the eggnog had to be unspiked — he'll put his nose in the glass to check it too in the morning."

Charles looked down at the plate again, at the lumpy bread-covered form in its center. "Peanut butter and jelly, eh?"

"It's his favorite sandwich. The way he sees it, it's nothing but the best for Santa." She kissed him quickly. "Do it for me?"

"Well," he said. "If you put it that way." He set the plate down on the mantel, next to the glass, and chewed it and swallowed.

"My God. It's gritty!"

"He must have used crunch style peanut butter," Annet said. "And lord knows what else he had on his hands — he's only a kid." She took the rest of the sandwich from Charles and put it on the plate on the mantel, then kissed him hard. "But it means so much to him . . ."

. . . and Timmy's eyes finally closed of their own accord as he drifted off to sleep, his hands still clutching the box of rat poison from the kitchen that he'd used to make Santa's snack extra special. He dreamed, not of sugarplums and reindeer, but of the crummy trick Santa had played the last Christmas. The clothes and the cheap toys. How, for a whole year, he'd planned to get even.

He slept very soundly, not even hearing the screams that began to echo downstairs, and he dreamed about Mommy's new boyfriend, Charles, and how much nicer *he* was than Santa.

COMES THE NIGHT WIND, COLD AND HUNGRY

Gene Michael Higney

When the doorbell rang, Cal Freeman sighed. It could only be his neighbor and cross in life Selma Huff. Selma had just joined the Jehovah's Witnesses, and Cal seemed to be number one on her converts wish list.

Every evening it was a booklet here, a donation there . . .

He sighed again as he opened the door. The sudden, chill wind gusted against his face, wiping away the only percentage of a friendly smile he could muster.

The sigh caught in his throat like a sharp-edged bone when he saw, outlined from behind by the yellow streetlight . . . a clown.

A clown on his front doorstep. With a painted clown grin that showed more teeth than he remembered clowns usually displaying. Baggy bright drawers . . . red nose . . . wild red hair under a chewed up and holey hat that sprouted a bobbing plastic flower from its brim.

Now, under the big bright lights of a circus tent, a clown might be . . . amusing.

But a clown in the night . . . in the dark . . . the chill wind whipping his ludicrous plastic flower about crazily . . .

Then Cal saw the gleaming arched fingers of the metal garden claw . . .

✦   ✦

It was the third night of terror.

No one in Payaso Falls would have believed it could have gone on for *that* long. Just how much time, they asked each other over neighborly cups of coffee, or cold brews, how much time would it take the cops (such as they were in this mosquito-bite-sized town) to find some maniac dressed in a clown suit?

The other question they asked each other was, of course, who *was* it?

Still not totally rejected was the idea that it could be one of the citizens of Payaso Falls themselves; though most preferred to think it had to be a stranger, an outsider; some transient who dropped off the train that passed half a mile north of the town.

That was it . . . a stranger . . . *had* to be . . .

Still others thought . . . a transient *clown*? A maniac who was clever enough to glide so easily in and out and around town, finding people's weak spots, vulnerable points, unguarded entrances . . . well, he couldn't be a *total* stranger.

They only knew he was a clown because old Mrs. Gehrig had "happened" to look out her window at the Wilberses after hearing what she swore were muffled screams, and had seen a rather tall, yes, *clown*, officer, emerge from their home with a bloody knife dripping chocolate syrup colored spots down their driveway.

The part about the screams may or may not have been pastime, because the entire Wilber family had been found hacked open and spread fairly evenly throughout their living room. As though just before their deaths they had been gathered there to watch some favorite show on television. Only their television was in the family room down the hall. They only used their living room when entertaining guests.

After Mrs. Gehrig's description of the clown, the Sheriff, Devlin Martin, speculated that they had gathered in the living room to watch something else . . . some *one* else . . . and had been given another kind of show altogether.

Sheriff Martin, heavy-set, salt and pepper-haired, and nobody's coward, had shuddered while Mrs. Gehrig described the clown.

He'd loved to go to the circus when he was a kid. His father, the greatly loved and respected Reverend Howard T. Martin, had taken his family every summer the circus came to town. Sheriff Martin would have taken his own children more often if his job permitted, but it didn't. And now that his wife had left for good and taken the kids with her . . . that was the end of his going to the circus.

Now, it seemed that the circus had come to him.

He couldn't shake the image of the clown, bulbous nose, baggy pants, striding down the driveway in the light-pocked darkness, knife at his side . . .

Martin swore to himself. They'd get this guy. He'd drafted a few of the feistier guys from Lefty's to help search the town's scuzzier hiding places. Just call them deputies and they're an instant, enthusiastic posse, ready to hunt whatever, Martin had grinned.

In the meantime, he figured, the townies should be safe enough. No one in his right mind would be going out after dark until the killer was caught. But, he thought sardonically, the maniac didn't seem to be waiting for people to come out . . . this clown made private appearances.

Freida Rusch had just put on the final coat of red that would stick in the memory of her nails. She wiggled them tentatively in the air, satisfied with the after-image they left in her eyes. As soon as her red blouse was out of the dryer, she was off. The dishes in the sink could wait until tomorrow. They'd only been there a week. One more day wouldn't hurt. And tonight that new country group was playing at Lefty's. No way she was going to miss that, killer or no killer. Besides, she'd have to be safer in a bar with a ton of people than she was here in this drafty sewer of a house she'd never even wanted, except for her mother died and left it to her. She was trying to sell it . . . but Lord knew there weren't many buyers in Payaso Falls. People were moving out, not in. And she had every intention of being one of the ones on her way out . . .

When her washing machine went on, with its unusual clank and buzz that you could hear all the way from the basement to the next county, Freida hoisted herself off the couch, dressed in slacks and brassiere, and clomped down the solid basement steps her father had built with his own two hands.

"What the hell . . . ?" Freida asked several times of no one in particular.

The dryer had gone off. By itself.

Now how long ago had that happened, and what was her red blouse going to look like; probably a wrinkled mess . . . damn.

Her face had never contorted into the particular expression of fright, alarm, and shocked laughter that it suddenly wore when she was confronted by the sight of a capering, squatting, dancing clown.

"Wha—?" was all she could manage as the clown spun a circle, then stopped short, with his left hand extending toward her a bouquet of plastic flowers, his lopsided grin and blinking, different colored eyes begging her wordlessly to smile her approval.

Freida couldn't move.

Not even when the plastic flowers squirted a stream of water into her eyes and face.

Not water . . . she thought as the searing agony exploded through her eyeballs and ate into the nerves behind them, and as her skin wadded up into blisters that popped like crackling chewing gum. Not water. . .

Clowns are supposed to squirt you with water . . .

. . . And it's not supposed to hurt . . .

She felt her eyes run down her cheeks.

Sheriff Martin looked down at the unrecognizable Freida Rusch. Flash cameras didn't help make the scene less ghastly and otherworldly. He couldn't believe this was really happening. He'd had a few beers with Freida just the other night. She was sloppy but happy drunk. Inoffensive. The worst thing about Freida Rusch was her housekeeping.

Who would do this to her? *Acid . . .*

Whoever it was had to be beyond psychotic. Who the hell would think to stuff plastic flowers into the gaping, mushy-fleshed face of his victim?

And *arrange* them?

The coffee was hot, the way he liked it, and Karen was smiling at him, the way he liked it. Martin sipped first, then blew, and Karen laughed. Just the way his kids used to laugh when he'd done that for them.

Daddy, you're such a CLOWN . . .

Karen was enough years younger than the Sheriff for him to think of her as a daughter. Sometimes. Other times, he thought of her as she wanted him to, a friend, lover, would-be second wife.

Karen of the chestnut rich hair, and eyes like those of a baby deer. Karen who could have had any of the young men in the town, but who only accepted dates with Sheriff Devlin Martin, whenever he had the time for her.

And who waited patiently for him those times when he hadn't. As in the past four days, since the murders had begun.

Her laughter now warmed away some of the chill that had settled inside him. Whatever new insanities the world brought into being, as long as there were people like Karen to balance it out, it would not tip totally over the edge into some nameless, endless universe of madness.

Martin's father used to describe Hell that way. Maybe he was on to something.

She placed a warmed donut in front of him. He was about to turn it down, thinking of his middle-aged spread in comparison to her youthfully slender figure, when a voice behind him caused them to look away from each other.

"So ya found the son of a bitch yet or *what*?"

"G'morning, Harley. And how are you this morning?"

Harley was having none of it. "Don't gimme that crap. I don't find you funny, y'know? Like *some* people do."

Harley planted his bulk two stools away from the Sheriff, in the process actually making Martin look small by comparison. Harley Sheen made good psychological use of his size in his business, which was selling grain and feed, and to win arguments in Lefty's bar on a practically weekly basis.

Martin had had to run Harley a few times when the damage got a little too expensive, and the fighting got a little too raw. Harley hadn't liked waking up in a cell with black eyes given him by the town porker, rather than honestly won in a decent barroom brawl.

The six or seven people in the café heard Harley's question clearly, and while they did not all share Harley's antagonism for Sheriff Martin, they were all undisguisedly interested in the answer.

"We're checking on some leads right now. And every part of town is getting a good going over," Martin replied mildly. "It won't be long now."

"Bullshit," Harley spat.

Karen pressed her lips together, unwilling to trust herself to speak. Harley, with the caginess that comes from long years of awareness of peoples' dislike, noticed her reaction to him.

"'Scuse *me*, Missy. I'm just a plain man I speak plain. The cops here don't know nothin' about who's doin' these killin's. I know bullshit when I hear it. Ands I'm hearin' it."

"Well then, do you want some coffee to wash it down?" It was out before Karen could stop herself.

Laughter pealed throughout the café, and when Martin joined in the expression of surprise and pleasure, it was worth enduring the venomous gaze Harley was giving her.

"Real funny!" Harley bolted upright with surprising speed for a man of his size. "Whole town's just *full* of clowns, ain't it?"

The laughter died as quickly as it had begun, and Harley stomped out of the coffee shop, satisfied at the palpable atmosphere of unease he'd left behind him.

Karen's eyes did not meet Martin's again until he said, "Hey, girl. It's okay. He had it coming."

"It's just . . . I hate hearing anybody talk to you like that. You don't deserve it, Dev." Karen wiped the clean counter in front of Martin, as though by doing so she could erase the memory of Harley's voice. And what he'd said.

"He's more right than wrong," Martin said quietly. "We don't know *what* the hell is happening out there."

Mindy wore her Care Bears pajamas to bed that night, even though her older sister Carla had told her they were stupid looking. Carla was doing a lot mean things lately, even more than she used to do. Mommy said it was because Carla was having Changes inside or something. Well too bad for her. Mindy still didn't like her, and wouldn't forgive her forever for saying that the Care bears were stupid looking. Mindy loved the Care Bears, and Smurfs, and—

Now what was Carla doing? Last week she'd sneaked out of the house and around the porch to the window outside Mindy's bedroom, and scratched on the glass, just to scare her. Mindy had been real scared too. So scared that Mommy had let her sleep with her and Daddy. And now Carla was doing it again. Only not scratching, but . . . she was out there for sure.

Mindy went to see.

Her eyes opened wide with surprise. And delight.

There was a clown outside! A real honest to goodness clown! Right on her very own porch! He was scampering and dancing and twirling and he had a long, long umbrella with colored ribbons hanging off its corners. Funny clown!

Mindy was speechless with excitement.

The clown clambered up on the white railing of the porch, then did a graceful, floppy sort of jump, and landed on the porch without even making a sound.

Funny funny clown.

Then he bowed, looked up right at Mindy, and grinned his lopsided grin. His umbrella closed up tight. Like magic.

And he pointed with its shiny bright point . . . at the front door.

He wanted to come in!

Ecstatic, Mindy hurried out, the flap on her Care Bear pajamas open, to go and let in the funny funny clown . . .

The Payaso Falls daily newspaper was using nine out of its ten pages to eat Sheriff Devlin Martin alive, or so it seemed.

The phone in the office only stopped ringing when Martin took it off the hook; people were seeing the maniac clown everywhere. If they weren't seeing him, then they had proof positive that they knew who he was. Generally, it was a disliked family member, or a neighbor who had unruly pets. Much of Martin's time was spent explaining that more than a longstanding grudge against another townie was required for him to arrest someone.

Before long, however, he'd become privy to a list of hates and grievances that he'd never known existed, even after living many years of his life in a town where gossip was the main export. Wives were shockingly ready to turn in their husbands, fathers their sons, and a few sons even returned the favor.

What the hell is happening to us? He wondered. It would have broken his father's heart; he'd loved this town. And all he'd ever preached about love and faith was deeply felt and lived. Unlike some of those television preacher-types who talked about faith but lived money . . .

His deputy volunteers had succeeded in unearthing two love nests frequented by local teenagers, identified as such by the scattered condoms and beer cans, two terrified hobos of indeterminate age and incredible filth, and nothing else.

The hobos were immediate suspects, naturally, and, as such, were about to be beaten senseless by the deputies, until one of the bums made it clear to them that the other was blind and could not be left alone for any length of time.

When Martin inspected the first hobo, he found arms skinnier than his own wrists, and muscles near non-existent from years of drinking sterno-and-unknown-substance cocktails. Both the hobos together could not have overpowered Freida Rusch, much less a family of two adults and two teenagers.

Then they found the other families. Slaughtered hideously. While the hobos were being "questioned."

Still, when the hobos were released on Martin's say so, the town council threatened to fire him. There went their easy solution.

Everyone wanted the State Police to be called in. Yesterday.

"I used to think nothing this awful could happen here," Martin whispered to Karen, who was sound asleep next to him. That was when he best opened his heart to someone, he found, when they were asleep and couldn't hear him. He'd done that with his wife, too. Maybe if he had talked to her more when she was awake . . .

Karen shifted slightly, her hair wisping down over her eyes.

"I used to think," Martin continued, after assuring himself that she was still asleep, "that whatever craziness happened out there, it would . . . you know . . . *stay* out there. In the cities. In the places where crazy people go to lose themselves. Stuff like this doesn't . . . *shouldn't* happen in places like Payaso Falls. I mean, we have our troubles, like everywhere. I've been busy enough what with drunk fights and feuds and speed happy kids . . . but nothing like . . . *this* . . . How do you get a *hold* of somebody like this? How do you *understand* what's happening inside his brain? He's doing more than killing us. He's . . . *infecting* us . . . the bastard's infecting us with the craziness that's happening all over the rest of this country. Kids killing their parents. Mothers killing their own kids. Drugs. But it used to be so far away from us . . . It always used to be somebody *else's* craziness."

He grit his teeth and twisted and wrinkled a handful of sheet, wishing it were the killers throat.

"But now the bastard's come *here* . . . He's made it our craziness now . . ."

"If I don't get him . . . if I don't stop him . . ."

He started as a hand brushed against his forehead.

Karen was awake. Looking at him with her huge, heart-softening eyes. "You'll find him," she said. She wanted to ask him what he'd meant by "infecting us," but decided it was better he thought her asleep while he'd been talking. So instead, she just repeated, "You'll find him."

"Is that what you really think?" he asked, his arm encircling her shoulder.

"It's what I'm really afraid of," she answered.

That night, Mary Lemmings shot her husband Biff dead as he tiptoed into her bedroom. He'd tipped a few with some friends over at Lefty's and thought he'd make it in without the wife knowing, as he had countless times before.

She was waiting for him, as she had countless times before. Only this time, she held on tightly to his shotgun and her excuse. The gun was for Biff, and the excuse was for the cops.

". . . oh, my God, Sheriff Martin . . . Oh, my God! I thought he was the killer! I thought for sure it was that maniac clown come to get me . . ."

She practiced her excuse (without the benefit of much acting talent) over and over into the wee hours, waiting for Biff. She thought about little else, except the nest egg they'd set aside. And how she and Rolly Lipscomb could finally leave Payaso Falls, where their affair had been a poorly kept secret for more than six months.

She had blown Biff's head pretty much off, and paused only to regard the mess on the curtains and wall.

" . . . oh, my God, Sheriff Martin . . ." she repeated carefully as she edged around Biff's still weakly twitching form and made her way toward the phone. " . . . oh, my God . . ."

"OH, MY GOD!" she screamed in earnest, and quite convincingly, at the grinning clown face in the window next to the phone table.

Backing up in horror, she stumbled once over the extended footrest of her nearly new recliner, and righted herself in time to see the window glide upward.

By itself.

She felt icy air lick her face and ears like an invisible, hungry tongue. ICY AIR? In the summer?

The bastard was trying to get in!

But the clown just stuck his head in briefly, darted a glance toward the bedroom, on the floor of which lay the remains of Biff Lemmings, and then looked back at the stunned Mary, only to give her a pop-eyed, tongue waggling, crazy clown face, and disappear into the darkness.

Mary Lemmings wasn't taking any chances, however. She ran across the room, heading straight toward the spot on which she'd deposited the shotgun.

When the clown somersaulted through the open bedroom window, she screamed and tried to slow down, but her feet slipped in the splotches of red and grey goo that had been the head of her late husband, and she fell face forward, her head landing on Biff's blood-spattered chest.

She reeled back, dizzy from the impact, and saw the clown caper up and down on her bed, the wild frigid wind fluttering his baggy pants, his tongue lolling in and out of his mouth, and his pop-eyes rolling and gawping independently of one another.

People's eyes don't do that, Mary Lemmings wanted to scream, but she was a practical woman.

She reached for the shotgun instead.

Grasped it by the barrel.

Swung it around.

The clown seemed to stop in mid-air, then drift downward, eyes riveted on Mary and the gun she was even now aiming at his head.

Knowing she had to make this shot count, Mary Lemmings aimed carefully and pulled the trigger.

Practical though she was, she could not think of another thing to do beside scream when the gun made a stupid popping sound and out of the barrel sprang a stick with a cloth sign on it that said: BANG.

After that, all she did was scream.
Because she knew it, it was the clown's turn.

By the time Payaso Fall's three police cars and one ambulance arrived, the entire street was populated with bathrobed, pajamaed citizens, flashlights bobbing and dancing over each others' curlers and pillow-permed hair.

Sheriff Martin wended his way through the grumbling, frightened, but more curious than either crowd, and into the Lemmings's house.

The warmth of Karen's body against his had long since cooled, and Martin felt chilled and alone as he passed by his glaring, or imploring, friends and neighbors and entered the house along with the other officers, and the medics.

He swallowed, hard, when he saw Biff Lemmings' body sprawled across the bedroom floor, the head a memory.

One of the paramedics was throwing up.

It was bad, Martin thought, but not *that* bad. Surely this guy had seen worse than *this* . . .

Martin started to snap at the medic but found that words would not come when he saw that Biff's gaping maw of a neck was not the reason the paramedic was sick.

It was because he'd seen what had become of Mary Lemmings.

This is evil, was all he could think. Pure evil. If there *was* a Hell . . . this was how it would start.

She'd been propped up between two upright lamps, her arms extended outward, neither foot touching the floor; strung between her right and left hand, dangling down under both her feet, was a length of her own intestine.

She looked like she was jumping rope.

Who the hell was swinging on the backyard swing at 4:23 in the goddamned a.m.?

Ben Gifford threw his half of the sheet aside, nearly smacking his wife, Sara, in the jaw. If one of those kids was up again he'd wail the tar out of them, and he didn't care what his old lady said about stepfathers having to be twice as loving. He'd about had his fill of these spoiled brats anyway . . .

He consoled himself with thoughts of what physical violence he could wreak on his stepchildren, until he reached the window where he could easily see the tire swing which suspended on large, creaky chains from a massive old tree in the yard.

It was probably that pain in the ass, Matt. That kid could give Midol cramps . . .

Ben Gifford squinted to verify his identification of the offending child on the swing.

Instead, he found himself wetting himself.

There was a clown on the swing.

Back and forth he went, the clown . . . the clown, Ben thought wildly, his heart trying its best to explode outward through his chest . . . the clown.

And the creaking swing went to and fro, to and fro, but so slowly . . . so very slowly . . . it didn't look right, it was like slow motion in the movies almost.

A wind seemed to have whipped up during the night; Ben felt its arctic chill through the glass.

But . . . a wind that rustled the leaves of the trees so slowly . . . ? Could that be right? Was he dreaming? That had to be it. A nightmare. Some ugly mistake by his brain.

No. There was no mistake. It was a clown, and his painted weird face was stuck up in the air, like he was drinking in the moonlight, goggle eyes staring right at Ben, greasy grin all red-lipped and twisty . . .

In and out of the shadows, the creaking swing went to and fro, from moonlight to dark, to and fro . . .

To his subsequent embarrassment, when Sara touched his shoulder, about to ask what he was looking at, Ben Gifford passed out cold.

Too busy trying to revive her husband, Sara didn't look out the window.

Nor did she pay attention to the slow creak of the swing.

The creaking stopped soon after anyway.

Just about when the freezing wind died away

◆   ◆

Ben Gifford, happy to be alive, phoned Sheriff Martin and informed him politely and helpfully of what he'd seen in his yard, eliminating only the details about his having wet himself and passed out cold.

He told the Sheriff he was planning to take his vacation early to get the wife and stepkids out of Payaso Falls until the killer was caught. Sheriff Martin was impressed at the tone of concern in Ben's voice when he said he'd rather die than have anything happen to his family.

Old Mrs. Gehrig called Sheriff Martin to tell him she'd seen the clown again through her binoculars, gamboling across a neighbor's lawn, and she was certain that he was in reality Jimmy Jalene, that nasty young man with the hot rod that wakes her up nearly every night and exactly when does Sheriff Martin plan to arrest him?

If even a *few* of the people that Martin talked to were correct, he was dealing with a maniac clown who could be in several places at once. This did not compute.

Sheriff Martin also talked to the Governor himself, and found that he was to "cooperate fully" with the State Police and the Federal agent who was at that moment being flown in to underline the fact that Sheriff Devlin Martin was incompetent and could not even catch a renegade clown.

That's how Martin explained it to Karen when he stopped at the café, despite the sensation of every eye being on him, and every mind in town wondering how he had the nerve to stop the mystical act of police investigation for even a moment's rest until the psycho who was decimating the population of Payaso Falls was located and lynched.

He assuaged his feeling of guilt by not having anything to eat, and by committing the further act of penance of not putting any sugar in his coffee.

He just had to see Karen. Needed to see Karen, more than he needed the rest, since he'd been awake and on the go all night long. He needed a friendly face, because everybody else in town, including his own officers could not seem to meet his gaze, and even more than that he needed to find the crazed lunatic who was at the bottom of the madness . . . more than his desire to tear apart the devil who had entered his much loved little town, Devlin Martin needed to see his friend. His love.

And she was there for him. Her hand placed over his, gently, cooling his feverish hate and desperation. Her eyes warming the icy loneliness that threatened to freeze solid what was left of his heart.

"My Lord, girl, I want to get the hell out of here."

She smiled. "Say the word, Dev. Just say the word."

For an instant, it sounded like the greatest idea he'd ever had. The greatest idea *anyone* had ever had. Quit. Pack up and leave Payaso Falls for good. Leave it to its own brand of madness. Leave it lay there, vulnerable to the thing that stalked its innocent people.

But *were* they? Innocent?

It didn't matter. He could no more leave his work now, than he could when his wife had given him her ultimatum. *Leave the job or I leave you.*

Even then he could not leave the job. And there had been no horror dressed as a clown back then, no hell-spawned, grease-painted demon gutting the life and happiness out of his community, and his friends . . . well, *once* they were his friends.

Sheriff Martin shook his head ruefully, and Karen nodded. Wordlessly, she poured his coffee, and, still wordlessly, she touched his hand again. He did not drink his coffee, because that would mean moving his hand and ending their contact.

He yearned to take Karen in his arms. Leave with her. *Be* with her. He ached to lose himself inside her gentleness and sanity. When he saw the tears forming in her eyes, he almost matched them with his own. He couldn't allow that.

Instead, he coughed gruffly, stood up abruptly, and said, "I'll see you later, kid. We've got a State search going. They don't think we did it right the first time."

"Say the word, Dev," was all she replied.

When this was all over, he realized with a start, he just might be able to say that word.

Calley, the part-time office worker who manned (or WO-manned, as she liked to put it) the office for Payaso Falls's Police Department, radioed Sheriff Martin that Harley Sheen had been involved in another fracas over at Lefty's, this one a little more serious than the other times.

When Martin arrived, Lefty and several other men had cornered Harley with a combination of pool sticks and baseball bats. Harley had contented himself with clutching Rolly Lipscomb hard against his chest, and occasionally taking solid punches at his head, further spreading Rolly's already broken nose across his blood-smeared face.

"I've got 'im!" roared Harley when he spotted Martin entering the cool confines of the bar. "I've got the clown!"

"What are you talking about, Harley?" Martin asked calmly. "And quit punching Rolly, willya?"

"I'm tellin' ya he's the clown! He *tole* me he seen Freida before she got kilt!"

Sheriff Martin leaned over Harley, trying to ignore the pathetic expression in Rolly's eyes. Up-until-now-handsome Rolly Lipscomb had seen most of the available ladies in town. And quite a few of the ones who were not supposed to be available. Martin happened to know exactly where Rolly had been during two of the nights in question. Making love, not mayhem.

"Let's talk about this," Martin said, and then he punched Harley's lights out.

With a sigh, he motioned for the other men to help him lift Harley and put him in the police car.

✦   ✦

When he awoke, Harley Sheen's head felt like a train was running at top speed from ear to ear and back. The roaring in his ears, the ache in his jaw, the shadow of the bunk bed over him, the stale concrete smell . . . he knew where he was alright.

And he knew who put him there.

Ducking his head to avoid slamming it against the metal bar of the bunk above, Harley Sheen sat up on the lower bunk that squealed its protest under his weight, and considered just how he might best tear the head off Sheriff Devlin Martin. Just when he'd had that bastard Rolly Lipscomb. Just when he had the maniac in his grasp, that stupid, worthless porker screwed him over.

Rolly all but admitted that he killed Freida. Hadn't he said he'd seen her before she died? That was good enough proof for Harley.

The pig would pay, that was for sure, Harley thought, but first . . . maybe, he'd better sleep just a little while. The way his head felt . . .

Harley lay back, nestling his skull into what there was of the flat pillow with the overstarched pillowcase. Then he felt it.

"Shit!" Harley said. "It's fucking freezing in here!"

The bunk overhead squeaked.

Shit, Harley repeated to himself. There's somebody else in here. Sheriff Porker's got some goddamned nerve!

Harley's eyes flew open wide as the thought occurred to him that the person in the upper bunk might be none other than Rolly Lipscomb. What an opportunity!

The springs squealed again as a face flashed over the edge of the upper bunk and looked down at him.

Harley's eyes opened even wider and he screamed in spite of himself when he saw the grinning, upside down, grease-painted clown face, and the eyes . . . the eyes that bugged so far out . . . so very goddamned far out . . .

"HI, HARLEY!" said the clown, with a giggle.

When Calley came in with the ham sandwich she was supposed to hand to Harley through the bars of the cell, she was all set to hear the usual insults and grossness.

Instead, a definite quiet emanated from the cell, much to her relief. Harley was probably still out like a light. So much the better. She'd just slip the sandwich through the slot in the bars . . .

That was when she saw that someone had already tried to do the very same thing.

Only they had tried to do it with Harley's entire body.

A great deal of Harley Sheen had been yanked through the unyielding bars of the cell, though there was still quite a bit of him left on the other side, in matching puddled swamp of blood, bone shards and chunks of twisted, compressed flesh.

"Holy shit," muttered Calley, and she absently took a bite of the sandwich.

Then she fainted.

While Sheriff Martin wished to prevent a panic, there was no way he could hold back the horror that gripped his own chest as though Harley Sheen had managed finally to latch onto his heart and squeeze and squeeze . . .

Only Martin, two medics, and Calley had seen the mess that used to be Harley Sheen.

Mostly they had stood together, unusually close together, in fact, and surveyed the hideous damage. They all wanted to say things like: "Who the hell could do something like this?" and "Do you know how strong the bastard would have to be to be able to do this . . . to somebody as big as Harley?" and "We're not even safe in a fucking jail cell!"

But no one said any of these things.

Aloud.

One of the medics was whispering audible prayers. Martin wanted to join him but his mind was numb and he could only remember something he'd been taught by rote, before he could even read or write. It sang through his head in the choppy rhythm of childhood prayers: "Angel of God, my Guardian Dear, to whom God's love commits me here: ever this day be at my side, to light and guard, to rule and guide. Amen."

Any other time, he would've mocked the idea of such a prayer. Now, Martin shuddered. Maybe prayer was all they had left.

The door behind them opened. They all started, and turned around quickly. Martin had his gun unholstered in a flash, which did little more than impress and upset the others, because it was only Doctor Medina from the hospital Payaso Falls shared with two other nearby small towns.

The doctor raised his arms in mock surrender and said wryly, "This is why doctors don't make housecalls anymore."

✦   ✦

" . . . pushed him halfway through the goddamned bars!" Martin hissed. Karen held him closer. Closer still.

"First thing I thought he got *pulled* through. But Doctor Medina said *pushed*."

Karen shuddered. She understood the significance of the word. "Pushed" meant, among other things, that the killer had to have been *in the cell with Harley.*

They had not moved in fifteen minutes from the tiny hallway that led into Karen's apartment; actually the back part of an old house redone after World War II to house a son who never returned. Karen had tried to coax Martin in, but he'd insisted he could only stay a moment. He had to get back out to supervise what was amounting to a major evacuation of Payaso Falls.

Nothing official was happening, of course, but a great many citizens decided, after hearing the rumors initiated by Calley's story of what she'd seen and heard in the jailhouse, that this would be the ideal time to visit relatives and friends in another town.

The one main road that connected Payaso Falls with the major highway, and thence the outside world, was busy; the town emptying out what there was of its population.

State police supervised. More confusion was caused by the incoming people than by the outgoing; TV crews from local stations, squads of deputized volunteers from nearby towns, intent on flushing out the maniac, and general out-of-town gawkers hoping to get a glimpse of one of the death houses, or, better still, an actual gory victim.

The Federal Agent did little more than talk on the phone to unknown listeners, and Sheriff Martin had grown tired of the name-calling and threats.

He needed Karen.

Again, she was there for him.

"I don't know what the hell I'm up against," he whispered sourly into her sweet-smelling hair.

"What we're up against," she corrected.

He held her away at arm's length, probing her eyes with his. "I want you to leave, Karen. Pack up some stuff and go and stay over at—"

"Forget it."

He knew she'd say that.

"I'm serious. I can't be out there hunting down some God know what while I'm worrying out of mind about you being here all alone."

She knew he'd say that.

"I'm . . . scared for you, Karen. I love you." He said it with barely enough air to give it volume, but she heard it anyway. He'd meant her to hear it. No matter what it cost, he didn't want to go back to talking to someone who was asleep. You never knew when you'd next see the person. Or if. Better to say what's in your heart and take the chances on their response.

"I love you too, Dev. Don't ever doubt that. I love you just the way you are, and I'll love you that way forever if you want."

He had no idea she would say that.

"After tonight," he whispered, "after tonight I'm . . . *we're* outta here. I'm through. It's bigger than what I can fight. I . . . I can't fight insanity, Karen."

"Let me come with you tonight."

He knew she'd suggest that. And she knew he'd say no.

They both knew she'd end up doing as he asked.

He waited while she packed a valise, and he saw her to her car, checked its back seat while she waited, hugging herself against a bitingly cold wind that had suddenly arisen, and, assured that it was safe, helped her in.

They kissed for what seemed like an hour; nowhere long enough.

"I'll call you from the hotel in San Luis."

He hated like hell to see her pull away toward the main road out of town.

He'd have hated it even more if he'd seen what was in her trunk.

As he drove through the dark, deserted streets of Payaso Falls, he had to fight the sense of unreality that threatened to render everything that had happened little more than the remnants of better forgotten nightmares.

This couldn't happen here. He kept saying it as though the sentiment was original with him. Gradually, the abandoned houses, with a few brave exceptions, convinced him that, indeed, the madness and evil that seemed like a vague, incomprehensible force out there in the cruel world had invaded Payaso Falls in a very personal, corporal form. An indiscriminate, coldly, brutally evil *something* had singled out this town for slaughter and destruction, and the turning of neighbor against neighbor, family member against family member. And was succeeding.

Almost worse than the cold-blooded killing, was the chilling effect the murderer's presence was having on people who used to live with one another in more or less harmony.

It may be that there was no power on earth that could stop a thing that could do . . . what this maniac had been capable of. Never very big on the supernatural, Martin now had to admit that the presence of the clown . . . God that sounded stupid . . . but the presence of the clown was a fairly convincing argument that *some* force other than the human kind was at work.

How had he gotten into that cell with Harley?

How had he gotten *out*?

Past Calley? No window? No *way*.

Hardheaded reality be damned; there was *something* out there. And if you called it supernatural, then that's what the hell it was. Might as well call it like it is and figure out what the hell to do about it.

It stood to reason, as far as Martin could tell, his thoughts as dark as the streets he now patrolled, that only another force, equally supernatural, could combat the invader.

But what force could *that* be?

Nothing presented itself to Martin's mind until he passed the white clapboard church in what was good naturedly referred to as Payaso Falls's downtown area.

He slowed the cruiser to a near standstill, and gazed up at the steeple, in which hung the first bell from the first church ever built in Payaso Falls, some hundred and something years ago.

Church? God? Oh, boy.

Be reasonable.

Okay. He tried. He didn't like what came out of his mental computer. If there was something out there . . . something . . . *evil* . . . which seemed fairly evident, might it not stand to reason that there was good as well?

His father had believed.

Where was his father's faith now that *he* needed it?

Why did it always seem to Martin like evil was so much stronger than good?

Maybe evil was easier to summon up than good? Maybe it was easier to lose faith than to get it?

The church looked so picturesque and peaceful. How could something that pretty and gentle hope to compete with the thing that shredded Harley Sheen and gutted the Wilberses and Freida Rusch, and—

And why was he wasting his time thinking about philosophy or religion or whatever the hell else you'd call it?

Martin was about to dismiss the thought of the supernatural altogether, and start all over on the basis of the escaped maniac theory, because it was the only idea that wouldn't make him sound like an ass when he made out his final reports . . . before he resigned . . . when—

He felt the blast of wind and the cruiser's wheel shuddered under his hands.

He shivered. Cold? Now?

As though a voice had called him from above, Martin looked up.

The bell in the steeple began to swing.

The wind gusted again. Stronger. The bell advanced.

Slowly. Soundlessly.

And against the direction of the wind.

Sheriff Martin knew the church was empty. He had seen Reverend Ogilvie and his family leave Payaso Falls early that very day. No one was supposed to be in that church.

Slowly the huge bell rocked forward. Then backward.

Martin waited for the bell's deep toll, but no sound came.

Still the bell arced farther out. Then back.

In silence.

The wind was strong . . . but there was no way to explain it's movement against the wind unless . . .

There was someone up there moving that heavy, ancient bell back and forth, back and—

Someone was clowning around Even as he thought the stupid expression, Martin regretted it.

He parked the cruiser, wincing as the fierce air slapped his collar up into his face so it stung with pain and cold.

That was when he saw him.

The clown astride the bell.

His baggy pants flapping and sounding like applauding hands in the winds. His grease-painted face glowing against the black black night, his toothy, red-smeared smile reaching ear to ear as though able to open wide enough to swallow the town whole.

The bell floated forward under the weight of the clown, who straddled it with a gleeful, ecstatic abandon that chilled Martin's blood worse than the icy wind.

I've got you, you son of a bitch, was all Martin could think as he raced forward, gun drawn, eyes squinting against the painful, searing blasts of air.

I've got you now, he repeated, as he kicked his way into the church and ran down a side aisle toward the steeple entrance, his boot heels clattering like machine gun fire into the dark stillness of the church.

He forgot to call for backup.

When the tire went flat, it did so without the loud gunshot pop that would have made Karen jump and gasp. Instead, the successive, resounding slams sounded like someone was beating on the top of the car with an iron fist.

Karen kept a firm hold on the steering wheel though it jiggled roughly under her grip.

Front tire, passenger side, she decided, as she pulled the car to the side of the road.

Wouldn't you just know it.

Of course here.

Of course now.

The old side road to San Luis was a typical shortcut: deserted and dark, and seldom used because there was nothing in San Luis that wasn't in Payaso Falls so who needed to go there?

Karen set the parking brake, and got out of the car.

Circling quickly, she went to check the tire.

Just a delay, she instructed her prickly nerves.

Change it and be on your way, girl. Let's not act like a Friday The Thirteenth movie victim.

She stared down at the betraying tire.

Her heart pounded. Harder. Her eyes rebelled and went out of focus. Her breathing wouldn't start up, and she thought there was a good chance she'd pass out.

She shook her head and looked again.

No, it was still there.

The little clown face sticker. The kind you put on a kid's homework paper for a reward. It was right there on her hubcap, grinning at her obscenely. Next to the jagged piece of metal that had imbedded itself deep into the tire.

Deep enough to let the air out a little bit at a time, as she was driving . . .

She kicked the clown in annoyance.

Of course it kept on grinning. What else would it do?

Hugging herself against a cold that was not outside her, Karen hurried around the side of the car to the back.

To open the trunk.

✦   ✦

He half expected the clown to have disappeared by the time he arrived in the bell tower.

No such luck.

Martin threw the door to the steeple open with such force, that it slammed and recoiled back at him. He stopped it with his elbow and found himself not ten feet away from the grinning lunatic.

This close, he could see the rolling eyes, the lolling, waggling tongue, and something else. Something that told Martin all he'd ever believed about the safe sure laws of the visible universe was dead wrong.

If the clown had been an oven, Martin would have been burned to a cinder. But instead of searing heat, what emanated from the very person of the maniac before him was a cold so intense, so scalding, that Martin had to fight the temptation to reach up and feel his face to see if there was any skin left there.

Behind the clown, the giant bell swung upwards, almost sideways, its thick clapper striking its side with no effect whatsoever. Silence. Dead ice silence. The quiet of a glacier in a midnight arctic sea.

He was lost in an ocean of cold and silence. Alone with the creature in garish paint and hideous eyes.

Only the wind is screaming, Martin thought wildly.

"You will be too, in a minute," said the grinning clown.

✦   ✦

"Damn," Karen muttered, when she had to double back to the driver's seat and get the keys. "Can't open the trunk without the key, bright girl," she berated herself out loud, hoping the sound of her own voice would drive back that dark . . . that reaching, grabbing cold that was scrabbling at her clothes, her hair, her eyes . . . but her frightened, almost whining voice did little to comfort her.

She thought about Devlin Martin. How much she loved him. How good things would be there for them both once they'd left Payaso Falls.

She put the key in the trunk's lock.

As the clown's grin stretched wide, wider, and his goggling eyes rolled apart and together again, the wind blasted like grains of freezing sand into Martin's eyes. He fought to keep upright, leaning into the blazing cold and forcing himself to ignore the agony it cost him to raise his gun and point it at the clown.

Reflected, suddenly, horribly, in the clown's eyes, as if done deliberately to throw Martin over the brink into despair, Martin was certain he saw . . . Karen. Alone also in the windwhipped light, reaching to open a door which would somehow unleash the waiting, other side of the clown . . . the side that revealed himself as he really was. The hideous extensions of the freak before him that in some inexplicable way enabled it to be in two places at once.

Two places at once . . . *Karen* . . .

The striking, dead silent bell, howled a message at Martin, an important message, if he could only . . .

The silent bell. Choked into silence like that stiffening, dying faith that it represented.

Dying faith. Jesus God, he thought, is that *it*?

The clown squealed with an ear-splitting screech of victory.

And Martin knew without doubt that he was looking at a horror that was not human and never had been. An evil that so delighted in its own misshapen malice that it was an affront to sanity and goodness, hope, and faith—

Faith.

Even as his gun went off again and again, Martin knew it would do nothing to the thing that stood before him in the mocking shape of a clown.

Martin stopped doubting even before the first bullet struck the chest of the clown and was instantly transformed into a polka dot on its rag-tag shirt.

Another bullet. Another polka dot. The clown cackled dementedly.

Martin would have laughed had his face not been near frozen with fear.

The clapper struck the church bell yet again.

Soundlessly.

As soundless and affectless as had been Martin's belief, just an instant before, in pure supernatural evil. And good.

Martin lowered the gun as the clown drifted toward him, its ragged-gloved hands reaching, reaching with too many fingers.

"I know what you are," Martin said quietly into the shrieking wind. "And I know how to stop you."

And against his own hard-come-by reasons, against his own stubborn rebelliousness toward his father's calm and assured faith in a God of goodness, against all his carefully accumulated doubts and despairs, Martin forced himself to say the words into the devil's breath of wind, into the approaching, hellishly mocking face of the madness of the universe:

"Angel of God," Martin recited, "my Guardian Dear . . ."

It did not matter to Martin that the gloves encircled his throat and the hungry wind tore raw red needle-width strips of skin from his face, not that his voice sounded as it had when his father knelt beside him at night while he recited the words that once reflected what he'd believed as a little child.

Back when he'd known and not doubted the truth.

"The Lord is my Shepard . . ." said Martin. And at that instant, staring into the face of evil . . . he believed it again.

The deafening thunderclap of sound coincided with the intake of Martin's breath.

The majestic gong of the church bell pealed like the voice of all the thunder that had ever sounded over the face of the earth.

This time the clown's scream was one of agony, and Martin, released from the thing's grip, fell backward, his head feeling as though it had been struck by the very bell that now tolled as if it would shake down the church beneath it.

"Yea, though I walk through the valley of the shadow of death," he whispered. "I will fear no evil . . ."

The clown's face sagged inward and then bubbled outward, stretching, changing colors at the same time as its body erupted with countless squirming wormlike pustules, each with a mouth that screamed hollowly and then writhed inward on itself to resolve into the shape of a thing so alien, so maddening, that Martin closed his eyes and felt hot tears course down his raw cheeks.

The clown-facade was no more; in its place was the disgorged unspeakable living detritus of hell, the asylum of the universe.

Its eternally hungry and insatiate mouths, its blind malevolent eyes, its scrabbling, pincered, chittering legs rimmed with erupting sores born of nameless, hell begotten diseases . . .

Again the lightburst thunderclap of the bell's music, faith given voice given sound given might; and the obscene thing before Martin exploded into uncountable fragments of darkness that spattered the black night sky and then were swept swirling and screeching away on the last vanishing gusts of the freezing, hungry wind.

The bell tolled once more, and its rich, bottomless voice sang over the silent town, settling finally into a hushed, steady, soothing tone that lay over everything like the memory of a cool gentle rain.

Shakily, Martin rose from where he'd fallen, the warm night air caressing his aching face as he knew Karen's hands would when next they were together.

He started down the stairway from the bell tower, the sound of lost faith and hope recovered, only a memory now. But a memory he knew he would take with him forever.

Karen had ignored the inexplicable fear she'd suddenly had about opening the trunk. Stupid, really, and it had just lasted for an instant. She'd imagined the clown leaping up at her out of the car trunk. Then, angry with herself for being such a baby, she flipped open the trunk just as the church bells in Payaso Falls sounded out across the night.

Naturally, there was nothing in her trunk except what was supposed to be there.

It was somehow quite soothing to hear that beautiful old bell, tolling away while she replaced her flat tire with the spare and then prepared to head off to San Luis.

It seemed as though she hadn't heard it in a long time, now that she thought about it.

Maybe, she thought hopefully, it's a signal that everything is okay in town. Maybe they'd all be able to go back in the morning and everything would be . . . well, maybe not the *same* again, but at least . . . back to normal.

As she drove away, she found herself saying a prayer for Martin's safety.

She knew it had been answered when his police cruiser came up behind her just outside San Luis.

They held each other for a very long time, and then turned around and headed back to Payaso Falls.

Back home.

Martin had so much to tell Karen, and he would not be waiting for her to fall asleep anymore before doing so.

CEMETERY DANCE INTERVIEWS DEAN KOONTZ

Bob Morrish

In between a publicity tour for his latest novel, some rewrites for the film version of *Phantoms*, and a variety of other chores, Dean Koontz recently found the time to answer a few questions for *CD*.

CD: Your penchant for mixing/crossing traditional genre boundaries is well known. Which of your books do you feel are most successful at blurring the genre lines?

DK: MR. MURDER was well-liked by mystery-suspense readers and critics, yet at its core is a solid science-fiction premise, and many of the ramifications of that premise are pretty horrific. Indeed, the recent sheep and monkey cloning has brought the moral and ethical issues to the attention of the general public. At the same time, there's lots of humor in MR. MURDER—maybe not as much as Donald Westlake would work into one of his comic crime novels, but a lot. WATCHERS seemed to capture suspense, science-fiction, horror *and* mainstream audiences, which wasn't as true of, say, HIDEAWAY or DRAGON TEARS. But there's an infinite number of ways to combine genres, and some are bound to please more people than others. The fun for me is in the challenge of it, finding new forms of fiction, new ways of telling stories, unexpected juxtapositions of mood and material.

CD: Tell us about some of the resistance you met from publishers when you began mixing genre elements in your work.

DK: Tremendous resistance. When I delivered LIGHTNING, my publisher wanted me to put it on the shelf for "seven years" because she was afraid it would destroy my career at the very time that I had finally begun hitting hardcover bestseller lists. We argued for six weeks, but finally she went ahead with the book. To her credit, she later acknowledged that I was right, that the public *was* ready for a novel that blended time-travel with elements of the suspense novel, the adventure novel, the comic novel, and the biographical novel that spans a character's entire life. This publisher is a very savvy woman, right far more often than she is wrong, so I can't say I blamed her for trusting her instinct. There's *still* so much resistance to genre-bridging that I'd never recommend a young writer try it. You have to be very sure of your intentions and confident of your skills, because if you try to mix genres, you're going to be called upon to justify it book by book and to stand your ground even when everyone in your professional life is assuring you that you are wrecking your career. This can be exhausting—stealing time away from *writing*.

CD: In the last few years, you've begun using greater amounts of humor in your books. Can you trace the development back to any particular cause?

DK: Early in my career, I wrote a comic novel—HANGING ON—that was well reviewed. But it didn't sell. I looked around and noticed that very damn few comic novelists made a living at it for any length of time. Being stubborn but not stupid, I gave up comic novels for suspense—but knew the time would come when I could start slipping comedy into the books and get away with it. WATCHERS had a storyline in which a thread of humor was not only justifiable but essential. I liked the experience so much that I incorporated more humor in LIGHTNING—and even made one character a stand-up comic so her constant stream of funny lines seemed natural to her. I mean, there are a lot of funny accountants out there—well, maybe not a *lot*, maybe two or three—but readers would find it harder to believe these humorous lines springing from an accountant than from Thelma in LIGHTNING. There wasn't much room for humor in INTENSITY, and only slightly more in SOLE SURVIVOR, but everything else since WATCHERS has included humor to one degree or another. Why? Because life is funny. The human experience is both a tragedy and a farce—and I can't imagine writing well if I didn't give voice to both aspects of that experience.

CD: You use female protagonists extensively. Why did you decide to do so? Do you feel there's a particular book in which you have been most successful in creating a strong female protagonist.

DK: I began using female protagonists when they were virtually unknown in hard suspense (as opposed to romantic suspense, where people like Daphne Dumaurier had been using them for years). Another writer once flabbergasted me by saying in print that I had a formula—always a female character as major as the male lead. Excuse me? Formula? This is *life*. There are *two* genders—well, three if you consider Dennis Rodman—in real life, and stories in which one sex or the other is relegated to the background never strike me as stories that could be *real*. Using women in roles equal to male roles, portraying them as equally smart and courageous and indomitable and tough—that's simple reality. Anyway, I don't always have equal male and female co-leads. INTENSITY has *no* male lead, only Chyna Shepherd and the villain! So there. Hah. And judging by reader response, I'd say that Chyna is my most successful female character to date.

CD: In recent years, you've written two dog-centric novels—WATCHERS and DRAGON TEARS. Why?

DK: Because I'm always fascinated with viewpoint in novels.

Out of interesting and convincingly rendered viewpoints comes the plot, the theme, the very soul of the book, because stories are first and foremost about people. And when I say "people," I include dogs. My kind of dogs.

Somewhat anthropomorphised but definitely not humans in costume. From a dog's viewpoint, I can say things about the human condition that might seem too harsh if said by a human character, because the dog's observation is colored by his innocence. In WATCHERS, I never really went wholesale into Einstein's viewpoint; there was never a scene done through his eyes. I just didn't feel confident enough to do that yet. By the time I got to DRAGON TEARS, the confidence was there, and I found the right note for Woofer's p.o.v. almost at once. In spite of the highly simplified language, the viewpoint was so *rich*. I loved writing those scenes so much, creating the entire doggy perception and idiom, that I was tempted to bring Woofer back for an entire novel told in his voice. Now *that* would have driven my publisher right over the edge!

There's also Rocky, in DARK RIVERS OF THE HEART, a totally different dog from any others I've done—and a mirror of some aspects of the hero. And Scootie in TICKTOCK. And I'm doing a novel—the first of those for Bantam—which involves a dog in a major role. I think I was a dog in another life. Maybe if I'm really lucky, I'll be a dog again some day.

CD: You've commented in the past about envy among writers: ". . . I discovered there are some writers who consider writing to be every bit as competitive an exercise as the Iditarod Dogsled Race." Do you still see a lot of this? Are there any anecdotes you'd care to share—with names censored?

DK: Many writers are fine people, honorable and well balanced. But as a profession, we have a higher than usual percentage of self-absorbed bastards with no sense of humor about themselves. One evening, reading the newspaper, I came across an article about a thirty-year study of 15,000 people who earned all or a significant part of their income through creative writing of one kind or another—and the headline of the piece was EIGHTY PERCENT OF WRITERS EXHIBIT EVIDENCE OF SCHIZOPHRENIA AND MEGALOMANIA. I showed the headline to Gerda and jokingly said, "Can you believe it's only eighty percent?" But I was only half joking. A well-known writer once became so disturbed when my (now former) British publisher praised one of my books that he went out of his way to find a bad review of it and sent it to the publisher in London with a note to the effect that "not *everyone* liked it." My publisher was so startled by this that he sent me the other writer's correspondence with the advice that I better watch my back.

I've got a hundred of these—but I'll save them for my memoirs. For my money, you can bet that when you see any author attacking another by name in interviews or with apparent casualness in essays or by the cowardly tactic of slipping disparaging remarks about other writers into the mouths of characters in his books, you are looking at an author who is desperately unhappy, deeply unsure of his own worth, and in need of building himself up by tearing others down. It's all stupid and sad. I have many close friends who are writers, but the majority of my friends are in the construction trades—masons, cabinet-makers, painters— largely as a result of the fact that Gerda and I have remodeled and built so many houses over the years. All of these people are craftsmen of real talent and some of them are artists by any definition, proud of what they do—but I have *never* heard one of them express an envious thought about a fellow tradesman or attempt to enhance his own reputation by belittling the work of others. They make damn good friends.

CD: You've not yet been fortunate enough to have one of your books creatively and successfully adapted for film or television, and your frustrations with the filmmakers who've mutated your work is well known. In your fiction career, your eventual success was seemingly due, in some part at least, to your dogged persistence and sheer force of will. Have you ever considered trying to bring that determination to bear on the Hollywood scene, in an effort to see one of your books successfully filmed? Or is the film industry just too political and too collaborative (and too avaristic) for any one writer to have that substantial of an impact?

DK: Well, I've just seen the director's cut of the miniseries based on INTENSITY, and it's quite wonderful. That was a case in which I got to choose the screenwriter—Stephen Tolkin—who did a phenomenal job. There are moments in the second night that I itch to change, but overall it is tremendous television. For the first time, filmmakers succeed in capturing the essence of what I do—the thematic cross-currents and especially the emotional content. They realized I'm not a horror writer. I've said I'm not a horror writer so often that no one even hears me say it anymore—but these people grasped that they were making psychological suspense with a spiritual element, and they did a knockout job. It airs in the autumn. Meanwhile, I wrote and exec produced PHANTOMS for Miramax/Dimension, with Peter O'Toole and Joanna Going and some other solid actors. I had total control of the shooting script, by contract. I've not seen a director's cut yet, but I've seen Joe Chappelle's assemblies of several primary sequences, and the picture looks as if it is going to be absolutely terrific. Again, I convinced Miramax to stop thinking of PHANTOMS as a horror story and to start thinking of it as science-fiction suspense. The moment I turned their heads around on that, everything fell into place, and now they are ecstatic with the dailies and the cut footage they're seeing. I'm sure we'll work together in the future. And when I finish the book for Bantam that I'm working on now, I intend to write the screenplay immediately and attempt to set up the production in such a way as to give me even more control than I had on PHANTOMS. I find that when I have a strong element of control, when I don't have to argue my way through endless—and generally useless—script-development meetings, film can be worth my time and energy. A strong element of control is the key—and hard to win, except when the studio badly wants the property and can get it no other way.

CD: Is anything else headed for the screen right now?

DK: Because I had such a good experience with Mandalay and the Fox Network on INTENSITY, we gave them an exclusive shot at SOLE SURVIVOR. Our hope now is to put together the same team. Done properly, eschewing sentimentality, handling the subject of loss and spiritual redemption with gritty realism, SOLE SURVIVOR could be a powerfully emotional piece of film. Even with commercials for deodorant and corn chips popping up every twelve minutes! And ABC is developing a miniseries based on MR. MURDER, with Stephen Tolkin doing the script, which looks very promising.

CD: Getting back to your "dogged persistence and sheer force of will": Discussing your novel TWILIGHT EYES and its character Slim MacKenzie, you've referred to "the iron will with which Slim has tried to bring order to—and make sense of—a world that he knows is infinitely bizarre and perhaps senseless." I thus can't help but wonder whether Slim is reflective of his creator. Do you think he is? Taking the point further, I'm sure there are bits of you strewn through all of your books (what an image!), but are there any particular characters that you feel are reflective of yourself, or that you especially identified with while creating them?

DK: I am not the Outsider, the monstrous killing machine from WATCHERS. Well, come to think of it . . . as a kid I was always an outsider, with a small "o," so I know what it feels like to be in the cold looking in on a place of warmth and laughter. So maybe I *am* the Outsider—which is why I could give the reader so much empathy with the beast at the end. There's certainly a lot of me in Regina, the disabled girl in HIDEAWAY, in her wide-eyed sense of wonder about virtually everything in life and in her curious relationship with God. Marty Stillwater, the writer in MR. MURDER, shares many of my own attitudes, especially as to the meaning and purpose of fiction, which he expresses in a scene somewhere past the middle of the book. I am very much like Chyna Shepherd in INTENSITY—or would like to think I am. I identified so strongly with her and with her journey from an abusive childhood to a life of decency and hope that I could literally feel her terror and exhilaration and despair as she was struggling through that story. The characters who use humor to cope with life—Thelma in LIGHTNING, Holly in COLD FIRE, so many others—are all reflections of me. When people do hurtful things to me or when life throws me a really scary curve, I eventually turn the experience into an amusing anecdote—which has given me such a fund of funny anecdotes that Tom Snyder just asked me to do his show for the fourth time this year! So even terrible pain can become prime material for book publicity!

CD: You've mentioned that in the course of doing research for WATCHERS and other novels, you've done a lot of reading in the field of criminal psychology, and that you've found that many widely-held notions are seemingly ill-founded: "the hard scientific data that is available seems to disprove most of the assumptions behind large areas of psychology. Antisocial behavior must not be caused primarily by social ills or childhood trauma because truly vicious criminal activities—the worst species of evil—don't correlate with those causes in any consistent manner." If that's the case, why do you think that such beliefs are widespread? Does the media serve to propagate this thinking? If so, why? Also, do you think your strong interest in this field is somewhat attributable to your own dysfunctional upbringing?

DK: Widespread beliefs are often ill-founded, even those that appear to be based on solid intellectual ground. After all, it was once rather unanimously held that the sun revolved around the earth. Or look at Darwin. I believe that large elements of his theories may be correct. But for a century and a half, his theory enjoyed largely unassailable status in the scientific community; it was "Theory" with a capital T and seemed as monumental as the Rocky Mountains, as timeless as the stars. Yet in the past couple of decades we've seen the Theory stood on its head by Steven Gould's "punctuated equilibria," which was desperately needed to explain the lack of any observable proof of random selection through gradual mutation—and such issues as irreducible complexity. Darwin believed—as did virtually all the scientists of his age—that the smallest unit of matter was the cell, which he called "carbonized albumen." Atomic and subatomic particles were unknown in 1858—which is one reason why Darwin's theory is now plagued by such thorny problems as irreducible complexity, which even the most brilliant of the hard Darwinists have not adequately answered. And in our own age, quantum physics and chaos theory have radically altered our previous perceptions of the fundamental nature of matter, energy, and time.

So if even the hardest of hard sciences are periodically forced by new discoveries to discard what seem to be absolute truths for new theories, why should it be surprising that in fields like psychology and other "soft sciences," a lot of what we think we know about human behavior and motivation is pure bunkum?

The facts are that ninety-nine percent of all violent career criminals are diagnosable sociopaths who lack the capacity for empathy, and there is no overwhelming or halfway even clear correlation between childhood abuse and sociopathy, poverty and sociopathy, or social-political oppression and sociopathy. Indeed, because most if not all violent sociopaths exhibit similar disturbing behavior by the age of three (torturing insects and then small animals), there's an unnerving amount of evidence that points toward a genetic cause. And boy does *that* possibility lead us into a tangle of moral and ethical questions, especially if the mapping of the human genome eventually allows us to determine the exact genetic damage that reliably identifies a sociopath. Anyway, there is not one case on record of a genuine sociopath being rehabilitated—yet our laws, our system of justice, even our fundamental political assumptions are predicated on the Freudian belief that *anyone*, given adequate therapy and led firmly enough to deep self-examination, can be rehabilitated. Even most of modern psychology has begun to distance itself from Freud and the religion of victimology that arises from his theories, yet our culture and society remain so saturated with Freudian attitudes that we persist in thinking of ourselves as victims, all victims of what our parents did to us, what our culture and society did to us. There is not a shred of proof that Freud's theories are correct, and much proof that they are not, yet as a culture we hold fast to them.

Because, as you ask, the media propagates them? No. The media *does* propagate them, but that's not why we embrace these untruths as truths. We embrace them because they excuse our worst behavior: If each of us lacks free will, if each of us is only a product of what his family, his culture, and his society did to him, then none of us is fundamentally to blame for what he does. What an enchanting idea! You can be a right bastard to others, lie and cheat and steal—and remain a victim. You and the Menendez brothers! Several years ago, I began to realize that *all* modern fiction uses Freudianism as the basis for character motivation, whether the authors of those works are always aware of it or not. When I look back at my own WHISPERS, for instance, I see the ultimate Freudian psychology at work in every character in the book—yet I was not aware of how slavishly I followed the Freudian faith while writing it. Some time ago, I made a conscious determination to stop using Freudian psychology as the underpinning of characterization. Since then my characters are defined and given depth by their actions, their reactions, and attitudes; they are possessed of free will and the power to make moral decisions; they are not defined solely by their backstories, by childhood trauma and the limitations of their socio-economic status and whether they suffered bed-wetting episodes when they were nine. Some critics don't get this at all. In their postmodern hipness, they are ironically reactionary and dogmatic: They feel a character *must* be defined by the psychological damage he sustained as a child and adolescent. This psychological background detail, lathered on, is the only thing they recognize as characterization! Tedious. If you think about it, the best characters ever to walk through the pages of fiction—those of Dickens, for instance—were created before anyone had ever heard of Freud.

As for whether I am interested in psychology in general and aberrant psychology in particular because of a dysfunctional upbringing . . . You bet! My father was a violent alcoholic who held forty-four jobs in thirty-four years, who was later diagnosed as sociopathic, and who made two attempts on my life, the second in front of a lot of witnesses, which landed him in a psychiatric ward. After growing up under the thumb of a deeply disturbed man, I'd have to be brain dead not to be interested in the source of sociopathic behavior, the issues of nature versus nurture.

CD: Unlike a lot of people who've undergone such weirdness and trauma as a kid, you seem to have turned out fairly...well, *normal*. Do you ever see reflections of your father's behavior in your own behavior?

DK: Normal? Well, yes, relatively normal. For a number of years I did believe that Betty Crocker was the secret master of the universe and a figure of towering evil. But I'm better now.

I know Betty Crocker is not the secret master of the universe. The secret master of the universe is Richard Simmons. All hail his name. All hail his name.

My father was sociopathic. You have to understand what this means: He completely lacked the ability to empathize with the feelings and needs of others. Like all sociopaths, he was convinced that love, honor, courage, and all the better human feelings were a hoax, that no one really felt these things any more than he did, that everyone simply faked these things in order to manipulate others. Sociopaths recognize no needs but their own and are narcissistic in the extreme. Were I to exhibit behavior like this, my wife would smack me upside the head.

CD: One other childhood question: When was the last time you returned to Bedford, PA? Do you know if the house you grew up in is still standing?

DK: I returned in 1989 for various reasons. The house I grew up in was not much of a house: four tiny rooms, a tarpaper roof and no indoor plumbing until I was about eleven. But it was still standing. Relatives thought it would be interesting for me to go back and see the place, to remind myself how far I'd come. They had even arranged with the folks living there to let me make a visit. We pulled up in front of the place, and I was so overcome with a sense of oppression that I could not go inside. I could think only of my mother, of what she had endured there, and I couldn't bear to walk through the door again. In fact, I never got out of the car. We stopped—and then drove almost immediately away. That is the past. Life is about the future.

CD: You've been quoted as saying that ". . . my editor at Putnam has said that all of my books, in one way or another, are about the remaking of families, some of them unconventional but nonetheless happy." Given the central role that families play in much of your work, I can't help but wonder why you've never had children of your own. Any comment?

DK: Two of my father's brothers committed suicide. I believed I saw elements of my father's mental condition reflected in others in his family. My wife and I wanted children . . . but when we were first married we had a hundred and fifty bucks, a used car, and low-paying jobs. We were too poor to afford a family. By the time we could consider having children, we had endured so much from my father (because he continued to play a role in my life as an adult) that we seriously had to assess the risk that any child of ours might be like him. If sociopathy can be genetic, then it might conceivably skip a generation. We did not want to be responsible for bringing into the world anyone who, regardless of upbringing, might be a danger to others.

CD: You've described your religious beliefs over the years as "Protestant, then Catholic, then agnostic, now firmly back in the believing camp again, though with no firm idea of the nature of God." What prompted these changes, most particularly the recent change back to believing?

DK: The move back into the camp of believers has actually been taking place since before I began writing STRANGERS and has progressed steadily since—and one of the motors driving me, oddly enough, is my lifelong interest in science. I read a lot of science, much of it obscurely published, and if you have been following much of the work in molecular biology, quantum physics, and chaos theory over the past decade plus, you will be aware that some scientists—a minority but with quite a few of the best and brightest on its side—believe that they are seeing powerful evidence not merely of an ordered universe but of a created universe. This is a hot debate in some quarters. But even Francis Crick, who won the Noble for discovering the double-helix structure of the DNA molecule, has found it difficult if not impossible to explain the diversity and complexity of life on earth with the standard theories—and thus suggested that all life here was probably engineered and seeded by an extraterrestrial intelligence! Begs the issue, doesn't it? If life here was created by ETs—who created the ETs? The older I get and the more observant I become, I am also further convinced of a meaning and purpose to existence simply because life is so full of fascinating *patterns*, complexities, subtle connections that I was too self-centered or preoccupied to notice when I was younger. There's the odd *synchronicity* of life, which Jung explored at length but never adequately explained, and year by year I become ever more aware of it. If I ever get the chance to meet Richard Simmons, I know everything will be explained. All hail his name.

CD: When asked about writing sequels, you've said, "The only novel to which I've contemplated writing a sequel is WATCHERS, but even that might never happen. There are two basic reasons for not doing it. First, new ideas grip me, and I'm more excited about those than I am about returning to older ideas." This makes perfect sense to me. *However*, I'm intrigued that you have taken the time to revise some of your older works—most notably INVASION and DEMON SEED —before re-releasing them. What does revising an older work amount to, if not "returning to older ideas." How do you distinguish your tendency toward revision from your aversion toward sequels? Finally, what about a WATCHERS 2? Are you any closer to someday writing such a book?

DK: Generally sequels are boring because the characters in the subsequent books do not grow and change the way they did in the first novel. Their natures freeze, and they become less like real people; they mutate into collections of eccentricities—because that's easier for the writer and because readers often *want* to see precisely the same traits and behaviors exhibited by characters that have become old friends. It's comfortable fiction. As a reader, I'm guilty of it too. I loved Rex Stout's series of Nero Wolfe mysteries—but over literally dozens of books, Nero Wolfe and Archie Goodwin and all the characters in Stout's milieu remained *exactly* the same, unchanged by their experiences. This is true in 99% of sequels. One of the few series in which repeating characters underwent fundamental—often subtle—psychological change was in

John D. MacDonald's Travis McGee books. I'm not nuts enough or vain enough to think that I could easily step into McDonald's shoes.

Revising an old book is an utterly different exercise from writing a sequel. You look at a book written in your twenties and wince at the naiveté, the clumsy use of language, the themes inadequately explored. Yet . . .there's something in the concept or the characters that still intrigues, that begs to be revisited, reworked. Sometimes this leads to a *totally* new novel like WINTER MOON (which, nominally, started with INVASION), and sometimes it results in the very same story so utterly recast that it *seems* like a new book, as in DEMON SEED. None of us can go back in time and undo a terrible mistake that has affected his whole life or be gentler and kinder to someone whom we treated poorly back then—but a writer can revisit early books that were not well done (either because of financial pressure or inadequate technical skills) and remake the past a little. It's fun. But I'd never write a *sequel* to any of those books, having revised them.

That said . . . I will reveal that I am launched on a trilogy that features the same lead character. I found a premise of such interest to me and a character with so much capacity for depth and growth and change that I became excited about seeing if I possessed the ability to wring the full potential from the material. The idea is that the books could be read in any order, each standing entirely alone, yet the central character has a major character arc within each book and is not the same person at the end of each that he was at the beginning. It's easier to announce this intention than it is to effectuate it!

As for WATCHERS . . . if I ever come up with a story that feels like the equal to the first, I might write the sequel. But I would not want to toss out a continuation that is a pale reflection of the original.

CD: What's the story on the new look? The mustache, the hair?

DK: I had the mustache for twenty-eight years. When I shaved it off, I looked as if I had a *milk* mustache. My upper lip was dead pale . . . and frighteningly longer than I expected. On first glimpse of that upper lip after so many years, I could easily embrace a theory of ancestor apes! As for the hair . . . One day it occurred to me: Hey, if they can safely transplant a human heart, hair should be a snap! I'd thought about it for years, never saw any procedure I liked or trusted . . . and then did. Vanity, vanity. But life is about change, after all. On the downside, it hurt. Not as badly as a heart transplant, of course. And while I was going through the process, I also had gum surgery and a horrendous two-hour extraction of a tooth, the roots of which were fused to the bone—all of which was a *lot* more painful than the hair. I hasten to add that this was not a surgical package deal, scalp and gums and teeth all handled by the same doctor at Scalpels R Us. Anyway, friends of twenty years have walked right past me, and a few have even spoken with me for five or six exchanges before suddenly recognizing me from the voice. It's taught me a lot about how fragile our physical identity is and how few visual signals we use to recognize one another. Shave off a mustache and restore a hairline and you suddenly become a stranger. After years of being recognized, I have recovered my anonymity—which is a wonderful thing. It won't last more than a few years, because I do television and because new photos will appear on future books, but for a while it's cool. The whole experience is interesting, like *living* a masquerade, and I know I'm going to get an intriguing book out of it soon. Anyway, I take considerable comfort from the fact that even if lifelong friends don't recognize me, I will always be recognizable to he who knows us by our hearts and souls, he who knows of every sparrow's fall: Richard Simmons.

AFTER THE DANCE

David B. Silva

It began in innocence. You stumbled across an old July, 1943 copy of *Weird Tales* in your father's trunk in the attic when you were ten, and you read, "Yours Truly, Jack the Ripper" by Robert Bloch and had nightmares for a week. A year or two later, you got to stay up and watch *The Twilight Zone* for the first time. It was the "Nightmare at 20,000 Feet" episode, and even today, when you think back to that moment when William Shatner pulls back the curtain to find the creature's face pressed against the glass, you get shivers down your spine. Then there was "The Sixth Finger" episode of *The Outer Limits*. And something called *The Exorcist* by William Peter Blatty. And *'Salem's Lot* by some guy by the name of Stephen King, who wrote as good a story as you had ever read. And . . .

. . . and

. . . and you might as well have thrown in the towel by then, because the wonder of it, the dangerousness of it, had you by the throat. You were hopelessly entangled, amazed and curious and hungry for more. Always hungry for more.

This was how I found my way to the horror genre.

It's how many of us found our way to the genre.

How Richard T. Chizmar found his way, I'd be willing to bet. Though in Rich's case, I'm inclined to believe that other forces were involved, that it was, in fact, his calling from a very early age. His heart was a little bigger, his vision a little clearer, and he was willing to work a little harder than the rest of us, and so the call was made and he answered. That's the only way to explain how *Cemetery Dance* has become the premiere horror magazine of the '90s, riding on the back of a single man.

I first met Rich over the phone not long before he started *Cemetery Dance*. He was a young, enthusiastic guy, excited about the genre and eager to start up a magazine that would make a difference. He was raw out of college, if I remember correctly. A business major. This was in early '88, I believe. *The Horror Show*, a small magazine I was editing at the time, was doing well. *Cemetery Dance* was just beginning to take form in Rich's mind.

We talked about our love for the genre, about horror's long and proud tradition, about what it takes to publish and edit and layout a magazine by yourself. We talked about mailing lists and how you attract quality manuscripts, about distribution and postal problems, about printers and sitting on the living room floor, stuffing envelopes. But most important of all, we talked about responsibility.

This was why I took such an immediate liking to the man: he understood his responsibilities. Publish a magazine with honor and you can't escape them. Rich knew, before the first issue of *Cemetery Dance* ever saw a printing press, that if he was willing to accept money from complete strangers for a magazine no one had ever heard of before, he owed them the best magazine he could produce; and he owed it to them on time, as promised. He knew that if he were to use a writer's work, he owed that writer the best possible presentation of that work, and that the writer deserved a prompt and equitable payment for his or her labors. He knew that for every Stephen King story he might accept down the road, he had a responsibility to read and pay attention to the works of all the future Kings out there who had not yet made a name for themselves.

Rich knew all of this.

He knew that he wouldn't be alone, that he would be a part of a larger community and that he had a responsibility to give back to that community the way its long tradition had given to him. He knew that as the mantle would be passed down to him, it would be his responsibility to help other magazines start up and succeed, to help the Horror Writers Association grow and prosper, to refer writers to other markets, to share the tradition as often and as freely as possible.

Rich knew all of this, and he acted on it with pride and consistency and a genuine love for what he was doing.

The premiere issue of *Cemetery Dance* debuted in December of 1988. Heavy stock. Black and white cover. 48 pages. Almost entirely fiction and poetry. Filled with names like Steve Rasnic Tem and Barry Hoffman and Bentley Little. $3.95.

There were other names as well, names that you hadn't heard before, some that you haven't heard since. That was one of those responsibilities we had talked about. And there were mentions of the Horror Writers of America (as they were known then) and SPWAO (the Small Press Writers and Artists Organization, which has since ceased to exist), and a handful of other small publishers, all flopping boneslessly down similar paths like straw men, trying to find their own means of keeping the tradition alive.

Rich had done himself proud.

He had done the genre proud.

Things do not always go the way they are planned, however. They rarely do. In my own life, my mother came down with ovarian cancer and after a long battle, finally succumbed in early 1989. In Rich's life, the battle with cancer was his own. To our relief, it was a battle he won. Good things *do* happen to good people.

After my mother's death, I stepped back and took a look at things and decided it was time to close shop on *The Horror Show*. After Rich's long battle, he stepped back and took a look and got excited about *Cemetery Dance* all over again. I was surprised by this, to be perfectly honest. So surprised, I brought it up to him once. You know what he told me? He told me that if he had lost his battle with cancer, he still would have been grateful for all the wonderful events, all the wonderful people, who had made up his life. He was a fortunate man, he said. And now that he was feeling better, he was looking forward to renewing the energy that had been lost while he had been fighting the good fight.

You would have been startled to see the improvements between the premiere issue of *Cemetery Dance* and its follow-up. Sixty pages now.

A nice mix of fiction and nonfiction. Excellent artwork. Even some photographs. These are all things you might take for granted today, but eight years ago, for one person working alone at home, this was very impressive. Very Impressive, indeed.

In the most current issue of *Cemetery Dance* you'll find 112 pages of fiction and columns; interviews and book reviews. A four-color cover. Superior artwork. Cover price: $4.00. Rich once said all he wanted to do was make certain that each new issue was slightly better than its predecessor. But Rich is less a talker than a doer, as he has proven time and time again. There isn't a magazine on the market today that can match the breadth and quality of the material you find in each and every issue of *Cemetery Dance*. Yet, each time out, he manages to continue to top himself.

This piece isn't really about *Cemetery Dance* as much as it is about the man behind the *Dance*. You already know this, of course. The simple truth is . . . it's impossible to separate the two.

It's been a number of years since I first met Rich over the phone. To this day, I have yet to meet him face-to-face (we both take claim to a degree of shyness, even awkwardness in social situations). *The Horror Show* folded shop in 1990. *Cemetery Dance* has gone on to become the backbone of the horror genre for thousands of readers, proudly carrying on the long tradition.

And it will happen again.

Somewhere down the road, a ten-year-old is going to spend an afternoon sifting through all the papers in his father's old trunk, in a back corner of the attic, and he's going to come across an old copy of *Cemetery Dance*. He'll read it, cover to cover, because when you're ten you still believe in the magic. He'll read "Herman" by Richard Laymon, and "Halleluja" by Hugh B. Cave and "Pandorette's Mother" by Melanie Tem. And the stories will stay with him for weeks, maybe months, maybe years. And he'll be hooked, drawn into the rich, imaginative tradition the way a thousand others have been drawn before him.

And as Rich has known from the very beginning, the tradition will carry on.

David B. Silva
Oak Run, California